REUNION . . .

The scent of her intoxicated him. It rushed to his head in a tangle of jonquil and rosemary, keen and urgent. All his emotion exploded within him, reawakening buried pleasure. He wanted to put his mouth on hers, to crush her soft, yielding body into his. He longed to steal her golden fire for his own.

She raised her face to his. The innocent beauty of her engulfed him as he traced the sweep of ivory flesh and the swell of her curving breasts with his eyes. Her bare arms rose to clasp around his neck. She brought her body closer, and desire pounded through him. Still he would not touch her until she made a soft sound and stretched to find his mouth. Sleek and dreamy, she gave a gentle sigh like the brush of summer wind in the trees. Her body melted against his in a familiar, well-loved motion, searing him, making him taut with need. . . .

"Janet Lynnford's love of history comes through on every page. A vivid tale of a jaded noble and an industrious young woman destined to find love. Enjoy!"

—Kat Martin

"Captures the lush sensuality of the Elizabethan period with effortless skill. Rich in passion and intrigue and blessed with a bright, vibrant heroine and a winning hero, *Pirate's Rose* is a delightful romantic adventure that kept me turning pages long past my bedtime."

—Teresa Medeiros

Lord of Lightning

Janet Lynnford

A TOPAZ BOOK

TOPAZ
Published by the Penguin Group
Penguin Books USA Inc., 375 Hudson Street,
New York, New York 10014, U.S.A.
Penguin Books Ltd, 27 Wrights Lane,
London W8 5TZ, England
Penguin Books Australia Ltd, Ringwood,
Victoria, Australia
Penguin Books Canada Ltd, 10 Alcorn Avenue,
Toronto, Ontario, Canada M4V 3B2
Penguin Books (N.Z.) Ltd, 182–190 Wairau Road,
Auckland 10, New Zealand

Penguin Books Ltd, Registered Offices:
Harmondsworth, Middlesex, England

First published by Topaz, an imprint of Dutton Signet,
a division of Penguin Books USA Inc.

First Printing, July, 1996
10 9 8 7 6 5 4 3 2

Printed in Canada

NOTE
This is a work of fiction. Characters and incidents either are the product of the author's imagination or, in the case of historical figures and events, are used fictitiously.

This book is dedicated

To Ann Bouricius, Karen Harper,
and Beverly Shippey
with my heartfelt thanks for all your support.
Your friendship is a treasure greater than gold.

To all the women of Central Ohio Fiction Writers.
I have never had a greater camaraderie than with you.

To Leah Bassoff, a fabulous editor,
and Audrey LaFehr and Andrea Cirillo.
My thanks for all your efforts on my behalf.

To Linda Lael Miller,
Kat Martin,
and Teresa Medeiros
for generously helping to launch my first book,
Pirate's Rose.

To the ladies of
Lace Makers of Central Ohio,
a chapter of the International Old Lacers:
Carol Lassak
Joyce Tate
and Nancy Davy.
My thanks for sharing with me
your knowledge of lace-making history and construction.

And to my family, both geographically near and distant.

Part One

Chapter 1

West Lulworth, Dorset, Southern Coast of England, June 1574

Margaret Smytheson curled in a chair at her father's bedside, a gleaming length of bobbin lace streaming from the lace pillow in her lap. Made of pure flax, the geometric shapes unfurled in an orderly, soothing manner. Tonight she needed that soothing. Within arm's reach, her beloved father slept, but only after twelve grueling hours of fighting a fever. With damp squares of linen, Margaret had wiped his arms, his chest, his burning brow. She had spooned cool broth between his lips, then doses of an herbal brew. Over and over she had plumped his pillows and straightened his coverlet. When she could do nothing more, she had held his hand and treasured his tender thanks.

Now it was midnight, and though she ached with exhaustion, she also tingled with relief. His fever had abated! He slept peacefully for the first time in days.

Leaning across her lace pillow, Margaret placed the back of her hand gently against his pale cheek. The Squire of West Lulworth, once hale and vibrant, now so ill. But her efforts had helped. He was cooler now—at least she thought so. Releasing a deep sigh, she sank back, letting her fingers caress the two dozen bobbins, lined up across her pillow. For a few minutes she would permit herself respite and escape into her lace making. She also needed to finish this piece of work.

Cool ivory, polished wood—the feel of the bobbins sent her rejoicing as they leaped from the pillow into her hands to obey. *Left over right, right over left.* When she was four, she had found the town lace makers, crept to their doorsteps each summer morn to watch while they worked in the sun. Her father had chanced to follow one day and seen her rapture. "Would you like to try it?" So complete was her absorption, his sudden question had startled her. But he had asked an old dame to teach her the art—fulfilling her dearest wish.

Pattern of beauty, pattern of grace. The bobbins crossed and flashed, etching their rhythm in her mind, just as they had when she was four, drawing her into their enchantment. Her father had bought her a pillow that very day, covered in sapphire fabric. Twelve years later it lay on her lap, her lace shining against its stunning blue.

Cross, twist, place a pin. A motif bloomed beneath her fingers, perfect in shape, pure and right. The lace was her strength and her refuge, born of her fingers. Away flew her father's suffering, their lack of money, her mother's anger. Calm suffused her being—deep, penetrating calm.

Letting her eyelids close, Margaret continued. She felt the patterns, lived the patterns. At four, she thought God had given her magic. Or was it her father? *You have a gift, daughter. Never forget—it will be with you long after other things pass away.*

Her eyes flew open. The words were so clear. Had he spoken? No, his eyes were closed. He slept peacefully. But he had said those words to her over and over while she grew up, when he sat by her side, watching her fingers fly.

"Let me see what you've done tonight," he would whisper. "You're a miracle, Margaret. Your fingers are fast even in poor light." He would squint in the dim room in mock surprise. "I'd wager your fingers are faster than the hounds of Sherborne."

Margaret would smile at him and shake her head.

"Nay? But I think they are. They're faster than the queen's swiftest stallion—one of those fabulous creatures from beyond the Mediterranean."

She would purse her lips, shake her head again. It was their favorite jest, and they were favorite companions, giving each other such joy.

A pebble rattled against the open windowpane, shaking Margaret from her reverie. Jumping up, she hurried to the window and peered into the dark with a throbbing, hopeful heart. A tossed stone at half past eleven could mean one thing only: Jonathan Cavandish loved her still.

Don't go, a warning voice pricked her conscience. She should stay with her father, in case he needed her. Too often she had left him in the nine months since she had met Jonathan, pursuing her frivolous pleasures. She should stay where she belonged, here at her father's side.

Torn by indecision, Margaret hesitated. Conflict warred inside her, tearing her apart. She loved her father; he treasured her in return. But Jonathan's handsome face rose in her mind, coupled with his rich laugh. Each time she saw him, her heart turned itself inside out for him, eager to do his bidding. He made her smile, he made her soar with pleasure. And tonight, she desperately needed his magic touch.

Whirling about, she caught up her lace pillow and headed for the door. She would have to do both tonight—see Jonathan *and* finish this piece of lace.

"Margaret, are you there?"

The back door stood ajar, Margaret noted, as Jonathan's enthralling voice drifted up to her at the top of the stair. She must have forgotten to close it the last time she went to the pump. Their house was always topsy-turvy, and servants didn't stay because they were rarely paid. But she forgot those troubles as Jonathan's voice called, luring her away from her cares.

Holding her lace pillow level in front of her, Margaret made her way down the stair, avoiding the boards that creaked. She could do it since she knew their pattern. Her left foot went here, her right one, there. At sixteen, she knew much about patterns. Wooden floor patterns, lace patterns, the patterns of her days. This was another pattern—slipping out to see Jonathan, the squire's daughter and the merchant's son, keeping the secret from *her* mother and *his* father, who forbade them to meet.

That she didn't understand. Or did she? Whenever she tried to think clearly about whether she was meant for Jonathan, Margaret couldn't, especially not now. Because when he put his head around the open door, then stepped into the kitchen, the sheer beauty of his face and form blotted out every rational thought. Her breath caught in her throat.

"Margaret, my sweet, are you well?" his husky voice

greeted her. "How is your father? I haven't heard from you in three days."

The urgency of his questions wrapped around her, along with his tenderness. Add to that his magical hands—his clever, gentle hands that she loved so well—and she couldn't resist. She needed him with such urgency that she let him guide her out of doors, into the privacy of the secret dark.

They paused in the neglected courtyard, where weeds poked their heads through cracked bricks, and he folded her into his arms.

"How is your father? Is his fever gone?" The kindness of his questions, the genuine concern shining in his autumn brown eyes, made her tears start. He was far too good for her, better than she deserved.

"He's improved," she managed to force out, though she was suddenly, heartbreakingly unsure of that fact. "His fever is down at last. I can take a minute with you, but no more. I'm sorry I didn't send word," she mumbled against his shirtsleeve, her head cushioned against his broad, comforting chest.

"You must not think on that." His fingers twined in her hair. He always forgave her, she thought, even when he didn't know what he was forgiving. "You must not worry about me. You have enough worries already. Tell me, have you cared for yourself as well as your father? You don't leave him to eat or sleep, do you? You don't take any time for yourself."

"I stay in his chamber in case he needs me," she admitted. "But I have eaten. And I sleep on a pallet near his bed."

Jonathan's hands smoothed her hair back from her face, gently tipped up her chin. "You must walk with me in the meadow. I'll wager you haven't been out since I saw you last."

Guilt struck her. She hadn't been out; she shouldn't be now. Breaking away, she crossed the courtyard, tripping on a broken brick. Seating herself on the sagging bench beneath the apple tree, Margaret removed the protective cloth that covered her work and rearranged her bobbins. "Oh dear," she sighed deeply. "I have to finish this piece of lace. Come sit with me while I work." She took up her bobbins and began.

He followed her to the bench looking perplexed by her sudden action. "Margaret, a storm is coming. Your lace would be safer inside."

Margaret glanced up. The wind had risen, the sky was turning dark. But for nine months, he had coaxed her away from her lace, with every good intention—so he could give her the gifts of friends and laughter, things she had never had. How could she tell him?—that when she didn't make lace, when she tarried with him instead, her family didn't eat? No one else knew it, so why should he.

"I know you're worried about your father," he stated, propping one foot on the broken bench end. "So I'll tell you what. I'll send for the physician on the morrow."

"Jonathan, you've paid the physician twice already," she protested in despair.

"And I'll do it again."

Conflict warred within her. To accept and be with him, to decline and remain free. "I thank you, but I'll do it myself," she said at last. "And don't you dare do it anyway, like the other times. I have not been a good daughter. I must mend my ways."

He looked astounded at her words. In the past she had accepted meekly, even when he went against her wishes. How could he know she had cared for her father long before he came along. Tonight she would finish this lace, tomorrow, sell it. She would pay the physician and have coins to spare.

"You have been an attentive daughter," he told her, clearly surprised by the change in her. "No one could say you were not."

"I could," she contradicted, another thing she'd never done with him. "Since we met, I've spent hours with you, even whole days. I should have declined, but I'm weak and gave in."

Her response seemed to puzzle him further. "You are too hard on yourself by far. I know your father needs you, but you have needs, too. Four days ago we met for scarcely ten minutes. And before that, I didn't see you for a week. We used to see each other daily. Come walk with me in the meadow. You need the fresh air."

"Oh, God." She buried her face in her hands. It wasn't working, her attempt to tell him. "I want to, but he needs me more."

"I don't mean to be selfish. I apologize if I am."

"You're not selfish," she mumbled from behind her hands. "You're generous to a fault, that's what you are, always helping people. Saving that fisherman from drowning, pulling the widow's child from the well. Bringing herbs to sick folk and bread to those who are hungry. You bought me new slippers when mine were full of holes. You brought us food. You had the pump mended when it stopped working. Always playing the hero, doing things for me when I—"

"I'm not playing at anything," he said rather sharply. "If someone needs help, I lend a hand. You've needed help, Margaret."

"Oh, Jonathan, I sound like an ungrateful wretch." She wiped at her eyes furtively, hoping he wouldn't notice her tears. "I do thank you for the things you've done, but I'm trying to explain that you can't keep doing them."

"Of course I shall keep doing them." He peered into her face, probably thinking her crazed. "I'll do more once we're wed. Your father may be a squire, but mine is prominent for a merchant. In five years we'll both be one-and-twenty. I'll have a share in my father's business and can support a wife. We can decide what we want, not what our parents want." He gave her a loving smile, took her pillow and set it on the bench. "Now then, that's settled. Come for a walk and stretch your legs."

Conflicting emotions battled within her—ripping her apart. For seven years she had wielded power in her household, ordered things to please herself, basked in her father's affection. Now Jonathan had stepped in and taken over, and though it went totally against her nature, she had let him, at least for a time. Because she needed what he offered.

Seeing her indecision, he put his arms around her, and she leaned her head against his shoulder, clinging to him hard while he smoothed her hair with kisses. "Only for a minute," she whispered finally. Lovingly she laced her fingers with his, lifted his hand and cradled it against her cheek. She would pay for this, but not until much later, she hoped.

Chapter 2

Leaving her pillow and her cares behind, Margaret let Jonathan sweep her into the dark. No, she told herself, he was not playing at anything. He was a hero, natural born. One with a magic touch, too. Just now, gliding with him along the uneven meadow path, she learned something amazing—the night was not all black.

"The night is beautiful, Margaret," he whispered, as if reading her thoughts. "Let me show it to you. Let me teach you to love it as I do."

She saw poorly in the dark, stumbled on roots and stones. But Jonathan was a magician in the dark—surefooted and clever, and as she leaned against his strength, his arm woven around her waist to guide her, the darkness opened up to offer more than hidden hazards. Grass and trees swayed and bent in a dance of midnight emerald. The sky changed to the deepest shade of plum. The rising of the storm moaned around them, sent the trees tossing along with her heart. Though her father needed her, and she loved him dearly, she also wanted Jonathan. She had a burning, craving need for his magic in her life.

When the rain began, they sheltered beneath some trees. Jonathan stripped off his doublet, held it over their heads. Water formed in warm beads on her cheeks, and he smoothed the drops away with his magical fingers. "I love you, my Marguerite." His choice of the daisy's French name fell softly on her ears, reminding her of the day he had nicknamed her, because of her ivory skin and golden eyes. His voice husky with longing, he sent the tip of his finger to trace her sensitive mouth. Bending over, he removed his finger and replaced it with his lips.

The wind circled around them. She felt marvelously

alone with him, as if blown to an enchanted place at the center of the world. His loving lips demanded, and she answered him with eager daring. Lightning flashed and broke into a thousand shards around them. The shooting light seemed to pierce her body as thrills from his flesh leaped to hers. As her lips drew sustenance from his, she rose up on tiptoe and clasped her arms around his neck, clinging desperately. Thunder exploded, shaking her world and her emotions. Guilt and want warred within her. She needed him, wanted him, but she also needed her father, and with a pang of foreboding, she realized she couldn't have both.

"Jonathan, stop a moment." She broke the kiss, overwhelmed by a storm of guilt equal to the wind's gusting. "I shouldn't be here. I must go in."

"I know you must. But one more kiss first."

She couldn't resist him. She never had, and that was the trouble. Tilting up her face, she met his lips with hers. His kiss warmed her body, streaking through her veins the way lightning raced across the sky. If only he could solve her problems, lift them like a burden from her shoulders. But he couldn't, and she must not ask him. She had to manage her troubles alone.

"Where were you?" Lady Eleanor's accusation greeted Margaret as she mounted the last step and moved toward her father's door. Her mother's face was tight and pale.

"I went out for air, Mother," Margaret said hurriedly. "But now I'm going in to Father. Come and see him. He is much better—"

"No, no, I can't." Lady Eleanor fell back several paces from the door, a fearful look on her face. But she regained her composure quickly. "My health is fragile, as you know. Your father begs me not to risk catching his fever. I will see him on the morrow," she finished briskly. "At any rate, I just wanted you to know that my father's men and his lawyer from Yorkshire have arrived."

"Another lawyer?" Margaret puzzled aloud. For years her mother had engaged in lawsuits. That was where all her husband's income went. "How can he help?"

Lady Eleanor cleared her throat and clicked her fingernails together in her usual nervous gesture. "He will settle my latest case, the one about that piece of property meant for your dowry. The other men are escorts. When your father is gone, they will take us to Yorkshire. We will live at Clifton Manor with your grandsire. And, mind you," she went on more sternly, "you're to forget this merchant boy. You are descended from nobility, as I told you last night. Your grandsire didn't like it when I wed with your father, a lowly squire, and we quarreled over it. But he and I are reconciled now, and he'll find you an appropriate noble match."

Margaret stared at her, aghast. "But Father's going to get well. He's much better. Just come and—"

"Enough of this pretense," her mother cried, suddenly losing all composure. "He isn't going to get well, Margaret. He's dying and you know it." She caught herself, obviously groping for self-control. "But you need have no fear. You're granddaughter to an earl and can live in wealth and comfort from now on. Don't deny your heritage. Welcome it and be glad."

Margaret shook her head, her mind spinning in painful confusion. "But I'm not going to Yorkshire. My life has always been here, with Father."

"Margaret, listen to me." Her mother spoke slowly and deliberately, as if to someone feeble-witted. "Your father knew we would have nothing when he died, so he made your grandsire your legal guardian. And your grandsire writes that he is eager to welcome you to Clifton. He will treat you with esteem, just like your father did. Your father wants us both properly cared for. You were always obedient to him, if not to me. I should think you would want to honor his dying wish."

A haze descended on Margaret, a swirling fog. She had read the will last night, but had cast it away after these shocking disclosures. Suddenly, without warning, she was granddaughter to an earl. Her mother had married low in taking the squire and had kept it secret all these years.

But her father wasn't dead. He wasn't! Pushing blindly past her mother, suddenly needing to see him, she entered his chamber. Here was the person who loved her. She lavished her care on him, in return for his wonderful tenderness—for the love he generously gave her ever since she could remember, whether she deserved it or not.

A gust of wind swirled through the chamber as she entered, blowing out the single candle. Her mother hadn't come to close the windows. Quickly Margaret pulled the mullioned casements shut, closing out the accompanying spate of rain.

"Here I am, Papa." She forced a cheery greeting as she turned to the massive four-postered bed and felt for the tinder box. Rubbing flint and steel together, she made a spark and lit the candle. "Shall I fetch a cool cloth to—"

Margaret froze. Her father lay in the center of the bed, more still than she had ever seen him. His eyes were open wide, staring at the canopy above.

"Papa?" Holding her breath, she leaned over the bed to touch his cheek. It was warm, but not hot with fever. He was fine. He had to be.

With trembling hands she groped on the nearby table and found the looking glass. Holding it to his lips, she waited for the telltale sign of life, the fogging of the glass. A minute passed. Then another. The crystal surface remained clear.

With a cry of despair, Margaret dropped the glass on the bed and flung herself against the bedside, tears scalding her eyes. Sobs shook her body as despair engulfed her. Dear God, what had she done?

"I only went for a few minutes," she whispered, raising her head, stretching out one hand to touch his beloved face. "I was terribly, horribly wicked to leave you." The shuddering tremors in her chest fragmented her words. "I'll do as you wish, go to Yorkshire to my grandsire. Mother will be happier there, and I know you want her happy. I know you love her, as you do me. But oh, Papa, I wish I had stayed with you every minute." She couldn't bear to admit it aloud, but he knew. This was all her fault.

With her entire life in shambles, she sagged against the bed, unable to check her weeping. Then she remembered—outside, her lace pillow lay forgotten on the bench, rain oozing through it, ruining all her effort. She sobbed harder against the counterpane, shaking the bed.

She had given in to weakness, and here was her punishment: her beloved father lay before her, his dear lips forever silenced. Stretching out one hand, she ran her trembling finger along his cooling cheek, then closed his eyes while her own sight blurred with more tears. Next she would lose Jonathan as well. In the short nine months they'd been together, she had deceived him utterly, played soft and clinging while he spoiled and cared for her—that was the type of woman he wanted, and she was neither. She was willful and did things her own way. With another heart-wrenching sob, she knew she had to end things between them. For his sake, to save him sorrow. She had known this ugly truth all along.

Jonathan awoke early on Saturday, still exhausted from arranging the details of the squire's funeral. Two full days he had labored, paying for everything from his own savings, though he never mentioned it to Margaret's mother. Instead he saw her lawyers, arranged every detail because he cared deeply for Margaret. It was his gift to her. Her father's death had devastated her, had shocked all of them. No one had believed the man so ill.

He should get out of bed, Jonathan realized, and try to meet with Margaret. He was still troubled by the way she had talked two nights ago. He must manage to see her alone today.

"Jonathan? Are you awake?"

"No. Go 'way." He turned over sleepily and buried his head in the pillows, not wanting to see his older sister Rozalinde. Besides, he had been having a wonderful dream and he didn't want to leave it, that he held Margaret in his arms.

"I have to talk to you, Jonathan. A letter just came from Margaret." Rozalinde's voice was full of urgency.

"Why didn't you say so?" He sat up groggily, impatiently ripped it open, scanned the few tearful, apologetic lines. A numb disbelief swept through him. He stared at the letter, then at Rozalinde, stunned. "This can't be right. What does she mean, she has to live in Yorkshire, her father wanted it that way?"

"Oh, Jonathan, I'm sorry to be the bearer of bad news. None of us knew Margaret's mother was the daughter of an earl, although it explains why she always acted so proud, as if nothing in our town were good enough for her. At any rate, now that her husband has died, Lady Eleanor is taking Margaret to live with the earl, who's wealthy. As I understand it, a noble marriage is being arranged for Margaret—"

"That's madness! I've got to see her." Jonathan leaped

out of bed in his nightshirt and fumbled for his stocks. "Go. So I can dress."

"They left Lulworth some time ago, long before daybreak, Jonathan. Those men who came two days earlier were sent as escort."

Jonathan looked at her, astounded. So much was happening so fast, he couldn't take it all in. "Then I'll follow them. I need a word with her. She must decline this other marriage. She loves me. I know she does."

"I agree, Jonathan, but you'll have to hurry to catch them."

"I will," he muttered as he tugged on his stocks and his sister closed the door. "Believe me, I will."

Three months later, Jonathan rode into the Cavandish stable yard on a new bay stallion. His mother and sister jumped up from their seats in the garden. "Jonathan, my son," called his mother, "where did you get that amazing horse?"

"I'm off for the Netherlands at week's end. I have a commission in the queen's cavalry, thanks to Rozalinde's husband." He dismounted with a flourish, but he wasn't smiling.

"Oh, Jonathan, I know you've talked about the Netherlands before, but please don't go to war. Is it really so bad as that?" his mother pleaded.

He stared at her as if she were witless. How could it be worse, when the woman you love was snatched out from under your very nose at dawn, when you rode hard after her but never caught up? Then she wrote to say she must wed another, that her beloved father had wanted it that way. "Margaret's grandsire answered my second letter," he told his mother, wanting her to understand. "After he refused my offer for Margaret's hand. He said not to write to her again because he would intercept my letters. And that by week's end, she would be wed to someone else. It took the letter well over two weeks to get here. So," he finished briskly, "I'm off for the Netherlands."

"Troth," exclaimed his sister, "it sounds as if Margaret's in prison."

"Exactly. And here I am, not able to do a thing about it. We're both sixteen and underage. And for some reason I can't understand, Margaret seemed determined to leave."

"Something must have changed her mind, Jonathan." Rozalinde patted the bay stallion's sleek neck. "I'm sure she loves you, but other things can get in the way of love."

"The only reason I stayed in Lulworth this long was because of her. I never wanted to be a draper like Father. I'm sorry, Mother." Jonathan put an arm around his mother's plump shoulders as she groped for her handkerchief. "But I can help the people over there who are oppressed by Spain. They're unfairly taxed, then imprisoned, tortured, and their lands and goods confiscated if they protest. Besides, if they're defeated, Spain will come after England next, so my help is needed. I can fight for things I believe in."

"You might see about an apprenticeship in Germany during leaves," Rozalinde suggested, apparently recognizing his mind was made up, but equally determined to lure him away from the battlefield. "You were always interested in armor, and Germany has the best armorers, so they say."

"I may do that." He might as well, he thought grimly. It didn't matter what he did now. Nothing mattered. Not since he had lost Margaret. He might as well serve others, because there was nothing more he wanted for himself.

Chapter 3

Clifton Manor, Yorkshire, England, June 1579

The Spanish called him El Mágico Demoníaco, The Demon Magician, for escaping from their most impregnable prison in the Netherlands. The women shortened it to El Mágico, for turning their heads and snaring their hearts with his magical charm. Queen Elizabeth made him her chief intelligence agent in the Netherlands rebellion against Spain. He had fought in countless battles and come home a hero, with bevies of females worshipping at his feet.

Margaret Smytheson Longleate sat behind the Venus statue in her grandfather's knot garden and thought about this legend. The maids had gossiped about him for an entire se'nnight, so enthralled they forgot their chores and had to be reminded. The serving men were just as bad. Everyone at Clifton Manor whispered tales of his exploits, the rumors coming straight from London. The grave dangers endured by the hero were legendary. They said he was impossibly daring! Heartbreakingly romantic! Everyone was ecstatic, half hysterical with excitement. Because he was coming here to Yorkshire to recruit men.

Margaret couldn't share their enthusiasm. War heroes weren't romantic. This one might have raised the siege of Lieden, but he had also been shot in the arm and almost died. He had saved scores of Antwerp families when unpaid Spanish troops pillaged the city, but his best friend had been killed. He might have led the Brussels *coup d'etat,* seizing the council of state from the Spanish, but he had been captured later at the battle of Gembloux. The noble captain had sacrificed himself and saved hundreds of his fellows, but for certes nothing romantic had happened during his ugly sojourn as Spain's guest.

No, Margaret thought, the man wouldn't be magic. He would be like her grandfather, who had also seen war. But she was out of time for thinking about El Mágico. She had sly, manipulative Robert to worry about, she remembered wearily, peering out from her hiding place behind the statue, praying she wouldn't see him. Ducking back, she breathed with relief. No sign of him. The scent of marjoram wafted to her, and she inhaled deeply, held the air. God, how she missed her father since he'd died, the person she had most trusted. Bereft of his love, she reached for her own style of magic. She must rely only on herself.

Breath escaped Margaret, a glad sigh. Permission granted. Leaning against the base of the statue, she closed her eyes, sought her familiar haven. Lace making. The *point d'esprit,* her favorite pattern, entered her thoughts soothingly, along with the bobbins. Eagerly she conjured the feel of them. Cool ivory, polished wood. The real ones were in her chamber, sitting on her table. She could fetch them. But no, she risked meeting Robert, and besides, in her mind she could feel them. *Cross, twist, place a pin.* The rhythm of the pattern grew inside her. *Enchanted motions. Flawless as dreams.* Though her empty hands lay in her lap, calm suffused her being.

Squeezing her eyelids tightly, Margaret thought of her father. *You have a gift, daughter.* His words came back to her, tender and loving, tearing at her heart. Tears wet her face, and she thought hard of the lace. It was her strength and her refuge. After all these years, the rhythm was a song inside her. Each time she took up the pillow, the song awoke. . . .

The sound of someone clearing his throat snapped Margaret back to the present. He came skulking into the grape arbor several dozen paces away, watching her with predatory eyes—Robert Weston, Viscount Solsover, heir to the earldom of Rodminster. The cherished calm of the lace disintegrated. She stood up.

He must have come from the kitchen gardens, she decided. As usual, he managed to trick her, a common practice of his. From his vantage point, she was fully in view behind the statue. Only low hedges and raked gravel walks separated them.

Margaret dodged around the statue and headed for the yew maze. Today she couldn't tolerate his company. More than anything she wanted to escape.

"Margaret, stop. I have important news."

Reluctance dogged her feet. She paused on the far side of the sundial, looked back. What could be so important? That he once again planned to badger her to visit his bed? Or did he just intend to attack?

He crossed the gravel toward her in long strides, seeming sure of himself, convinced he deserved her favors. She knew otherwise. The problem was getting him to accept it. His thick skull took new ideas at a rate she deemed tedious.

Today was no exception. He came straight for her, rounding the right side of the dial. Automatically she dodged left to escape him, their movements mirror opposites. When he changed direction, she did, too. Right. Left. Back and forth.

"Robert, I told you no! I won't bed with you, no matter how many times you ask me." Margaret clapped one hand against her side, panting. "Accept and let it end."

"You don't mean that, Margaret," Robert cajoled. "You delight in teasing me, saying one thing but meaning another. Come now, give me what I need."

Margaret frowned as Robert's gaze moved over her body. She was uncomfortably conscious of the way her breasts threatened to spill over the top of her black brocade bodice. Vaguely she remembered her mother had bid her to wear this gown, laced it so tight she could scarcely breathe. Now it attracted Robert's interest, Robert's attention. A man who didn't believe anything she told him. A man who crept up on her when she didn't expect it, who waited for her in deserted passages. With distaste she remembered his clammy hands groping, his unwanted thighs pressed against hers. . . .

What he needed was a good dose of saltpeter. She wouldn't say so, would store away the thought, along with the other rude things she wanted to say to him. But how long could she hold them in?

"I don't want to give you anything," she said firmly. "I want to be left alone."

He came around the dial plot after her. Margaret sidestepped and darted to the other side.

"Margaret, you cause me great torment. You know how

I long for you. Do me an unending kindness. Let me give you one tiny kiss."

"Your kisses are not tiny, Robert." As Margaret backed away from him, she felt the sole of her slipper skid on a slick place. With a thrust she righted herself and hurried around the dial.

Robert's rapier clashed against his legs as he blundered after her, taking a similar slide on the mud. "You've had your fun, Margaret. You've made sport of my feelings. Now 'tis time to yield. I've asked your grandfather for your hand."

His words reeked of desperation. Rob pursued a different female each week. Only as a last resort would he tie himself to one in particular. "In truth?" she taunted, unwilling to believe him. "What did he say?"

"He agreed. Since you've been widowed a year, we're to wed."

Margaret stopped short and stared at him. "You jest."

Robert looked dead serious. "No, I'm tired of waiting. Since you won't bed with me, I asked for your hand. Your grandsire said yes."

For a second, the garden swam before Margaret's vision. Then rage ripped its raw path of insult through her. The meaning of the seductive dress, worn at her mother's insistence, gripped her. The thought absorbed her wholly, her sense of betrayal deep. No one knew better than her mother what she had been through.

One of Robert's huge hands snaked into view. As he strained for her, he collided with the heavy face of the dial. It tilted on its marble base and began to fall.

"Catch it. 'Twill break!" Margaret clasped her hands in dismay. "Grandsire's favorite dial."

Robert fumbled for the heavy disk and caught it just before it plunged to the ground. "There. I've rescued the silly bauble."

But Margaret had gathered up her heavy black skirts and taken to her heels. Hoping to escape, she ran.

An oath burst from Robert's lips. Without looking back, Margaret heard him as she tore down the path of a hundred yews. Then she turned to head up the avenue of limes. On she ran, around the corner at the Mars fountain, along the north terrace beyond the great house. She would lose him in the maze. She knew its twisting pattern well, and he, being a visitor, did not.

A minute later she came to a junction where four paths met among ancient, towering yews. Screened by their thickness, she entered the maze. She hurried until the stitch in her side once more throbbed. But by then she left the maze by the far exit. It brought her to Clifton's west side, where the drive made its first proud approach from the main road. Now she could stop for a minute and decide what to do about this new catastrophe. The river Esk flowed nearby. Soon she would take refuge in company by seeking Patience, who would be there with Bessie. Her cherished child loved dabbling in the water with twigs and leaves.

Sinking down on a marble bench, Margaret plied her fan vigorously, trying to still her pounding heart and cool her flushed skin. She would go in a second, as soon as she caught her breath. Nearby several gardeners trimmed the shrubbery while maids and children raked the gravel drive smooth. The late June light beat on her velvet-clad shoulders. In fact she burned all over, but it wasn't from the sun. Thoughts of her grandfather rose up, thoughts of her mother. Now she realized they had meant her for Robert. While she engrossed herself in her lace, they had planned her future. Without even asking. God's eyelid, how dare they do such a thing again!

Anger poured into her, came to a rapid simmer, culminating in a full boil. Images of her last decision multiplied in her head. She clenched her fists, thinking of what she had done to win her grandsire's affection. For the sake of the name Clifford, a family she hadn't known existed, she had wed as he requested. She could still hear his deep voice ringing with conviction, saying, "You, granddaughter, are my final hope."

He took her to see the hereditary estate: the huge crop fields, the rows of tenant cottages, the iron mines among the Yorkshire hills. All must pass to a male with pure, noble bloodlines. Her son, her grandsire told her, must be his heir.

His wish had seemed so reasonable, along with his flawless logic. And she *had* wanted to please him. Sixteen, she'd been, bereaved of her beloved father, desperate for an anchor in a sea of tumultuous sorrow. Who else should she turn to but the guardian her father had selected. She had made a muddle of her life up until then, had had to do penance for her many errors.

What followed hadn't been just a bad marriage—it had been a disaster! Not her fault entirely—Oliver had been impossible—yet she blamed herself. Woe and betide, to think she could tolerate someone managing her life for her. But most of all she blamed her grandsire. She had clung to the hope that he might cherish her, that he might take her father's vacant place. Foolish thought—her grandsire didn't cherish anyone. He was much too intent on enforcing his rules.

The turmoil in her mind brought Margaret to her feet. She didn't want to think about it. She wanted to be with her child. Best hurry though—any time now Bessie must go to the house to assist with supper. Mary would fetch her, then take her place. Knowing Mary—foolish, inept Mary—she would let Patience get into mischief. Even at two, her child could lead the maid to believe anything. Propping one foot on the bench, Margaret flicked away the mud on her velvet shoe, then prepared to set off.

How she yearned for her father. If only she hadn't deserted him when he most needed her. If she had nursed him diligently the way he required, he would most probably still be alive today.

She writhed at the idea, burdened by remorse in layers. Like layers of onion she peeled away pain, but found only tears, ever more tears. Her mistake. Her grievous mistake, teaching her life's rules the hard way.

When a mounted party came through the black iron gates guarding Clifton's entrance, Margaret's eyes lit on seven men, all riding quality mounts that showed signs of careful grooming.

Clifton's portly gatekeeper waddled out of his lodge to greet them, crying the name El Mágico with joyous acclaim. This must be the expected war hero and his traveling fellows, but she wasn't interested. Besides, Robert had burst through the yews, puffing from his run and demanding her attention. He looked comical in his ornate court costume, sweat-stained, with his lace ruff askew. "You tricked me," he growled, voice low and tinged with fury. "That blasted dial couldn't break."

Margaret started to say she *had* tricked him about the

dial, with pleasure, but just then a shrill female scream from the direction of the river tore the afternoon air. That had to be Mary. Which meant Patience was in trouble!

An answering explosion of terror plummeted through Margaret. She had waited too long!

Chapter 4

Jerking around in the direction of the scream, Margaret bundled up her massive black skirts and tore down the nearby path. She raced along the broad trail toward the river, around a turn, and down the hill to the water's edge.

Sure enough, Mary had changed places with Bessie. Now she hovered on the riverbank, wringing her hands and wailing. Midway across the river, the splashing figure of her daughter clung to a branch caught among some rocks, fighting the drowning pull of the river Esk. The too-slim branch was bent taut.

Margaret reached Mary and passed her. "Get to the house and summon the physician," she shouted at the maid without stopping. "At once!" Mary took off for the manor, scuttling like a guilty goose. "I'm coming, Patience," Margaret cried, charging into the water without pause.

Liquid ice sent its shock through her as the water rose all the way to her thighs. Still swollen from earlier spring rains and melted snow, the river raged stronger and deeper than she had imagined. Her expensive black skirts billowed as she moved, then soaked and sank, but she had to ignore them. Her baby's face was scrunched with terror as she clutched the branch, her fingers blue with cold. Please, Margaret prayed as she slogged forward, don't let her lose her grip!

Halfway there, the water grew deeper, swelling to her waist. With each step, Margaret fought the greedy grasp that dragged at her leaden petticoats and massive farthingale, pulling her off course and downstream from Patience. Flailing with both hands, she battled her way back while the river's ominous roar filled her ears like laughter, ridiculing her efforts. Within several yards of victory, her farthingale snagged on something underwater and caught fast. Struggling with the skirt, she wrestled to pull away.

"El Mágico's a-coming, my lady! Don't fear," cried a voice Margaret recognized as the porter's from atop the hill behind her.

Twisting around, she started. One of the military party, a striking bearded warrior clad all in black, sprinted toward the river, stripping off his doublet as he came. She had a fleeting, astonishing impression of muscular strength in motion before he plunged into the water, just as she had. Unlike her, his booted legs sliced through the water with the ease of hot steel through butter.

"Stay back. You'll fall," he ordered tersely. She had a split-second encounter with his charismatic, smoky brown gaze before he flashed past her so fast he was almost a blur. Sprays of water from his wake nearly blinded her as he launched himself at Patience, who lost her grip on the branch at that very instant.

Margaret screamed in horror as the two of them, man and child, disappeared beneath the surface of the water. Freeing herself with a frantic yank of tearing skirts, she fought her way toward where they had both gone down.

The river erupted in a dazzling fountain of water several feet downstream, and El Mágico emerged, cradling her child. Patience had locked her hands in the fabric of his dark shirt, and she coughed and gagged while he rapped her on the back. Thigh deep in water, the heavily bearded magician stilled, massaging her child's back with a circling movement. While Margaret stared in amazement, Patience vomited on his arm. He merely shifted Patience to his other arm and rinsed it off in the running river, whose strength had dwindled compared to his amazing bodily power. Moving toward the shallows, he spoke calming words while Patience's lungs expanded and her tiny body drew in air.

"Hurrah, Captain Mágico!" yelled the porter, whipping Margaret's gaze back to the hill. With consternation she remembered they had an audience. The gardeners and the rakers lingered with the porter, excited by the spectacle but afraid to come near. They were supposed to be working but had tossed aside their tools and followed to see the uproar. Everyone stood awestruck, peering over each other's shoulders, watching El Mágico make the rescue. She dragged her gaze back to her child. "Saved her, didn't he, my lady?" the porter's deep bass boomed out. "Magic, just like we 'eard tell."

Margaret couldn't answer. She was staring at El Mágico's hands, mesmerized. She always noticed a person's hands first. His were beautifully sculpted, with long, powerful fingers full of grace. They seemed eerily familiar, wrapped around her baby. She knew them from somewhere, but she could not quite think . . .

"God's eyelid!" Margaret's mind reeled as recognition hit her, knocking the words out of her as well as her breath. Her world tilted wildly as joy bloomed inside her for one marvelous minute, spread with lightning swiftness through her veins. Because Jonathan Cavandish stood before her rocking her child, a man with a face like a god and the body of a warrior, just above an arm's length away.

A hundred times she had walked along this very river in the past five years and wished him here, the boy who had once loved her. Now he appeared like magic at the moment of crisis. But bobbins and bolsters, he wasn't a boy anymore!

Margaret stared at his hands, wanted to stare at the rest of him if he would come out of the water. If he had appeared like magic, the way he had changed was also magical. He'd grown impossibly tall, his sculpted facial features hardened from boyish beauty into sleek, elegant manhood. His chest and shoulders, the same ones that had once sheltered and comforted her, had widened with muscle—the fabric of his wet shirt strained with it. The sleek mustache and full beard gave him a sensual look that had disguised him temporarily. Not for long did she fail to recognize him. And from the sudden blaze of intensity in his eyes as they meshed with hers, she knew he recognized her as well.

"You've ruined your clothes," she blurted as he straightened Patience's wet smock. "You must let us replace them. Your boots will take days to dry." He wore a knee-high pair of fine black leather, at least they had looked fine before he plunged into the water. But they were nowhere near as fine as his heavily muscled thighs that rose above them.

"Marguerite." His voice, deeper than she remembered, twined itself around her consciousness as he pronounced her nickname with a caress. "I would have thought 'Hello, Jonathan' a more appropriate greeting, but you always had your special way of doing things. Kind of you to care about my clothing, but you've ruined yours as well."

His gaze lingered on her, asking a hundred questions, about her mourning black and more. She was suddenly conscious that her wet widow's weeds molded to her flesh like sodden plaster. Glancing down, she had to resist the impulse to cover the twin peaks of her breasts showing through her wet bodice. When she looked up again, he sent her a lightning-swift grin and quirked one eyebrow, something only he could do. It was just like in their Lulworth days, only then he had done so much more than just look.

"I'm sure my clothes will dry and be none the worse," he continued, "but even if they are ruined, 'tis a small thing for the sake of a child. I know you agree."

Margaret stood in the cold water, her mind growing as numb as her toes. Jonathan straightened a lock of Patience's wet hair with steady hands, seeming perfectly collected, not the least ruffled by their unexpected meeting. A tumult of memories swooped down on her—of leaning her cheek against his warm shoulder, of tracing his handsome face with shy fingers while his arms pressed her close. Jonathan was here! her unruly body cried, wanting to celebrate. He was here at last!

"We have stood in the water long enough." With sure movements he grasped her elbow and propelled her toward the bank. He surged out of the water on powerful legs, then turned and caught her hand. His warm fingers closed around her cold ones with a shock that traveled up her arm and into her body, all the way to warm her soul. As she emerged, dripping, dragging the weight of her wet gown, she knew he inspected her further, taking in the elaborate braiding of her hair, her rich gown drawn tight at the waist, the low swoop of her bodice across her breasts. His lingering glance sent hot pins of pleasure nipping through Margaret's belly. Then he nodded, as if in approval, which made her drop his hand fast.

"I don't understand," she said. "You're this El Mágico that everyone talks of?"

He inclined his head in a slight bow over her child. "It is my dubious honor to be the bearer of the name in question. I prefer Captain Cavandish, but people like the other label and it has unfortunately stuck." He sent her a rueful gaze.

Her spirits fell. The laughing, jesting boy she had known—wounded in battle dozens of times, seeing his comrades die around him though he came through by some miracle, sacrificing himself for others, even a prisoner of war? "I can't believe . . . But that's horrible, not the name, but how you earned it!"

He nodded soberly. "None of your serving folk would agree. They think I've come to entertain them." Without taking his eyes off her, he inclined his head toward the hill.

She glanced that way. Every female's face had turned hopeful and starry-eyed, imagining his lovemaking. The men's expressions were a cross between worship and envy as they yearned to join him, hoping his wondrous skill with war and women could rub off on them.

Robert stood to one side, his face reflecting boredom, one foot braced on a boulder while he picked his teeth with a gold toothpick. How like him to stand idle while her child was drowning. Margaret looked away in disgust.

"We must take this child inside," Jonathan told her briskly. "She needs something hot to drink, as much as she'll take, then bed. Someone was lax, letting her in the water. Can you think how such a thing came about?"

A cold breeze ran through Margaret. "She must have fallen. It was my fault; I should have come sooner." Empty-handed, she shivered in her wet clothes and stared at the pair of them as Jonathan caught up his doublet and swaddled Patience. Her child snuggled against him, drinking in his body warmth, a contented smile on her cherub face.

"Your fault? It seems to me 'twas the fault of the maid who watched her. She is not fit for tending children. I'll speak to the earl about it."

He didn't wait for her agreement. Ever the man of action, he set out for the house.

"Stop! Wait!" Margaret gathered up her skirts that now clung like shrunken tent silk to her whalebone farthingale and hurried after him. There he went again, taking charge the way he used to. But she was no longer the young girl pretending to be helpless to please the man in her life. "I don't want you speaking to the earl about the maid. I'll handle it. And you must give me my child now," she cried, trying to catch up. "I didn't need your help in saving her.

I was about to do it myself. Pray be so good as to hand her back at once."

"This is your daughter?" He stopped and stared at her intently. "Then I refuse to apologize for saving her. And I seem to recall a past disagreement about the things I did for you. Are we going to quarrel about them again?"

The rich tones of his voice fell on her ears, beguiling her as of old. "You're the one making the quarrel," she insisted, determined not to back down. Plunged from joy into chaos, she felt like a box of jumbled bobbins that had just been shaken. "I thank you for saving my child. I appreciate the kindness. But I was about to do it myself."

"On that topic I have to differ with you," he said in a strict tone, probably the one reserved for his cavalry unit. "I have a great deal of experience with emergencies—more than most people. I would have been remiss to hold back."

Margaret's temper slipped the first notch—her nasty, troublesome temper that refused to obey her. The battle recommenced inside her—the thrill of seeing him again mixing with frustration—he always pushed his way in and neatly took over. When they were her tasks to handle. Hers! All the things she had hidden from him, the things she really was inside, longed to burst forth. He had never suspected, had been so sure of his strength and her helpless nature.

"What I'm telling you," she cried, "is that not everyone likes being rescued. Your deeds may be needed by some but not by me. Not anymore. I would rather you asked first."

He stopped again, this time so suddenly that she ran into his elbow. "Margaret, you've changed. I want to hear about it. Pray go on."

By heaven, what was she doing? Margaret wondered as she righted herself from their collision. Just the power of his gaze was enough to wilt her willpower, make her cave in and pretend to be what he wanted. His deep brown eyes probed hers, demanding the truth. Their smoky hue had always enchanted her, like exotic tea from the mystical east. But he was right. For some time she had needed to tell him these things. They were bursting to get out. "I'm sorry," she said, steeling herself to the task, "but I deceived you back in Lulworth. That was wicked of me and I'm paying the price for it, as well as for everything else. But you see, it's not that I've changed. I was never the girl you wanted. I'm not the person you thought I was at all."

His gaze intensified, if that were possible, making the blood creep up her chest and neck and flood her cheeks. Oh, the temptation to burst into flame; he had always aroused her passion. They were picking up exactly where they had left off five years ago, but with one difference. She must not deceive him this time. Her entire body quivered as she awaited his next question. She knew what was coming . . .

"Then who are you?" he demanded, staring her straight in the eye.

Chapter 5

"Who am I?"

Jonathan cradled his delicate burden and listened to Margaret echo back his question in seeming bafflement. Once more the astonishment of seeing her again swept over him. She was even better than he remembered—still radiant with the beauty of finely textured skin highlighted by amazingly gold-blond hair, the flare of her lip and nostril, flawless.

Lord in heaven! She had grown more vibrant than ever—a mother, beautifully blossomed. Her body, still slim and willowy, was now the epitome of graceful swells and enticing curves. Though he would see more of her if she didn't wear that monstrous barrier of a farthingale. How he would like to see her without it, without anything, in fact, hair floating down her back in a golden tumble. He'd always loved twisting his fingers in that gold, catching the drooping flower of her lips with his own. . . .

"The trouble was, I let you dominate me," she was saying, apparently oblivious to the way he was staring. "When what I really needed to do was . . ."

"Go on," he urged her, pulling himself together, trying to let the past be the past. Yet it drew him undeniably, his time with this sweet maid whose nimble feet had flashed beneath her simple skirts when she ran with him across the meadow or laughed with him on the shores of Lulworth Cove. Nimble feet and equally nimble mind, her thoughts shining deep in her golden eyes. "You were about to tell me the truth. I prefer that you did."

"You prefer it? What of me?" she shot back, evidently ruffled. "I was the one contorting myself, trying to be something I wasn't. God's eyelid, how can you ask who I am?

Can't you tell?" she demanded, growing more distressed. "I know who I am. Why does no one else?"

"We all hide part of ourselves at appropriate moments," he consoled her. "You need not feel ashamed of that."

"You don't understand, you never did." She shook her head, as if despairing. "You're much too generous, and in the past I took advantage of that, letting you do things when *I* should have been doing them. I never even thanked you properly for my father's funeral, though I didn't know about it at the time. My mother seemed to think the lawyers handled it, but I looked at her papers after and saw no trace of expenses. I guessed you had done it and I never even wrote to you. I'm wicked, I tell you, and 'tis time you knew."

The strength of her outburst astonished him. But then she was entitled to it, he decided. "There now," he gentled. "You're overwrought, that's all. 'Tis the strain of the accident. You'll be yourself anon."

"That's what I'm trying to tell you. I am myself. This is how I am."

An odd little shock jolted through him. At the core of his being, where his dark need for revenge dwelled, a dim spark of gold light flickered—Margaret's light. A tiny swell of pleasure followed. In the year since his escape from prison, he had felt nothing but grinding hate for the man who had tortured him. Inside, memory of that demon was an ever-present river of darkness waiting to sweep him away. What a relief to feel something different. Only minutes in her company and she awakened things long dead in him: surprise, curiosity.

"What you're telling me," he said, motioning for them to continue toward the house, "is that you have a temper. I never knew that. How did you manage to keep such an interesting part of yourself hidden? From me of all people. You should get angry more often. It well becomes you, makes your eyes flash gold and your cheeks turn to rose."

She hurried after him, having to take two strides to his every one. A tinge of color like ripe berries had indeed crept over the beautiful ivory flesh of her graceful neck and worked on warming her face. "That's not at all what I'm trying to tell you!" she cried, running to catch up.

"I know. There's more." He sighed with resignation. "You're telling me you didn't really want to do things my way all those years ago. You didn't delight in my every thought and idea, the way you suggested. Well, well, the truth comes out at last. 'Twas obvious something was wrong between us, even before you left Lulworth. Now I know what it was. I knew it was too good to be true."

"Too good?" She did have a temper, that was quite evident. Words fairly flew from her. "I was horrible, the way I acted, fawning on you, idolizing you, letting you solve my problems and take control. You treated me like glass, likely to break and twice as delicate, and I encouraged you. I drove myself mad, trying to be what you wanted. Even when I tried hard, I was terrible at it. I should never have let it go on."

"If you believed that, why did you?" He appealed to Patience, who was rubbing one chubby cheek against his chest. "Did you know she had a temper, little imp? Why did she hide it from me?"

"She knows!" Margaret cried, well on her way to a frenzy. "Everyone at Clifton knows! But men don't like willful women. If I hadn't hidden it, you would never have liked me, most certainly would never have noticed me in the first place. And after I went to all the trouble of—" She clapped her open palm across her mouth, an appalled look on her face at what she'd said.

Jonathan stopped, so astounded he was speechless. By heaven, the joke was on him. He had thought he chose her, that he did the wooing, when all along . . . Throwing back his head, he let loose a howl of laughter so intense, the child started. But she settled right away as he continued, laughing until tears wet his eyes. Once started, he couldn't stop. Would wonders never cease, this woman was full of surprises. For the first time in eighteen months, he could laugh.

"What is so amusing, pray?" she demanded, a suspicious look on her lovely face.

"*I* am," he managed to say, bringing his mirth down to a chuckle. "I was so cocksure, never imagining a woman might do the choosing. Full of the folly of youth." He wiped his eyes and resumed his progress toward the manor house.

"So there you have it," she said, her framed skirt clashing and bouncing while she hurried beside him. "That's why we never suited. I prefer doing things my own way. Alone. That's how I am."

"Is your way so different from everyone else's?"

"I fear so." Her face got a sudden haunted look about it.

He instantly perceived that she had suffered since he saw her last. A shot of anger surged through him—that emotion still came readily, along with the desire to protect her from whoever had done her damage. But that would have to wait until later. "Here we are," he stated as they approached the massive manor doors.

Margaret shook her head in surprise as the house loomed before her. Her chest heaved from their rapid walk. She was out of breath and out of temper, and she didn't want to end her talk with Jonathan. She had thought explaining would clear the air between them, but she felt worse than ever.

"I take it your grandsire didn't warn you I was coming." He courteously let her mount the steps first.

"The two of you exchanged letters?" She immediately bristled, though he delivered the words without a trace of triumph. So her grandsire had known Jonathan was coming, mayhap even of their former Lulworth connection. "Oh," she huffed, narrowing her eyes at the thought. "Wait until I speak to him. He thinks females haven't the wit of cabbage worms, despite our last five years."

"I would only come with his prior invitation," Jonathan said. "I regret he didn't share the information with you."

"He didn't," she said grimly. "And why did he invite you? Our servants are all paid wages, so you can't recruit them."

He guided her through the doors, though he carried the burden. Leaning near, he whispered conspiratorially in her ear. "Pray don't say that too loudly. I'll recruit in the village to keep up the pretense. I would like to say more, but it must wait until later. We'll exchange details then."

Margaret tingled all over as he came near her. "There won't be a later," she stated as firmly as she could.

"Are you sure? Have you become a seeress? I thought your skill was lace."

"God's eyelid!" She stared at him in amazement. "You still turn serious things into jests. Would you stop your monstrous teasing and give me my child!"

He finally obeyed her orders, chuckling as he relinquished Patience. But Patience didn't want her. She set up howl and struggled to get back to the warm giant, a performance she had reserved until now solely for her mama. Mortified, Margaret winced as she took her child, doublet and all. Then she felt the captain's hand on her shoulder, steadying her while he shifted the doublet to keep Patience covered.

Please, no! Let her not respond to his touch! She shut her eyes tightly, gripped Patience, and braced herself to bear it. Because the scent that was uniquely Jonathan swept over her, sweet woodruff soap, along with horses and leather. Memory of his searing kisses rose up inside her, bringing her scents of summer, the mesh of his lips against hers. Out of the bounty of his generous nature, he had tried to help her. But she couldn't let him this time. The last five years had filled her with a raging need for independence, which meant she must resist his enslaving magic with all her strength.

"There you are, Mistress Willful." He arranged the doublet, then rubbed her shoulder with a familiar massaging motion that reminded her of sunlit days on the cove with him, trysts in the meadow, kisses in the woods. "Run along now and warm your child. She's like her mother, you know." He leaned close again and whispered in her ear. "A rare flower."

Margaret struggled to find her breath, which was lost somewhere in the pounding of her heart's hammer.

"One last thing," he admonished, holding his voice to that husky, intimate murmur. "You must give up this thought that you're wicked. You don't begin to know the meaning of the word. I've seen enough wickedness to know."

She stared at him, captured by the thin edge of tension underlying his words. His dark eyes had grown darker, like the center of a storm. And he said he had seen wickedness? Good God!

Once she had loved him but let him go. Without knowing it, she had sent him away to the cold arms of war. Now he was different—no longer the laughing, gregarious boy she'd known in Lulworth. The charm was still there, heightened into alluring, magical charisma. But inside him, she sensed the flowing darkness. Had she done this to him?

Remorse assailed her. Would she never be free of it? It

tore her in two, both in the past and now. Yet surely, for her father's sake, she had had to do her penance. She had been wrong for Jonathan, and he, for her. He ruined her self-control, made her weak and irresponsible. Not his fault. It was hers, really. When she was with him, her will weakened. Just now when he had touched her, she had wanted to melt.

Clutching Patience to her, she fled up the stairs, praying for deliverance. Yet as her feet padded on the stairs, one after another, inside her head the question formed—what was Jonathan doing at Clifton if he hadn't come to recruit men?

Chapter 6

Jonathan stood just inside the massive front doors, arms crossed at his chest, and watched her go. Lord, it was wonderful to see Margaret full of flash and fire. What a work of art she had become!

And she had a daughter—a daughter by another man. A stab of jealousy ran through him at the thought. But he brushed it away, choosing instead to see Margaret's image in the little imp—she was just like her mother, sweet as a comfit with her thickly lashed eyes and delicately curved cheeks. Seeming docile but unquestionably willful. Else why was she in the river when she had no business there?

Yes, Margaret was entirely correct, he hadn't thought her a willful woman, nor had he wanted one at sixteen. His father had taught him women should be soft and helpless so that men could spoil and cosset them. Most were like his mother—charming and chattering, loving gossip as well as gowns. Except for his sister Rozalinde, who was as willful as they came and, he had thought, the exception.

Which brought him to his immediate problem. He had practically told this new Margaret, this willful woman, his secret reason for being at Clifton. It was all because of the flash in her hazel-bright eyes, the astonishing texture of her ivory-gold skin, the silk-spun shimmer of her hair. She wore that hair drawn stiffly back in a tight coiffure that hid its rare beauty. Along with a grotesque court costume of mourning black with an artificial shape he detested. Yet even those things failed to subtract from her loveliness, from the stellar shine of her nimble spirit. He held on to the light she kindled within him for as long as it lasted.

When it was gone, he took the thought of their meeting and examined it methodically, just as he did when working minute, interlocking pieces of armor. Having seen all its parts, he put it away. He was an armorer, after all, as well as a soldier. Just as he'd trained his body with rigid military discipline, so had he trained his mind. Nothing must interfere with his work, not even Margaret. He had forced himself to forget her . . . until now.

He shrugged and turned away. It was best she had wed another. He had nothing to offer a woman anymore, now even less than when he had been a lad. Because his recent experiences had shrunk his capacity to feel the softest of human emotions to precisely zero. Only one-and-twenty and already he was a ruin of a man.

"That's all," he said to the servants clustered around the front entry. He pasted on his public smile and made a shooing motion with his hands. "The drama's over. Back to work."

The manor folk gave way before him as he came down the steps. Most meandered reluctantly back to their tasks. A few, however, came forward to be recognized, more because they were the boldest than for any other reason. Two housemaids in starched coifs and staid blue-and-murrey livery waited until he passed to bob deep curtsies. They smiled hopeful smiles, turning up eager faces while they dipped and rose, striving to catch his eye. Once, before his time in the Spanish prison, he would have had the buxom one with the bright cheeks. A brief lingering, a flirtatious word or two, and later that night, an exercise in amour to ease his bereaved soul. Not now. He nodded to them in a friendly manner but passed on by.

The gardeners from earlier crowded forward to touch their caps and shake his hand. The porter from the gate had also followed them to the house. Now he scuttled forward, shook Jon's hand, scraped a hasty bow, and headed back to his post. "The little mistress ye saved is a favorite here, Captain," he called over his shoulder. "We're grateful to ye. So's her ladyship. Don't let her tell ye otherwise." He sent Jonathan a knowing look and hurried up the gravel drive.

He called her his "ladyship." Jon turned the idea over and over. *A noble's wife. Dressed in mourning for someone.*

A boy of perhaps ten dashed up as Jonathan headed for the stables. The lad nipped Jonathan's sleeve, then raced away, shouting to his fellows, who bent over shovels in a nearby flowerplot. "I did it," he chortled in high glee. "I touched El Mágico!"

"I want to join the cavalry someday!" another cried to him. "Would you take me on?"

"When you're older, we'll see if it's really what you want." He gave them a relaxed salute. How well he knew the exuberance of youth, the hot lust of longing to achieve. Would that he could still feel the things they did. They had no inkling of what they could lose.

They stood stiffly at attention as he headed toward the stables. He was about twenty paces away when a whoop rang out from all six boys in concert. Their devotion gave a slight lilt to his lips.

It was wiped away immediately as another man caught up with him and put out one hand. "Robert Weston, Viscount Solsover."

"Captain Jonathan Cavandish, of Her Majesty's cavalry in the Netherlands." He and the viscount shook. Jon recognized the same coxcomb who had burst out of the bushes earlier and talked to Margaret. He had also noticed the knave stayed on the hill during the entire rescue and refused to move. He still held the gold toothpick between his teeth. Jonathan strode on toward the stables, not wanting to talk with this buffoon, knowing he must.

Solsover swung in beside him, jerked his head back toward the manor house. "So how do you know Margaret?"

"My family lived some years in Dorset, for my father's health before he died." Jonathan immediately sensed the reason for the viscount's interest. "I knew nothing of her Yorkshire relations until the squire passed away."

"Spare me the details." Robert pulled a face. "I've heard the story more times than I cared to. Loving father. Died tragically. Mother reunited with her father who disowned her when she married beneath her. All a bunch of farafiddle. Margaret in black for a year after, flapping like a crow. I tried to get her to take it off." He grinned and winked at Jonathan, confirming the double meaning of his words. "But her grandsire betrothed her to Oliver. Pity."

"What of you?" Jonathan wanted to get to the root of the matter. "Where are you from?"

Robert waved one hand vaguely. "Various parts. The family estate is in Wiltshire, but the house is ugly. I prefer my house nearby. 'Tis how I met Margaret. She's to be my bride." He grinned, his sensual mouth widening with satisfaction.

Jonathan frowned at an espaliered pear tree. "Despite the fact that she's willful?"

"You said it a-right. She is willful. But I'll break her of that once we're wed. Plan to enjoy every minute of it, too."

"What happened to the father of Patience?"

"Died of a fever in the Low Countries. Best that way, really. Picked up the pox from his whores in London."

Disgust overwhelmed Jonathan. Here, beyond a doubt, was one source of Margaret's trouble. He was used to men with rough manners and little polish, but this man had no niceties whatsoever.

"Aren't you wondering if Margaret caught it from him?"

Exasperated, Jon checked his rapier and kept walking. He didn't need to encourage this weasel to spill his story. Aye, and the name he had chosen on the spur of the moment fit him, too. Despite being handsome, he had close-set eyes and a sharp chin.

Solsover matched him stride for stride, chuckling. "She didn't. She wouldn't let him back in her bedchamber after his last trip to London. There was a terrific quarrel, believe me, but there always was between them. Oliver left for the Netherlands directly after. Nothing else for him. You missed meeting him because he died before he got to the fighting. Could have used some battle glory to send him off. No son either. Nothing but sniveling Patience."

Jonathan frowned again, this time so fiercely a gardener who had been staring leaped back to work as if reprimanded. "I'm glad the child is safe. Pray she doesn't take ill."

"Why do that?" The viscount took out a leather case and put away his toothpick. "Little beggar would be better off out of the way." He snapped the case shut. "She's a nuisance."

Jonathan shook his head, thinking that was no way to speak of a child. Especially Margaret's child. His mind staggered under these new pieces to the puzzle.

Robert laughed, as if divining his thoughts. "The child's worse than her mother. All of two and twice as willful."

Jonathan had had enough. He searched the grounds and spotted his first lieutenant. Giving a brief excuse, he left the viscount to join his friend. They headed for the stables and the rest of the men.

"I didn't know you had a sweetheart in Yorkshire. You never said a word," Cornelius VanderVorn, his first in command, greeted him.

Jonathan glanced at his friend, with his Dutch blue eyes and shock of white hair, and rolled his gaze heavenward. "I knew her years ago, nothing more. Took you long enough to join us, by the way. I expect you were keeping busy in London. Find yourself a doxy or two?" He lowered his voice. Servants were still within earshot. "Is the ship in sight?"

"Spotted off the coast yesterday, as expected." Cornelius took his voice down a notch as well. "Tonight's the night." He then raised it and went on more loudly. "I did visit the Green Lattice Tavern and enjoyed a drink of ale with Gert. She was cordial enough, but all she did was talk of you. I told her you wouldn't be in London for weeks, and when you arrived, you were busy," he added hastily as Jon cast him a scowl.

"Don't look at me that way," Cornelius continued. " 'Tis hardly my fault the lasses ask for you. How is it you're always surrounded by beautiful women, Cavandish, everywhere you go?" He winked at Jonathan.

"You grow wicked, Cornelius. You think of only one thing."

"No more than you."

It was an old jest between them, but now it was merely ritual. Because they both knew for Jonathan, since his escape from the Spanish, it was no longer true.

When they came to the long, rambling building that was the stable, the new recruits were walking their horses to cool them. Saddles had been removed, bridles replaced with light halters. Stable boys lugged buckets of water for the animals. The whole area smelled of dried clover and hay and just the right mix of oats and cracked corn. Jon nodded with approval as the head stableman hurried up.

"Captain, I've saved the best feed for your chargers." He drew his thin figure smartly to attention.

Jon returned the compliment. "I am deeply appreciative."

"A pleasure to serve the great El Mágico." The fellow

beamed, showing a tooth gap. "We've been a-hearin' about yer progress through Yorkshire for the past se'nnight. We welcome your visit to Clifton Manor."

"Did you do this to these folks?" Jon asked Cornelius in an undertone as they moved to take their horses.

"What, give them El Mágico fever? Not I!" Cornelius swore, hand on heart.

But it was quite evident the fever had spread like a virulent sickness, incapacitating people so they couldn't work. Several comely maids who gathered freshly dried linens from nearby bushes dawdled at their task, making it last as long as possible so they could stay in the vicinity. A child with a small band of weeders talked excitedly to his companions while pointing at Jonathan. The laundry maids gathered in a gaggle, put their heads together, and began to giggle, tossing coquettish glances over their shoulders. Four men working on the thick yew hedges bordering the stables paused in their trimming to smile and wave at him. Jonathan nodded in return as he took Phaeton's lead from the lad walking him.

He chirped to the stallion. The majestic head came up, ears pricked forward. They rambled off toward the riverbank.

At the river's edge, Jonathan stopped and leaned against the massive warmth of his animal, one arm looped around his neck. Phaeton's head swung around. He poked Jonathan in the chest with his muzzle—his touch compassionate. Jon rumpled Phaeton's forelock and rubbed his head and ears. "You're not too tired, old fellow? That's good. I didn't want to exhaust you. Have a drink. Have two, one for me." Jonathan had seen to none of his own needs yet; Phaeton's came first.

The stallion lowered his head to the water. His muzzle broke the surface, neck muscles rippling smoothly beneath his curried coat. Pulling off his hat, Jon tried to let the ordinary comforts of the day enfold him. Vigilant against bad memories, he sought equilibrium. Most days it came slowly or not at all.

He stared into the water, swift-flowing and darkly swollen from recent rain. A moment of laughter with Margaret, wonderful as it was, didn't change things. Obsession ruled him, its torrent as strong as this river's current, sweeping him away. And as long as the darkness claimed him, as long as his life was dominated by a single purpose, he must pursue it. He would stamp out the Spaniard who had created this ravenous dark.

Another animal's hooves came into Jon's range of vision, along with the booted feet of his master.

"Ho there, my friend."

Wearily he raised his gaze and looked into the open, sunny face of Cornelius, but couldn't share his friend's good cheer. The demon that the Spanish had named him for *did* possess him. They spoke the truth more than they knew.

"Can I be of aid?" Cornelius asked softly, sensing Jonathan's black mood.

" 'Tis nothing." Pushing back his thick, hot hair with one hand, Jon fanned himself with the hat in his other. He thrust away his irritation, not wanting to loose it on Cornelius, instead putting on the jovial facade he preferred.

"An excellent set of new recruits, these men. I congratulate you." Cornelius let his rangy chestnut gelding step into the water beside Phaeton. The pair acknowledged one another, then lowered their heads to drink.

"All I do is mention the methods used by the Prince of Parma in governing the Netherlands and men join up. I told the story to a group at Bishop Burton, of how he advises his king to let him invade and conquer England after he has subdued the Netherlands. I got a number of pledges. And three volunteers more." He nodded toward the clutch of men returning with their horses from downstream.

Cornelius studied them, then his captain. "It's you that inspires them. Not just the cause. Those who can't join up reach for their shillings. Men volunteer to be near you."

Jon put on his hat, shook his head cynically. "I'm just an armorer, Cornelius. 'Tis time to go inside before your brain is further fried by the sun."

He turned to Phaeton, who tossed his head, sending droplets of water flying. Brushing them away good-naturedly, Jon gave him a friendly slap on the neck and led him back toward the stable. Taking up a brush, he began to groom his animal's sleek flesh.

Cornelius followed suit with his chestnut. "This Earl of Clifton," he said, lowering his voice, "what do you know of him? Will he welcome us? Do you think he'll make a pledge?"

"He'll pledge." Jonathan continued his care of Phaeton without pausing. "He fought in numerous actions with old King Hal. The earl appreciates the importance of war."

Chapter 7

"Patience, my sweet, the physician says you are well. But let me see for myself." Margaret knelt before a blazing fire in her chamber, beset by a hundred overwhelming emotions. Men weren't magic, she told herself, seething with turmoil. They were impossible beings who thought women helpless and treated them accordingly. Over and over she repeated the words, trying to convince herself while she anxiously clucked over her baby, moving her chubby arms and legs, searching for signs of visible damage, finding none.

She sighed deeply and gave up the litany. Most men weren't magic; this one was. From the day she had first seen him, she had known it. He had fascinated, aggravated, allured, and frustrated her—doing things for others, making himself the hero. Well and good, except when he did things for her and *she* was supposed to do them. How well she had learned she couldn't pass her duties to others. She must handle them herself or tragedy could follow. Look what had happened to her father. And Patience! She must concentrate on her child. "Does anything hurt?" she asked.

"No hurt." Patience wiggled on her back and grinned at her mother, basking in the attention, enjoying the freedom of being without her wet clothes.

Margaret bent down to kiss her baby, letting their play hide her agitation. Once she had managed to escape the Magician, she had rushed all the way to her chamber and bid a maid make up the fire. Then she had peeled the sodden garments from Patience—first the loose kirtle and bodice, then the little white embroidered smock.

"Ruined?" Patience sat up and grasped a piece of Margaret's limp skirt. It hung from her hand, bedraggled like a dead crow.

"Ruined," Margaret confirmed, remembering how she'd stripped off her own ornate ensemble—gown, black brocade kirtle skirt, and forepart—and flung them in a soggy mass on the floor, terrified by her devastating joy at seeing Jonathan. "Come let me warm you," she coaxed, controlling the chaos inside her. "The river was like ice today. We don't want you to catch a chill."

They were both utterly naked—something her grandsire would disapprove of. Catching up a woollen blanket, Margaret enveloped them both in its softness and resettled on a thick Turkish carpet before the fire. "Surely your toes and fingers are freezing." She wrapped her hands around the little pearl-tipped rows of toes lined up in sweet precision, bent over and breathed warmth on them.

"Tickles!" Patience giggled. Slippery as a silk satin ribbon, she rolled out of Margaret's grasp. Within moments, she was playing with a box of extra bobbins.

Margaret sighed with relief as she watched. Despite the accident, Patience seemed her usual, happy self, less bothered by her wetting in the river than Margaret. Still, though the crises was over, she felt her throat tighten. Unexpectedly, she gave way to tears.

Lord in heaven, she thought, rocking back and forth, she had almost lost her child. Although she had hated her marriage, this beautiful being was the result of it, and she could never regret Patience. If that were so, she couldn't regret her marriage either. Of course Patience wasn't the son Oliver and her grandsire had demanded, but to Margaret, that made her all the more cherished. *Here* was her love, *here* was her precious duty. Never must she let anyone usurp her place.

But then Jonathan had appeared, taking charge as usual, and she had let him. Remembrance rushed over her as the past repeated itself. Her father, Jonathan—she had been torn in two between them. The impossible dilemma, which should have ended at her father's death, returned in full force to haunt her.

'Twas all because she was headstrong, her mother used to say. Her father had softened the word, calling her determined. Both were true. Long ago she had accepted herself and her nature, despite the trials they sometimes brought her. Her father had taught her to cherish who and what she was. Now Jonathan called her Mistress Willful. Breathed from his lips, the name became almost an endearment.

Margaret stopped herself. She was mad if she thought that, a candidate for St. Margaret's Hospital in London, the infamous Bedlam. Here she was, slipping easily into romantic musings when she mustn't even think about him.

Pressing both palms to her cheeks, she shut her eyes, again overwhelmed by his unexpected appearance. Joy fought with despair, though clearly joy was winning. Without question she must guard her heart with vigilance. Because if she didn't, without her agreement it would desert her breast and hurry to lay itself like a supplicant at his feet.

She thought again of his face, so greatly missed these five years past, now so greatly changed, his dark eyes stormy. Shortly he would meet with her grandsire, discuss his secret business, whatever it was. A deep desire to hear Jonathan's voice engulfed her—that warm, comforting voice she had yearned for. Dare she indulge her wishes? Like the piercing of her lace pins, an indiscretion could draw blood.

No, no, she assured herself. It would do no harm to listen. Besides, the peephole was meant for protection, and she should protect herself with knowledge. She would learn his secret in order to understand.

She would take Patience with her. In a few minutes they would slip down the back stair. Blinking her eyes, she forced herself to wipe away the last tear.

"Mama no sad," Patience piped, struggling to her feet. She patted Margaret's arm comfortingly and gazed into her eyes.

Margaret returned the gaze, her heart overwhelmed by the tender display, the trust mirrored in those thickly lashed, innocent eyes. "No, love. Mama no sad," she whispered, rubbing her cheek against the curly brown mop of hair. "Mama is glad you didn't drown. How did you fall in?"

"Jumped," Patience pronounced with satisfaction. "Pat swim."

Dismay filled Margaret at this revelation. "We play in the pond sometimes, but never the river. It runs too fast."

"Magic save me."

Margaret grimaced. Even the innocent ears of her daughter had picked up what the manor folk called him—El Mágico. Patience resettled in Margaret's arms, a contented look on her face, failing to notice her mother's disapproval.

"Patience, you must listen to me. You cannot hope the captain will save you whenever you have troubles. You must learn to handle your problems yourself."

Margaret cast a glance at the captain's doublet, lying in a heap on the floor where she had dropped it. How he had changed, yet he clung to his hero habits, probably now more than ever. He was the exact opposite of her husband, despite the fact that Oliver had been thoroughly the courtly gentleman before they wed. Once the vows had been said, she learned the truth. His needs and comforts came first, especially in bed. She would never forget the suffocating weight of his body as he swived her nightly, trying for an heir—the horrible stench of his beer-thick breath, the rhythmic bang of his hips against hers until he finished, then left her without a word.

"Besides, the captain won't be staying," she reminded Patience. "After his talk with great-grandsire, he'll be gone."

At the mention of her feared great-grandfather, a stricken look came to Patience. She clapped both hands over her eyes.

" 'Tis all right," Margaret said, rearranging the blanket. "I won't let great-grandsire shout at you for going in the water. I know," she changed the subject, speaking cheerfully, "we'll go down to his chamber. He won't be there," she added, gently prying away Patience's hands from her face. "We'll listen at the secret hole."

Patience nodded in instant agreement. She liked the peephole. Margaret looked about for clothing and found clean smocks for them both. Time grew short. She might miss Jonathan's secret if she delayed further. Wrapping the blanket more firmly around the pair of them, she opened the door and slipped from the room.

Chapter 8

They arrived at her grandsire's chamber without meeting any servants. The door creaked open at Margaret's touch. The faint scent of musk soap assailed them, slyly staking its claim on the senses before one thought to resist, just like her grandsire. Heavy brocade draperies muted the light, making the massive four-poster with its hangings loom like a ghost ship in the semidark.

Deadly quiet. Patience gripped her mother's arm and shoulder beneath the blanket with sharp little fingernails, but Margaret gave her a reassuring pat. She approached the farthest wall from the bed.

A series of polished wood ornaments studded the wainscotting at intervals. A fleur-de-lis. A lion's head. A fish with curved tail. Then the series repeated. Handsome patterns, clever patterns, made by an ingenious architect. Taking a chair, Margaret silently thanked him as she selected a fleur-de-lis, pressed it left until it clicked. Patience reached for a fish, swung it on its hidden pin. A tiny hole appeared. It allowed one to see and listen, disguised by the concealing eye of a matching fish on the other side.

"You first," Margaret mouthed the words to her daughter. She pressed a finger to her lips. "Don't let them hear you. 'Tis our secret we're here." Patience peeked; she listened. She tired of the game in seconds. Two men droning of grown-up business failed to hold her interest. She scuttled away to finger the fascinating chess pieces her great-grandsire forbade her to touch.

With her turn arrived, Margaret gripped the seat of the chair. She shouldn't be here, but she couldn't help it. Once again Jonathan's hypnotic presence invaded her serenity. Drawing a shaky breath, she placed her eye to the hole.

Her grandsire's comfortable wood-paneled cabinet looked as usual—opulent yet formal. Despite a fire crackling in the grate, despite the bank of mullioned windows looking out over the lush spring garden, no one relaxed in this room save the earl. From here he conducted business and ruled supreme.

Adjusting her view, Margaret found her grandsire—William Clifford, twelfth Earl of Clifton, Viscount Henley, Baron of Great Driffield, Coxwold, and Marston. Jonathan probably knew about his military and political history in his prime. He would also know of the earl's ruthless skill in outmaneuvering his enemy, his merciless punishment of his foes. Those qualities had won him a handful of battles in the past. Now he used a cane when walking, but he needed no such prop for his authority. Regal in his carved X-chair, he studied his guest with narrowed eyes.

She shifted her view, searching for Jonathan. He did not sit in a lowly chair, as expected. Instead, he lounged by the windows, cutting a striking figure in dark clothing against the light. He seemed not the least discomfited by her grandsire's grim inspection. His face was arranged in a pattern of quiet intensity. She heard the murmur of his voice. Hurriedly she pressed her ear to the hole.

"Someone from my household?" The earl's answer, full of fury, came to Margaret clearly. "Meeting a messenger? No, by God, that is not true!"

"A Spanish messenger," Jonathan's voice corrected calmly. "Sent by King Philip of Spain. Without question there is some movement afoot to piece together a plot. One or more of the actors are located at Clifton Manor."

Margaret's eyebrows shot up as she took in this information. So *that* was his purpose here. If it shocked her, it obviously shocked her grandsire more. For the first time since she had known him, he seemed dumbfounded. Margaret strained to hear more.

"You will have to prove it before I believe you." Her grandsire's voice cut like a whip through the mounting tension in the room. "A traitor hiding in my household? It couldn't happen without my knowledge. I know all of my servitors well."

"It might not be one of your people, my lord," came Jonathan's calm, logical voice, outreasoning the man who believed he had invented reason. "It could well be someone passing through. One of the weeders you hired, a traveling peddler, the workers who sow your grain. You have to consider that."

"I don't have to consider anything I don't want to. You have been nosing around my manor since you arrived. An impertinence." His tone implied he would not stand for it. But his next words conceded the possibility. "What do you make of the plot? The usual plan to murder the queen?"

Murder the queen? God's eyelid! Margaret swallowed thickly, unnerved by this news. She was also unnerved by her grandsire's unusual concession to Jonathan. Could the captain's hero power shake even the invincible earl?

" 'Tis impossible to know at this stage," Jonathan's voice continued, confident and in control. "But I consider it a strong possibility. Spanish plots brew, suspicious characters enter and leave the country. They generally hide behind clever fronts of legitimate business, so we stay vigilant. The traffic up and down the eastern coast to Scotland is particularly heavy of late, so when I intercepted a communiqué that named a date for contact at Clifton, I wasn't surprised. Frankly, I wondered if it was you."

"I!" her grandsire cried, incensed. Margaret heard him leap to his feet, despite his ailing knees. "Damnation, but you go too far. I stood for the queen when she was only a princess. I was with her father at the Field of the Cloth of Gold. If you think I will tolerate insults from you, despite your war heroics, you are utterly mistaken. No matter that you come from the queen."

Margaret put her eye to the hole, trembling for Jonathan, wondering what would happen next. Well she knew the earl's anger, how his face mottled red, his huge fists clenched. Drat this hole, for failing to offer both view and hearing at the same time. As she watched, Jonathan smoothed his mustache with one hand, the casual gesture belying any inner tension. He studied her grandsire, no doubt doing the work of an interrogator, noting facial expression, body posture, eye movement. He would spot the lie if there was one. She returned to listening with bated breath.

Jonathan's easy laugh rang out in the room, full of approval. "Be at ease, my lord, I was merely making certain. You know the importance of checking everyone; you've done the same yourself. I've heard the stories of how you protected our queen when she was yet a princess."

There was a pause. To Margaret's astonishment, her grandsire broke into a hearty guffaw. "Clever, Cavandish," he barked, "using my own tactics. For a second I wasn't sure what you were up to. But I shall forgive you. In fact . . ." There was a scrape of wood as he opened the drawer in his worktable. "I'm willing to do more than that. I'm willing to aid your Netherlands venture. Very worthy, your work."

"My thanks. But the best thing you can do is perpetuate the ruse that I'm here recruiting."

Jonathan's modest answer annoyed Margaret. He had just done the impossible, besting her grandsire in discourse. Yet he seemed not to realize it.

"Nay, I wish to hear more of your endeavors," her grandsire insisted. "And I insist on making a pledge. One hundred pounds."

Margaret's mind reeled. A hundred pounds? Her miserly grandsire?

"I thank you for your generosity. With that I can outfit an entire new company. 'Twould be a definite benefit to the war effort, which Her Majesty will appreciate. I'll assemble the men, train and equip them as soon as I get back to London."

"When will you return to the Netherlands?"

"That I cannot say. Her Majesty wants me here for a time, though I am eager to be off."

With a pang, Margaret heard the impatience in Jonathan's voice and wondered how he could yearn for war.

"In all likelihood she wants you fully recovered from prison," said the earl. "A man can't fight if he's half dead."

Margaret bit back a gasp of horror. Half dead? Ugly images rose in her mind—of Jonathan in that dank Spanish prison, wracked by terrible pain.

"I was not half dead," came Jonathan's terse answer.

"Close enough, I'll warrant. Now don't go on the defensive with me." Her grandsire snorted. "I know full well how it was, believe me. But you don't like the subject, so we'll speak of another. Why does the queen hold you back?"

Jonathan sounded more relaxed when he spoke again. "Who knows why women do the things they do. She's nervous and short-tempered these days. But I must return to the Continent as soon as possible. As soon as I can recruit the balance of men."

"As to that," interjected the earl, "I need all my men in service, so you'll have to settle for the pledge. Except for the traitor. You're welcome to him."

"My thanks, again. If I can find out who he is." Margaret heard the grin in Jonathan's voice. They were coconspirators, he and her grandsire.

"You think you won't?"

"Anything could happen tonight. And probably will."

"You must sup with us, stay the night. Your men can bed down in the great hall. Plenty of room. Which makes me think. You are of an age to take a wife, yet you are a bachelor."

"And like to stay that way. A soldier doesn't make much of a husband, always absent from home and apt to be killed."

"A well-dowered, unmeddling woman would be a boon to you," the earl urged. "I have a niece who will be at table tonight. She would come with a comfortable sum and a sizable piece of land."

Margaret winced at the turn in the conversation, knowing the niece in question was five-and-twenty, recently widowed, penniless, and eager for a new husband. Her grandsire believed in taking care of his own, so had agreed to see her wed again. Margaret felt a surge of unbidden jealousy.

To her chagrin, Jonathan's answer sounded suspiciously positive. "Land could be welcome. We will join you at table and thanks. My men will appreciate a roof over their heads. They're new to training. But after we sup, I must go to the village. I'll recruit men at the tavern. The rest you'll hear when we next see light of day."

Silence followed, and Margaret wondered what was happening. But she dared not remove her ear to look, in case she missed their words. "The servants say we owe you a debt of thanks," said her grandsire at last, "for saving a drowning child."

Margaret started. How unlike her grandsire to explain himself to another, yet he continued his odd, halting speech to the captain. "I assure you, the maid responsible will be discharged. She's been lax since she was young."

"She's been with your household since birth?" Jonathan's seemingly innocent question probed to the heart of the matter. A lifelong servant turned out would most likely starve.

"Aye, and learned naught in all those years."

"My father had such a servant once. He set the woman to washing trenchers. The worst she could do was drop them. Being wooden, they never broke."

There he went again, Margaret muttered to herself, intruding on her affairs. She had told him *she* would handle Mary. Even so, he attacked her grandsire's callous intention, subtly shaming him, and she had to applaud that. She hated Mary's laxness, hated the need to defend her, but she had planned to fight her grandsire's wish to discharge the maid. Everyone made mistakes, she thought grimly. She had made her own in the past, with far worse results than Mary's.

She jumped when her grandsire laughed a second time. "You amuse me, Cavandish. You have an odd way of looking at things." He changed the subject. "As for the child, she jumped in the river intentionally, I am told, so she will be properly punished. She must be taught never to endanger her life again."

Punished? Sudden fear throbbed through Margaret's head. What did he mean? Jonathan asked the question for her, moving smoothly to the new topic, not the least put off by the shift.

"I agree many things are of danger to small children, my lord. Yet I wonder if punishment will help her learn. She is yet young, as I understand. No more than two."

Margaret gripped her blanket, waiting for the answer. Away flew all thoughts of Jonathan, of his spy hunting, of her grandsire's apparent admiration for him. She focused on the issue of Patience, tension tightening her muscles.

"She will be three come September," replied her grandsire, once more the commander in his element. "She understands things far in advance of her age. A few strokes with the cane should suffice, nothing extreme. Enough to remind her to obey."

Margaret clenched her teeth until her jaw ached. He would not cane her child! She would never permit such a thing!

"Will the mother consent to the punishment?" continued Jonathan's rational questioning.

"Her mother is an unmanageable wench, just like the child, but I will rule them both."

Margaret jerked away from the hole, unable to listen further. Her mind flew among the many things she had heard, each competing frantically for her attention. One rose above the others with startling urgency. Her grandsire plotted to beat her daughter. He must not succeed!

Leaping to her feet, she swooped down on her baby, caught her in her arms and hugged her. Then she slipped from the room and made for the refuge of her chamber, taking the stairs two at a time.

Back in her room, Margaret shut the door and, putting Patience down, leaned against it. She quaked inside and out. Never since her child's birth had her grandsire threatened Patience physically. True, beatings were a regular thing in the household. Among the servants for breaking rules, for wasting time or shoddy work. Among the older children of the household, the birch ruled. But Patience, being the youngest and still an infant, had never been beaten. Margaret had believed her child exempt from the rule. Now she learned, to her horror, her grandsire did not.

She imagined the scene, knew exactly how he would plan it. All household children—both family and servants—were required to witness the fortnightly punishments of those who had broken manor rules. He terrorized them all while one received the blows. But not her child! It was time she demanded the right to live on her own.

Having made the decision, Margaret drew a deep, shivering breath and tried to calm herself. Whatever happened, she must not frighten Patience. No child should live with the fear of a beating. Nor would Margaret agree to raise her by someone else's rules.

"Let's have some fun," she forced herself to say playfully. "I will ring for hot milk, and later we'll have supper here. What do you say to that?" She sank down before the fire, arranged her blanket, then stirred the embers and added wood.

"Want Magic," Patience insisted, her bottom lip emerging, petulant. She had seen him through the peephole and knew he hadn't left.

"I know, Patience." Margaret sighed deeply. "We all want magic in our lives." She clung hard to her calm, but her insides twisted and gnarled, her thoughts doing likewise. She had so many troubles; they grew worse by the moment. Her other disturbing problem probed at her. Wed with Robert? How could her mother or grandsire think she would agree? Robert, the lecher, Robert, the hypocrite. Who cared that he was a distant cousin to Queen Elizabeth? This time she wouldn't accept her elders' plans passively. Like Athena, the warrior goddess, she must gird herself with weapons and prepare for battle. It was time she made changes in her life.

Catching Patience to her, Margaret nestled her baby in the crook of her arm and deliberately opened the blanket to the fire, letting its heat scald her cheeks and forehead. Tilting back her head, she felt the searing blaze on her bare neck. The earl ran a proper household, would be scandalized to see them. But from now on things must be different. She would not accept meekly, nor train her daughter by example to do the same.

But, oh, for some respite from these cares and burdens. Margaret's gaze instinctively sought her favorite refuge—the pristine, dark blue lace pillows, two of them sitting on the shelf of the great mahogany court cupboard. The third one, the original gift from her father, reposed on her table, the lace she had produced piled in a snowy heap of crisp, jagged stars. How she longed to take that pillow and escape to the lace maker in the village, her friend Bertrande Capell. They would work side by side until the patterns soothed Margaret's mind, blocking everything else around her. But she had done that too often in the past, especially when she first came here, when she had had to decide about Oliver. Look where it had led her. She dared not obey her instincts. Plans were being made behind her back.

"What was so important, you couldn't answer my summons?"

Margaret jerked around, her guard going up. Her grandfather's forbidding figure loomed in the open entry. She had no way of knowing how long he had stood there, watching her. He had glided into her chamber, showing his true colors, creeping up on her as silent and stealthy as the fox.

Chapter 9

Margaret turned away from her grandfather, refusing to be cowed into submission. "Patience fell in the river." Resolutely she concentrated on her child, who had thrown herself down behind the blanket at the sound of her great-grandfather's voice. Margaret felt her tremble and reached out a reassuring hand. "I think she will not take sick, but I could not come to your chamber as you asked."

Her grandsire leaned heavily on his ebony cane, his enormous, knobby hands wrapped around the gold ball adorning it. His formidable frame, clothed in stark black, had shrunk over the years; still, he towered over Margaret. His broad shoulders hunched slightly, but he had not lost his power. He controlled his household, his estates, his many servitors with a surety she had always respected. What he lost in physical stature was made up for by strength of will. From her place by the fire, Margaret saw the determined set of his jaw, the astute gaze of his piercing blue eyes recessed in cavities of wrinkles. Unlike his aged skin, nothing about his character sagged. It reminded her that those who made him angry were usually sorry after, but just now she was not sure she could hold back.

"So," he said in ominous tones, "you required me to come to you? Up the stairs."

"You could have sent word asking how she did." Margaret knew his knees pained him, though he never said so. It showed in his posture, his limp, the set of his lips in a tight line. Today she refused to feel guilty. She stared into the flames.

"I expect *you* to report to me regarding your child's health."

"That's not the issue and well you know it. How dare

you pledge me to Robert," she cried. Her outrage erupted, and she leaped to her feet. "Without telling me. Without my consent." Patience huddled on the floor at her feet, covered by the blanket.

"We are talking about your child."

Margaret scowled as they stood face to face, both their indomitable wills clashing. "Very well," she ground out. "Your subject first, then mine."

Her permission seemed to anger rather than please him. "Your child must be disciplined for what she did today, Margaret. She deliberately went into the water, and I will give her just punishment. Five strokes with the cane tomorrow at noon."

Rage flared before Margaret's eyes. The room swam with it. How dare he say this where Patience could hear. How dare he even think it. "I will not permit it," she cried passionately. "She is too young to equate a beating tomorrow with what she did today. She will not understand—"

"She understands far more than you think." His shout silenced her, a first taste of his own anger. "She understands enough to steal the sweets from the high shelf when you're not looking. She sneaks the chess pieces from my chamber when I've said they're not to be touched."

Margaret's eyes followed his pointed stare. With dismay she beheld a white chess piece lying on the carpet. She had failed to notice it until now.

"She endangers her own life and you refuse to teach her? What manner of mother are you? You will let me discipline her and she will learn quickly to obey rules meant to keep her safe."

She will learn nothing except to hate you, Margaret thought, the tempest in her inner mind raging as Patience cowered at her feet.

Her grandfather observed her silence with stern satisfaction. "As to our other business, Robert has honored you by offering for your hand. I was going to tell you this night."

"He told me himself." Margaret struggled for control, knowing he had purposely attacked Patience first, her weak point, to make her vulnerable in this one. "I'll not accept."

"You will understand the wisdom of my choice. Look at your child."

"I do look at her. She is perfect in every way, but you

don't acknowledge her. You make plans behind my back to beat her and tell people you'll manage me. You—"

"Margaret, you were listening to private business from my chamber." His frown ploughed deep furrows in his high forehead. He threw a glance at the chess piece, now knowing exactly how it had come to be there.

Margaret lifted her chin, refusing to be ashamed. "You trusted me by showing me the hole."

"That device is meant for household security. You're not to use it except when I tell you." He didn't sound the least trusting now. "You might be a model wife and granddaughter if you would but obey. If you could learn to see the benefit to you of my plans." His manner shifted subtly. Yet Margaret recognized the shrewd assessment he gave her. "I told you Oliver would produce the type of child we wanted. She has good blood in her veins. She's sound of mind and limb. Unfortunate that she is a girl, but we will try again."

"We?" she cried. "You made me think I was part of the bargain last time, but now I know better. The esteem you promised was empty. I'm nothing to you but a vessel to deliver the goods." She stopped, drew a deep, shaking breath, trying to deny the pain inside her. "And despite Patience's perfection, I cannot believe Oliver's breeding was impeccable."

Her grandsire made a dismissing motion. "His lineage was excellent. The trouble was his mother; she overindulged him. Mark you, spare the cane and your child will end the same."

For the first time he acknowledged there had been something amiss with her husband. But it gave Margaret small comfort. "I'll not take Robert for such a reason."

"Margaret, you are small-minded." He appealed to her with that lucid logic of his. "He is related to the queen. And he's rich, with estates throughout England. As a widow someday, you will have one-third of it all."

"I am already a widow and where is my jointure?" Her opening arrived and she leaped into the gap without hesitation. "Do you let me have it, so I can make decisions of my own? No! You give me only a modest allowance for trifles."

"I see no purpose to giving you money when I provide every comfort and convenience your heart could desire. I have told you no expenditure on your behalf or your daughter's troubles me." He gestured toward Patience without looking at her. "What does trouble me is your attitude, Margaret."

"There is nothing wrong with my attitude. The things that shape it are wrong."

She expected a reprimand for this outrageous statement and would ordinarily have gotten one. But just now he was searching for her weakest point. She wouldn't wait for him to find it. "I have just turned one-and-twenty, Grandsire. I wish to see the banker and draw upon my personal funds," she stated firmly. "I intend to set up my own household with Patience and live—"

"I will not permit it." He cut her off with a slash of his right hand. "The funds you refer to are safely invested, and I alone manage them for your future security." He went to the bellpull and jerked it hard.

"You'll not beat my child," Margaret cried, bending down to gather Patience in her arms. She was in a rage again, barely able to contain herself.

"You require rest to calm yourself," he stated.

A tap sounded; the door opened. A maid hovered uncertainly. The earl waved her in brusquely without a glance her way. "Remove this child and tell the nurse to put her to bed. That's the proper place for her after a near drowning. Then send someone to dress her ladyship for supper. She joins us tonight in the great hall."

Margaret started to open her mouth, to say she would not join them. She closed it sharply, knowing she dared not break the cardinal rule of the household by contradicting her grandfather before the servants. She had learned to live with that rule, thinking respect a fair exchange for his bounty. But no more. She whispered in Patience's ear that she would visit her later, then waited in stony silence as the girl took her. Patience cried anyway, holding out her arms to Margaret as she was borne away.

"I wanted her here," Margaret flared as soon as the door closed.

"You said she would live." His answer was calm, calculated.

"That has nothing to do with it. I wished to care for her myself."

"She is as well off with someone else. You will lie down now," he ordered, "and rest until the maid arrives." He limped to the door. "Then you will dine with the viscount and accept his offer. Leave off your black gown and wear one of the new ones your mother selected. One of the colors."

"I am still in mourning for Oliver." Margaret stood tight-lipped, not moving from her stance before the fire.

With a crash, he slammed his cane on the bare wood floor, crossed the room, each step punctuated by another bang of the cane. He would force her, Margaret thought sadly as he flung wide the clothespress to reveal a dozen garments hung on brass hooks. Again he yanked the bellpull.

"Remove the black gowns," he ordered Bessie, who answered the call. "Tell Roberts to burn them. And tell him to deduct a shilling from your pay this se'nnight. You were late again to table this Sunday past."

Bessie's face crumpled as she began to sob. Hiding her tears behind the heap of black gowns he had flung at her, she ran from the room.

"You needn't have done that," Margaret cried the instant the door closed. She clutched the blanket around her. "You could have let me give the gowns to the parish almshouse." She wanted to cry that he shouldn't have fined the maid, either, that the girl had been late because she went to care for her aged mother. But he wouldn't care, she thought dismally. He lived his life by rules, and they came first.

The earl let his eyelids sink to half mast. "I've waited a year for this proposal. You'll not put the title in jeopardy." She heard the threat in his voice, saw his huge chest rise and fall as his breath came faster. "With your cousins too young to breed, you are the only one who can fulfill this obligation. Otherwise the queen could grant the title elsewhere. Or confiscate the land and let the title go dormant. Your mother, aunts, and cousins would be turned out of Clifton. Think of it, Margaret. All because you are stubborn beyond belief."

Margaret closed her eyes against his arguments. He, too, was stubborn, and unlikely to die soon, despite being five-and-seventy. Drawing a deep breath, she opened her eyes and played her highest card. "The queen hasn't approved this match with Solsover. How do you know she will?"

"That's none of your affair. I'll handle Her Grace."

Margaret noted his subtle change of expression. So he hadn't asked the queen yet, and Her Majesty might not like the plan. "I won't wed with Robert and you won't beat my child," she declared roundly. "I won't stand for either one."

Her grandfather eyed her coolly. "I will discipline both your child *and* you if required." He crossed the chamber and picked up Margaret's lace pillow, the one given her by her father.

"You're making a muddle of the bobbins," she cried, tugging the blanket close and following him.

"I'm taking it to my chamber, Margaret." He tucked it in the crook of his arm and regarded her. "I'll take the others as well, if I must. When you're ready to comply with orders, you may work your lace again."

She felt herself flush, her skin turning hot with rage. How dare he think to punish her by taking away her lace.

He strode to the door, his limp hardly noticeable in his victory. "I expect you at table, promptly at seven of the clock. And you are never to sit in your chamber again half clad. 'Tis unseemly."

Margaret despaired as he closed the door with finality. It hurt to admit she had misjudged him. Another thing hurt even more: as she had listened through the spy hole, her grandsire's voice had rushed over her, filling her with longing. If only he spoke to *her* the way he had to Jonathan—in a voice deeply paternal, full of empathy. But he didn't feel that way about her; he considered her a weak, inferior woman.

He didn't know it, but her grandsire had just put his seal to her decision. She must take Patience and leave. She couldn't do it until after supper, but she would bide her time and make her move when the moment was right. Because she was not a man, had not known war, and they would never see eye to eye.

Chapter 10

With her grandsire gone and her decision to leave Clifton firm, Margaret sank into the chair before her looking glass. God's eyelid, but she had thought she was making progress in softening his heart. How many times had he proved her wrong the next minute?

Feeling restless, Margaret rose and crossed the chamber to search deep in a coffer. Finding what she wanted, she held up the garments so she could see them in the glass. The simple kirtle skirt required no farthingale. The bodice was a rich, satisfying saffron gold, the color Jonathan used to say . . .

She stopped herself. It was no use thinking of him again. Having donned the clothes, she found the reflection in the glass more pleasing. But something was still wrong.

All of a sudden, she erupted into a frenzy of action, tugging the hairpins from her tight, intricate hairstyle, brushing the stiffness from her locks until they glittered on her shoulders the way she preferred. Both the plain gown and the hair change cheered her.

So did another thought. The image of Bertrande came to Margaret, enclosed in the enchanted circle she always imagined. More mother to Margaret than her true mother, this one friend understood her. Because despite being a French refugee who fled to England with her niece and scarcely more than the clothes on her back, despite her poverty and the fragility wrought on her by age, Bertrande was the keeper of a rich heritage of lace patterns. Within her guardianship lay the wisdom of her ancestors. That Margaret served as protégé to this great artist made her feel truly blessed.

Once she had thought she must live without her mentor,

but now Margaret thought otherwise. Three days hence, Bertrande and her niece were moving to London, since there wasn't enough lace business here to keep them alive. Well and good, she and Patience would join them. For the first time it struck her what she left behind—a luxurious manor full of people, yet there was no warmth here. It was cold both in body and in spirit, made so by her grandsire. As cold as the freezing waters of the river Esk.

So resolved, Margaret arranged her kirtle skirts and tied on her favorite lace-trimmed apron. She would slip up to see her child now, then go down to supper. Before she went, though, she paused by the court cupboard and opened a carved wooden box.

My miracle, my Marguerite. The inscription etched in the bobbin reminded her of the day Jonathan had given it to her. He had given her a nickname as well, called her the French name for the golden-eyed daisy, because of her eyes and her similar name. *Marguerite.* Her lips warm from his kisses, his hand pressing hers.

A quiver ran through her, a stab of longing. The instant she had studied his hands, large and powerful, closing around her daughter, she had recognized him. His magic stole over her, cast her back to the hour of their first kisses. Summer's eve, after the daylight had died. She had slipped from her home, met him in the meadow. His father disapproved, her mother forbade her. She had defied them all in order to find out.

Impossible he had wanted to kiss her—she, the quiet one, who hid in her lace. Margaret couldn't believe it. Not until he pulled her close, brought his wondrous male body against hers and proved it with his lips. Now she remembered how her head swam, giddy with excitement, her pulses racing. He had touched her, held her with those magical hands. He had made her love him, though she had tried to resist, knowing she should stay home, content with her father. But each day the lure of Jonathan's magic wore on her, tempting her away. He enticed and beguiled her, with his tender deeds and his jesting ways. Until she had reaped the bitter fruit of her weakness. The grip of remorse tightened on her, the old recurring pain.

They were better off parted, she reminded herself. Jonathan liked a woman to be clinging and helpless, someone who needed his strength. But she had her own strength, her own independence. Once she had kept it hidden, but no longer. She had shown it to him clearly by the river, because now she had nothing left to lose.

She left the chamber, her step definite. At the nursery, she peered through the half-open door, trying to see who was on duty. She couldn't tell, but someone must be. Pray whoever it was wouldn't run tell her grandsire. It made her furious when he barred her from Patience. Squaring her shoulders, she swept into the room.

She had expected Susan, the usual woman who relieved the nurse. But the stool stood empty by Patience's bed. She had expected to find her child red-eyed and crying. Instead, a giggle sounded from down by the chimney piece. She whirled in surprise toward the far end of the room.

Chapter 11

What Margaret saw made her insides run to jelly. Patience played contentedly on the floor by the hearth, but she wasn't alone. El Mágico sat cross-legged, holding her in his lap and making her smile. With her chubby legs stuck straight out before her, her little white smock twisted to one side, Patience peeped into the deep recess of his dagger sheath. He had a finger stuck through a mounting hole so he could tickle her nose. She jumped and laughed.

Margaret stared. She couldn't stop herself. Just looking at him gratified the senses—the way his hair fell in soft layers across his forehead, the clean sweep of his cheeks down to the unfamiliar beard and mustache that accented the sensual curve of his mouth. She would never have expected to find him here. The nursery was a female domain, where children of the household came at birth with their wet nurses. Not Patience. Margaret insisted on nursing her personally, and her mother, weak vessel that she was, had for once supported her. Her grandsire capitulated to what he called "women's affairs."

But at six months, her child had been snatched from her, weaned forcibly at her grandsire's orders. 'Twas time for Margaret to conceive again. They needed that heir.

Banished to the nursery, Patience cried unceasingly. Many nights Margaret crouched outside the door waiting for the nurse to doze, then slipped in and nursed her baby. Many times she had slept on the floor beside the cradle. During her child's illnesses. During fights with Oliver.

Now Jonathan was here to charm her child . . . and her.

Weakness swirled around her, wrapped her in a fog of pleasure. She longed to hold the moment—to let her hungry gaze devour him. Despite her desire, a warning sounded. She must beware. Danger lurked here for her foolish heart.

Enough gaping, Margaret scolded herself. She must send him away before she committed some new indiscretion. With a twitch of her apron, she mustered her courage and marched herself across the room.

He looked up at her footsteps. His eyes blazed with a welcome that pitched her into a well of confusion. "I would like my child now!" The words hurried from her mouth, tripping over one another. Shifting her gaze to Patience, she bent down. "Pray give her to—"

Patience hollered. She latched on to the captain's arm and buried her face in his armpit. Like a burr, she clung to him and refused to let go.

Jonathan shot Margaret a brief look of apology. "I fear she has no wish to stop her play. Mayhap you would humor her. If you have the time."

Margaret retreated. With as calm a step as she could muster, she crossed to the window seat. Only half conscious of what she did, she tucked her skirts tightly around her thighs and sat.

Patience ignored her mother. Gleefully she turned back to the captain, discovering his wooden shirt buttons. Entranced, she tugged at them one by one, climbing the row. When she reached the top, she spied his short, pointed beard and grabbed for it.

"Ouch. Stop." Jon craned his neck away, grinning. "I'll have to shave this off, little maid, if I'm around you much. You'll pluck me bare. Ouch. That's attached to me, Mistress Patience. Leave off."

Patience wouldn't. The stiff tickle of his beard fascinated her. She explored it with curious fingers and yanked again.

"She's not been close to many men with beards," Margaret explained, embarrassed. "I suppose it's novel to her. Patience, stop," she admonished. "You mustn't do that to the captain. 'Tis most rude."

"No harm done." He smiled reassuringly. "You recall I have five younger brothers and sisters, and now a young nephew, so I know something of children. And of their mothers. After talking to the earl, I guessed you would wish to be with her." He nodded toward Patience. "He said he forbids it when the child is overwrought."

"You discussed me with my grandsire?"

"It was necessary," he told her firmly.

"I hope you paid no heed to anything he said. At least about me."

"He said you were unmanageable. But I'd already heard that. From the best possible source." He sent her a sympathetic smile as he continued to play with Patience. Bringing out a huge white handkerchief, he found a thimble on the floor and made it appear on his finger beneath the cloth. The next moment, it disappeared.

Margaret watched their play, crossed her legs nervously and uncrossed them. It came to her in a rush, what he had done for her—smoothed the way so she could see her daughter, with no one the wiser. It unsettled her completely, while he remained serene and composed. He didn't suffer inner turmoil like she did. He wrapped women easily around his little finger and thought nothing of it. Her child was clearly one of them. Yet if rumors were true, what she felt for him now was no different from what hundreds of other females felt. She clung to the thought like a charm against panic. He didn't need her, didn't want her. She studied the chimney piece and took a fortifying breath.

But her gaze was drawn back to him over and over. He had a face as intriguing as the magic he was named for. A face full of secrets, compelling her interest. Seeing him raised a myriad of questions inside her. Despite the danger to herself, she must have answers, especially to those most pressing. What exactly had the Spanish done to him?

"You must tell me about your adventures in the Low Countries," she began. "We are eager for the news."

"We? I can't think Patience is interested."

She bit her lip hard and blushed scarlet.

"You didn't used to do *that*."

She started, shocked out of her wits. Did he mean her blush or what she was thinking. But he couldn't see her thoughts, could he? He couldn't know the indecent things she was imagining. "What do you mean?" she choked out.

"You're biting your lip. If you don't stop, there'll be nothing left of it." He sent her his most engaging grin, the one that probably made women shed their smocks for him. " 'Tis new to me, that's all."

It wasn't all and they both knew it. Not with the way he studied her lips, as if wishing to devour them. His teasing penetrated her defenses, leaving her tongue-tied in his presence. "I pray you, just tell me the news."

He talked for a while, about the peace talks at Breda and the siege of Alkmaar. While he talked, he spun Patience's top for her, making it whirl in a rainbow of colors while his tales whirled through Margaret's thoughts. No wonder women worshipped him and men joined him. He spun stories of exotic, intriguing adventures. It took some time for her to realize how much he wasn't telling. "You tell me only the outside of things," she interrupted. "I want to know the rest."

"The rest?"

He raised his left eyebrow, that seductive, subtle move. It unnerved her, his questioning her right. She asked him to share his innermost thoughts, an act of intimacy and trust. But she *would* ask him. This might be her only chance. "Yes," she persisted, meeting his gaze steadily. "What happened to you on the inside. What you felt."

He didn't answer for several moments. "You're good at keeping your secrets. I have my own . . . The viscount tells me you're going to wed with him."

Margaret winced. She asked for intimacy and he went straight for her jugular. "The viscount is an idiot. Pay him no heed."

"It's not true?"

"He never pays the least attention to what I tell him. Like most men."

"Not all men are the same."

"I've failed to see any difference."

"Some are better-looking than others."

"Who cares about that, pray?"

"You do," he said gently, "if you're going to wed the viscount. He's attractive, you'll have to admit."

"I'm not going to wed him." Agonies, he teased her again. He had always done this, tried to get a reaction out of her, though what reaction he wanted, she wasn't sure. Especially now. "I told you I was not."

"Marguerite, you didn't. You should say what you mean. It seems to me, from your earlier words by the river, that you never have."

He was right. She bent her head, frustrated, heartsick. She dared not ask for intimacy if she couldn't give it herself. But she could never tell him what had happened—that he had seduced her from her duty and she had let it happen. That because of her grievous faults, her father had died. She flashed him a glance, watching him warily.

"From now on, let there be truth between us. You owe me that much."

Margaret felt color stain her face, her exposed neck down to her bodice. She did owe him something, having let him go. "You make me sound . . . dishonest. Keeping secrets, not telling the truth. Like a thief of some sort." Her voice dropped to the edge of a deep, unreleased sob.

Jonathan saw her blush and saddened for her. Yet she was a thief. For reasons he had never fathomed, she had once stolen his heart. It would happen again if he had anything left to steal. But he didn't. His empty chest ached, as torn and ravaged as his body had been in prison. "I'm not suggesting anything of the kind," he forced himself to answer calmly, "but you insist on wielding the power. Keeping secrets is power in one form."

"I don't need power." She sounded defensive. "I just don't want to be controlled."

"You think so?" A sudden knowledge came to him. "What of your lace?"

"I don't see the connection." Her confusion looked honest. "I love my lace."

"But that's why you love it. Because when you work it, you're in control. No one can touch your realm." He watched her steadily to see her reaction, knowing he had stumbled on the crux of the matter. *That was how you bore your life in West Lulworth,* he all but cried in triumph at his discovery. After years of puzzling, understanding burst upon him. Now he knew why she had buried herself in her lace.

His triumph turned immediately to despondence. Desperately he wanted what she had. To be rid of this torment inside, to be cloaked in serenity like hers. He gathered up Patience and went to Margaret. Going down on one knee, he bestowed her child on her like a gift.

As Patience left him, holding out her arms to her mother, Jonathan felt the crush of his weighty solitude. It grew as Margaret clasped the child to her breast and buried her face in Patience's tousled hair. Entranced with the two of them, he knelt there. For the second time that day—the first was earlier on the riverbank—he felt the stirring caused by a woman. The sensation surprised him. That dank Spanish prison had pared away his illusions about himself and the world around him. Stripped him bare of pretensions. He hadn't even a place left for the excesses of the flesh—he had come to admit that in his stark cell with its musty odor of death. Face to face with naked reality, he had known the truth. For four years, indulgence with women had shielded him from the agony of losing Margaret. Once he had escaped, he had let them go. The attractive widows, the comely noblewomen, the lusty doxies who longed to have him in bed. No more could they act the balm to soothe his wounds.

But now Margaret appeared once more in his life. Like a sleeper coming awake, he opened his eyes and saw her as a vision before him. Like a swimmer rising to the water's surface, he breathed her in as air and lived. His gaze feasted on her—the flesh of her face was more than just beautiful. Her long lashes fluttered as she blinked, and he drank in the petal texture of her skin tinted with its subtle shading, rose and ivory, the color of morning. The architecture of her mouth drew to a graceful bow, wrought by the clear separation between lip and skin. The outward glory of her mirrored the inward beauty. The small spark he had felt upon first seeing her came alive inside him, like the tiny wick of a rushlight floating in its pool of dark. It cast a steady light, making the first, fragile inroad on the midnight of his soul. God, if only he could cast away the demon inside him and be innocent again.

"Why do they call you a demon?" her voice demanded, bringing him out of his thoughts, shocking him with how closely hers touched his own.

"Isn't it obvious?" If he had become a demon, he had learned it at the right school, at the knee of the grand master. Inspired by the whip, singing like a lusty maiden longing for his flesh.

She seemed afraid to pursue the subject and instead changed it. "Why are your hands so rough?"

"I'm an armorer. They're rough from my work."

"I thought you were a draper," she blurted, looking disconcerted by this information.

"My father was a draper," he explained patiently, taking out his favorite hammer, the one with the mother-of-pearl inlaid handle, and balancing it in one hand for her to see.

"But he gave me the choice of my future, and I discovered I wanted to be an armorer. For four years I've apprenticed to a master armorer in Germany whenever I took my leaves."

"So you like it?" Her soft voice drifted to him, low and hesitant, its texture silky like the lace she made.

"I've become quite good at it. Though it's not to me what your lace is to you. I wish it were."

Margaret heard the starkness of his words and was struck by them. While she watched him closely, the darkness spread to his eyes again. She sensed just beneath the surface the quiet desperation in him, a wildness like a wrathful spirit wanting to break loose. His body might have changed over the years, might have grown taut and hard. But it was not just well conditioned. It was spare to the point of hunger. Something deep inside him reached out to her, and the answering cry rose within her, the urgent need to redeem him—though her commitment lay with her child. "I understand the magician part. That was always there."

"In truth?" He looked skeptical. "What magic did I ever work?"

"You made me laugh."

Patience had nestled in her arms and dozed off. Margaret rocked her gently, unable to tear her gaze away from Jonathan.

"No wonder. You had little to laugh about, with your house so quiet, with the failings of your father and mother."

"My mother had her failings," she said carefully, guarding her temper, "she still does. But not my father."

"I merely meant they kept you too much to yourself."

"You wanted to change me, make me more like you."

"Was that so bad? I wanted you to get out more, to have friends. I introduced you to other girls about Lulworth. One of them became a favorite companion. You did benefit, didn't you? If so, what does it matter if I did it or you did yourself?"

As he spoke, she watched his wondrous fingers manipulate the little hammer with its beautifully curved head of chased brass. An armorer's hammer, for making curves in steel. When he hung it at his waist again, she suddenly recognized his belt. She had given it to him for a New Year's gift some months before they had parted.

Jonathan tucked the hammer securely back in its loop,

waiting for Margaret to answer. She didn't, though. When he looked up suddenly, he caught her unguarded expression—soft and pained and full of longing.

An acute stab of desire wrenched through him. He seized on her longing greedily before he remembered he had nothing to give her in return.

With difficulty he checked himself by coughing, turned away and brought himself under control. "The time for supper draws near. I told the nurse to return just before it was announced. Mayhap this is a good moment for you to slip away." He received no answer, so he rose up and came to the window, gently took the sleeping child from her. Patience grunted and resettled in his arms, perfectly content with the change. He moved across the room toward her bed, then looked back.

Robbed of her child once more, Margaret sat alone in the window, her bright hair lit up like a halo by the late-day sun, an expression on her face full of that blessed longing. Was it her daughter she couldn't bear to part with, or him? He had no time to consider, because she rushed toward him suddenly, bent over Patience, and gave her a fervent kiss. "I love you, my sweetheart," she whispered. "I shall see you anon." Then she flew from the room in a flurry of saffron kirtle and golden hair.

As she left, the thought struck him forcefully, and he felt the agony of it. Though he had nothing to give her, he wished she had meant the words for him instead.

Chapter 12

"More pickled eels, love?"

Margaret sat in the great hall of Clifton among the family and servants lining the long table. Her gaze shifted from Robert's obsequious smile to the platter of eels offered by a servant. "My thanks, but no." Neither the eels nor Robert tempted her appetite. If only supper would end and the desired moment arrive—she could refuse his offer and escape.

"Come, come," Robert insisted, taking the spoon and serving her anyway. "You should eat more, Margaret. I like my women with a bit of flesh."

"I said no and I meant no, Robert," she snapped, not caring if her mother heard from where she sat, not caring if the servant or the entire table heard. "You never listen to what I say. And I'm not one of your women, so if I'm lacking flesh, 'tis none of your affair."

"Tsk, tsk." Robert shook his head at her and dismissed the servant. "You have been a crosspuss of late, I must say." He wrapped blunt fingers around his wine flagon, brought it to his mouth, and drank. "But I have a cure that will put you right. I'll show it to you as soon as we're wed."

Margaret shuddered. "I said I have no intention of wedding." She narrowed her gaze at him as he picked up a roasted dove and bit into it with relish. Grease dripped from his chin.

"Sure you don't want these eels?" he asked, not heeding her words in the least. "I'll eat them if you don't."

"You're impossible!" she hissed. "I refuse to speak to you further." She twisted in her chair and set her back to him. She heard the clink of his knife as he confiscated her trencher and dug in.

"A shame," he said calmly, "to waste perfectly good eels."

Margaret seethed. Her plan might not work after all. She had meant to refuse his offer tonight in a grand gesture of defiance, but at this rate he wouldn't listen. Without meaning to, without the grand gesture, rejection *had* leaped from her lips just now, yet he ignored her. He assumed, like her grandsire, that a female had no choice.

Two could play at his game—she would ignore him. Resolutely she turned her attention elsewhere, watching the busy feet of servants as they hurried back and forth from the kitchens, treading the woven rush mats covering the stone flags. The many echoing voices scattered in the vast, high-ceilinged room, drifting up to where they were lost in the masterwork of hammer-beamed rafters. Her gaze drifted also until it lit on El Mágico. He was in his element tonight, looking every bit the Magician, garbed in stark black. The minute he had entered the hall, men crowded around him, maid servants connived for his attention. Once at the table, he had been seated to her grandsire's left and plunged into discourse with him. Now they sat knee to knee, trading war stories and talking armor. She could tell because Jonathan had whipped out his pearl-handled hammer to demonstrate a technique. Without question, here were men who saw eye to eye.

In fact, she hadn't realized that Jonathan bore a marked resemblance to her grandsire in more ways than one. Both ordered the people around them, both possessed uncanny skill at inducing others to adopt their way of thinking. Though they worked from different motives, both were dangerous to her. Tonight she must remove herself from their reach.

It took effort to send her gaze elsewhere. As soon as she did, she recognized her latest folly. Jonathan had enchanted her in the nursery. He would do it here if she let him. She hadn't even realized she was so drawn by her craving to be something to him—whatever he happened to need at the time. In Lulworth, he had wanted a coy, docile maiden; she had became that. Now it was a healing spirit, so she dropped her duty and forgot everything in her eagerness to probe and listen to him. During that hour in the nursery, she should have been preparing for her departure. She meant to pack clothes and necessities for Patience. Instead she had lingered with him, all but forgetting supper. If she had any hope of escaping Clifton tonight, she must close her mind to him and attend to her affairs.

Yet if he needed healing, she ought to do it. Especially when he so generously tried to help her. Especially because it was her fault . . .

The confusing tug of war recommenced inside her. When Jonathan distracted her from her duty, life went awry. She must have a care tonight, or her bid for freedom could end in failure. Her child would suffer first.

At last the interminable meal ended. A servant removed a remaining trencher, and her grandsire flung down his napkin. Then with a final glance down the table, he scraped back his chair. His once-powerful body straightened momentarily, then hunched into its usual position over his cane.

"God-den to you, Cavandish. Best of fortune recruiting in the village." Margaret saw him nod to Jonathan, who had also risen. "Your men can bed down here in the hall. Always have room for fighting men. I have business to attend, but the rest will have music. You're welcome to partake."

The two men saluted each other. Margaret felt the usual oppressive silence in the hall as the earl limped toward the door.

The minute he was out of sight, the musicians began a tune on crumhorns and recorders. Lilting strains of the galliard "Sweet Marguerite" rang through the hall, the song Jonathan used to sing to her. Bittersweet memories wove through her mind, their patterns both joyous and painful. The man who had made them stood across the hall, talking to the vicar, his face in shadows so she couldn't catch his expression. Did he remember?

For a second she allowed herself a luxury—she dreamed she was plain Margaret Smytheson, able to hide behind her father's name and obscurity. When she had first seen Jonathan crossing the green in West Lulworth, life had been much more simple. All she had had to do was trip and spill her pail of milk to bring him running to her aid. The warmth of his hand as he helped her up lingered in her memory, as sweet as the music running through her mind.

The dream dissolved as a different hand gripped her elbow. Robert's hand, clammy and nagging.

She evaded from long habit. The need to escape him swept her from her seat. She moved around the great hall's edge, unable to tolerate his touch. In fact, she couldn't tolerate anything at Clifton. The hall oppressed her, with its ancestral banners, pompous reminders of Clifford duty. She would go to the village, make plans with Bertrande. When the men brought more logs for the fire, she would slip out unnoticed, collect Patience, and leave.

The cushion dance began. Margaret's twelve-year-old cousin Dorothea chose a partner from the captain's men, a dark-haired young man with a winning smile. When he knelt on the cushion, she darted a kiss on his cheek and bid him join her. Instantly he hopped up, sang his part, in turn selected Mary, their ten-year-old cousin. When five couples held the floor, all the young cousins were chosen. Willing female dancers dried up.

Margaret waited in the shadow of a pillar while three servants heaped wood on the fire. A blond fellow who had come with the captain, a Dutchman with burning blue eyes, leaned against the chimney piece, watching. His gaze flickered from her to Jonathan, making her uncomfortable. As did the ever-growing bevy of maid servants and kitchen girls peeking from behind the screens, awaiting their chance to mix with the cavalrymen.

Giggling erupted from those very maids. With a start, Margaret found Dorothea before her. One of the captain's men lurked behind her, holding the cushion, an excited grin on his face.

"Join us, Margaret," came Dorothea's expected plea. "I want you to dance."

"I'm going to Patience. You have your fun."

"It's no fun without you," Dorothea wheedled. " 'Twill cheer you. Come, try."

A sudden thought assailed Margaret. Robert sat at the table, watching her, his lids half dropping to hood his hateful gaze. This was the way to refuse him, before the entire company. With everyone as witness, she would make her intentions clear.

A slight guilt weighed her, but only for a second. She threw it off, set herself free. The power to choose. The power to decide. They were hers if she took them. She intended to claim them tonight.

She knelt on the cushion. The recruit bestowed a proper

kiss in the air above her and bid her join them. After that, all eyes turned to Lord Robert. 'Twas expected she would choose him. The music continued, bold and merry, the folk in the hall clapping, keeping time. She sang her part with relish, let her voice ring out.

When the music paused, as it was supposed to, Margaret paused also, holding the cushion before her. Dancers and musicians waited. Robert regarded her intensely, his expectation showing. It seemed everyone had known of his impending offer. Everyone but her. She hadn't wanted to. She had shut out the signs, wished them away while she lost herself in her lace.

Smug self-satisfaction—she saw it in every limb and bone of him. Too long she had gone without care for her own comfort. For the first time in five years, Margaret dug down inside herself and called on her reserve of courage. She found it stored in quantities so large, it amazed her. How had she let it lay dormant so long?

The viscount slid forward on his chair. His heavy lips parted so she could see his tongue. He ran it over his teeth and upper lip in a thoroughly sexual suggestion, telling her he was eager to lay his claim.

Revulsion struck her. She turned away and scanned the room, studied the men who had come tonight, intending to choose one of them. The hall had fallen deathly silent, the crowd waited. If she didn't choose Robert, he and the earl would be wroth.

Her wrath would equal theirs. Her needs mattered. She could and would make her choice, but she didn't want just anyone. Her gaze lighted on Jonathan and lingered. While she watched, while the vicar harangued him on some favorite topic, with an almost imperceptible movement Jonathan turned her way and winked.

She stared harder, not willing to believe it. He invited her to use him? That couldn't be.

But when he propped his hand on his chin and slyly crooked a finger at her, she believed it. He understood her loathing for Robert and offered to aid her. With a defiant twitch of the cushion, she walked straight for him.

She flung the cushion at his feet, as if it were a gauntlet. She stepped back.

Chapter 13

The captain broke off his conversation with the vicar. The religious man melted into the depths of the hall, embarrassed. Margaret was past caring. She ignored the audible gasp of the manor folk present, registering their shock. She had gone beyond the boundaries permitted by proper society and delivered Robert a horrible insult. There was no turning back now.

Jonathan's eyebrows rose in pleased astonishment, as if he did not understand the gravity of her action. "You wish me to partner you, lady? How thoughtful of you to think of me."

But his voice wound its way around her, a lazy, reckless drawl that dared her. When she heard it, she wanted to laugh—a bold, savage laugh. Of course he knew what she was doing. He had encouraged her. "I reserve the right to inspect the gentlemen present and select the most fitting." She felt a vast satisfaction in her newly discovered independence and wanted him to share it.

He chuckled as if he recognized it, while stroking her body with his gaze. That gaze wasn't like Robert's, which made her feel sullied. This one made her tingle in places deep within.

"Fitting is hardly the word. I am anything but in your case."

"You shouldn't listen to my grandsire. I know he suggested you wed with my cousin. Don't do it if you would rather not."

"You know of his offer?" He raised his eyebrows again, but this time she saw his genuine surprise.

"I do."

"But how ..." He rolled his eyes heavenward. "Don't

tell me. I'm probably safer not knowing. But I wasn't referring to your grandsire. It's my judgment, not his." He scanned the hall briefly, then signaled the musicians. "If we're to dance, we'd best have a pavane instead." Courteously he offered his arm.

The cushion dance had been broken, shattered by her deliberate failure to choose Robert. A change did seem in order. She took his arm as the musicians nervously launched into the new piece. Dorothea and the others followed, trying to pretend nothing was wrong. As they moved into the first figure, Margaret heard the angry thud of Robert's boot soles as he left the hall. Insulted. Never to return. A stab of jubilation soared through her.

"Pleased with yourself, aren't you?" Jonathan sent her a conspiratorial grin as they glided forward.

She let his magic wrap around her with a delicious shiver. "I'm sending a clear message, though I doubt he's clever enough to heed it. Now, sir, let us change the subject." She let him guide her through the steps, marveling that he, who once hated dancing, executed the steps with ease. "I don't remember your being such an accomplished dancer."

"Your compliment is backhanded," he answered. "As it happens, I've changed over the years. In more ways than how I dance."

God help her, she could just imagine some of those ways. His innuendo turned the tingle to a flare of heat inside Margaret. It lit up the pit of her belly, twice as intense as before, making her quiver. Each time they parted, each time his hand reclasped hers, her entire body threatened to mutiny, to overthrow her tight control and fling itself into his arms. "Why is the cushion dance less fitting than the pavane?"

"Because in the cushion dance, I would have had to kneel on the cushion. We both know what would have happened then."

Margaret started, swept from triumph into confusion. So he did remember the first time he had said he loved her. He had bid her kneel on the cushion, used the dance as a blatant excuse to kiss her. Later, he took her out into the dark where he had kissed her until she was dizzy, whispered words of endearment, his breath warm by her cheek. The memory put her in such a heat, she turned the wrong way for the next step and ran into him. "My dancing seems to have deteriorated," she apologized. "Mayhap we should stop."

Obligingly he drew her into a recessed alcove. "You will have consequences to this dance and the partner you chose. Can you manage them? I fear it wasn't wise."

"Of course it wasn't wise." Margaret knew he had seen right through her, but then so did everyone else in the hall tonight, including Robert, which was exactly her purpose. "But I intend to decide for myself from now on."

A mixture of emotions seized Jonathan. Longing stabbed him, mingled with regret. When he had seen her scan his men, searching for a dancing partner, he had been cut to the quick with jealousy. How could he not urge her to come to him?

She had answered his slightest signal. Unfair of him to call her. Grossly cruel. Yet when she approached, he found himself engulfed by the welcome fragrance of her, and the rare light shining in her eyes. Now he sent a longing gaze to skim her body. Her arms, folded at her chest, emphasized a soft swath of cleavage revealed by her kirtle bodice. He liked this garment better than the black one. In fact, hadn't she worn this same thing in Lulworth, when their love was new and just being with her brought him a blinding rush of exultation, along with the urgent wish inside him to . . .

He stopped himself. His loins had tightened. No woman had interested him since prison. He had seen the truth there—Margaret had been the ideal of his youth. Nothing could touch that memory. But he was a bare shadow of what he had once been, had less to offer her now than when they first met. All the old barriers of class and her family still stood between them, wider and more formidable than the frigid water of the river Esk. By no means could he let this go on.

"With regret, lady"—he gave a slight bow—"I should bid you god-den. My thanks for your company. And my apologies for bypassing the cushion dance, but I gave up that particular dance years ago."

"So did I," she answered quickly. "Tonight is the first time I've danced it in years. I never danced it with anyone else."

He knew what she meant—she had never danced it with anyone else since him.

"But the pavane accomplished my purpose," she hurried

on. "My point is made. And I promise to repay the favor soon."

Repay him! God, he had loved the way she used to repay his favors. As he recalled, so did she. She hadn't meant it that way, though. Color seeped into her face as she, too, remembered and blushed at her error. " 'Tis not necessary," he said. "I absolve you of the debt."

"I will repay you," she insisted with quiet dignity. "You offered to assist me; I accepted. Therefore I owe you a debt. I will be in the village tonight, at the thatched cottage nearest the smithy. I stay there often. Call on me if you have need."

"If I am in the village, your best course would be to stay out of my way."

"I know more about the manor folk than you do," she answered sharply. "I know all the comings and goings here. If you're in danger, I might be able to help."

"You have danger enough of your own to deal with." He jerked his head in the direction last taken by the viscount, determined to squash her interest. "He'll be quite unruly now that you've riled him. Though I must admit it was worth it, seeing him leave. For that reason alone, I couldn't resist."

A tiny bubble of laughter escaped from her, and he winked at her, sharing a second of mirth at Robert's expense. "Sure you don't need help managing him? You will let me know if you do?"

"The viscount has the wit of a mud clod. He is no threat."

" 'Tis best not to underestimate your opponents."

"My grandsire is the one to be reckoned with," she answered calmly. "Now, if you will excuse me, I have other matters to attend. You have served me graciously, and I give you my thanks."

Whirling on her heel, she headed for the door. Her slippers slapped resolutely on the cold flagstones, reminding him of Robert's earlier exit. Jonathan turned away, the warmth from her presence fading within him.

By heaven, if only he had room inside for something beyond this hate.

He searched his soul, but found nothing beyond the cold dregs left by the inquisitor—a man so diabolic, he thrived on people's pain.

Behind him, the hall came to life again. Hushed gossip and chatter started up, everyone probably speculating on what would happen next. Jonathan went out a side door and was moving past the kitchens toward the stable when a young lass stopped him. It was the little wench Dorothea, hugging his doublet to her flat chest.

"I'm to return this to you, Captain, with thanks for its use."

She extended it toward him, and he took it, noting the garment had been dried and brushed. "My thanks to you, young mistress. God-den." He turned to go.

"Might I ask you a question, Captain Cavandish?" The childish voice arrested him.

He stopped, curious despite himself. She had a bald approach.

"What's it like to become El Mágico Demoníaco?"

Jon grew thoughtful. "I'll tell you, Mistress Clifford, since you ask. It was like a bad case of the sweating sickness. In the heat of it, you want to die. And the rest of the time, you're terrified you're going to live."

She gaped at him, shocked. A war hero was supposed to mouth platitudes about loving victory, no matter what he felt inside. "But, my lord captain," she whispered, rubbing one slipper against the back of her calf, confusing his title in her consternation, "you're magic. How can that be?"

"Think about who christened me El Mágico Demoníaco," he said gravely, seized by a sudden desire to be understood by someone. "Our enemies, not our friends. Though it seems exciting to you, I have no pleasant memories from earning that name."

His response unnerved her. She stared at him for several minutes. "My apologies, sir. I was remiss to ask," she whispered before she turned tail and fled. Jonathan remained sober as she disappeared. He had shocked the wits out of her. With most people, the truth usually did.

As he headed for the stables, his thoughts divided. What had he done tonight? A mad, reckless thing. He had supported a rebellion at Clifton Manor that would see ugly consequences, then had left Margaret alone to cope with them. He must somehow help her, but it had to be later. He was due at the village to complete his mission. There was no time to lose.

* * *

Margaret entered her darkened chamber and felt her way to the court cupboard where she located the carved box. Prying it open, she drew out some papers, a coin-filled purse, and the lace bobbin. Thrusting them into a larger purse, she strapped it to her waist, then turned and headed for the nearest stair.

When she reached the nursery, she stealthily opened the door and went in. Her grandfather wouldn't follow her here. He disliked the nursery filled with female children. Tiptoeing to Patience's bed, she looked down on her sleeping daughter.

Leaning down, Margaret smoothed the dark hair from her daughter's brow and kissed her. Then pulling back the linen, she gathered the girl in her arms.

Patience sighed as she settled in the familiar embrace and lay her cheek on Margaret's shoulder but did not fully awaken. Arranging her warm burden, Margaret checked the nurse and saw she dozed undisturbed by the fire. Gathering some of her child's clothing, she made a bundle. Then she took a blanket and wrapped it around Patience. With both in her arms, she slipped to the door and lifted the latch.

The door creaked open, but neither Patience nor the nurse nor the other three girls, deep in slumber, showed signs of hearing. With breath held tightly in her lungs, Margaret took a last look around the room. It was time to burn her bridges behind her. So resolved, she fled into the night.

Chapter 14

Margaret strode through the darkness toward the distant lights of Clifton Village, feeling every stone gouge through her thin-soled slippers. How she wished she had worn something more serviceable. With a wry grimace, she realized that the men in her life must consider her like these slippers, beautifully ornamental but ultimately useless in the face of crisis.

She knew it wasn't so. Ever since she had sold her lace to care for her father, she had known her strength. Now the time had come to shake off her grandsire's bonds and care for Patience the way she should have from the start. Now she would pursue the future she wanted.

Hugging herself and her baby with anticipation, Margaret renewed her speed. But halfway to Clifton village, which lay near the sea, Margaret heard hoofbeats drumming on the road behind her. She ducked off the beaten track behind some bushes, unwilling to be seen. Who could it be, riding at this time of night?

She didn't find out, though, because Patience shifted just then and Margaret had to rearrange the blanket. By the time she looked up, the rider had vanished. She slipped from the shadows and continued her journey. She had much to do tonight.

She thought of Jonathan, the way he had appeared today like the magician he was named for. Confusion overcame her again, as always with him. He had tied her emotions in knots for the brief year she had known him. Three months acquainted, another nine in love. How well had she understood him, or he, her?

Very little, that was evident. Now he had changed further, held mysterious secrets within him. Those secrets frightened her, especially when she remembered her grandsire's words to Jonathan—*A man can't fight when he's half dead.*

How she longed to help him, to banish the darkness from his eyes. It had vanished for a second in the nursery when he brought her Patience and knelt at her feet with such agile grace. For a moment, he had seemed once more the young, carefree Jonathan. She longed for that time with an intensity she dared not admit.

Shifting Patience in her arms, Margaret sought her destination. Bertrande's cottage lay in the distance, nestled beneath a sheltering spread of trees. As she drew nearer, another set of hooves pounded on the road behind her. Again she dived for the bushes. Was everyone bound for the village tonight?

This time she risked discovery and tried to see the passerby by peering through the branches. Swathed in an all-concealing cloak, the mounted rider hid himself from prying eyes.

She shrugged, thinking little of it. Probably one of the men come with the captain, craving a more exotic lass or a taste of tavern wine.

Margaret's hopes lifted as she drew near the cottage. She breathed in the night air, filling her lungs. It smelled fresh like it had this afternoon in the garden. But that was her grandsire's garden. Here she was beyond his jurisdiction. Light flared within her, filling her with lust for freedom. Pressing her cheek against the soft hair of her child, she let out a sigh of thanks. Patience would go unbeaten, as would her spirit.

Her destination sat away from the road, separated from the public way by a stone wall. It clustered with the smithy's forge, the local tavern, several other neat private cottages. Scraps of music floated to Margaret from the tavern, where the host and his paid entertainers cheered guests in the public room.

She reached the gate, opened it, and went down the path. Pausing before Bertrande's door, she steeled herself, then pounded firmly. The slight shock of hard wood against her knuckles resounded through her body, startling her. Let them answer quickly, she prayed. Let them not be asleep.

She blinked as the door opened and light flooded her

face. A young woman of medium height with curly black hair gaped at her in surprise.

"Marguerite!" The younger girl grasped her hands, pulled her inside. "*Mon Dieu*, you walked all this way with *la petite*?"

Margaret nodded as she stepped over the threshold. Gratefully she entered the simply furnished chamber and saw the glad scene awaiting her. Bertrande sat by the fire. Slowly, she raised her regal head and turned toward Margaret. Peace radiated from her, while the firelight caught the glint of her snowy wealth of hair, crowned by a pristine, lace-trimmed cap. Though her wide gray eyes were all but blind, they still reflected grave caring from the serenity of her oval face.

Margaret waited while Marie hurried to draw back the curtain at the far end of the room and rearrange the bedding. A minute later she returned for Patience. Trustingly Margaret let her child go to her friend. The soft voice of her daughter floated across the room as the two disappeared behind the curtain. Margaret heard Marie's French murmurs, the drowsy answers from Patience as she was tucked into the cozy bed.

Bertrande reached out one hand to her, beckoned, and swiftly Margaret crossed the room. Going down on one knee, she placed her head in Bertrande's lap. Closing her eyes, she let out her breath while the long, slim fingers twined in her hair.

"Marguerite, I am glad you come to us." Gently the old dame shushed the beginning of Margaret's explanation as she stroked her hair. "There is time enough to tell me. For now, lean against me."

Relieved, Margaret steeped herself in the comfort, grateful no words were required. Here was one who had cherished her for five years past. Here, for the present, she was at peace.

"A drink would strengthen you." Bertrande pointed to a comfortable chair. A kettle of water steamed on the hook over the fire. Within minutes Margaret found herself settled, a cup of hot brew in her hands, the restful scent of chamomile permeating the air. She sipped, scorching her tongue, then blew ripples in the foggy surface until she could drink. The chamomile burned a calming trail down her throat, into the pit of her stomach. Something deep inside her uncoiled. It was overwhelming, this warm feeling, after the day of tension. Suddenly, tears threatened. She battled them silently, refusing to let them spill. It was nothing, this moment of weakness. She would be over it in a flash.

Bertrande kept her gaze to the flickering fire and let Margaret rest in the silence. So many times before they had sat here in just this way. But tonight was different. The part of Bertrande that had seen seventy years opened to Margaret, spread throughout the room, a vast, sustaining presence. Margaret felt her waiting, as calm and patient as the hills and moors of Yorkshire. It seemed that the patience she held was a primal force, sage and solemn, like her father's patience. If only she, Margaret, possessed such patience, something she never managed. Her plans longed to spill from her lips in a babble of excitement, but she must wait. She sipped more of Bertrande's herb brew to rally her courage, knowing she would need it before the night was out. The comfort spread throughout her middle and radiated to her extremities. In a minute she would speak.

Marie came back just then. Seating herself at the table, she reached for her plain sewing and inclined her head, waiting for someone to begin.

"What have you come to tell us, Marguerite?" Bertrande's sober voice broke the quiet. "This is not just a friendly visit like we usually share. Out with it at once."

Margaret bent her head for a second, realizing what Bertrande was to her, mother and mentor, offering the key to her memories. The firelight shone on her friend's finely textured skin, still fresh with her youth's radiance though age had woven it full of creases. She had been a beauty in her youth; that beauty still shone from within. That was her wealth, though she had lost nearly every material thing she owned. Yet she shared what she had freely with Margaret. Here Patience whiled away happy hours, playing merrily with cups and spoons on the floor. Here Margaret's thoughts and feelings were cherished by her friends.

"I have made a decision," Margaret began slowly but determinedly. "So pray do not try to convince me otherwise. I am leaving Clifton tonight and taking Patience with me. If you will permit, I will meet with you later and we will travel to London. We will start your lace business together, as I have wished." She awaited their protests, their attempts to convince her of the danger. But she would not be swayed.

Bertrande smoothed her starched white apron, her hands decisive. "*Eh bien,* we will make our plans."

Margaret's heart soared with hope. "You won't try to stop me or send me back?"

Bertrande reached out her hand and placed it on Margaret's. "I know you would never do anything on whim, Marguerite. I trust your choice."

Margaret placed her other hand over Bertrande's. "May I never make a wrong one. My plan is to leave here tonight when my grandsire doesn't suspect it and ride west. By the time he knows, I'll be long gone. I can then double back to throw him off my track."

"You must go south to Scarborough instead," Bertrande said promptly, "to Master Hale. I buy my thread from him, as you know. He will hide you at some farm nearby. A few days later you can go to Ripon. He will arrange for you to travel with someone. Whoever it is, a farmer or a dairyman, can't keep you safe from your grandsire, but he can protect you from ruffians. Marie and I will go as planned with the carpenters three days hence."

Margaret nodded eagerly. "I will meet you at Ripon. I have money, so I will pay—"

"You have given us too much already," Bertrande broke in. "We would not be making this journey at all save for your help, nor would Master Foster and his son, Master Paul. Your gifts to them last winter meant the difference between life and death for their family, all five of them, and for us. We would risk our lives to repay you."

"I don't want you to risk your lives," Margaret hastened to say. "You have already risked much to poverty. No, no, I only desire that you should meet me at Ripon. Grandsire will not equate my disappearance with you because you will be sitting right here when he finds I am missing. When you leave three days hence, 'twill be just as you originally planned, as everyone knows."

Bertrande nodded briskly. "That is well. Now then, what of Patience? How will she travel? Marie, bring me those baskets, the ones we take to market when we go."

Marie brought the baskets and put them on her aunt's lap. Bertrande explored them with her hands. "I think these will do. Patience will ride in one, your things in the other. They will hang on each side of the horse, roped in place. 'Twill serve if Patience will be still."

Margaret reached over to take the baskets. "I thank you again, for not trying to convince me to stay here. I will manage with these to Scarborough."

"After that, Master Hale will see that you ride to Ripon with someone carrying goods," Bertrande continued. "Locate the carpenters' guild and wait in some out-of-the-way place until we arrive. Once we are joined up, you might pass for Master Paul's wife, who left for London this week past, going to her mother. She took the baby with her, but the older son remains with his father. Patience might pass for their child."

"Oh, no." Marie put down her sewing, looking distressed. "Won't her grandsire recognize her? She cannot hope to deceive him."

"My grandsire is not capable of the hard riding required to follow me," Margaret said. "I feel guilty, playing on his lack of strength to escape him, but I cannot—"

"Nay, feel not guilty," Bertrande soothed her. "Were you evenly matched in strength when he asked you to take Oliver? *Non, non,* he took advantage of your wish to win his approval. I absolve you of any guilt here and now."

"Bien," Marie agreed, "that is well, but what of his men? They will follow you, as will Lord Robert. What will we do?"

"If a search party comes upon us," Bertrande said, "Marguerite can feign illness and ride in the closed cart. Let me think. We will suggest it is an unknown fever. Or mayhap the small pox. Lord Robert would not wish to risk his delicate skin." She thought hard, her brow wrinkled with concentration. "We will take an indirect road and hope they do not find us. Beyond that, all we can do is pray."

Margaret's heart raced with jubilation. Might they be together as she wished? "Once we get to London, I have money to get us settled." She pulled forth the small purse from her waistband and spread the coins on the table to count them. " 'Tis only four pounds, and we must lease a shop, a place for us to live, buy food. But I think we can manage, since we can sell our lace—mine as well as yours. I'd care for you both, so you need not fear—"

"*You* care for *us*?" Bertrande's voice was astonished. "Of course you will not. We must care for ourselves."

"But you will help us find noble buyers," Marie threw in enthusiastically as she wound thread on a bobbin. "Let us not quarrel. We are going and all will be well. In London, we will eat meat twice a week, like we did in La Rochelle." She gazed at the kettle standing in the hearth. "I would wish for a glorious piece of venison. Or some fresh lamb." Her expression turned dreamy and she stopped winding the bobbin as she imagined the food.

They were silent, thinking of the two women's desperate flight from La Rochelle, of how they had selected their destination in England blindly. Yorkshire hadn't worked out well for them at all.

Margaret slid her guineas back in the purse, drew the strings tight and refastened it to her waistband. "Yes, let us take things as they come." But she knew she would care for them. They needed it, and it was her dream. Just as she had cared for her father, who had accepted silently and let her do it. She would do the same for her daughter and these friends she loved.

Chapter 15

The hour grew late for the lace makers who rose at dawn each day to take advantage of the light. So Margaret did not protest when they moved to retire. Marie went to put out the cat, leaving Margaret and Bertrande alone.

"Marguerite, I did not wish to speak before Marie, but I would not deceive you," Bertrande said. "Our journey will be fraught with danger, as I think you know." To aid her weak eyes, she reached for Margaret's hand and took it in her own.

Margaret felt the warmth of her friend's fingers and drew on her strength. "I know my grandsire will challenge me, and he has the advantage of wealth to aid him. I have the element of surprise on my side, but that is all. I must be clever and outwit him."

Bertrande scanned her sharply. Margaret knew she had full skill of appraisal despite being blind. "Cleverness can be useful, but sometimes it is no defense against might. I know little of the friends you might call upon, but if ever there was a time to seek them, it is now. This is your most desperate hour—your success or failure in this venture will decide the course of your entire future. I urge you to call up every last source of help you hold in reserve."

Margaret shifted, uncomfortable with Bertrande's words. They frightened her, and she had not, until now, felt frightened of her grandsire. But Bertrande was right. He had the power to change her life irrevocably. Until today, she hadn't believed he would go against her wishes in matters she considered important. Now she knew she had judged him wrong. "I have few friends I can call on. Those I could, I hesitate to ask. It would make me beholden in ways I could not repay."

"That is a hard choice, but one you will soon be forced to make," Bertrand replied emphatically.

"Do you mean I must choose the lesser of two evils?"

"I pray it should not be that bad. But remember, no one lives alone in this world. Nor can you."

"I won't obey my grandsire any longer," cried Margaret. "I want to be myself again. I want to make my decisions alone."

"And so you shall," Bertrande told her gently, "but there is more to it than that. I would speak the truth to you. Will you hear me?"

Margaret bowed her head. "Aye, *ma tante*."

"Don't play meek with me. I am not your grandsire, to be fooled thus. There is no meekness in you," Bertrande admonished. "Hate my words if you wish, but heed them. You must take a husband. You said you would hear me," she insisted, raising her hand as Margaret strove to protest. "The queen has ultimate authority over her nobles' marriages. You must go to her and tell her the man you choose."

"But that is the problem." Margaret wanted to weep, she was so frustrated. Everyone bade her to wed, even her dearest friend. "I wish to remain unwed."

"You can't do that and well you know it," came Bertrande's disheartening answer. "It is your destiny to serve your family." With her sensitive fingers she felt Margaret's face, tracing her mouth, no doubt recognizing that it had stiffened into rebellious lines. "Besides, you are a woman made to wed and mother children. Best make the choice while it remains yours."

"How can you say that?" protested Margaret. "Men are difficult to live with. They expect to be the center of attention, demand that everything be done their way."

"So it has been with your grandsire and Oliver," Bertrande soothed her. "But this next time can be different. You must search for harmony with others, just as you had to learn to harmonize your bobbins when you first learned your lace. The right tension of the threads is essential. The roles of the weavers and the passives are distinct."

"Men always want to be the weavers," stated Margaret stiffly. "They force the woman to take the passive role. But I want to be the weaver. I want to dominate the pattern. At this point, I refuse to accept anything less."

"*Eh bien.*" Bertrande continued to soothe the rumpled feathers she had deliberately stirred earlier. "Take the part of the weavers and enjoy it. You have the strength in you now. But think on this—without the passives, there is no ground on which to build the pattern. Without the foot of a piece, there is no anchor for the motif. Each thread is important, each plays its necessary part."

"If I can play both at once, well and good," insisted Margaret. "But I will not play the passive to my grandsire. Not ever again!"

"Ah, but lace making requires that you switch from one to the other at the right moments. At the point where dominance and strength are required, you work the weavers. But you must work the passives when it is their turn. Now then"—Bertrande caressed Margaret's hair, clearly intending to change the subject—"I regret to lay a heavy burden on your shoulders, yet I must. It is one of the few things I can do to protect you. You must give up your lace for the duration of this journey. Yes," she insisted when Margaret gasped in dismay. "If you are seen working it, it will give you away to your pursuers. You must not even own a lace pillow. For your safety and your daughter's, you must obey me in this."

Tears stung Margaret's eyes, the tears she had not shed before her grandsire or her mother, or even Jonathan. No matter which way she turned, her lace was forbidden. For some unknown reason, the loss of her father assailed her at that moment, as fresh and grievous as if it were only yesterday she had laid him out in their parlor, washed his dear face for the last time, then arranged his arms across his chest in his best shirt while the women of West Lulworth assisted her and her mother cowered in her chamber, terrified to face their loss.

"Ma chère petite," Bertrande comforted, "I grieve for your trials, but you have within you a source of solace. Close your eyes and you will see."

Margaret did as bid. As her lids descended, the outer world died to her. Blackness like Bertrande's near blindness swirled before her. The darkness of impenetrable night.

"When other people close their eyes, they see nothing," continued Bertrande's voice. "*We* see our patterns. For me, they make my world a place of beauty and harmony. Think of your favorite pattern, Marguerite. Draw on its strength."

Gladly Margaret called up the image of the point d'esprit, imagined the placement of the pins for the curving leaf pattern. At last she could let the mystery steal over her. Even without pillow and bobbins, the pattern formed in her mind. Relief poured into her soul as she entered that secret place where the crisp geometric shapes ruled. Fear fell away as the threads crossed and twined in her mind, forming the heart of the pattern, its melody humming clear through her spirit. In such moments she felt her father's presence, standing at her back, firm in his loving. *You're a miracle, daughter. You have a miraculous gift.*

"It is time, Marguerite." Bertrande's whisper came to her, layering its love with the memory of her father's voice. "As you move forward in your life, you must do so in your craft as well. Your days as my pupil are done. Listen well!" Bertrande ordered, catching her hands as Margaret tried to say she would always be Bertrande's pupil and love the role. "I have taught you all I know. Having mastered the stitches themselves, you must apply your unusual skill to designing your own patterns and copying valuable patterns whose secrets have been lost. You could not do this as a novice, but now you are ready. Let the creator within you awaken, Marguerite! Look at me."

Margaret heard her mentor's words, obeyed the orders, and opened her eyes. She was immediately gifted with Bertrande's smile, that curve of her pale lips lighting up her face to reveal her inner beauty. With a sigh that mixed both joy and sorrow, Margaret went into her friend's arms and clung to her. Bertrande was right, she yearned to test her own power of creation. It was something she unconsciously had longed for as she planned their London lace business.

The realization filled her with exhilaration and froze her with fear—she was on her own. In another minute she must rise and enter an unknown future. But she couldn't help wondering, as she readied herself for the challenge, if Jonathan was part of the new pattern, or if she must struggle on alone.

Chapter 16

The clock struck ten in the village of Clifton as Jonathan leaned against one of the clustered trees near his rendezvous point. He had finished his recruiting at the tavern and welcomed with enthusiasm another man to their cause. A few minutes earlier he had met with Cornelius beneath the trees, then they had separated. The Portuguese ship stood anchored offshore. Soon the courier they sought would arrive.

Cornelius had swaggered off to the tavern, pretending to be lonely, seeking ale and company. The gathering place was new to the area, built of young timber and boasting two staircases, one outside, the other within. Mullioned windows graced it, including the second floor made up of rooms for private parties. Yet as if the owner had run out of money, the structure's roof was thatch. Odd, that. Odd, too, to see such an outlay of expense in this remote part of Yorkshire, but Jonathan could think of reasons for it, most of them having to do with Spanish money exchanged for favors.

Cornelius would sniff out the details. Even now he mingled in the public room, gathering information, plucking it from unsuspecting fellow drinkers like ripe fruit as the night progressed and their tongues loosened. Soon they would gain even more than information—the Spanish courier and his English contact were set to meet here.

Standing in the shadows, Jonathan focused his thinking. Everything he was or had been fell away, subsumed by his purpose. Tonight he began the slow dance that would lead him to his enemy. With surety, he felt the inquisitor's presence in this plot deep in his gut.

Margaret. In the midst of his concentration, the name

intruded. It haunted him like the light breeze off the sea, reminding him of her achingly sweet qualities. She had offered to help him tonight in the village. If only she would—in ways beyond her intent.

He shook his head to clear it, meaning to jettison that thought. Never before had he experienced trouble shutting out everything around him. He wouldn't let it start now.

But the unbidden thought of her persisted. Suddenly a companion thought pierced Jonathan's mind—an image from the past. As a lad in West Lulworth, he had stolen from home to see her. When he had crept through the lonely darkness, when he had peered through the squire's window, there she sat in a pool of light so gold it glittered like a living halo. And when he tapped on the glass, she had looked up and smiled on him, her eyes like the rising sun.

A shock ran through him as he realized. At the time he had been too foolish, too young to understand. He had thought her lace making boring, when he had been the bore. Now he knew. She gave heat and light like the purest of fires sought by the armorer to temper his steel. And at the core of her, in the hottest part of her luminous center, lay the fuel that gave her that golden, glowing serenity. It was the strength of her soul, shining from her amber eyes.

He needed purity like that! He required peace of mind. How well five years had taught him it was not easily found. Like the painstaking tests he did of woods and charcoal, searching for the perfect fire, he had sought this miraculous element. Never had he found it in womankind, until he saw Margaret again.

Yet he could take no peace from her. It was either the hate or this gnawing, hollow feeling for him. But the void within preserved his sanity. After an experience like his, you had to empty yourself of feelings to survive—like a too-full pack, throw out the excess baggage. Travel light and lean and alone.

He had done that. Inside, he was blank and emotionless, his energy fixed on destruction. Because of it, in the past six months he'd grown as inhuman as the man he despised.

Seeing Margaret made him remember—what it was like to know the full range of emotions and be sensitive to every shade and nuance of them. But remembering wasn't the same as feeling. Praise God for that, because to feel anything, even pleasant emotions, meant opening up to the torturous ones. He must not run that risk—already the pleasure she had brought left him writhing in anguish as he knew its futility. Hate must suffice for him, and he had that in excess. The old church stories of hellfire had come to life for him, embodied in his tormentor. Jonathan would never forget his voice, for it haunted him nightly, his face always hidden by its black mask.

Though she was loath to leave, Margaret at last tore herself from Bertrande, prepared to return to the manor. She had left her mare there on purpose so no one would suspect her intentions. Now she would fetch her, then return for Patience. She hurried to be ready, sorry she had kept her friends from their much-needed rest. Now Bertrande let her out the door and Margaret started off.

As she went up the path, she thought on Bertrande's words. Must she be a wife in truth? No, she would not do it! She could never find a man who was trustworthy, who would let her produce the required heir, then leave her in peace.

Troubled by the thought, she stopped just outside the gate, though she wasn't sure why. Something made her linger. An odd premonition. An unnerving prickle of anticipation at the back of her neck. Her eyes adjusted to the darkness, and she scanned the trees, the smithy, the nearby tavern. The drink business was brisk tonight at that establishment, the largest in the parish. As she looked, her gaze halted at the base of an oak tree. Beyond rough bark, its trunk had shape and substance that hinted at a man's molding.

Margaret squinted, rubbed her eyes, and looked again. A naked rapier blade glinted to catch the moonlight. She went completely still inside.

The line of the rapier guided her until her eyes found the man holding it. El Mágico leaned against the tree, blending as if he were part of the trunk.

The sight of him was more than expected. It sprang on her like full-blown moon madness. Spontaneous and unpremeditated, the thought swept through her: he was a magician, just like they said. Slipping through moonlight, appearing unexpectedly, disappearing without a trace.

He used his magic to call her. Instinctively she went to him, unable to resist. As he stepped away from the tree, his tall form was gilded by the witching hour moon, his brown hair became a nimbus radiating light. He shifted on those light, silent feet, and the rapier at his hip glittered, emphasizing the power of his pelvis, reminding her of his paralyzing charm. It drew her blindly. The expression on his face, veiled by day, was thoroughly disquieting by night, bared to show his passion. Years ago she had loved that look, because it meant he wanted her. An answering shot of excitement launched itself through her middle and shimmered up her spine. Crossing both arms over her stomach, she tried to hide her yearning. God's eyelid, she was mad to feel this for him again.

"Margaret." His voice wrapped around her with sensuous sounds. "I was just thinking of you, and *voilà,* you appear."

Because he was right, she rushed to change the subject. "You are in great danger," she warned. "I feel it. The English contact knows you are here."

He looked around, shrugged his powerful shoulders in that nonchalant way of his, and grinned at her. "I don't see the welcoming delegation."

"Nor will you." His easy humor irked her. "They have the sense to stay hidden. You vex me to death, standing here in the open, taunting danger, daring it to come get you. I'll never understand how you do it—turn horrible things into jests."

"I've lost my former touch, I assure you."

She caught the dark note that slipped into his voice as he spoke. It hurt her to hear it, just as it had in the nursery. "You must let me help," she insisted impulsively. "I told you I would."

A generous offer, Jonathan thought as he forced himself to study the woman before him objectively. Her bright hair reflected moonlight in the most bewitching manner. Her movements showed the beauty of every bend and curve of her form. He let himself appreciate her but went no further. The golden fire he had imagined earlier burned within her, lighting up her eyes, but he couldn't have it. The way he was right now, he would steal it with ruthless violence and leave her broken. No good could come to either of them. He must send her on her way. "I might welcome help," he said pleasantly, "but I cannot see a role for you. Good of you to offer, but I think not."

"You don't listen, do you," she snapped back. "I told you before, I know the comings and goings at the manor. I know everyone and their tasks, and I instantly recognize anyone new."

"So?" He crossed his arms at his chest, maintaining his emotional distance. Her spark of temper amused him. It was fresh and vibrant, even better than the old Margaret, but he felt nothing for her. No, that was a lie, he felt a mad lust for her, but he wouldn't act on it. Not and keep his honor intact.

She seemed used to being put off and equally used to ignoring it. Without his invitation, she tilted her head to one side in a fluid gesture and plunged into naming suspects. "First there are the weeder people. They arrived Thursday last. Grandsire has them every spring and early summer, you understand, but their numbers always differ and so do the members. It could be any of the men among them but you'll know them at a glance. They wear roughly cobbled shoes, so be sure to look at his feet."

"Whose feet?" With a jolt, he found he wasn't paying attention. While she had been talking, he had feasted his eyes on her, let himself drift off, he wasn't sure where to. Her beauty drew him along with the sound of her voice, both burning themselves in gold on his brain.

"The man, when you catch him," she scolded, evidently noticing his lapse of sanity. "Or is it men?"

He grimaced. "Is there any part of my talk with the earl you didn't hear?"

"I heard the important parts." Her answer was full of earnestness. "You must take care. It could be one of the folks who begged charity this night and last. There were three of them, a peddler, a traveling cobbler, and a lad. Or it might be one of the field-workers. They travel like the weeders, in bands with changing members. They come to help us several times each year."

"What of the viscount?" It was difficult to listen to her properly. He had to force himself.

"Robert?" She gave a dry laugh. "Unlikely."

"Why is that?"

"Robert has no interest in intrigue beyond whether the queen will renew his license to tax imported wines. He spends his time chasing anything in a—pardon, I shouldn't talk of that, but you catch my meaning. Robert isn't capable of keeping a secret nor of speaking to others in secret."

"I never underestimate my enemies. I advise you to do the same."

"So you said before, but Robert isn't an enemy." She cupped her hand to her mouth and confided in him. "He's a sloth, not a danger. He's much too dense for that."

"I'm sure he does his thinking with the nether part of his anatomy," Jonathan drawled, again amused by her. "Especially where you're concerned. But I intend to be wary. You can never be sure."

"You're wary of the wrong things. I tell you I'm sure of Robert. Never surer."

Jonathan wasn't listening. He should have been, but it was happening again. Each time he tried to hear her words, he couldn't. He was drawn into another world where he might indulge himself in her beauty. It left him feeling off balance and disoriented. Her voice trailed away as she saw how he looked at her. Her silence was a relief.

She said not a word, but looked at him with wide, thickly lashed eyes. He saw that golden glow within her, felt its magnetic draw. In his middle, a dark hole of appetite starved for her. He let his eyes feast on the soft, surprised arch of her brows, the lush warmth from her body, the gauzy cloud of her hair. A rush of pleasure washed over him. Followed by the inevitable wrench of pain.

Lord, he had to stop it! He threw up a plate of steel, riveted it into place. He must suit himself in armor both stalwart and formidable, to keep out both good feelings and bad. If he admitted to one, the other would follow. Because of her. She held the power to make him feel again.

Suddenly he was more terrified facing her than he had ever been as he planned to kill his enemy. The man who had tortured him would die a slow death beneath his hand while he, the Demon Magician, felt nothing except a sense of justice done.

Yet Margaret threatened him—she, the embodiment of innocence. Once he had loved her with a pure, virtuous love. Now he was no longer virtuous. He had been corrupted irrevocably.

"If you really want to help me," he said softly, driving the words out with effort, "you would remain silent. Don't talk anymore."

"And do what instead?" she whispered.

"Nothing, I suppose." He spoke harshly and averted his face, staring toward the tavern. "Just go away."

"That isn't what you were about to say." The sweet modulations of her voice reproached him.

"It doesn't matter," he insisted vehemently. "Go about your affairs. Do what you were about to do." He refused to look at her. *Leave,* he willed her silently. *And be quick about it.* But she didn't. Once more her sweet voice subtly attacked.

"It has to do with prison, doesn't it?"

"You don't know a thing about it," he ground out, wanting to frighten her, wanting her to run like a scared rabbit before he crushed her with his insane desire. "Nor should you."

"I don't," she admitted with a self-possession that unnerved him. "But I know what you need."

Chapter 17

What he needed! Lord, Jonathan thought, he knew just what he needed right now, but Margaret couldn't provide it. If she did, she would become as mad as he, given who and what he was, a lunatic full of hate. True, she had studied him with intensity in the nursery, probed at him closely. But without the experience, she couldn't know what had happened to him. "Men understand these things. Women can't," he stated firmly. To his surprise, she emitted a soft laugh.

"Men like my grandsire? He might understand, having been a commander who took prisoners and extracted information from them. That has nothing to do with it. He doesn't understand what you need."

"And you do?" he sneered, hoping sarcasm would hurt her. But she was made of sterner stuff, because she remained unfazed.

"My grandsire knows nothing of feelings. You should be able to tell that."

He dared not do it—give in to what he wanted. He was a ruin inside and out, unable to feel normal emotions without going mad as well. And he pursued an enemy who might well destroy him, which was fine as long as he killed the whoreson, too. He had nothing to give her. It was essential he warn her away. "If you had any sense at all, you'd go while you could. I'm dangerous to us both."

"I don't care. I'm going to help you, despite what you say."

He couldn't believe it. This wasn't the Margaret he had once known. This woman was reckless and daring to the extreme. "Is that so," he said, firmly applying scorn. "Just what would you do?"

"What I used to do."

He shouldn't have asked. Her words turned *him* reckless and daring inside. He should have walked off and left her standing, because he could see the tremors shaking her, the building of her excitement like he used to arouse. Earlier, in the nursery, he had warned himself sternly away from her. Now he tried to warn her, but to no avail.

It was his fault she wouldn't listen. He had saved her child from the river, then smoothed the way so the two of them could meet in the nursery. He had helped her reject Robert, though only with a foolish dance. These things reconnected them in ways neither of them could resist.

Now, as if in a dance, she extended one foot gracefully and stepped forward in a lithe, supple motion. She came within a breath of him, her head bowed so that her soft hair just brushed his beard.

The scent of her intoxicated him. It rushed to his head in a tangle of jonquil and rosemary, keen and urgent. All his hate, his one emotion left since prison, exploded within him, confusingly mixed with reawakening pleasure. The hunt was on for his enemy, yet in this particular instant the mad lust to kill churning inside him turned on her. It changed to primitive arousal. He wanted to put his mouth on hers, to crush her soft, yielding body against his hard one. In short, he longed to steal her golden fire for his own.

He dared not move, because the ravaging dark inside urged him on. This is what he was afraid of! He would take what he wanted without consideration, douse her fire, and leave them both to smoke in the sun. It took all his strength to resist her. She had been used badly by her brute of a husband and he ought to protect her. He must not destroy the precious treasure she held.

In that moment of temptation, that particular instant when resistance came so hard, she chose to raise her face to his. The innocent beauty of her engulfed him. Holding to his control, he traced the fine line of her throat with his gaze. It fell away in a sweep of ivory flesh to meet with the beginning swell of her curving breasts. Her bare arms rose to clasp around his neck, just the way she used to. As her body came closer, desire pounded through him. He would not touch her in return.

She made a soft sound as she stretched to find his mouth.

Sleek and dreaming, she sighed like the brush of summer wind in the trees. Her body melted against his in the familiar, well-loved motion, searing him, making him taut with need.

Her lips meshed with his, and suddenly her golden fire flared within him, chasing the dark. It felt wondrous after his many months of pain. He pressed her mouth open beneath his, his tongue driven and starving. The impact set her quivering against him, and still he didn't touch her. He kept his arms straight at his sides.

But he needed her sweetness to stanch his torment. His hands longed to devour her, wanting all she had to offer, her beautiful waist, her flaring hips. But control ruled him, even when every muscle in his body clenched with delight in her, even when she nestled those tantalizing hips against his own. The heat in his loins kindled as she took his right hand and placed it against the graceful vertebrae of her back. Scarcely venturing to breathe, he let the fingers of that hand explore her beauty, evoking her rich music.

It was too much to hope he could restrain himself longer. He tempted the demon within. Besides, the pain would come soon. Just because he hadn't felt it yet didn't mean it wouldn't swoop down and ravage his spirit. Another minute and he must draw back.

But the heaven of that minute! Her lips caressed his, her tongue darted as she kissed him. Again he felt the burn of her light within him. It lit up his soul like the fires of heaven, scourging the dark. Urgently he tasted her brightness, wanting more of it. He drank in her sacred flame with all his being.

Margaret struggled with her own excitement as Jonathan's lips pressed against the sensitive places he knew so well on her neck and shoulders. She shuddered, full of joy that this was real, that at last she truly touched him. No matter that whenever he kissed and caressed her, she became a hopeless snarl of indecision. It had happened to her in Lulworth—everything she had meant to do and be was swept away by his magnetism. In such moments, she became whatever he needed or wanted. Just now she sensed he needed the comfort only female tenderness could bring.

Her willpower fell away, just as predicted. His mouth

returned to explore hers, hot and aching. All the things she loved about him swept over her—the new strength in his widened shoulders, the honing of his body to maturity, the craving for her in his eyes. They made patterns of passion cross and braid in her belly as her fingers searched him, driving him to greater excitement, though he kept his hand firmly on her back and roved no farther. His other hand denied itself, resting at his side.

Yet he kissed her. Not the sweet, gentle kisses of their youth. These kisses spoke the language of mature lovers. His tongue dove deep, and to her, he tasted of wild night wind and her own defiance. Because she couldn't help it, she gathered his hard, masculine hips against hers while her hands explored his firm, muscled back. There were odd creases in his shirt beneath his jerkin. She wanted to smooth them away, but she forgot about them a second later as she rubbed her full length against him, loving the feel of him, the feline swell of her breasts against his chest, the wet shock of pleasure starting between her legs.

His response showed he sensed her enjoyment. He had always been sensitive to her moods, if not her every thought and feeling. He couldn't read minds—he wasn't that sort of magician. Or was he? She let her mouth slide away from his, and when he didn't follow, she marveled. He let her control their contact the entire time. Even his hand at her waist fell away, and she leaned freely against him, feeling the tender rub of his cheek against her hair. Her nostrils thrilled to the powerful scent of him—leather and woodruff. She wanted the moment to go on and on.

But her time was fleeing. Though she reveled in his touch, he diverted her from her purpose. Even now she should be fetching her mare and Patience. Still she lingered, unable to tear herself away.

It was good when his head whipped up suddenly as if he had heard something. She searched the dark but detected nothing herself. He turned toward the tavern.

"Damn," he breathed. "It may be too late."

Margaret stiffened. Prickles of fear ran through her. Too late for what? He looked silent and sinister, scrutinizing the darkness, swearing softly. And it wasn't about her.

"You're going?"

"I shouldn't have tarried." His gaze swept the area intently. He took two strides away. "There's going to be trouble." He cast one last glance at her over his shoulder. "Stay out of the way."

No sweet words. No farewell or even an apology. Just that terse order. Having given it, he melted into the woods.

Chapter 18

Like magic, Jonathan became one with the trees, disappearing on those stealthy feet. *He's not magic, he's not.* Margaret bit her lip, repeating the litany. He was utterly wrong for her, making her weak and foolish. Despite the thoroughness of her logic, her need whispered otherwise. His heroics made her ordinary heart yearn.

Shortly after, she saw him glide up to the tavern and climb the nearby spreading tree. Stepping deftly from branch to branch, he took a stance by one of the windows. She couldn't tear herself away, watching him perform his sorcery. A knot of pain grew in her chest, an obsessive, blinding want.

At the same time, her mind ran in circles, her fists clenched spasmodically. A flood of fear for his safety washed over her. Tiptoeing among the trees, she grasped a thick trunk and clung to it for cover. The gnarled bark roughened her hands as she searched the threatening dark.

She spotted the treacherous figure just as he stepped into the clearing, raised a pistol, and pointed it with expert aim toward Jonathan's tree. God's eyelid, he would kill Jonathan! Hurtling herself across the short distance, she launched herself at the gunman's raised arm.

In a split second, a dozen things happened. The man's arm swung up. The pistol exploded with a deafening roar. Margaret's weight threw him off balance and he reeled backward. They hit the ground together, her chin connecting with painful force against his shoulder bone. Stunned, she lay half on top of him, unable to move.

In the tree, Jonathan heard the shot. Discipline kept him frozen in position. The Spaniard, visible through the window, turned toward the sound, alerted to danger. At that moment, a cloaked, masked man entered the room to join him. Jon's time had come.

He catapulted through the flimsy window. Glass and wooden mullions shattered in a shimmering sweep of sound. He landed on the traitor and bore him to the floor with his weight.

They struggled, rolling across the floor in a frenzy of arms and legs, raising such a racket that everyone belowstairs would hear them. Ending on top, Jonathan thrust the cloaked one back, his muscles straining to pin his adversary to the floor. The Spaniard loomed behind them. Jon sensed him seeking the right opening to lunge in and free his friend. Where the devil was Cornelius? With all his might Jon wrestled the cloaked monster, but the English traitor fought him with a vengeance, kicking and biting, meaning to keep his identity unknown.

Outside, Margaret scrambled away from the assassin and stumbled to her feet. Gripped by terror, she put distance between them, tripping on hillocks and branches as she went. Finally she paused and dared to look back. He didn't follow, and she stared at his still, dark form. It was then she noticed the blotches. Creeping back, she strained her eyes in the dark, ready to retreat if he moved a muscle. Apparently that wasn't possible. She gagged at the sight, tasting bile in her mouth.

Turning her head away, Margaret staggered to a safe distance and vomited in the bushes. Hot rushes of nausea swept through her as she emptied her stomach, and the horror of what she had done became clear. She had meant to ruin his aim but had done much more. The gun had blown away the entire side of his face.

Jonathan maneuvered around behind his opponent and wrenched the man's arm hard behind him, heard his snarl of pain. Just as Jon thought he had him, he glimpsed the Spaniard from the corner of his eye. The short, swarthy fellow had sidled over to the fire, held his foot poised.

Jonathan shouted, hoping to distract him. Too late! A burning log flew into the chamber, propelled by the Spaniard's kick. The piece skittered across the room and lodged by the window. The hanging drapery, lilting askew from the broken frame, caught fire. In a thrice, a roar of flame licked its way up the wall, heading straight for the dry thatching.

Jonathan made a split-second decision. Releasing the cloaked figure, he went for the burning cloth. The many wooden cottages of the village and the stone ones with thatching could catch fire in minutes. Lunging across the room, he yanked down the fabric and stamped out the flame, then fell on the one man he was still certain to catch. The Spaniard hit the floor heavily beneath him, but the traitor had moved to the hearth. Clasping the poker, he gave it a mighty swing, spewing the room with burning logs. Laughing diabolically, he straightened his mask and charged out the door.

Margaret saw the fire first. The tinder of the roof was bone dry inside. It flared like an inferno. With a scream, she made for the tavern door. As she approached, a man hurdled through the door, crashing into her. Hands gripped her, clammy claws. "Robert!" she cried, but he tore away. A cloak with enveloping hood and face mask covered him. Fear soared through her. It wasn't Robert. Looking down, she saw the stranger's roughly cobbled shoes. He whirled and raced away into the night. Margaret searched for Jonathan as she dodged the other patrons who poured from the tavern. But he wasn't among the crowd, nor did he appear when the host and barmaids emerged last. Had he left by the back stair?

She rushed headlong around the corner, hoping to see him. He wasn't there either. Scanning the area, she saw the blaze make its first leap to the neighboring thatch. The cottage of the French lace makers burst into flame.

Patience! A sick feeling engulfed Margaret. Again it was happening. While she attended to Jonathan, her true duty went ignored. She ran for the cottage as if the hounds of hell panted at her heels.

"Wake up," she shouted, bursting in the front door. A roar of heat forced her backward. A sheet of flame blocked her way. In a panic, she darted to the back where a window looked over the sleeping area. With a stout stick she smashed the glass she herself had provided several months ago, her arms pumping as she cleared the window frame of its razor-sharp points. She was trying to guess how she might jump high enough to climb inside when, without warning, El Mágico materialized at her side.

Without a word he flung himself through the window. A second later he handed out Bertrande, coughing and gasping. Once on her feet, Bertrande staggered against Margaret, who braced her and screamed for Patience. Marie came instead, wheezing and stumbling. In a fit of fear, Margaret left her friends together and ran to the window. Where was Patience? Where was her child!

El Mágico appeared in the narrow gap, her child cradled against his chest. He poised there an instant, looking wild and magnificent, his beautiful face in shadow, his splendid, muscular body crouched for the spring. The fire roared behind him in the cottage, licking its way close. As Margaret clenched her fists, her entire body tensed with terror, he leaped. His feet touched earth, and he urged them away from the cottage, striding ahead to lead the way.

"Patience! I must see her." Margaret hurried after him, finally catching up when they were away from the fire. "Please," she pleaded, grasping his arm, "give her to me." The sleepy bundle of warmth he held opened one bewildered eye and, seeing her mother, held out her arms. Tears of relief wet Margaret's cheeks as she gathered Patience to her. "Thank God you are well, my love," was all she could murmur, her mind dazed with the speed of events.

"Her bed was low to the floor. The smoke had not yet found her." The Magician stood in the semidark, fists planted on hips. "She will recover quickly. So will the others once they clear their lungs." He nodded to where Marie and Bertrande clung to each other, looking like a pair of ghosts in their night rails. "If the four of you will stay here, I will save what I can of your goods."

"What? You mustn't go back. You . . ." She had no chance to tell him more. He sprinted away, leaving Margaret to gape after him. Without hesitation, he returned to the burning cottage and vaulted through the window, entering the dangerous depths.

A rain of goods followed, accompanied by Marie's mad scramble to haul them away from the cottage. Clothing, bedding, lace pillows, Bertrande's precious box of lace patterns, cooking pots, basins, baskets, and bobbins hurdled through the window. Bertrande regained her wits enough to gather up a kirtle skirt and bodice and pull them on over her night rail. " 'Tis well he brought me out half asleep," she muttered as she reached to take Patience, gesturing for Margaret to help Marie. "I would not have left without my lace equipment. Now 'tis a tangle. Find me some shoes, if you can *mon amie.* My feet grow cold."

Margaret turned to do her bidding but stopped short when she saw the progress made by the fire. Racing to the window, she shouted a warning. "Jonathan, the roof looks about to fall in."

He fairly flew from the window carrying a last bundle. Just in time, too. In a blaze of heat and burning debris, a portion of the thatch collapsed. Without the sign of a qualm, he caught up a box and strode to where Bertrande sat with Patience beneath the trees.

"Here is your box of lace patterns, mademoiselle. I fear it has suffered a sore toss from the window." He crouched beside her and placed the box on her lap.

"My patterns are important to me," came Bertrande's answer. "But things can be replaced, and a life cannot. I owe you great thanks for preserving mine."

To Margaret, it seemed some silent communication passed between them—some agreement of intimacy and trust—because Bertrande reached out, and Jonathan clasped her frail hand, his broad palms enveloping her slender one. Margaret saw him smile on her with an expression she couldn't quite fathom—as if he, the Magician, found her magical. He leaned over her friend, and Margaret heard the murmur of their secret exchange. As she stood alone in the shadows, loneliness pierced her like a pain. *She* craved his secrets, *she* wanted his attention for her own. Yet she must claim nothing from him, because once more he had worked his spell on her. She had committed murder for him tonight, as well as ignored her child's needs.

Still, she couldn't help watching them. Bertrande withdrew her hand at last and touched Jonathan's head, as if in a blessing. Finished with their talk, he rose, gave Margaret a quick nod, and headed back to where the fire still raged.

Margaret tried to feel nothing. She groped in the dark for shoes for Bertrande, while Marie wrapped her aunt and Patience in blankets against the night's chill. Done, Margaret almost bumped into the neighboring widow who wandered, moaning desolately. Her burned cottage was little more than a hulk.

Taking the woman's hand, Margaret offered comforting words, parted with several shillings to help her begin anew on the morrow. Then she settled her with Bertrande, along with clear instructions to move if the fire came closer. Having made the three as comfortable as possible, Margaret beckoned to Marie and they hurried to help fight the fire.

Chapter 19

As Margaret came broadside to the tavern, where men and women pitched buckets of water and beat the flames with brooms, blankets, and shovels, shouts reached her ears, something beyond the screams ringing through the village. A lad stood at the far end of the wood, crying distraught words she couldn't decipher at first.

"A dead man. Come look!"

She understood him clearly as she drew near and recognized the miller's young son. With horror, she remembered the body of Jonathan's attacker, who still sprawled where she had left him.

As always during a crisis, El Mágico came striding. The tangle of folk rushing about made way for him. With him came a breath of calm as he reached the lad and took him gently by the shoulder. The two spoke for a moment. Then Jonathan lifted his head and found the boy's father, who took his son off to fight the fire. Margaret threaded her way closer to watch Jonathan examine the body. She stood separated from him by the rushing crowd.

No one seemed to know the dead man. Margaret certainly didn't, and she knew everyone in the village. People charged past for buckets of water at the well. Around them rose the hubbub of comings and goings, shouting, and panic. Jonathan searched the dead man's pockets, then started to turn away.

"Who killed him, that's what I want to know." The tanner passed, heading for the well to fill his bucket. "Captain, any idea?"

"None. Did you do it?" Jonathan asked the tavern's ostler as he followed the tanner. He seemed a likely possibility since he would have been near.

"Not I." The ostler shook his head. "Wish it were, since he tried to shoot you. But I don't know him. Never seen him before tonight."

An indignant murmur ran through the nearest workers. Who dared try to murder the Magician?

Margaret moved forward until she felt the fire's heat dancing on her face. Jonathan looked up at that moment and saw her for the first time. "I did it," she said clearly. "I saw him come into the clearing and aim for you. I hit his arm to ruin his shot. I didn't mean that to happen"—she gestured toward the dead man's ruined face—"but it did." Once again, the appalling magnitude of her deed burst upon her. Never had she thought to do such a thing!

Jonathan's eyes narrowed as he took in her meaning. Suddenly he was beside her, his voice penetrating the night's madness, his fingers closing on her arm. "You killed a man for me?"

Margaret nodded. They were the only still ones in a churning sea of humanity. Frantic workers darted past on either side, intent on their urgent business. Flames flickered behind Jonathan, transforming his handsome face, making him both magician and demon. The look he gave her was lit up with passion, bringing heat to her straight from the inferno. His arms clasped her against him, making her burn again. One more kiss tonight and she would fall prey to his spell—never to be free again.

"You should have stayed away," he admonished, his voice rough with caring. "You endangered your life."

"Something had to be done," she parried, the answer coming despite her better judgment. "So I did it." She met his look, daring him to protest.

For an answer, he stared deeply into her eyes. His gaze was full of darkness, eating into her with its loneliness. It struck her then—*she* must bring him the light. Because when he closed his eyes, he didn't have her healing patterns. The dark threatened to stamp out his spirit's strength.

Take mine! she wanted to cry to Jonathan. He had only to beckon, and despite the danger, she would give him whatever he required. As if he knew it, in the midst of the night's upheaval, heedless of who saw, he brought his mouth down on hers in a hungry kiss.

The wildness of his embrace engulfed Margaret. The strength of his arms rushed through her mind and stoked the embers within her. Twining her own arms around his middle, she felt his deliciously taut muscles and let every reasonable thought within her bow to her weakness. Things she held dear were threatened tonight—her chance to escape, to protect her child—things she had fought hard for, yet she could not break away from him. His touch sent energy springing through her like a renewed purpose in life.

"Cavandish!"

He broke the embrace for her, whipping around at the shout. Margaret beheld the Dutchman struggling with their Spanish prisoner. The spy twisted himself free and ran. In a flash, Jonathan launched himself in pursuit. Margaret gasped as Jonathan left her. She clasped one hand to her chest, trying to catch her breath.

The Magician suffered no such aftershock of their passion. With a leap he brought the Spaniard to the ground and rose scowling. Without pause he ordered the Spaniard up and to work.

"That's right. Make him help us, El Mágico," someone called. Several people applauded. A woman shouted, "Aye, make him fight the fire he started." A chorus of agreement rose from the villagers.

Margaret heard Jonathan growl something to the Spaniard. Brushing back his greasy forelock, the prisoner reluctantly picked up a shovel. Under the captain's malevolent gaze, he sullenly began to beat out the fire. Cornelius shackled himself to the prisoner so he couldn't get away. Once the two were at work, Jonathan picked up another shovel. Margaret hurried to do the same.

Everyone worked with a will, but the night reverted to chaos. Folk ran from one cottage to another, shouting the alarm as the flames spread. Margaret fought beside the tavern keeper and the goat herd, the midwife and the herb woman. The score of traveling field hands and weeders camping nearby turned out to help. Vessels of all sizes were used to lug water from the wells and river. And still the wicked sparks leaped, devouring the wooden timbers and combustible thatch.

Trepidation mixed with fear in Margaret. Her own purpose could be lost tonight in the fire, yet she couldn't desert the people who were dear to her. Her time in the village had taught her each person's name and lot in life. Now their suffering filled her heart with pain.

Working with Marie, she managed to save most of the local midwife's belongings before her fragile cottage gave in to the flames. In the blinding light of the blaze, Margaret put her soot-blacked arms around Hortense and consoled her. The squat little woman who had delivered Patience two years ago buried her face in Margaret's shoulder and wept. After that, Margaret's purse grew even lighter as she gave away more shillings, but what else could she do?

Through it all, she caught glimpses of the Magician, flitting in and out of firelight, appearing and disappearing. At one point she watched him truss up the Spaniard, fastening him securely to a tree. After, he returned to the fight, directing others, offering his strength.

Margaret paused where she stood and stared into the night at his compelling figure silhouetted against the leaping flames. He dominated them all, commanding people's awe, their abject devotion. Like lightning, he sprang into her life again, making her like the others, awed and abject. She bowed her head and returned to her work, wanting to resist him, but even then, she understood. He reappeared, and the passions she thought were dead within her once more burned high and wild like this dangerous, all-consuming fire. The thrill ran through her as she thought of giving herself up to that fire, and against all reason, she longed for it, wanted it more than anything she could name.

To work! she commanded herself. She must fight the fire before it destroyed everything of value. It demanded her attention, and grateful for the distraction, she wiped her sweaty face with her sleeve and continued beating the timbers. But when her grandsire appeared among them with his servants, who brought buckets from the manor so a relay line could be formed from the river, Margaret knew the fight was in good hands. The time had come for her to leave.

Rushing to collect Patience, she told Bertrande her purpose. Under cover of the tumult, she walked back to Clifton. After washing at the pump, removing the soot from her face and arms, Margaret found her mare and settled Patience in the basket. Mounted, she turned south for Scarborough. Within, she carried her last glimpse of Clifton village, illuminated by the fire. At the center of the action, the commanding figures of the earl and Jonathan worked side by side, fighting with like-minded determination their common enemy, the threat to the ordering of their lives.

She defied their ordering! She let change propel her forward. All the rest of the night, Margaret rode with Patience steadily southward. Exhilaration streaked through her, swift as the wind rippling her hair, whispering of freedom. Her escape from Clifton, hastily conceived and imperfectly executed, had to succeed. The appearance of the fire, along with the Magician claiming her grandsire's attention—everyone's attention—convinced her of the rightness of her timing. The rhythm of Circe's hoofs beat steadily on the bare ground, drumming out a new litany: she was sure of it, sure of it, sure of it. The uplifting refrain resounded in her ears and with Patience sleeping peacefully in the basket, Margaret urged Circe onward, reveling in the silky rush of her animal's pace. It moved her forward away from Clifton, into unchartered territory, blessedly away from the guardianship of men.

side by side, fighting with unrivaled determination their common enemy, the threat to the existence of their lives.

She seized their chance. She let elation propel her forward. [illegible] steadily eastward. Exhilaration surged through her swift as the wind ripping her hair, whispering of freedom. Her escape from Clifton, hastily concocted and imperfectly executed, had to succeed. The appearance of the vicar, along with the Magician claiming her grandfather's attention—everyone's attention—convinced her of the rightness of her timing. The rhythm of Circe's hooves beat steadily on the hard ground, drumming out a new litany: she was sure of it, sure of it, sure of it. The uplifting refrain resounded in her ears, and with Patience sleeping peacefully in the basket, Marianne urged Circe onward, reveling in the rhythm of her animal's pace. It moved her forward away from Clifton, into uncharted territory, blossom away from the guardianship of men.

Part Two

Chapter 20

London and the Guild of the Honorable Merchant Drapers, June 1579

Elation, that's what it was to him. Two weeks later, just north of London, Jonathan bent low over Phaeton's neck, the two of them reveling in motion. This was freedom; this, his passion, to follow a target and not be discerned. One moment silent and subtle, the next, startling as lightning, he raced on swift feet after his unsuspecting prey.

Several leagues later he glimpsed Margaret's traveling party, and a sudden, ridiculous urge came over him—to let her know he followed them, to tell her he had diverted the earl's men and kept her safe.

It took all his control to rein in Phaeton with a light touch and guide him from the road. They slid behind a hedgerow, vanishing cleanly. He would respect Bertrande's request to keep Margaret in the dark. The good dame had asked it of him. He had met with her after the fire and received her instructions. He would use his strength as he was meant to—to guard Margaret's safety, to shield and aid the weak.

But was she weak? In the solitude of the hedgerow he pondered the question while a bird chirped in the spattering drizzle of rain. For twenty-one years, he had thought women wanted protection. Less than a day at Clifton with Margaret convinced him otherwise. Such an error! His quiet, retiring Margaret was a figment of his imagination. In a matter of hours, this new woman defied her sole provider and fled from his wrath. She paused to save people from a raging fire, then took off on her own with her child and little more. And the keystone to it all was this—she had killed a man for his sake.

Wishing it had never happened, he swung down and adjusted Phaeton's girth to make him more comfortable. As his fingers slid over the wet leather and buckles, he realized what irony fortune brought. When he was no longer worthy of Margaret, destiny bound them together. He had saved her child, but she had *killed* for him. Such a sacrifice for her to make!

Because killing changed the soul, even if it was done for a noble purpose. How well he knew that truth firsthand.

With the girth refastened, he stroked Phaeton's mane, working out a tangle. Bertrande had seen the burden of war he carried—pain, regret, and his stoic acceptance of death. Beautiful crone, full of sorcery—from the minute he had seized her in the cottage and carried her from the fire's treachery, she had put her magic hands on him. When he had knelt at her feet, her serenity had flowed over him like a balm.

That richly coveted peace—he had sensed it deep within her, just as he had sensed it hidden in Margaret. Despite Bertrande's near-sightless eyes, she knew his longing. She had given him his charge because of it—*Fly on silent feet, use your power,* she had told him. *Protect Margaret with all your strength and skill.*

Then, too, he pursued Margaret for reasons beyond Bertrande's urging. Pieces to this Yorkshire puzzle fell together. He, too, was being followed. He knew it as surely as the sinister voice that haunted his dreams.

Of course *he* lay behind it—his enemy, the Netherlands inquisitor, was a moving power behind the throne. Events at Clifton confirmed Jonathan's suspicions. He had uncovered another serious plot, with the inquisitor lying at its rotting core like a worm.

For these reasons he had left his prisoner with Cornelius and followed Margaret to see whom she would draw. Solsover? The earl? The man who followed him wasn't Solsover, nor was he the earl's man. And the cloaked, masked man hadn't been one of the weeder folk, as Margaret claimed. He hated to speculate on the truth of the matter, but danger was growing. If the worst happened . . .

He led Phaeton out from behind the hedgerow and remounted. As he pursued Margaret, he vowed not to let the worst happen. He must prevent her further involvement in the fight against Spain.

Tired. He was so tired. William Clifford sat before the fire in his cabinet, staring into the flames, brooding. Everything in his well-ordered life had been firmly under control of late. Until two weeks ago, two aggravating weeks.

To think that his honey-haired wench of a granddaughter should give him the slip. In the middle of the night, no less, with her child and nothing more. It was an outrage! Never had he believed she would do such a dangerous, foolhardy thing. Stubborn girl, didn't she see he just wanted what was best for her?

"Might we go after Margaret, Father?" The timid, nagging voice of his daughter penetrated his thoughts like the grating of a crooked armor rivet making a bad join. "I don't know what has gotten into her, but I would like to see her wed to Solsover as soon as possible. Mayhap if we—"

"We can't go after her because we can't trace her," he snapped, heartily wishing he had a hammer like that Cavandish fellow carried with him—a well-crafted, pearl-handled one used by armorers. Damn, he'd spent too much time talking armor with him, but Eleanor drove him to distraction, sitting behind him at her embroidery. Right now he would like to use that hammer on her—his daughter's crooked personality needed straightening like a bent nail. "My men haven't found her," he went on. "You saw what happened to Giles." The humiliation of that event ate at him: opening a mysterious coffer sent by an unknown benefactor and finding his chief man bound and gagged. Clearly someone was protecting Margaret. If he hadn't been so furious, he might have congratulated the knave on his cleverness. Damnation, but it filled him with choler, which brought on the old cramp in his gut. So bad, he had agreed to see the physician, something he abhorred, pottering old villain with his vile-smelling concoctions that didn't help.

"Might we hasten to London ourselves?" Eleanor asked. "Margaret will surely try to see the queen, but if you intervene first, you might be able to influence Her Majesty. Addlepated chit—to think she would turn down a match with the queen's great nephew. How she got so stubborn, I'll never know."

" 'Tis your fault," growled William. He took up the

poker and jabbed the logs. His knees ached abominably, nagging him just like Eleanor. And the fire's heat did no good, wasn't even pleasant with the weather turned mild. Margaret's face kept coming back to him, angry and outraged as she argued with him in her chamber. Where was she now? a needling voice asked him. Was she safe? Was she well? "If you had seen to her personally when she was younger," he told his daughter, "she might have turned out better. She might have even had some respect for you. As it is, she depends utterly on herself." He stopped, amazed by what he had just said. His granddaughter was as independent-minded as he.

"And what of you?" Eleanor's tone leaned dangerously toward the shrewish. "Did you give her attention while she was here? Of course you did. But did she respect you, for all that you gave her your esteem?"

Alas, no, he realized silently. She didn't respect him, nor had he given his esteem—not the way she wanted. He hadn't thought it mattered at the time, despite the pleasure he had taken in their arguments, which she invariably lost because he was master, because he must guard her welfare and decide what was best.

He shifted in his chair, uncomfortable from more than his blasted aching knees. He didn't like to remember Margaret's face because it sent a clear message of what she felt for him. He never bothered with other people's feelings; they hindered your work and were a damned nuisance. But Margaret forced him to admit one thing: only hate would drive her to leave.

She hadn't hated him in the beginning when she had first come to Clifton. He remembered how she had looked that day, bright-eyed with tears but smiling bravely, sliding from her mare and rushing to him across the courtyard. She had curtseyed and given him pert answers to his questions. Then suddenly, for no reason, she had flung her arms around him, called him grandsire, and clung to him, kissing him on the cheek. No one had done that since his Bessie. Sweet, beautiful Bessie, branded as a harlot because she was his doxy. The only woman he had ever really esteemed.

Margaret reminded him of that woman. Bessie had been tender and bright, though her lowly birth precluded their marriage. Frankly, such a thing had never occurred to him. Bloodlines were bloodlines, his father had said, to be maintained like a good piece of land or a noble household. If well nurtured, they enhanced the dynasty. And that was what they were building, a Clifford dynasty, with power and the ear of the sovereign and the freedom to do as they chose.

Now, at seventy, confined to his chair by the pains in his body, it occurred to him to wonder. If he had wed with Bessie, would he still be sitting here alone, with nothing but his pain and his caterwauling daughter? For the first time in his life, he questioned his choices, and cursed Margaret for making him do it. Blasted chit, she tied him in knots.

"I'm for London." William rose so fast, the wrench of pain in his knees made him groan. With his usual discipline, he suppressed it. "I will find her before it's too late."

"I'll ready your things immediately." Eleanor stood, ever obedient.

But he saw the question in her eyes. Before what was too late? she wanted to ask him. He wasn't sure what he meant himself.

Women were mysterious creatures, their heads full of nonsense. As he left his cabinet, he heaved a pained, exhausted sigh.

Chapter 21

"'Tis immensely odd," Margaret complained to Bertrande some days later as her party plodded along just northwest of London. The seven of them had met up in Ripon, then traveled south together. "But my grandsire or Robert have not caught up with us yet. I cannot think what is wrong with them. They're monstrous slow." She knew she sounded miserable and out of sorts, but she couldn't help it, for she was both.

"You sound as if you want them to catch you. What ails you, Marguerite?" Bertrande admonished. She had asked to stretch her legs, which meant Margaret had to guide her as they walked behind the donkey cart, trailing the rest of the party who walked on ahead.

"The weather is what ails me," Margaret grumbled. "All this rain." Last night the sky had opened up and let loose a tremendous downpour. This morning it continued, wetting them through and turning the roads to mire. On top of it, her heels hurt, rubbed raw by borrowed shoes from Marie.

"You are out of temper for several days now. Be cheerful," Bertrande encouraged. "Patience is happy. Look at her laughing with Marie. And London lies mere hours away."

London, Margaret thought grimly. Two short weeks ago she had started her journey full of exhilaration. Master Hale had hidden her at a remote dairy farm, and for a small price hired someone to deliver Circe safely back to Clifton. She and Patience had slept in the dairy loft, where her child had kicked her feet in the rustling hay and chortled happily, loving their adventure and being with her mother. But for Margaret, too much had happened, all of it overwhelming. She had left her grandsire. She had kissed Jonathan again. She had killed a man! To keep her sanity, she shut the thoughts out. As often as she could, she imagined her lace patterns, sought their calming peace.

But today she must watch the road in case they were followed, which made her tense and irritable. Suspense plagued her. She had snapped at nearly everyone and had to apologize. She jumped every time she saw anyone remotely suspicious, a bad feeling following her. A torrent of rain pattered on the wooden cart ahead of them, and she plodded onward, watching rivulets weeping down its sides.

"Marguerite, I hate to say this, but you are one of the most stubborn people I have ever known," Bertrande continued as Margaret remained silent. "If you think to live your life alone, you are vastly mistaken. You are made to be a married woman. Accept the things you cannot change."

Margaret stopped in the middle of the road and stared at her. "What are you saying?"

"I'm saying that one may be independent and still have bonds to others." Bertrande pulled at Margaret's arm, insisting they move on.

"You've gone and done something. What is it?" Margaret's temper was set on edge. She slipped and almost fell into a muddy rut, which made it worse.

"I have done something," Bertrande told her adamantly. "Something you ought to appreciate. We will get to London in safety. That is worth much."

"You've told the captain!" Margaret groaned. "That explains everything. He's been protecting us. And to think, I was fool enough to imagine I had come this far because of *my* strength, *my* cleverness. I should have known better. *He's* controlled me the entire way."

"You *are* strong. You *are* clever. But still I told Captain Cavandish," Bertrande stated firmly. She, too, stumbled in a rut and clasped Margaret's arm tightly to keep her balance. "I told him to stay hidden, and he has obeyed me, which is better than I can say of you. Yes, I told him, and I refuse to regret it, so save your tantrums. You can't live your life alone."

"I don't expect to live alone." Margaret steadied her friend as best she could in the treacherous mud. "I have you and Marie and Patience. Master Foster and his son have offered aid and I accepted it gracefully. Why must I accept anything from him?"

"Because he is what we need just now!" Bertrande cried, venting her exasperation. "What *you* need. And for once I will do what I think best for you—my age gives me the right. You are welcome to like or dislike my decision, but I will not stand argument. *Vraiment,* Marguerite, you are *obstiné* in the extreme."

"Headstrong," Margaret stated, knowing deep inside why she was so obstinate—at least in this case. She was terrified of seeing Jonathan again, had made up her mind she must not. "My mother always says I am headstrong and it benefits no one. And in truth," she went on, getting more agitated by the minute, "the captain is a man; he'll want something for this favor. Surely you understand that, even though you never wed."

"'Tis true I never wed, but I did not banish men from my life."

She looked so serene, Margaret couldn't believe her. "But he renders a service that requires repayment."

"You have already done much for him. Friends do things for one another without thought of cost."

"Now I *know* the rain has gotten to you," Margaret muttered. "It's addled your brain. Men won't settle for friendship. They want something else entirely, at least the ones I've known."

"And how many have you known," scolded Bertrande. "Oliver—with whom you had the misfortune to be wed. You cannot judge by him, or by Robert or your grandsire. You might judge by your father or the captain."

Margaret squirmed at this—her father and Jonathan? Did Bertrande imply they were somewhat alike?

"Or another man I knew who settled for friendship, as did I," Bertrande continued, the tone of her voice changing, becoming dreamy as she delved into her past. Her near-sightless eyes gazed into the distance, and Margaret bit back a reply. She was about to hear another of Bertrande's stories, one likely to make her own hardships seem no more than foolish fancies. It would probably be good for her, so she hung on to her temper and searched for her calm.

"You assume I had no wish to wed since I am a spinster," Bertrande began simply. "Yet there once was a lad I wished to wed. Because he had not the money to care for me or any children, he was stubborn. He insisted he would not give me a life of poverty. For ten years I never took a husband, nor he a wife."

"I am sad to hear it," Margaret said, her voice constrained.

"Do not grieve overly. My Jacques and I were best of friends, which gave me great wealth. He was a baker in his father's shop, so often I would take my lace pillow and sit in their warm kitchen, working. Each time I looked up, he had a smile for me. Nothing gave me greater joy."

"Could you not have saved your money and wed with him eventually?"

"Aye, but you see, I lost him to the plague."

"The . . . plague?" Margaret gulped, stricken.

Bertrande's face was serene, resigned to the old sorrow. " 'Twas then I became the obstinate one. I nursed him during his illness, though he begged me to leave for fear I would sicken. I didn't." Her mild voice grew fierce. "I'm glad I stayed with him, to care for him and lay him to his final rest. So you see, I have more experience with being stubborn than you, Marguerite. I know what it means. You can chose to use it wisely, or you can use it foolishly." Bertrande gave her hand a heartening squeeze. "But whatever you do, remember, stubbornness can be very powerful. More powerful than you would guess."

She was stubborn and that was powerful? An hour later, Bertrande's suggestion still amazed Margaret. Whatever the trait might be, though, it kept her walking, despite the mud and misery. London lay ever closer, and now was no time to give up.

Patience, wanting her mother, insisted on being carried, while Bertrande again rode in the cart. Old Master Foster, in his native sabot with his wild white hair, trudged ahead of them, showing no emotion, as if he were used to it. Revived by the rain, the countryside unrolled its lush green sward around them, but the road had become a veritable bog. Margaret wrinkled her nose at the mud and tried to emulate her friend's stoic acceptance. She squinched and squelched along as best she could.

Chafe, chafe went her borrowed shoes against her sore heels, which were much like her temper, rubbed raw. The image of the Magician rose up to unnerve her further. What would she say when next she saw him? What would she do? Whenever she was with him, he inspired blind loyalty in her. Without thinking, she killed for him. Even now he turned her heart inside out . . . in dismay and in ecstasy. She would always turn herself inside out for him. The night of the fire the urge had been upon her, tickling her reflex, making her want to drop everything for him and abandon her dreams.

Steady, now, Margaret calmed herself as she walked. He wasn't here now, and as Bertrande said, she must use her obstinate nature to good purpose. Instead she fixed her mind on her future. With her lace earnings she would buy a house that was all her own, create a realm of peace for her child.

"Are your heels better, then?" Master Foster inquired. "Did the salve help last night?"

"They are, and I thank you," Margaret lied as she pulled her feet from the sticky mud, wishing for new shoes. But she dared not spend more of her precious funds to buy replacements. They needed the money for so many other things.

"Mayhap you should ride a while," the old man continued. His startling, bushy white brows wiggled as he spoke. "If you feel pain, you and the child must go back in the cart with the rest."

She felt pain, that was sure, though it wasn't the kind he imagined. Besides, there wasn't room in the cart for everyone. Young Paul rode with Bertrande, the two playing anagrams to pass the time. Bringing up the rear came Master Paul and Marie. "My thanks, but I'll walk awhile. It gives me something to think of besides my lace." Margaret shifted Patience from one hip to the other, her arms aching. "Or," she added beneath her breath, "the lack thereof."

She plodded on. The endless road rolled out to the north and south of them, a muddy brown ribbon twining over the land, empty of travelers in the sheets of rain.

Hoofbeats sounded behind them.

"Ho, Father, have a care," the young master cried from behind as a horseman bore down on them. When he showed no sign of yielding, Master Foster pulled the donkeys to the farthest side of the road. The rider flew by at a gallop. Water splashed in Margaret's face, followed by clods of mud from the horse's hooves. Patience began to cry, furious at being splashed.

Margaret brushed a dollop of mud from her nose, looked at Master Foster, and saw he sported a similar adornment on one cheek. She reached out to wipe it away from his leathery skin. They caught each other's eye and burst into laughter at the sight they made. "Don't cry, love," she coaxed Patience, straightening the little woollen cloak her child wore. "Look at me, I'm speckled like your favorite hen at the manor." She held out her own cloak with its new crop of mud dots. "Why do you think the rascal was in such a rush?"

"That's the second one in the last hour," Master Foster said, growing sober. "Probably both couriers, working for folk who think their messages so important, they have to be delivered fast."

"No doubt you're right," Margaret agreed. "But let us continue. Come, Patience," she said, giving a merry lilt to her voice. "London is not far ahead."

Chapter 22

"How much farther?"

Inside the cart, Margaret shivered as Bertrande's voice stirred the rainy afternoon's chill. She hugged Patience, who had fallen asleep, and tried to quell her jitters. "You have asked a dozen times in the last hour," she teased Bertrande, "and finally I can give you the answer you desire. In another few minutes, we will enter at London gate. I can see the city ahead."

"Which gate?" A sudden animation lit Bertrande's features. "There are many entries to London, or so I've heard."

"Aldergate, I think." Margaret licked lips that were suddenly dry. A tingle half of excitement, half of terror, shuddered through her. She peered through the open front of the cart, trying to see ahead, but the wooden roof limited her view. As always in populated areas, she and Bertrande rode inside while the men and Marie led the donkeys. There was no reason to suspect trouble, yet now that they had arrived, she was as nervous as a cat. The warm burden of Patience slumbered in her lap. Young Paul leaned against Bertrande's shoulder, drowsing. A welcome warmth suffused the interior of the cart.

Contentment evaded Margaret. She studied the travelers ahead of them, looking for possible danger. All she saw were two pie sellers, wooden boxes slung from straps around their necks, bound to sell their wares in the city. A fat vintner drove a pretty little two-wheeled cart, resting one hand protectively on a hefty keg while he guided the shaggy horse. Margaret scanned the others—farmers with empty produce baskets leaving, a lad with sheep. Three women gossiped as they walked, packs of woven goods on their backs. Four small children tagged after them, subdued by the lateness of the day.

"What could the time be, Marguerite?" Bertrande seemed restless for the first time on their journey.

The tension wore on her, the same as the rest of them, Margaret thought as she fidgeted, moving a cooking pot so its handle wouldn't poke her. "I cannot tell for the fog, but we are arrived, *ma tante*. There is nothing to fear."

Margaret hugged her cloak around her, wishing for wings that would fly them over the city walls.

Jonathan had followed the carpenters' traveling party openly for the last few miles. It didn't matter now if he showed himself. The moment of reckoning had come. He loosened his rapier in its hanger, getting ready. While he had watered Phaeton at a stream several towns back, well off the road and thoroughly hidden, he had noted the passing of a galloping courier. The horse was fresh. A dry cloak flapped from the rider's shoulders. Fortunately, after that obvious warning, he had taken his own precautions, engaged a courier at the next village and sent him ahead on a fast steed. Alert, Jonathan kept his gaze trained on the gate.

First warning—at the gates to the city, a huddled mass of people clustered to either side, failing to enter. Second warning—as others approached the gate, instead of entering, they, too, turned aside to join the clusters. The murmur of unsettled voices reached him, people milling in agitation. Third warning—Phaeton's head came up, his ears pricked forward at the familiar sound of swords loosening in their scabbards. At last the crowd parted. Jonathan saw the row of horsemen barring the gate.

Jonathan swiveled in his saddle to assess the area. Then he checked the riders—two, four, five in all. No firearms. The law of London prevailed, banning such weapons from within five miles of the queen. He flew into action, moving Phaeton forward, off the road, and past the other travelers. He hoped the crowd wouldn't get in their way when the fight ensued. He would need room to maneuver. Because at the head of the men, he spotted Viscount Solsover. His suspicions were confirmed.

A shout rose, the cry of attack. Rapiers glittered in the light as the horses launched themselves forward, their riders rising high in the stirrups, brandishing their weapons. A massive gelding, bigger than the rest, pounded on iron-shod hooves up the road, slogging fast through mud and water. Every head jerked in the riders' direction. Swords drawn, the attackers closed on the crowd that had stopped dead in the road.

When the many people on foot realized the riders had no intention of stopping, they scattered. Children ran crying. Women shrieked. Pandemonium reigned as one of the pie sellers tripped and sent dried apple pies flying in all directions, bursting in sticky messes on the ground. The vintner's heavily loaded cart pulled off the road and stuck in a mud hole, one wheel mired to its rim. The two carpenters squeezed their donkeys as close to the edge of the road as possible without falling in the ditch, but they were not fast enough. The five riders skidded to a halt before their cart.

Huddled in her hiding place, Margaret heard the shouts and gripped the rough sideboard so hard her knuckles whitened. This was exactly what she had been afraid of. She shifted Patience and crawled toward the opening to see.

"Stay back," Bertrande thrust with unexpected strength. "Do not show yourself."

Patience sat up and looked at her questioningly. "Mama?"

" 'Tis nothing," Margaret's words came in a fierce rush. "I won't let it be anything. Nothing shall get in our way."

Bertrande slid forward, blocking her view.

"Come out, Margaret. I know you're there!" came Robert's petulant demand.

Margaret saw Bertrande grimace at the sound. She searched for her frail hand in the dimness of the cart and squeezed it. "I will handle him." Choler swept through her, making her furious, reckless. "I pray you take Patience and let me slide by."

"Nay," Bertrande whispered back with urgency. "He means to take you prisoner. You must not show yourself. Stay hidden here."

"I won't let him." Margaret glared at Robert's knees, which were all she could see of him at the moment. "I'll tell him how little he pleases me and he'll leave me be."

"Non, non." Again Bertrande blocked her. *"Arrête."*

"I pray you, my lord, have patience." Outside, she could hear Master Paul speaking, his voice placating. The crowd had fallen quiet, waiting to hear the confrontation. The new silence was punctuated only by occasional squawks of chickens, the stomp of a horse. "I have my wife and her elderly aunt with me, as well as my two children and my sire. This woman you have named is not with us. I beg you leave us to our humble affairs."

"You, sirrah, will rue the day you aided this woman."

"Your pardon, my lord. I have none of yours. I have with me my family. You see, here is my son." Margaret saw his hand stretch into the cart. Young Paul climbed over the bags and bundles and was hefted in his father's arms.

Margaret wanted to shriek as she listened, realizing what would happen. Robert would punish her friends unless she stopped him. An angry urge sprouted inside her to fight her way from this suffocating little cave and attack him. She lurched to her knees.

"He is dangerous, *ma chère,*" Bertrande warned, staying her. "You must not put yourself in his hands."

"He's a fool," Margaret bit out. "Without wit to endanger anyone but himself." Though she wasn't entirely sure of that anymore. He had shown himself to be clever by being ready for her. One of the couriers must have been going to him.

Silence reigned outside. Robert's horse sidestepped—Margaret knew it was his, for it swung its hindquarters because he held the reins too tight, sawing the poor creature's mouth. A woman cried out in terror. Margaret imagined her dodging the horse's slicing hooves. She wanted to shake some sense into him, to make it clear she would never favor his suit.

"Margaret, come out here." Robert's voice rang with authority.

But Margaret heard the edge to it. He was losing patience fast. Determinedly she moved forward, wanting to tell him everything on her mind.

"Mais non." Bertrande stopped her. "I will go out first." Taking Patience, she reached for a quilt. "Let me wrap you, *doucette,*" she crooned. "You do not like Lord Robert, so let me hide your face."

Patience must have understood the essence of the old lady's words, because she didn't struggle. She let Bertrande lift her over the bundles and baskets and climb out of the cart. Margaret could see the back of Bertrande's skirt as she bobbed a curtsy before Robert while the senior Master Foster said their names.

Robert wasn't fooled. "Margaret, you waste my time," he barked. "I've traced you all this way. I know you're there, so get out here straight."

Chapter 23

From his vantage point away from the crowd, Jonathan observed the scene before the London gates coolly, knowing what would happen next. He'd suspected that courier, guessed he had been sent ahead by the man who had followed him from Yorkshire. Now he had proof: Solsover had been warned of Margaret's coming. The lazy slug had sat comfortably in London, awaiting the message. When it arrived, he came to the gate and she rode straight into his arms.

Except for one thing. The viscount hadn't counted on Jonathan. True, he had known Jonathan followed Margaret. That accounted for the superior number of horsemen he had mustered. But two could play the same game.

Jonathan scanned the setup of people, searching for someone. Sure enough, there was Cornelius, his white-blond hair disguised by a massive hat. Their other men, the trained ones and only a few new recruits, were close by. He counted them, picking them out easily in the crowd because of their superior mounts. He would wait until just the right moment, when Margaret needed him so sorely that she couldn't say . . .

She would say it anyway, accuse him of meddling. It astonished him, how impractical she was in matters beyond her lace making. Did she expect him to walk away, leave her to the devices of the viscount, who would carry her to the nearest church and a priest? Pharaoh's foot, but she made him angry! And now she would insist on arguing with the viscount. She gravely underestimated him. In a minute the verbal encounter would begin.

Margaret emerged from the cart, pale and bedraggled, her magnificent hair hidden by a frumpy-looking coif. The triumph on Robert's face annoyed Jonathan. With a snort of derision, he looked away.

"Robert, I've had enough of your nonsense." Her words rang out clearly over the tension-gripped crowd. "You must learn that you cannot threaten people. They won't tolerate it." She pointed to the two Masters Foster, then Marie and Bertrande. "Not these men, nor these ladies."

"You have no basis for bargaining." Robert's oily smile creased his face, his satisfaction visible. "Come here at once and mount up behind me."

"I'll not." Margaret faced him calmly. "With these people as witness, I tell you, Robert Weston, I refuse to have you. I thought I'd made myself clear at Clifton, but you force me to say it again. So be it. I refuse to wed with you. You must accept that as my final word."

Jon studied the viscount's reaction. Robert's smile had faded, replaced by a dangerous expression. Holy heaven, Jon thought grimly, didn't she realize what she was doing? She humiliated Robert publicly, a shaming he wouldn't endure.

Apparently she didn't realize. Or didn't care. Because in the next moment, Robert spurred his horse closer and reached down to grab her, but Margaret stood her ground. She shook her head firmly in the negative.

Jon's restraint crumbled. Suppressed anger surged to the surface of his consciousness. He'd had all he could take of the viscount. And of her, expecting to fight might with her intangible will. Now he must do his duty. With a shout, he signaled Cornelius, then drove his spurless heels into Phaeton's sides.

The horse shot forward like hailshot from a cannon. Jon's rapier screamed from its sheath as he charged Robert. The crowd, which had been primed for a fight, gave a hurrah of joy as he launched into action.

Margaret spun in astonishment at the shouts and gaped at what she beheld. The Demon Magician materialized out of nowhere, with what seemed like a legion of men. She leaped back with a hoarse cry, caught Bertrande, who still held Patience, and pulled them out of harm's way. Against the shield of the cart, Margaret stared as the rapiers of the two groups clashed.

The crowd reverted to chaos. People dodged the flying hooves, seeking shelter. Margaret heard the Magician's diabolical laughter reverberate eerily in the fog as he confronted Robert. He maneuvered Phaeton with a skill that was uncanny. His men charged Robert's. At the last minute the cavalry horses wheeled, whirling their masters' rapiers in flying arcs. Retreat, attack, wheel. The perfect precision of men and animals kept her gaze locked on them. Enthralled, she couldn't move as Jonathan and Phaeton ran circles around Robert. She glimpsed his handsome face as he whipped about, a study in motion, laughing, elated. For a second in the dream, she paused, musing, wondering if he belonged there, always at her elbow when she needed him. But suddenly, a new thought came to her. There was nothing left in the world that he loved but this—this fleeting galliard, a deadly dance of glinting steel, bonded with the fluid grace of his animal into an instrument of death.

The thought sent a bolt of agony through her. He wasn't like this when she had first known him. Changed irreparably. Unable to feel for others what he once had. Unable to feel for her. His heart, what might be left of it, was with his war work. Chin sunk in one hand, elbow propped against her middle, she pondered the painful questions, her mind lost in a confusing labyrinth, groping to find its way out.

Jonathan laughed with glee at the surprise on Robert's face when he made his first caracole on Phaeton. He would give anything to preserve that look in perpetuity. It took Robert only a second to recover his defenses, but it was the second Jonathan needed. He retreated, then turned Phaeton and stormed back into range. As the horse wheeled deftly, Jonathan reached with his sword. Steel engaged with steel. Jon drove his rapier point into one of the ornamental holes in Robert's cup guard. Phaeton pivoted on his haunches, Jonathan flicked his wrist, strong as an iron spring. Robert's sword jerked from his hand, flew through the air, and landed with a splash in a mud puddle, right at Margaret's feet. Jon caught a glimpse of her face as she jumped back, her eyes glazed, as if she were only half awake.

"Run!" he shouted at her, laughing furiously as if all the demons of hell did possess him. "Do you wait for an invitation? Run! Wait for me inside the gate!"

He pointed his rapier toward the city. Its entrance stood open, inviting.

Margaret gathered Patience to her, made sure Marie clutched Bertrande, and ran.

Jon returned to the fight merrily, the stimulating exercise to his muscles welcome. He flipped a hat in one man's face, nipped his sword arm until he dropped his weapon and bled freely. He unhorsed another.

"I want my duel, you poltroon," Solsover howled, spurring his horse while sawing on the reins, his conflicting orders putting it into a frenzy of useless motion. "I want satisfaction."

"You don't have the capacity for satisfaction." Jon grinned as he unseated his next victim. It was like child's play to feint at these fellows, draw back unexpectedly and make them lose their balance. He waved at the younger carpenter, who jumped out at the viscount's horse, waving his arms and shouting. The poorly trained animal shied and half reared. Solsover fell heavily in the mud.

Jubilation! Jonathan laughed so hard he had to clasp his middle. He knew he was an idiot to involve the crowd in this skirmish, but they were having a hell of a time, that was evident, and so was he. His men had one of the viscount's followers against the wall and were tormenting him with mud clods. Another group laughed at an unhorsed fellow who had climbed a tree to get away.

"To the city!" Jonathan shouted, taking the sword from his last victim and beckoning to the carpenters. The game little donkeys broke into a smart run, pulled ahead of him, and passed through the gates. As Jonathan followed, weaving his way through the milling crowd, he spotted the vintner. The rotund fellow had finally managed to free his cart from the mud hole and now trundled his load toward the city entry. In another minute, he would block the gates.

Jonathan swerved right, passed the vintner, and brought Phaeton to a halt, wheeling him on his haunches. As he looked back, he observed that Solsover had recovered his rapier and was hopping on one foot, trying unsuccessfully to remount his skittish gelding. The cart lumbered toward Jonathan, at that split second blocking the gates, forming the perfect barrier.

Jonathan signaled Phaeton, who lunged forward. With a flip of his blade, Jon severed the vintner's cart traces on the right, then swerved left and severed them on the other side. Freed of the traces, the horse moved forward. The cart stopped short, the mouth of the vintner a silent oh of surprise as his horse left him. The two-wheeled cart began to tilt.

Jonathan threw back his head and laughed as the huge barrel careened against the back of the cart, breaking it open with a resounding crash and falling to the ground. The barrel split like a ripe melon. Wine splashed everywhere, filling the air with its ripe smell. The mess effectively blocked the city gates. Two of Solsover's men, who just then reached the entry, reared back in confusion, unable to pass.

"Here," Jonathan cried to the vintner, who had leaped from his seat to catch his horse. "This for your trouble." He dug in his purse, and flung a handful of gold in the mud at the surprised man's feet. Dozens of people in the square, all of whom had stopped to stare at the spectacle, gave a cry at the sight of the gold, but the vintner dived for the money first, plucking each piece from the ground.

Phaeton reared to his full height, pawed the sky, and gave his great trumpeting neigh. Jonathan checked the square for Margaret. He would sweep her up behind him and take her to the guild hall. His blood roared in his veins with the heat of the fight, his triumph. At this moment he wanted her seated behind him, soft and yielding and clinging to him. But he couldn't see her anywhere. Phaeton switched his tail and danced sideways, expecting the signal to bolt. Jonathan gave a rough curse of frustration as he realized what had happened. He dashed up one street, got halfway to its end without finding her. Phaeton wheeled and they retraced their path, took another way, and returned unsuccessful.

Blast! Jonathan knew London well, and the myriad of twisting streets could hide a person for some time if they desired. It would be a contest to see which of three men would find Margaret first.

He had the advantage. Only he knew her intention to make lace and sell it, though the others would guess soon enough. Bending low over Phaeton's neck, he plunged into the city's depths.

Chapter 24

Holding Patience, Margaret ran until she couldn't run anymore, then stopped and leaned against a wall, her rapid breath making searing pains in her side. A tradesman looked at her oddly, no doubt questioning her behavior, but she ignored him. She must compose herself and get her bearings. Then she would find Bertrande and Marie.

Within minutes she spotted them coming more slowly after her. Margaret hurried to meet them. "We must find ourselves lodgings at once so we are out of the streets." *And out of danger,* she thought nervously. Robert was more clever than she had thought. She scanned the street they had chosen at random. "Have you any idea where we are?"

"It must be the street of the fishsellers." Marie pulled a face and waved her hand to indicate the odor. "Let us ask assistance at that shop."

A stout woman guarded the fishseller's entry, her white apron smeared with blood. She looked at them suspiciously until Margaret smiled and addressed her in well-bred tones. The woman unbent. Yes, she knew of some rooms to let. She happened to have some herself.

Margaret lost no time in indecision. In a scant few hours she had her friends settled in decent, furnished lodgings above the fishseller's. She stocked the kitchen and brought firewood, then there was cleaning and arranging to do. The remainder of the afternoon passed quickly in a flurry of work.

Suppertime arrived. They washed, sat themselves down in the single room serving as kitchen and dining parlor. Bread and cheese fortified them, along with cups of ale.

"I am sorry to lose the Fosters," Margaret said to Bertrande and Marie while feeding Patience chunks of bread softened in milk. "I would have preferred their company while we settled in."

"We must be parted from them regardless," Bertrande reminded her. "They will lodge with the young master's wife and his mother-in-law. We are now on our own."

On their own. Unexpectedly, Margaret found the thought confusing. How she had longed for this moment, yet now that it was here, she felt unsettled. Something was missing.

The image of El Mágico at the London gates flashed in her mind, startling as lightning, snatching her from Robert's clammy claws. Feelings wove through her, feelings for Jonathan, as soft as the smoothest silk for lace.

"Now that we are safely settled, you must stay inside," Bertrande was telling her. "I thank *le bon Dieu* for the captain. That one man who passed us on the road was undoubtedly a courier going to Lord Robert. The viscount is a formidable threat, so I pray you stay here in the coming days. Do not venture out on the streets."

"And how are we to find a shop, or do the hundreds of things that must be done to start our income flowing?" To Margaret's horror, the argument popped out in her most quarrelsome tone. Her nasty temper wiggled inside her, wanting to protest. She hadn't come all this way to sit, staring out the window. She had come to do things, to strive and to be!

With immense effort, she bottled up her temper. "Your pardon, Bertrande, but pray let us discuss it on the morrow. We will decide then who goes out and when."

Bertrande accepted her apology, but Margaret was suddenly assailed by an explosive attack of need for her lace. If only she had her pillow! She could all but see it tucked under her grandsire's arm. God's eyelid, but she wanted it now!

Clenching her eyes shut, Margaret summoned her patterns. Lace stitches took shape in her consciousness. Neat and precise. Pure in their geometry. Calm came flowing with them, blessed relief, and she let out an exhausted sigh. Here she was in her own home, able to do things the way she wanted. It was a veritable triumph that she had come so far.

But the way she had done it continued to haunt her—whenever she turned around, there was Jonathan at her side, as if he belonged there. Propping her elbow on the table, she leaned her head against her hand. Thoughts crowded in, all too confusing. And despite being bone weary, she didn't know if she could sleep.

Sure enough, Margaret's sleep, when she finally dropped off, was restless. All night, dreams gnarled and knotted, weaving her into their tangled skeins. The Magician's wish to dominate, her weakness wishing to let him—they twined together in the fertile plains and lush valleys of her mind. Lightning sizzled across her dreamscape. Stark midnight hovered. She sat alone with her lace pillow, working her bobbins—needing to immure her heart against the charms of men.

Jonathan plummeted out of nowhere on his mighty charger, taking her by surprise. Fleet-footed Phaeton, his iron-shod hooves sparking fire, black mane writhing like tongues of flame. And on his back the ephemeral Magician flaunted his weapons—his devastating touch and the heartbreaking pain in his eyes. The two of them sped straight for her, mighty muscles straining. Like molten quicksilver they came, gleaming with the night's madness, making her quiver with building desire.

The Magician drew near, his rapier glinting. But it wasn't by force that he would take her heart. Her torn, wounded heart, yearning for her father, yearning for someone to love—with her own scissors she carved it out in the dream and offered it to him. She pinned it to his sleeve like a badge for all to see. He tried to refuse, but she wouldn't let him. Because inside he held a hundred secrets, all of them ugly, fighting to get out. How she wished to release them, to wash his mind clean with her own tranquility. To soothe away the illness that gripped his soul.

The dream darkened. The rain arrived. Margaret moaned in her sleep. She must not love him, yet she couldn't help herself. If only she could! She put her whole being into escaping the dream. With a cry, she wrenched free and emerged into waking and the calm of her new room.

Birdsong trilled through an open window. Margaret focused on the pattern of sunshine shifting on the rough-beamed ceiling. It was just a dream that fled with waking. She had made it to London! Springing to her feet, she stretched both arms high over her head and praised heaven. At least for now, she was free!

The city beckoned, the street below her window all a-bustle. The brisk calls of hawkers shouting their wares drifted up. Slipping to the casement, Margaret looked out.

"Brooms! Buy new brooms! Fit to sweep your house clean!"

"Le-mons! Fresh, ripe le-mons, all the way from Seville."

London sunlight shone through the window, as bright as the crier's lemons. Smiling, Margaret whirled from the window in a rush of white night smock. Her gaze lit on her baby, who sat up in bed, eyes open wide with a wide, gay grin to match. They both laughed and hugged.

"Good morrow, Marguerite, and my merry Patience," Bertrande called to them from her bedstead. "Your laughter does my heart good."

"What a pleasure to hear a gay greeting," Margaret returned, crossing the chamber. The two embraced. "I'm going to find a shop for us today," she confided in Bertrande. "If you and Marie will keep Patience content."

"So you do intend to go out." Bertrande's disapproval was written strongly across her face. "You did say we would agree—"

"I cannot help it," Margaret cried, remembering her promise but unable to keep it. "I was a prisoner so long I can bear it no longer. I refuse to cower under the bedcovers, waiting for them to find me. I'll go freely about the streets and do the things I've yearned to do. I'm going to find a wonderful shop just right for our lace trade. Then I shall visit the Drapers Guild so you and Marie can become members soon."

To Margaret's surprise, instead of getting angry back, Bertrande chuckled. "I see that obstinate spirit in you fights to get out. And I can't imagine you quaking beneath the blankets. *Pas du tout.*"

Margaret's anger flew out of her as quickly as it had come. "You'll pardon my quickness to temper, but I cannot reap benefits without taking risks."

Bertrande nodded and rose from her bed, shooing Margaret away. She crossed the chamber to the washbasin, tweaking Marie's coverlet as she passed. Already she had memorized their lodgings, found her way with increasing skill.

"I wish you to wear my large coif when you go out, to hide your hair." Bertrande held up the cap. "I washed it last night and now 'tis dry. And I ask one more thing of you. You must make a plan, Marguerite. You cannot live long in London without one. I cherish your wish to stay with us, but the facts are the facts."

Margaret couldn't bear to listen that morning. Instead she put her lips against her child's arm and blew hard. Patience screamed with laughter at the funny sound and tickle. Margaret hid her face in the soothing scent of baby flesh and refused to think of her troubles. There was time enough later for that.

Margaret broke her fast with the others, relishing the hearty pleasure of bacon and bread. Then the door to the wide world beckoned. Promising her daughter a sugar plum from her shopping, Margaret set out.

The city was glorious, teeming with people. Margaret walked and looked and enjoyed. In the street of the habadashers, respectable houses and handsome shops lined the way like staid matrons and masters dressed up in well-kept timbers. In contrast were the courtesans of goldsmiths' row, who wore their transparent glass windows like wantons, enticing the passersby. Around the corner sat a row of goodly almshouses, built sturdily to endure. Churches graced every corner, and when the hour came, their bells rang out in bold contest, each striving to outdo the other and deafen the hearer. Thus it was she wound her way around to Threadneedle Street and the drapery district, her destination for the day.

A shop! She required the perfect shop. Not too large, not too dear. Behold, she found one. A beautiful little shop, empty and waiting, begging for her to take it. Blithely she paid the man and woman who owned it three month's rent in advance. She wanted to be trusted, so she gave them her gold. Upon taking possession of the key, she brimmed with joy.

"Can you make a sign?" she inquired of the man at the wood-working shop two streets over. "An oval one, painted a beautiful blue?"

"For certes, I can." He smiled at her.

She went to buy a table for showing their samples, then returned to see the finished sign. The man had painted the letters with gilding, setting its message in vibrant relief—THE FRENCH LACE MAKERS.

"There you are, *mademoiselle.*" The woodworker bowed as she paid him.

Margaret shivered in delight at being called "mademoiselle." For the first time in four years running, she felt as young and fresh to the world as Patience, whom she brought to the shop along with Bertrande and Marie. Patience loved their new shop. She cooed and laughed because she was glad, like Margaret, to be doing new things.

The sign went up. They cleaned the shop, washed the windows inside and out. Margaret then found the Carpenters Hall on Brode Street and was directed to the Fosters' new home. After fond greetings, she retrieved their belongings and had a man with a barrow take them to their home.

Back at the shop, Margaret arranged their table of samples before the window. A set of lace cuffs gleamed white against white linen, replete with festoons of rippled arches. White silk trimmings for ruffs and gowns glowed against dark velvet like a sky full of spangles. Passersby stopped to gaze in the window, to smile and nod at the beauty of their goods.

Then it was time to visit the Drapers Guild. Margaret found her way to the guild hall. When she asked for the master, she learned he was absent on business for several days. Her plan thwarted, she set it aside. She would have to inquire again for him soon.

Only slightly discouraged, she returned to the shop and retrieved her market basket. "Let me buy some fresh things for our supper," she told Bertrande and Marie. "You take Patience home, and I will be there anon."

"More sugar plums!" cried Patience, hopping and pulling on Margaret's arm. She had enjoyed the ones from the morning.

"We shall see. If you mind Bertrande and Marie, I might bring you a surprise."

"Take extra care," Bertrande hastened to warn her in a low voice, not wanting Patience to hear. "Watch the streets carefully for the viscount and return to us soon."

"I shall, I shall." Margaret hid her impatience. Bertrande meant well, but her warnings were vexing. Today, London seemed full of infinite hiding places. With a hasty farewell, Margaret left the shop.

The freedom of the city embraced her. Her feet seemed to fly as she rushed down the street and rounded the corner. To her astonishment, she crashed into a man's broad chest.

"Oh! Your pardon!" Her basket flew from her hands. As she groped to catch it, so did he, accidentally treading on her right foot. With a yelp of pain, she bent double, kicked off her slipper, and clutched her injured toes in both hands.

Chapter 25

"Ouch," Margaret moaned. "You've mashed my foot! 'Twas my fault, I didn't look where I was going. But it does hurt." The toes of Margaret's right foot throbbed painfully. While she assessed the damage, he knelt, took her foot in his hand, and she saw who it was. "God's eyelid, Jonathan!" She dropped her slipper and stared at his fingers, which were caressing her stocking-clad arch in the most delicious way.

Jonathan's wide-shouldered frame dominated the narrow street. His dazzling smile dominated her mind. "I am most sorry about your foot. Allow me to—"

"No!" She jerked her foot from his hand and backed away. "That is, no thank you. I mean not here. I mean not ever. Oh dear." She stopped, flustered by her reaction. Heaven help her, but she wanted to touch his face and stare into his smoky dark eyes, run her fingers along his magnificent arms and shoulders the way she had at Clifton and kiss his wondrous . . . "What I mean is, I must thank you," she said, pulling herself together, determined to bow to duty and not her insane wishes. "For what you did at the London gates."

His languid honey gaze slowly perused her, and she felt as if he poured molten desire all over her. The flare of her kirtle skirt from her hips, her bare arms and low smock cut just above her breasts, the way curls fanned at her neck—he praised every part of her with his eyes. Her body warmed, drifting in that honey.

"My pleasure." He gave her a tiny bow.

The air stuck in Margaret's lungs and refused to come out again. She would like to be his pleasure. She truly would.

"I hope I didn't frighten you with the noise," he went on, displaying his usual cool control of himself and his emotions. "A few of those men were new recruits in training. They get excited and shout a good deal."

"You didn't frighten me, you startled me. You're always popping up like a jackrabbit. I don't know when to expect you. Like now." She covered her excitement with talk—that rising, tickling excitement she shouldn't feel. "I didn't expect you to find me. At least not this soon."

" 'Twas rather easy, I'm afraid. The FRENCH LACE MAKERS sign was a clear clue. Tomorrow Robert will find you as well."

Dismay filled her at his words. "What else am I to call the shop?" she demanded. Suddenly she was aware that people were staring. What a sight she must be, loitering in the street with her shoe off. Hastily she groped for her slipper and jabbed it on her foot, forgetting her injury. It hurt abominably, but so did something else—seeing Jonathan again. She must keep a tight hold on her heart.

He made it hard for her. As she reached for her basket, he got there first, whisking it from the ground with dexterous grace. "Don't worry, I'll protect you. Are you going to market?" He held out the basket with a bow. "Allow me to show you the best places to shop."

"I do need some things, but I must go alone." She took the basket and, gripping it tightly, started off down the lane. "My thanks again, and adieu."

To her chagrin, he ignored her farewell. He caught up in a few easy strides and kept pace with her.

"I thought I just said farewell," she said a trifle acidly. "Was I wrong?"

"Not in the least, but you can't go alone."

That did it. He made her furious. She didn't like being ordered by anyone. "Jonathan, you make this most difficult. You're doing things for me again. I've tried to tell you *I* want to do them. Alone. Without your help. But I must explain myself badly because you haven't stopped yet. You do something for me every time I turn around."

"What do you expect, after what you did for me at Clifton?"

His words flowed over her, low and beguiling. Did he mean when she kissed him? Or when she killed that man?

Lord, both of them bound her to him so tightly, she couldn't get away.

A pair of gossiping old ladies in almshouse garb stared at them and chortled lewdly. Probably imagined a lovers' quarrel. Hurriedly Margaret moved on. "Let me understand this. Because of what I did at Clifton, I have to let you do things for me."

"That's right. Like helping you get to London," he replied. " 'Tis well I did, too. As early as Sheffield I had to divert your grandsire's men and send them west on a false trail. Their leader went back to Clifton with a message for the earl."

"Impossible," Margaret blurted out, dumbfounded at this news. "He would never have agreed to that."

"He couldn't help but agree." Jonathan chuckled as he guided her around a pile of refuse a housewife had swept out her front door. "I slipped in his window at night. A sound sleeper, that fellow. Child's play to bind him. I put him in my new coffer, the one the innkeeper sold me, had it transported to your—"

"You're mad!" Margaret cried, appalled. "He would smother in there! How could you do such a—"

"He didn't smother." Jonathan's forehead twisted into a puzzled frown as they walked. "The man had instructions to feed and water him regularly, and to allow him a short liberty during their day's journey. I assure you he's quite well, though a bit humiliated. He had plenty of air."

"You make him sound like a horse, with your feeding and watering," she insisted, becoming more agitated. "He's not! That was Giles Hampstead, my grandsire's chief man. He used to give Patience horsy back rides. He used to—"

"He could have given her a ride straight back to Clifton," Jonathan cut in sharply, clearly irritated with her. "Is that what you wanted?"

"Of course not, but I don't think . . ." She gave a sigh of despair. At this rate, she would never win the argument. Besides, the image of her grandsire opening the coffer and finding Giles did make her mouth curve up at the corners. She couldn't help it. "Now listen to me, Jonathan Cavandish," she told him firmly, squashing the temptation to giggle before she got started. "We must come to an agreement or we'll never get on. I am grateful for any help in avoiding

Robert, and my grandsire's men. But you must stop there. Agreed?"

"Agreed." He indicated they must turn at the corner.

"Then," she stopped, "I must bid you farewell."

"Lady Margaret"—he put on his most formal manner—"helping you avoid the viscount and the earl is not a single act, performed once and then finished. I saw you safely to London. I helped you at the gates. Now, if you go about town, you require escort. I might as well be useful while I'm at it. I'd see you settled in."

"I might have had no choice about being seen to London," she cried, thoroughly frustrated with him. "I know Bertrande told you to follow us. But I won't be settled. Not by you, I won't."

"I have to agree there."

His wry chuckle wrapped itself around her like thread around a bobbin, holding her captive, and the irony of her own words struck her. Never had a man unsettled her more.

What he did next was even more unsettling. He cocked his famous eyebrow at her. "How's your temper doing?"

"Nicely," she snapped, hurrying around the corner and into a street lined with produce sellers' stalls.

"Nicely? I don't think so. I think you lost it back there." He jerked his thumb behind them. "Care to tell me why? And pray remember to make it the truth."

"Yes! We don't see things the same way." She struggled to contain her voice so it wouldn't carry. "I have agreed to be protected, but you want to move in and take over my life. Do you want to decide what I eat for dinner, like you did in Lulworth because you supplied it? Do you want to chose my gowns?"

"I would like that, but I have my own pressing affairs to manage."

He grinned and sent her a knowing glance that caused her skin to flame. And those things he had to manage—suddenly she remembered. "Where is your prisoner?" she demanded. How lax of her to forget. "Did he escape?"

"Cornelius and the recruits brought him safely to the Tower. The important part comes when we see who he draws. We want his English contact."

"Oh, I near forgot to tell you," she said, remembering another detail, "but the man in the cloak at Clifton wore rough shoes. He must have come with the weeder folk. How does that fit in?"

"He didn't necessarily come with them. He might only have wished folk to think he did."

She fell silent, absorbing this information. "Then we can't identify him yet. There's nothing more to do until we get another clue."

"Just one moment," he interrupted. "We aren't doing anything together in this."

"There, you see." She arched her own eyebrows and sent him a superior smile. "You insist I accept your help but refuse mine. I could help you and the Spanish would never know it. They don't even know who I am."

"They know. After that night at Clifton, you can be sure they do. The danger is incredible, Margaret."

That dark look had come over him again. Stopping near a stall of cooking pots, she picked up a kettle, its iron handle warm from the sun. Whenever his agony showed, she wanted to help him, to throw away everything she valued to set him free.

"Your intentions are good," he was saying quietly, so the stall owner couldn't hear. "But you've already made a tremendous sacrifice for me." He broke off, and she knew why. They were already bound together by her actions. "I must have your promise that you will do nothing more."

She let go of the kettle, and his gaze caught hers. Her knees grew weak and quivery. The noise and stir of the street receded in the distance, and she felt isolated with him in a glass bubble of illicit bliss. First he had wanted the truth from her. Now he wanted her promise, and she couldn't give it. Because her heart was an unruly, untamable thing, unwilling to be held in check. If she saw Jonathan in danger, there was no telling what she would do.

"Do you promise?"

She shut her eyes and gripped her basket. The vine handle's narrow strips dug into her palms while she searched for an answer. Her body was as unruly as her heart, for it dearly wanted to embrace him in a fit of passion. She must change the subject, promise him something else.

"Why do you shut your eyes?"

His probing question, asked in that intimate tone of his which made tingles run through her middle, caused her lids to fly open. "I'll make you a promise." She rushed headlong into the words, avoiding the images in her mind. "I'll . . ." She groped for something, anything to distract him. "I would feel much better if I could repay you in some small way for your protection. What if I promise to make you a piece of lace?"

"Lace? Hmm." He stroked his beard, distracted, just as she had hoped. "I would like that. Would you make that one pattern you used to? The one with the edging like snowflake points?"

He *had* noticed her lace back in Lulworth, though he hadn't shown it, but had only scolded her for working it too much. "Do you mean the one with the three different points?" she said slowly. "Like I made for your sister's marriage gown?"

"Yes, that one."

"Lace it is," she nodded, glad her tactic had worked, though it distracted her as well. "And I'll do anything else I can," she added. "Is there something else you need?"

Lord, she shouldn't have asked. His eyes got that hungry look in them. She felt like a juicy tidbit, swinging before a ravenous wolf.

"You did something rather significant back at Clifton."

Without question he referred to the kisses she had given him. Her boldness reared up in her mind, immense in its power to drive her life in new directions. Five years ago she would have been aghast at her actions. But now her yearning spirit pressed forward, demanding she claim her independence. It was thoroughly frightening. And intoxicating.

"Mayhap we should discuss it another time," she said quickly, covering her alarm. "Just now, I think you had better show me those shops."

He obliged with good grace. She was intensely conscious of him at her side, his height and strength and supple movements making her giddy. She grew uncomfortably self-conscious. When he took her hand and placed it on his arm, which was bared by his rolled-up sleeve, the feel of his warm flesh lightly threaded with hair started the heat inside her, definite and discernable. "You said Robert would find me on the morrow," she said, searching for conversation. "How do you know?"

"I know a good deal about Robert's comings and goings

since we arrived in London. Would you care to know them, too?"

"Well, I . . ." She wasn't sure she wanted to know anything about Robert.

Jonathan stopped and pretended to look in a shop window at a weaver's loom. He nodded to a tanner's man who was passing by.

Chapter 26

The man stopped before Margaret and Jonathan in the busy street and touched his wool cap. "May I be of service, sir?"

"You can, my friend," Jonathan replied. "Do you happen to know the time?"

"I do indeed. 'Tis four of the clock just now."

Margaret stared at the two of them. It had to be later than that.

"Do you know a good place to dine? One that you would recommend?"

The man nodded briskly. "The Mermaid Tavern, sir. Many people like to go there."

"And after, what then?"

"Mayhap a play in Shoreditch. Or some like cockfighting."

"Alone or in company?"

Margaret glanced from one man to the other, thoroughly puzzled. What was this all about?

"Oh, in company," answered the fellow, pulling off his wool cap and twirling it on one finger.

The conversation continued, growing stranger to Margaret by the moment. At length, they finished. The man saluted and whisked off. Jonathan took her hand again and placed it firmly on his arm. "Pretend nothing happened," he said in a low voice. "Just walk."

"What was that about?" She gripped his arm and stared straight ahead, but loosened her hand quickly when she felt the firm definition of his muscle.

He captured her retreating fingers and held them against his warmth. "That was one of my associates. He's in training for reconnaissance. Didn't he do well?"

"I have no idea if he did well or otherwise. Nothing he said made sense."

"Robert went in to supper at the Mermaid Tavern at four of the clock with some cronies. He's been there ever since but appears to be considering a trip to Shoreditch later, either for a play or cockfighting. The fellow who followed us is doing so no longer because Samuel tripped him. He fell down some stairs."

"How did he know this?" Margaret dragged him to a stop.

"Let us walk on, pray." Jonathan spoke cordially, as if they were exchanging pleasantries. "Look at that lovely house." They strolled sedately. He pointed out the different flowers in the house's garden before continuing. "I have men working in pairs around the city, following certain targets. You didn't see Samuel's partner because he stopped to look at the goods in a stall. The pair of them report to others in fixed places, at the same time picking up the latest reports about Robert. Robert does the same, though some of his men are ill trained. Like the one who fell down the stairs. The fellow didn't even draw his sword."

"Do you mean to say they would have brawled in the street? In broad daylight?" Margaret was shocked.

"It happens all the time in London. More often at night. Haven't you been to the capital before?"

"Yes, twice," Margaret began, "just after my father . . ." She stopped, unable to go on as memory of her father's death, her past sorrow, choked her thoughts. Tears pooled in her eyes. "Never mind. Is this a good place to buy?"

"It was a difficult time for you," he said gently. "You needn't tell me if you don't wish to. Let us buy at the next place down."

He helped her buy milk and butter, bread and meat bones for broth. She got excellent prices everywhere. Because, Margaret thought with resentment, the women liked him so well. At the butcher's, a stocky dame smiled on him in a kindly manner and threw in an extra bone. Margaret didn't mind her. It was the lass at the dairy who bothered her. A giggling maid with deep blue eyes and a bulging bodice. Jonathan pinched her cheek and she stood on tiptoe to place a kiss on his, apparently a familiar ritual between them. And he seemed to know females all over London. The vendor's lass who sold lemons. The girl with meat pasties on a tray hung from her neck. This last lusty lass with rosy cheeks gave him a special price when he bought from her, along with a sly wink. Jonathan had kissed her hand and murmured some flirtation about relishing the pastry she rolled with her own sweet hands. Margaret could scarcely enjoy eating it after that. The crust stuck in her throat.

"You're jealous," he said conversationally as they stood in a doorway, eating. "You look about to explode."

Margaret choked on the pastry. She coughed so hard he had to pound her on the back. "Don't talk pish pash. The pastry went down the wrong way," she said tartly when she could talk again. "You can stop hitting me now."

He stopped thumping, but his hand didn't go away. It lingered, warm and intimate, on her shoulder. "Tell me the truth," he demanded. "Does it trouble you that I know so many women?"

"*They* trouble me," she huffed. "They're too forward by half."

"Don't you think I encourage them?"

She studied him seriously. Since he had asked . . . "No, I don't. They're mad for El Mágico, but they don't know a thing about you."

She thought a flash of sadness darted across his face. Placing his hand lightly on her back, he guided her toward the vegetable seller. "I don't know much about you either," he said. "You've been to London before and I never heard about it. Were you here just—"

"After my father died," she finished for him, her voice sunk to a whisper. She stared at the brown and gray cobbles as they walked, but her focus blurred. She had an unexplainable urge to tell him every detail. It was heightened by what he did next.

He slid an arm around her shoulders, gave her a quick, sympathetic squeeze. Before she realized what he was doing, he had her nestled against his side. "Go on," he urged.

"Mother met with lawyers all day while I stayed at our inn." It hurt too much to talk about it. How well she remembered her copious tears, the anguished ache in her heart. Both of them welled up inside her, even after five years. "I never thanked you properly when you paid for my father's funeral," she said, still studying the cobbles, trying to hold her composure. "You worked so hard to make it proper and lavish enough to befit his station. I would have had the money, but I let my pillow sit out in the rain that night. I forgot all about it, being with you." She cut herself off. She hadn't meant to say so much.

He halted before a stall loaded with parsnips and looked at her inquiringly. "What did the pillow have to do with it?"

He deserved to know, she thought with a tremor. But she feared this confession, feared he would turn away from her. "You asked for the truth, so I'll give it to you. I sold the lace I made, not just one piece, but many. Regularly. Long before I knew you. In fact, ever since I was nine. I used the money for food and other household needs because my mother spent everything on her lawsuits and gowns for London when she visited the lawyers. I made good lace and got good prices. I'll get even better ones when I start selling here." She lifted her chin proudly and awaited his reprimand.

"But your father!" His face was troubled, not angry. "He let this go on?"

"He didn't exactly know about it."

"I mean with your mother!" Indignation radiated from him. "He should have managed the money himself."

Margaret's back went rigid. "He loved her too well to deny her. He loved us both. The money meant nothing to him. When it came in, he let my mother manage it. He paid for our living with what was left. If it wasn't enough, he bought with the promise to pay later. I'm sure you can't understand, but he loved me above all else in life. He let me do whatever gave me joy." Her voice was haughty, she realized, but she hoped he could understand.

"If he loved you, he had a damn funny way of showing it," he muttered. "Never mind," he went on before she could protest. "I know your father loved you. I won't debate that. But what *did* he think happened to your lace pieces?"

"I let him believe I gave them away—to friends and others. I would say I hadn't finished one when in fact I had made three."

"And he never noticed?" Jonathan scowled at the parsnip in his hand. "How did you handle the money?"

She could all but hear him say it was not the place of a child.

"I would carry a packet to the butcher or the tailor as if bid to deliver it. And Papa usually left the servants' wages in special places—the cook's went in a little crock on her kitchen table; the maid's in a dish by her bed. He put the shillings there each Saturday. Except when he forgot."

"More like there was nothing to put there, whether he remembered or no."

She could hear the pity in his voice, and she wanted to cry out that she had been rich without the money. Her father had been the most precious gift of her life—a man whose mind lingered with matters of the spirit. He would tramp the woods and meadows for hours, gazing at larks building a nest or tempting the deer to eat from his hand. Once each day she would leave her lace and walk with him through dappled Dorset, drinking in the exercise and sunshine, enamored of the deep calm his protective presence brought. "My mother thought she was the strong one who kept the household together, but she wasn't," she insisted. "My father kept us together with the strength of his love, and he let me help any way I wanted. But 'twas small wonder your father didn't favor me for a daughter-in-law. He knew all about my lace."

"He did? How?" Jonathan looked astonished at this.

"He bought a number of my pieces for wealthy patrons. He understood things we didn't, back then. He saw right off we weren't suited. 'Tis easier to admit it now." But it wasn't. The pain in his eyes, pain felt for her, made her want to weep. "Go ahead," she said humbly. "Hate me. Be angry, I deserve it. I hid these things from you. I pretended I was the girl of your dreams when I really wasn't. I said at Clifton that I was wicked and it's true."

"You aren't wicked. Not in the least!" Jonathan couldn't believe the story he was hearing. His poor, gentle Margaret, forced to labor from the age of nine, when her father was in health and should have provided. But that wasn't it at all, he corrected himself. She had chosen to labor. What he had to learn was why. "You apparently did what you felt you had to, though I find it deplorable. I don't deny I thought you were different, but the true problem was your nobility, not our suitability. Your blood ties will follow you wherever you go." As he said the words, he thought she looked like an enraged mare, wanting to fling off a too-tight girth. She hated that nobility, as did he, the thing that had pulled them apart five years ago. But now he knew it was more than that.

"You wouldn't have liked me if you'd known," she insisted. "You wanted a sweet, helpless girl to care for, and I was neither. Admit it. Admit the truth."

"The trouble was, and still is, that you refuse to let anyone help you. I can help with your lace business. I can get you set up."

"I don't want you to," she cried, almost leaping down his throat, her face turned suddenly anguished. "I want to do it alone. I want to make the goods, find the customers, sell my product, reap the rewards. It's my dearest wish. Can't you see?"

"You want to do it alone? Or you want to do it yourself?"

"What's the difference?" she asked. "Just because I want to work, everyone thinks me mad."

"There's a great deal of difference," he told her patiently. "You can do something yourself but still have companionship. You accept Bertrande and Marie's company. Why not mine?"

"Because they don't order me around," she said. "Besides, speak for yourself. You're the one who wants me out of your business."

It was his turn to anger, and he did it quite readily. "That's because my business is dangerous. And you didn't promise, either, now that you bring it up again. It's not safe for a woman and I have to do it . . ." He was about to say "do it alone," but he shut his mouth with a sharp snap.

"Solitary Magician." She sent him a smug glance, but after that she lapsed into silence, and he thought she looked dazed by the rapid fire of conversation. "What were we about to do?" She looked around as if she didn't know where they were.

"Vegetables," he muttered, trying to sort through the many emotions tearing at him. "You wanted some vegetables, and here we are, so choose whatever you wish to buy."

Margaret did as she was told. She brought herself out of the confusing depths of their intimacy, focused her eyes, and found herself staring at a bin heaped with golden onions. Hurriedly she bought two, planning to make broth for supper. But the onions only reminded her of tears. Ever more tears.

Chapter 27

"Time to get you home," Jonathan said when Margaret had completed her selections. A semblance of normalcy had returned to their conversation, though they avoided anything with a hint of personal revelation. "Where do you lodge?"

"You don't think I'm going to show you."

"It doesn't matter if you show me or not. I'll find out where it is."

She wrinkled her nose at him.

"Temper." He wagged a playful finger at her. "Tell me why you're angry. Out with it quick."

"You're impossible to get rid of."

"Blunt spoken, aren't you. Fear naught. I have multiple commitments that claim my attention. I was about to bid you adieu." He nodded again to a passerby.

The fellow stopped in the street and whipped off his hat. It was the white-haired Dutchman. "At your service, Captain."

"This is Cornelius VanderVorn," Jonathan said. "He was with me at Clifton, if you recall. Cornelius, you know my good friend Margaret Longleate. Margaret, on the morrow Cornelius will be at your lodgings for you. What time would you like?"

"For me?" she asked, baffled.

"Someone must accompany you each time you go out. 'Tis quite dangerous, believe me. As soon as your grandsire arrives, 'twill be worse."

"But I don't want someone with me when I go out."

He looked at her sternly. "Temper, again?"

"Not temper. Privacy," she insisted with all the dignity she could muster. Really, he took things too far.

He sent her a disarming smile, then turned to his friend. "See the lady home, pray. He will be here at eight to escort you, Margaret," he said in parting to her. "See that you don't make him wait."

For the rest of the day, Jonathan went about his round of activities—drilling his cavalry unit, hunting down supplies and equipment—but all the time he carried Margaret's revelations with him: the haunting specter of a child, alone and laboring to keep her family fed. Now that fiercely independent child had grown into a bold, independent woman. No wonder she had resented him years ago when he did things for her. No wonder she resented him still. No one had ever helped until he came along, and by then, she considered it an intrusion.

Then there was the other trouble—she was right about the girl he had thought she was. Though he hadn't wished to be a draper like his father, he had craved a gentle, clinging woman like his mother to grace his home. Not that it mattered what he wanted anymore. He could no longer have any girl at all, gay or otherwise. Not while he still burned for vengeance. And by the time he had it, he would have sunk as low as the man he meant to destroy.

That vengeance was foremost on his mind, but he was making no progress in it, thanks to Elizabeth Tudor. He stood in her antechamber at Greenwich Palace later that evening, frowning at a draped easel. Slowly, he swung around to face his brother-in-law, the Earl of Wynford. "Tell me I've heard you wrong."

"I have it on the best authority that Elizabeth has invited the French Duke of Alençon to England." Christopher Howard, called Kit by his friends, rose with muscular grace from his seat by the window. "She wants to see him before committing to marriage. Worse yet, I believe Alençon's going to accept."

"I knew something was brewing when she wouldn't sign my papers to leave for the Netherlands," Jonathan muttered. Tonight the fit of darkness lay upon him worse than ever. He was immobilized in England, unable to pursue his prey. "She swore she would let me go when I finished in Yorkshire. But yesterday when I named my departure date, she refused to answer. Instead, she insisted I attend that revel last night for the French delegation. For that simpering Frog Alençon sent to woo her."

"I know, she insisted I attend as well!" Kit threw up his hands, his face mirroring similar repugnance. "I like Simier no more than you do. But you needn't have acted like a bore. You sat in the corner all night long."

"My thanks, you always were a forthright fellow." As Jonathan moved away from the easel to the middle of the ornate chamber, he sent Kit a wry grin. This was the man who had taken him to the Netherlands and helped him become a cavalryman of renowned skill. He didn't want to make him angry. "I regret not following your good example and behaving like a polished courtier. But I can't enjoy reveling when I'm supposed to be at the battle front. As long as she foists nonsense on me, that's how I'll behave."

"Your viewpoint is clearly the sensible one, but Elizabeth is far from sensible these days," Kit warned, leaning out the open window for air. "She's in love and resents anyone who offers insult, real or imagined, to her prospective husband. Remember that and have a care what you say."

"Oh, aye." Jonathan held his place in the center of the room, well away from the embroidered wall hangings, which he hated. This was the famous tapestry of "The Wise and Foolish Virgins." The many woven eyes of the women kept their silent vigil, guarding the room. "I'll have a care. But how much did you enjoy last night, having to watch while she giggled and blushed at Simier's compliments—not that I don't think she's entitled to them. But everyone knows while he captivates her the negotiators keep raising the marriage settlement. They hope she'll be so swept off her feet she'll insist her ministers agree."

"Ambassador Mauvissière displays France's greed." Kit wandered idly to the easel, flicked off the dust cover, and grimaced at the portrait. "I personally hope this marriage never happens. I'm suspicious of the entire affair."

"I'm more than suspicious," Jon interjected strongly. "Jean de Simier has a certain attraction, but he's no more than the duke's chief wardrober. Alençon is the one Elizabeth will be stuck with." Jonathan came around next to Kit and scowled at the portrait. "Cover him up, for heaven's sake. Look at that indecisive chin and beady eyes. He's weak-spirited, if I'm any judge of character." Jonathan moved away while Kit redraped the portrait.

"Of course 'tis a shame our queen lacks a husband," Jonathan went on, in his turn leaning out the window for a breath of air. "It just shouldn't be Alençon. He has no political clout in either France or Europe. He's spent his life fighting his older brothers as they became kings of France, then died one after another, so he's a hellion, and she doesn't need that."

"No, she doesn't." Kit looked grave. "She has enough problems."

Jonathan fixed himself in the center of the chamber again. He stared intently at a particular scene in the wall hangings. "I've heard some very troubling things, about Simier having access to the queen's private apartments. Last night he boasted of breaking into her bedchamber and stealing her nightcap to send to his master. One of her maids admitted the truth of it when I interrogated her."

"When you what?"

"Don't debate my word choice," Jonathan snapped. "Since I've returned, I've become involved in the queen's safety, and I don't like what I see. The maid said Simier teased her mistress in the most provocative manner while she blushed in bed, half naked. Do you realize how vulnerable she is if he can visit her private chambers whenever he pleases? I tell you, security is as lousy around here as a dog at the end of summer. The usher guarding the door must not be on duty at night, 'else how did Simier get in?"

"Come now, I don't think there's any danger from him," Kit answered. "The French may be mad, but they want a marriage, not a funeral. They wouldn't plot against her in that way."

"No," Jonathan muttered, "the French wouldn't, but some others we know would."

"Are you willing to do something about it?" Kit queried, gesturing toward the door, which rattled with approaching footsteps.

"I suppose." Jonathan looked dismal. "Though it means delaying my return to the Netherlands indefinitely."

"I know your reason for wishing to return." Kit sent him a sympathetic glance. "So I appreciate your willingness to stay. But let me do the talking to Elizabeth, will you? Agreed?"

Jonathan was about to answer that he would say what he had to, when he had to, but the double doors leading to the chamber swung open. Her Majesty strode in and dismissed her two women. At forty-five, Elizabeth Tudor was still comely, though comely was never the word for her, Jonathan thought. Strong and decisive, her character lent an awesome glory to a countenance that was no more than handsome, given a different personality. Today she was gowned in black rustling silk with no trim, her auburn hair dressed simply as if she had hurried.

"My Lord Wynford. Captain Cavandish. My thanks for coming," she greeted them as the doors swung shut behind her. She held out slender, beringed hands to each of them. As Jonathan bowed over her hand, he caught the strong scent of thyme and coriander from her pomander. "I have important tasks for you both," she said, coming straight to the point.

"We are ever your faithful servants," Kit replied smoothly, giving Jonathan a sharp glance as a reminder to stay silent. "What would you have?"

The queen's manner changed. Her businesslike expression left her as she drifted over to the easel and removed the dust sheet. With a dreamy smile she gazed at the portrait of her intended. "I must confide in you both," she went on. "Come here, pray."

Kit went to her, a model of courtly decorum. Jonathan followed with a show of reluctance.

"I have invited the Duke of Alençon to visit me," she confessed in a rush, "and I believe he intends to accept."

Kit regarded her steadily, but Jonathan gave her his blackest stare. Sure enough, the queen lowered her gaze and blushed. Highly unusual, he noted. The queen rarely blushed. She conducted state business in a forthright manner much like a man.

Kit broke the awkward silence, his voice and his words gently supportive. "How can we assist?"

"You must arrange for his journey," she told Kit, more in her usual manner. "Bring the duke safely to me across the Channel on the *Swiftsure II.* And you, Captain, must ensure his safety once he's here."

"*Your* safety is of greater importance, Majesty," Jon said strongly. "You are the one I wish to protect."

Elizabeth narrowed her gaze at him. "What," she inquired, changing the subject, "did you find on your journey north?"

"I brought back a Spanish prisoner," he told her, "and have him in the Tower. He is plainly a messenger, and I intend to learn who his English contact is."

The queen's face changed. Her nostrils became pinched as her regal calm fled. "God's blood, why can't they leave me be? Philip never got over my refusal to wed with him years ago. As if I would be the fool my sister was, selling England for a man's handsome face. And his wasn't that handsome. 'Tis probably less so now."

"Your Majesty, you have nothing to fear," Kit hastened to soothe her, even as he cast Jonathan a worried look behind her back. "Captain Cavandish will guard you, and we will both work with Walsingham to uncover any plots. This messenger is probably nothing, as is the delegation from Spain."

"Delegation? What delegation?" Both Jonathan and Elizabeth spoke at once.

"I've learned that King Philip sends a new delegation to discuss the import and export of fine fabrics and other goods." Kit made light of the information. "They will arrive any day now. I am certain they—"

"Bah!" ejaculated Elizabeth. "They're not coming to discuss trade. They want to protest the French marriage. 'Tis as plain as the nose on my face."

"Why would they do that?" Jonathan queried, suddenly suspicious. "Is there something new for them to protest?" He paused and scrutinized the queen closely. For the past year she had vacillated in her decision to wed with the duke. Now she invited him to England. "You haven't accepted him, have you? Tell us!" he demanded, ignoring Kit's warning look. "If you have, we deserve to know."

Drawing herself up rigidly, she glared at them. "You have no right to question me, Captain. When I make a decision, 'twill be the one best for my country."

Jonathan relaxed and smiled winningly at her. "That sounds more like the queen I know. You put my mind at ease when you talk like that."

Elizabeth continued to glare at him as she snapped open

her fan. "You are too familiar by far. And this room"—she turned to Kit—"is stifling hot."

"Sit down, Your Grace. I will fan you." Kit guided her to a carved, cushioned chair and seated her. He took her fan and plied it, stirring the air. She leaned back in the chair with a sigh.

"Sit." She waved Kit to a chair opposite. "Why can you not behave like your brother-in-law," she demanded of Jonathan, who had not been invited to sit.

"Because he is an earl and a courtier," Jonathan told her solidly. "Oxford-educated and all the rest. I am a plain-spoken merchant's son and a soldier. I say what I think and I hope 'tis to your good. Right now I think you should remove the court to another location, Hampton Court or Whitehall. Anywhere else but here."

"Why?" Elizabeth cast him a look of vast surprise, clearly caught off guard by the request. "We're settled here for now."

"This place has all the security of a barn with both doors open," Jonathan stated. "I can't keep you safe no matter what I do. I suggest Hampton Court. Your chambers there have fewer doors."

"The court spent the spring at Hampton Court," Elizabeth objected. "The privies are still being cleaned. I'll not go there, nor will I go to Whitehall, since everyone in the environs had the smallpox of late. I intend to pass the summer here."

"Then how am I to guard your person?" Jonathan demanded. "I requested permission yesterday to return to the Netherlands. You might as well let me go."

"Permission denied," she snapped. "God's blood, how am I to rule this country when my best men want to get themselves shot in battle. If you want to be killed, stay here and do it protecting the duke."

"I'll protect you, and the duke, too, if he happens to be nearby. But I warn you, I am less than effective here. I would wash my hands of the whole affair—"

"But you can't," Elizabeth finished for him in high temper. "I need you here and I'll have you. If you leave the country, I'll have you brought back. Pray you meet with Walsingham on the morrow," she went on to Kit, bringing her tone back to normal. "He'll await you at eleven of the clock." She turned and glared at Jonathan, who was frowning at that same scene in the wall hangings. "Bring this ruffian with you if he's not too unruly. If he is, leave him at home and give him his orders when you return."

He wouldn't come, Jonathan thought fiercely, realizing what he had taken on, protecting the queen. Involuntarily, his thoughts skipped to Margaret. Two women to protect, both of them impossible. Already it was a trying task.

Chapter 28

She had to make a plan if she stayed in London. Margaret sat up in bed the next morning, knowing Bertrande was right. "I believe I should request an audience with the queen today," she said while Bertrande helped with her hair. Her friend's nimble fingers worked on the wicked snarls, causing Margaret no pain. Her pain came from another source—her restless night. So restless, her plaited hair had unfurled and snarled something fierce. Oh, she pretended not to be troubled, but the wonderful, forbidden memory of Jonathan stayed with her, the way he probed about her lace, his face grave and caring. And he hadn't declared her wicked for what she had done!

"I do wish you would abide here." Bertrande reached for a hairpin and tucked up Margaret's hair. "But if you must go out, pray be careful, whatever you do."

"If I see my grandsire or Robert in the streets, I can hide." Margaret's fear since the city gates episode had lessened. She had to get out, to breathe and move.

"I know, *ma chère,*" Bertrande reassured her. "We will not quarrel. But can you not take a covered litter to court? How much money is left?"

Blast the money, Margaret thought as she donned her clothes. She would have to count it. After breaking her fast with Patience, Margaret spilled the contents of her purse on the table and did so. "I have but half a pound left." In dismay she indicated the shillings and pence arrayed before her. "We'll run short in a few more days."

"Can we not open the shop and take orders?" Marie ventured. "We might receive partial payments for promised work."

"*Non,* we require the guild's license before we sell a

stitch," Bertrande interjected. "Even if we had a wealthy patron and sold quietly to her, outside the shop, we could not do it for long. Word would spread of our duplicity, seeking the guild's approval but selling without."

Margaret nodded. "I fear Bertrande is right. The London Drapers Guild dominates the fabric trade." She rested a hand on Patience, who had wandered over to lean her head against Margaret's knee. "We must be careful with our money until Bertrande is admitted," she declared, fortifying herself for the wait. She felt dismal as she said the words, though, mostly because of the ones left unsaid. They were not sure Bertrande would be received. "I'll call at the guild again today," she finished. "Just now I must hurry to see the queen."

With that, Margaret went to purchase writing materials, returned and penned a letter to her grandsire's goldsmith who held her jointure. Then, knowing it was still well before eight of the clock, she placed her child in Marie's loving care and set off for Greenwich Palace. With some satisfaction, she gave Jonathan's man the slip.

As Margaret glided through the busy London streets, she remembered the other thing she must do—purchase the makings for a new lace pillow. She needed her own pillow to make lace for Jonathan. Not to mention needing her work for its own sake.

She must also be careful. Without question Robert would be out and about London, and soon, so would her grandsire. She walked swiftly across London Bridge, then headed east for Greenwich. If a nobleman approached by coach or on horseback, she would blend with the crowd, keeping her head down. If her face didn't show, they wouldn't notice her—not dressed the way she was. Her plain kirtle skirt and bodice, her hair bundled neatly at her nape and covered, were not especially suitable for a court appearance. But they did disguise her, making her look as unexceptional as the other women who crowded the busy road.

Margaret hurried but enjoyed the sights as well. Dairy maids with yokes of milk buckets headed for London to sell their goods, along with men and lads ladened with produce. Occasionally she saw a great lady or gentleman in a litter, their passage protected by footmen. How she longed for the money to make life easier for herself and her friends, for the protection afforded by wealth. She would have a garden for Patience to play in, cooler lodgings for Bertrande, who was troubled by the London heat. In fact, Margaret worried about her friend's health. Bertrande seemed unusually tired of late. If only she could have her jointure! Not for herself but for them.

She saw the water meadows of Greenwich long before she came within view of the palace. When at last the structure sprawled before her, she paused to study it. It made Clifton Manor look minuscule. Greenwich was not one building but many—a rambling, majestic edifice where the queen was housed, along with a chapel, tennis courts, kitchens, stables, and more buildings too numerous to name.

When Margaret rang at the gates, a man in black silk netherstocks strutted out from the porter's lodge. He clearly thought well of himself, to wear silk, and he wouldn't be hurried by a poorly garbed maid.

"Papers?" He wasn't old, but he appeared grumpy. He took her papers and studied them.

Margaret leaned over and pointed firmly to her name on her marriage papers—Viscountess Margaret Longleate.

"Longleate! Good gravy! Ho, George, come here smart." Another man appeared in similar livery—they both wore scarlet doublets embroidered with gold Tudor roses. "Escort the Dowager Viscountess Longleate to the privy chamber. Her Grace gave instructions to bring her at once if she called."

Margaret followed her guide, realizing a bad sign when she saw one. It meant her grandsire had been here before her, visited the queen, and reported her escape.

Ten of the clock struck in a nearby tower by the time Margaret reached the privy chambers. Her Majesty, she was informed, was working at state affairs but would see her anon.

Margaret stood alone in the queen's antechamber, the wait making her anxious. The longer she stood, the more uncomfortable a feeling crept over her. She had the sense of someone observing her, of eyes watching.

Whirling, she searched the dimly lit corners of the room. One of the embroidered wall hangings rippled, stirred by air currents. Margaret's gaze darted to inspect it. Her eyes halted at a woman's figure on the hanging. She stared hard at it. Was it her imagination, or did a real pair of eyes stare back at her? The dark pupils seemed to leap against their white background. They seemed alive!

God's eyelid! She turned her back on it, sure her imagination played tricks on her. She clenched her jaw and released it, determined to ignore the feeling. Her mind grew capricious, imagining ghosts.

Still, the feeling flexed its muscle, ever stronger. Someone watched her.

Margaret whisked around and strained her eyes to see. A faint light seemed to flit in the wall hanging. The figures in the tapestry watched her, pupils shifting, lids blinking. The hair on the back of her neck prickled, and she hugged herself tightly. If only the queen would come.

Chapter 29

The door at the far end of the room opened. A lady-in-waiting stood in the entry, beckoning. With relief, Margaret hurried to meet the queen.

"Your Majesty." Margaret sank into a deep curtsy, took the hand offered, and kissed it. "My humble thanks for this audience. I regret coming so unexpectedly."

Elizabeth's red-gold hair glowed in the morning light from the window, matching the gold thread in her jeweled, embroidered, loose coat, making her seem to Margaret both majestic and formidable. And she could tell the queen scrutinized her, summing up her circumstances and her person in one swift judgment.

"Be quick with your business," the queen commanded. "I am engaged with important matters of state." She withdrew her hand and sat on an upholstered bench. Pointing to a stool, she motioned Margaret to sit as well.

As Margaret told her story with quiet dignity, including details about her grandsire's choice of bridegroom, she saw the queen's expression turn from one of lofty impatience to that of keen interest. Margaret produced the letter to the goldsmith.

"Your request is unusual." Her Majesty drummed long, slim fingers on a tiny rosewood table beside her. "Our courtiers often appeal to us to solve their family quarrels, but never have I heard a request like this one. I am not sure I can sign this paper of yours. The Earl of Clifton would be displeased."

"I understand your hesitation," Margaret said, knowing full well the queen cared little for anyone's pleasure or displeasure outside of affairs of state. "But I sense you do not approve my grandsire's choice of Robert Weston as my bridegroom. If I might have my jointure, I need not wed him." Sitting on the edge of her stool, she held out the paper to the queen, silently pleading with her to sign.

The queen scanned it but did not take it. Instead she retrained her gaze on Margaret, a beginning sparkle in her eyes. "Do you think you can evade your grandsire? I will not conceal from you that he has been here. He wants custody of your person, and if I know him, he will gain it before long."

"Ah, but I know the tactics he will use to find me, and because I know him, I will evade him." Margaret saw curiosity grow in the queen's dark eyes as she said this. Could it be the queen found her situation entertaining, as she played cat and mouse with her grandfather? She might well win needed support for no reason other than that. Plying her words carefully, she sought to stoke that interest further. "You will find my defensive tactics intriguing, though I agree he is wily as a fox."

"Ah, but I know him of old," the queen stated. "He is a formidable adversary." She took up a feather fan lying on the table and stroked the brown, ruffled plumes. "So you evade him for a time. In the end when he finds you, what then?"

"If I have my jointure, I can pay guards to keep him away. And if you make it known you do not consent . . ." Margaret cast a yearning glance at the paper.

"I would rather make you an offer, Viscountess. When you're tired of evading the earl, come and live at court. I will provide you with access to your jointure. You may take your time to decide."

Margaret pondered this offer. Her mind leaped from one thought to another as she remembered the queen's reputation: Elizabeth didn't do favors out of kindness. She generally couldn't afford to. "That is, er, kind of Your Majesty. But do I understand correctly, you will give me legal control of my entire estate?"

"Generous, is it not?"

"Most generous, Your Grace." Margaret searched for words before she couched her next question. "What might I do for you in return?"

"There is something." The answer was rapid, and the queen smiled, holding her mouth closed to hide the two bad teeth she was rumored to have. "You may have the place of one of my ladies-in-waiting. Her son took ill and I sent her back to the country. I need a full complement of women to serve me at court."

Margaret bit her lip and pondered this new information. "I would be honored, of course, should you deign to give me a position at court. I know they are coveted."

"You will be well advised to take it. I will keep the post vacant for you."

"I need not take it now? I may take it later?"

"The porter at the gate knows you now. I will give him orders to bring you to me straight if you present yourself." The queen's dark gaze was locked on her, assessing.

Baffled, Margaret returned the look, the oddity of the offer striking her. She tilted her head and looked quizzically at the queen, unable to put words to her question, yet knowing there was something more.

"You are right," the queen said finally, gaining her feet slowly. She rearranged her jeweled coat. "There is something more."

"Yes, Your Majesty?"

"When I give you full control of your inheritance, I would choose the man you wed."

"Your Majesty!" Margaret's breath escaped in a rush of disappointment. "I wish to remain unwed, just as you yourself—"

"I may wed soon. The French negotiations proceed apace." The queen crossed to the easel Margaret had noticed earlier. A white cloth draped the canvas, keeping it from prying eyes. Elizabeth swept away the cloth. "You see here my latest suitor, François de Valois, the Duke of Alençon and youngest brother of the French king." She stepped back, studied the portrait, one fist on her hip, the other supporting her chin. "You are young enough to bear more children," Elizabeth went, catching Margaret's gaze with her own. "If I am willing to accept a woman's role, so can you."

It was Margaret's turn to cross the chamber and stand before the easel. She studied the dark-haired Frenchman, taking in the devilish tilt of his head, the impetuous gleam in his eye. "Your Grace, it is a hard choice, to take a man into one's life. I cannot doubt you have argued the idea back and forth yourself." When she paused, she saw by the queen's face that she spoke rightly. "I accepted the burden of one husband, but Dame Fortune set me free. Now my most important duty is to raise my daughter so she can respect herself. For that, I must remove her from the dominance of men."

"A woman, too, can dominate." The queen struck through the rhetoric to the heart of the matter. "If that is the issue to your way of thinking, the choice is yours. You can use your money to insulate yourself, if necessary. And remember, if I wish, I can force a husband on you and offer nothing in exchange. Instead, I have offered you control of your inheritance. I can arrange it legally so it doesn't belong to your husband. Go home, Viscountess, and think on my offer. Think on it well, for I do not like it when my gifts are spurned." A hint of anger edged her voice.

"Why don't you let the title go dormant, Your Majesty?" Margaret asked bluntly. "You could if you wished."

The queen laughed low in her throat, as if she had been caught in a mischief. "I'd thought of that, Viscountess, as soon as your grandsire requested an audience. But I don't really want that, nor do you, I think." She deliberated a second, then continued. "I want a loyal man in control of the Clifton title. A warrior to fight for me, with the strength to put down rebellions in the north and invasions from the Scots. I also require a clever man who knows about amassing money. No more of these spendthrift lords who think they deserve wealth even if their father's coffers are bare. I need this sort of man for earl and I intend to have one. I'll even send you a list of several choices. What could be fairer than that?"

Margaret shook her head in despair, not knowing what to say.

The queen fixed her with a stare, then suddenly let out an explosive bark of laughter. "Stubborn, aren't you. You're more like your grandfather than you know. Bullheaded, the both of you. You'd not wed Robert Weston, even if I wanted you to, which I don't. I have far too many questions about his loyalty and his interests to allow that. No, I will offer you some more suitable choices. Where do I send you word?"

She awaited an answer, and Margaret could not avoid giving one. "Send to the sign of the FRENCH LACE MAKERS in Threadneedle Street. Anything delivered there will reach me straight."

The queen nodded briskly, clapped her hands, and summoned her ladies. "Go home, Viscountess." She laughed over her shoulder. "Make your decision. And when you're ready, come to me."

Chapter 30

She could have her jointure if she agreed to wed. A scant half hour later, Margaret made her way back to the city, her mind in a morose muddle. Of all the outcomes from meeting with Her Majesty, she hadn't expected this one. What a dilemma she was in!

Margaret walked more slowly on her return than when she had come. The heat of the day was oppressive, and she plodded along the river path. A man with a bundle of kindling caught her attention. No matter what she did, stop for a drink at a well or for a brief rest in the shade, he, too, found an excuse for stopping. Whenever she looked back, he was there.

Determined to lose him in the city, she continued until she passed the bullpits and alehouses of Southwark, then recrossed the great bridge. There, she plunged into a crowd, which slowed down her follower. While he waded his way through people, she dodged down the next lane and stepped into a shop. To her glee, the man passed on by. After he disappeared, she doubled back and took a different street, making several turns. If someone as dim as Robert could play this game, so could she. Thinking herself clever, she headed for the guild hall, where she once more asked for the master. Great joy, he was in! A lad showed her through the vast meeting hall to a cheery, paneled room.

She was greeted by a stout, prosperous-looking gentleman in modestly styled trunk hose and jerkin, with crisp graying hair fringed around his face. As he indicated a chair and she sat down, she noted his guild badge and the excellent quality of his garments. Modest they might be, but the finest of fabrics had been used.

"I am Master Richard Thirstan, first warden of the Honorable Guild of London Drapers." He introduced himself cordially, his voice full of depths like a huge drum. "How may I serve you, mistress?"

"I am Marguerite Smytheson." She reverted to her maiden name, suddenly realizing she felt uncomfortable calling herself Longleate here. "I have friends who wish admission to the guild. I came to inquire as to what they must do."

"What is their product?" Master Thirstan asked politely.

Margaret caught the interested gleam in his eyes. So they did want new skilled craftspeople. "My friends are lace makers. They produce the finest quality of product available. I know there are only two other lace businesses in London, so their work will be in demand."

"Hmm, locally made is more desirable than imported." Master Thirstan seated himself behind his work table just across from her. He stroked his clean-shaven cheeks and fingered his quill pen. "It seems you have checked the market."

"I have." Margaret slid forward to the edge of her chair, warming to her subject. "I assure you, they will be a boon to your guild. How do they apply?"

He gave her an assessing look, as if counting how much she and her friends might be able to pay for the privilege. "They will need to make the request in person at our next guild meeting about six days hence."

"Six days?" Margaret almost shouted with frustration. They needed membership now. "Must we wait so long?"

"We only admit new members with the consent of the entire membership," he said in a sympathetic manner. "Do they wish to attend?"

"Yes, of course," Margaret said firmly, though frustration roiled inside her.

Master Thirstan took up his pen, dipped it in the inkpot, and poised it over paper. "What are the names of your friends?"

"Bertrande and Marie Capell."

Master Thirstan lowered the pen. "Your friends are women?" he asked a little sternly.

"Yes, they are," Margaret said, startled at his question. "You admit women, do you not?"

"Of course we admit women," Master Thirstan explained

patiently. "Sisters are always welcome to share in our holiday feasting and festivals, to aid us in our charitable works and help honor those members we lose to death. But usually they are wives or sisters of our brethren. Our working members are mostly men."

He put a slight emphasis on the word "working," as if women couldn't work.

"Mostly," she questioned him sharply. "But not all?"

"A few are widows of deceased members," he admitted. "They have been permitted to assume their husbands' places in the guild."

"And the others?" Margaret demanded, refusing to be put off.

"We have one or two unwed women with something exceptional to offer the guild who became members in their own right. But it does have to be exceptional."

"And what of Lady Howard, the Countess of Wynford? The others must have voted to admit her."

Master Thirstan's mild face assumed a shocked expression. "Lady Howard? What do you know of her?"

Margaret sent him a withering look, her hand itching to slap him. He assumed she could not possibly know a countess because she dressed simply and went about without a maid. "She and I grew up in the same town some years ago," she said tersely. "I knew her well."

"Oh, some years ago." Thirstan seemed to dismiss the idea that she knew the countess. "Well, you are misinformed about her ladyship. Her brother is the member. He assumed his father's place in the guild when Master Cavandish died. Do you know the captain? If he could vouch for your friends' character, that might—"

"Never mind the captain." Margaret was seething. She had best get herself out of here before she lost her temper. "My friends have something exceptional to offer," she said, looking him squarely in the eye. "They will be here for the guild meeting in six days. Pray name the time."

After that, she tried to escape, but he insisted on describing the way to the captain's workshop. " 'Tis one street over," he explained. "You get there by a descending stair." He put a patronizing hand on her shoulder while giving detailed directions. When at last he let go, Margaret hustled herself off.

Nasty, female-slighting poltroon, she thought furiously as

she strode through the streets. Oh, he seemed nice enough, probably had a lovely family, worked hard, and was honest as well. But women couldn't be members unless they were exceptional? How many unexceptional men belonged? Probably most of them fit that class. It made her so furious she wanted to snarl. She would buy the makings for a lace pillow now, she determined angrily. After meeting with that fool, she needed her lace even more.

She was so angry that she didn't look for the man who had been following her. She hadn't seen him since London Bridge, so she must have lost him in the teaming crowds. As she strode down goldsmith's row, she did notice the entrance to Jonathan's workshop. Just as Master Thirstan had described it, the stairway descended from street level. Poised on the top step, she peered down, but noted the door stood closed, the window dark.

She moved on swiftly, relieved at the excuse not to encounter Jonathan. In a hurry she found the proper shops and counted out more of her dwindling pence for her purchases. Cloth for a pillow cover, a special wedge tool for pounding the cover full of straw, thread to sew it with, needles, and flaxen thread. Clutching the bundle and a box of precious brass pins, she hurried back toward home. No fish bones or sheep's trotters to anchor her lace stitches. At least she had not sunk as low as that.

But when she stopped to buy two oranges from a hawker, she realized she was being followed again. The same man, keeping the same distance. How had he found her once more?

It was no use wondering. Tucking away the oranges, she wove her way through the crowded streets, needing to lose him. She brushed shoulders with men returning from work and women on suppertime errands. She hopped over the cobbles and dodged piles of refuse, hurrying . . . hurrying. Her stomach growled uneasily and she longed for a moment to devour her fruit. She hadn't eaten since morning. Ducking into a doorway, she peered around the corner to look behind.

"You there, bring me a flagon of ale."

She nearly jumped out of her stockings in sudden alarm. Robert! She knew his voice anywhere. Cursing her ill fortune, Margaret flung herself back into the shallow recess of the entry and pressed against the wall, listening. He had found her. Jonathan had predicted that today he would.

"Stupid knave, not that kind. Call the tapster. I'll order it myself."

He was sitting outside one of the alehouses, only a few doors away. For the first time true fear visited Margaret, making her throat go parched and dry as if filled with sand. He had set his snare for her, and when she was caught . . .

She didn't complete the thought. She cut it off, just as she cut off the thread at the end of a lace piece. With finality. Her soul starved for freedom, and here, for the first time in years, she had it. She would not give it up to Robert. Not on any account.

Breathless, she slowly edged forward to sneak a look. With Robert were her grandfather's men, paid to help him find her. They lounged before the alehouse, refreshing themselves with drink. Robert tilted his flagon, and she saw the bobbing of his throat as he swilled the ale. Someone, it seemed, had managed to placate him with a drink he found acceptable. Robert always wanted placating. As she watched, the man who had followed her slunk up to Robert. He was going to give her away!

She had to leave the doorway. Steeling herself for her next move, Margaret felt her coif to be sure her hair was covered. Then, lifting her chin, she left the shelter of the doorway, stepping out as if she lived there. After making a pretense of closing the door, she set off down the street away from Robert. As she walked, maintaining a steady pace, her heart slammed against her chest, in rhythm with her rapid steps.

"You, there! Halt!"

Robert's shout rang out behind her. A thrust of fear gouged her stomach. "Stinking cutpurse, halt!"

A ragged boy pelted through the crowd and collided with her, almost knocking her down. She staggered forward, catching his arm to keep from falling.

"Someone stop that lad!"

Margaret spied Robert coming after the boy. Irony of ironies, he must have just cut Robert's purse.

Chapter 31

The fear of the law was in the boy, for he wrenched away from Margaret and took off. Not knowing what else to do, Margaret cast herself after him in an all-out run. Whether Robert knew yet of her presence, she couldn't tell. But she mustn't waste time checking. She had to disappear.

When the boy dodged into an alley and whipped through an open door, Margaret charged after him. Rude to enter without invitation, but she couldn't help it. In the dimness, she flew into the boy from behind and knocked him flat. Struggling to keep from crushing his thin form, she picked herself up while her eyes adjusted to the gloom.

"Gotta lock the door," he cried, leaping up and slamming the door. He dropped down a stout bar. " 'Else I'll go to Newgate, sure."

He should, thought Margaret. He'd stolen Robert's purse. A hysterical giggle wiggled in her throat. She was glad he had cut Robert's purse. Glad! Yet she was in as much trouble as the lad!

"What'er you done," he demanded of Margaret, turning around to scrutinize her, "that he wants you, too?"

"Regrettably, he does want me," she said, trying to catch her breath, "though not for cutting his purse."

"Oh, ho, I get it." The boy grinned at her. "Gentleman not willing to pay yer price?"

By heaven, the child thought her a prostitute. "I suppose so," she admitted, panting with fear yet forced to see the absurdity of the situation. Hysterical laughter built inside her. "He wants me to warm his bed, and I'd get nothing in return."

"Right." The lad gave her the grim smile of a cohort.

Crawling under a table, he jerked open a trapdoor. "Down ye go."

Astonished, Margaret watched the boy scramble through the hole, disappearing into the unknown depths. She peered in after him, imagining what was down there. Spiders made their webs in holes like that.

The door came alive suddenly, jumping under the force of pounding fists.

"What's the meaning of barring the door," came Robert's shout. "I'll have the bailiff on you, you poxy boy. Give me back my purse! Margaret, are you in there with him? Damn it, come out at once."

Margaret dived for the hole, pulling down the trapdoor behind her, all but stepping on the lad's fingers as she backed down the ladder. When she hit the last rung, she had to grope for it in the dark. Terrified, Margaret shut her eyes and squeezed her pillow goods against her chest. The sweet scent of oranges drifted up, and she realized she squeezed them, too.

The lad smelled them, for he relieved her of one. Her eyes popped open to see him thrust the orange into his ragged purse without so much as a by-your-leave. When he lit a lantern, she felt better, but only a little. She had felt the sticky spiders' webs against her face as she had descended the ladder. At that point, a horrible banging commenced above. Robert would break down the door!

The boy took to his heels down the passage without a word of invitation. Clutching her bundle, Margaret bolted after his light.

The miserable hole went on forever, winding beneath the city in a veritable rabbit's warren of exits and entries, and she was helpless to do anything but follow her guide. They climbed into undercrofts of buildings, then dived into new tunnels where she had to dodge low-hanging ceiling beams. Twice they came to the surface, dashed from one decaying building to another, and descended into the bowels of London once more. The dark squeezed from all sides, the lad's lantern constituting the solitary light, bobbing ahead of her. Here, in the dark, the brimming pain in Jonathan struck her. He was like this tunnel—a maze of complicated, mysterious secrets. As his friend, she should wash away his pain.

Of a sudden, the lad stopped. Putting down the lantern, he fell to examining the contents of several purses he had cut, while gobbling her orange. The fruit disappeared so fast, Margaret wasn't even sure he had peeled it.

"Want some shillings from the purse," he offered, "since you know 'im?"

Margaret took two coins without speaking, needing the funds too desperately to refuse. Again the irony struck her. Robert would pay her keep without wishing to. Mad laughter bubbled inside her, wanting to get out. She managed to swallow it down.

After he had counted the money and pocketed it, the lad, who looked to be younger than her cousin Dorothea, took the other orange from her and fell to peeling it.

"What's your name? And how old are you?" she asked.

"Tim, and I dunno my age." He shrugged, noncommittal. "Not important, would you say?"

"I suppose not, given your occupation, but you should be apprenticed to someone, learning a trade." Margaret studied him by the lantern light. He had fair skin, at least where she could see it through the dirt, and dark hair that hadn't seen scissors in years. She sat down on the floor beside him, and he turned wide blue eyes on her that seemed innocent if she hadn't known better. One of them had been blackened—he must have been in a fight.

"No chance of that. Who's goin'a 'prentice the likes of me?" He didn't pause for an answer to his question but pointed at her bundle. "You could move faster if you'd get rid of that."

"Oh, I couldn't." Margaret patted the items inside to assure herself they were still there. "This is my lace equipment. Cloth to make the pillow cover, and a special wedge tool to pack in straw."

"You're a lace maker?"

Margaret nodded.

The boy leaped up, brushing orange peels from his lap. "You'll want to talk to Queen Mab. She always needs lace makers. She'll pay you, too."

Without further ado, he rushed off, and Margaret hurried after him. She didn't want to be left alone in the dark with the spiders. Why the crawling arachnids filled her with revulsion, she didn't know. They were God's creatures, put on earth as part of the holy scheme, and she did trust God's patterns. Closing her mouth, she put her head down, ignored the sticky threads, and plowed on.

At length they came to a door opening off the tunnel. Margaret eyed it dubiously, but the boy banged on it with his fist and went in.

The scene to greet her eye justified her trepidation. Squalor of the worst kind. In the flickering light of two stumpy candles, a bent hag sat enthroned on a chair, presiding over several ragged beggars who drew back and assessed the intruders—one was covered with evil sores, another balanced on crutches, the third sported the stump of an arm. The smell of sweat permeated the room. Her gaze was captured by one pristine thing in the room—a lace pillow, on which the old witch was making lace.

She was most assuredly a witch, Margaret thought with horror, unwilling to believe people lived this way. The floor was littered with dirt and the woman's shapeless garments were filthy. But she did not touch the thread with her fingers—that was the advantage of bobbin lace making. A cow herd could make it and keep it clean, handling only the bobbins by their spangles at the end, if need be. The old dame's gnarled fingers manipulated the bobbins, her movements swift and crafty. To Margaret she seemed the epitome of the dark, like a great spider, squat and bloated, with her lace stretched out in a web of evil, waiting to snare the unwary.

Margaret bit her lip nervously as fear poked at her stomach. Not even to escape Robert should she have followed Tim to this stinking place.

"Come to pay your week's due," the old woman spat, making a statement rather than asking. Her voice, like rusty machinery, grated on the nerves. Dark little eyes pinioned the boy with a stare. "Did you save me an orange?"

She had a keen sense of smell, Margaret realized, despite the overwhelming odors already clogging the room. Nothing much escaped her notice, that was sure.

"A-aye," Tim stammered, losing his cocky assurance. Slipping forward, he placed some money on the table before the hag. Three of the beggars leaped for it, but the hag was faster. Her cane smashed down on the money first, catching fingers and noses. The beggars slunk back.

"In my hand, next time, you poxy weasel," she snarled at Tim.

Her crabbed hand whipped out and she counted the money. Then she jerked her head and grunted. An uncouth giant of a man unfolded himself from a dark corner where he had sat, previously unnoticed. Tim's face transformed with fear.

The giant lunged, grasped Tim by the shirt, and throttled him while he pawed around for his purse. Finding it, he dropped Tim in a heap, where he gagged and choked on the floor. As the giant shook the remaining coins from the purse into the hag's hand, Tim scrambled to his feet and took a defiant stance, as if this were a common occurrence. It probably was, Margaret concluded, wishing she could leave, except she would never get out of the place without Tim. Besides, if there was even a remote chance of making honest coin, she wanted it. Though her heart warned her—none of the work commissioned by this woman would be honest. Clearly she had stumbled on a den of thieves.

"If you think to cheat me, I'll make you sorry," grated the woman. " 'Ear?" She turned her gaze on Margaret. " 'Oo's this?"

"This 'ere's a lace maker," Tim announced in a hopeful tone, seeming less intimidated now that his employer was pacified with the payment. "Thought she might make you some lace."

Margaret suppressed a shudder as Mab's gaze came to rest on her, and it was her turn to be inspected. In turn, she examined Mab, the straggling gray hair hanging in greasy strands around a leathery face drawn with valleys that Margaret knew were not put there by years of honest toil.

"Can you make French patterns?" the woman demanded, taking in Margaret's plain kirtle and bodice, her unadorned smock of inferior linen.

Margaret nodded. "Yes. I can do point de neige, point d'esprit, or even—"

"I need edging for a woman's ruff," the spider woman rapped out. "Make whatever, but make it good quality French. An ell of it, three days hence, an' I'll pay you a crown."

A whole crown! Margaret's heart swelled with excitement, and she struggled to restrain herself as she answered. "It's a short amount of time to complete such a project. May I make it no more than an inch wide?"

"If it's perfect."

"So, Black Jack's ship got caught, did it?" Tim interjected a bit slyly.

Mab shot him an evil glance. "I can bruise more than just your eye, boy, if you don't 'old your tongue. Mistress," she turned back to Margaret, "is it yea or nay?"

Margaret swallowed hard before agreeing. This was black market trade, both dishonest and illegal. Under normal circumstances she would refuse it, but her life was far from normal these days, and for Bertrande, Marie, and Patience she would walk through the fires of hell to provide. They must have money to sustain them until the meeting of the guild.

The evil-smelling woman gave her a meeting place where she must bring the lace to Tim in three days, at which time she would be paid if her work met the buyer's stringent standards. This last bit worried Margaret, but she ousted it from her mind. Her lace technique did not lack in any way. The buyer could not fail to be pleased.

As Margaret followed Tim through the tunnels, breathing a sigh of relief to be away from the woman she had mentally dubbed the Spider Queen, she figured how long she could stretch the shillings from Robert. Pity Tim had lost his share, yet he assured Margaret it mattered little. He would nab someone else's purse later.

"I'll say it again, that you should be apprenticed," she chided.

"By you?" he asked, grinning. "Will you teach me to make lace."

"I would, if you would work it faithfully," Margaret answered, meaning it.

He only laughed. "I'd 'ate sitting still all day, twiddling string. 'Twould bore the breeches off me. But I'll tell you what. If you 'ear of someone wanting a 'prentice for brewing beer or joining or such, I'd do it in a thrice."

Margaret promised to keep this in mind. She liked his open, sunny smile and his friendly way. He would have to give up thieving, though. She warned him as much.

Now if she could but return home safely without encountering Robert. She hoped that was possible, but it seemed London was not nearly as huge as she had imagined. He had found her within two days, and that boded ill.

Chapter 32

Tim guided Margaret back to the world's surface. As they emerged from a trapdoor in someone's stable, she felt like Persephone coming back from the Netherworld. The bright light of day had never looked so good. Yet fear gripped her. She hadn't yet made it to safety. And she had agreed to make illicit lace.

Her new friend left her not far from Threadneedle Street. She would have to be on guard now. Robert wouldn't have taken kindly to her evading his capture. Nor, she thought, to losing his purse.

Her palms were sticky and her smock clung damply to her chest and back. Margaret bit her lip as she walked, studying the street. A chimney sweep and his assistant trudged in the opposite direction with their brooms and ladders, both of them smudged with soot. A woman tricked out in wondrous colors and a huge farthingale minced down the street on high, cork-soled pantofles, her maid carrying the hem of her gown. No one appeared out of the ordinary, yet trepidation spoke sly whispers to Margaret. *Robert seeks you everywhere. Don't turn around. Run!*

She bolted around the corner into the next street, hearing male voices behind her, imagining one of them was Robert's. She didn't stop to prove her theory. Fear spurred her on. Vaguely she noticed she had turned into the goldsmiths' street. Metal riches gleamed in shop windows as she hurried by on fleet, frantic feet. The fabric district lay nearby. She must get herself off the street and out of Robert's sight.

Halfway down the street she felt conspicuous, running. Three women gossiping at their doorstep stared at her, and she slowed to a hasty walk. Straightening her back, she arranged her parcel and tried to look more decorous. She didn't feel decorous. She felt frazzled and frightened and she knew she should never have evaded Jonathan's escort. Yet she had because she prized her freedom. Though that made no sense if her freedom were ended by Robert. What she needed just now was to stop the torment of thoughts tumbling through her mind. She needed to drug herself with the soothing power of her lace.

She would never have the chance if she didn't keep going. Staunchly, Margaret hustled herself on, passing their lace shop in Threadneedle Street, which was locked up tight. Bertrande, Marie, and Patience would be at home awaiting her, praying for her safety. She remembered the key in her purse, now without coins to keep it company. But she had accomplished much today. Turning down the street toward the fishmongers' section of the city, she congratulated herself on her . . .

Robert! She slammed to a halt, shocked. He and his men loitered in the street, waiting for her. He started up at her appearance, a smile of triumph on his face. With a cry of anguish, she twisted around and bolted back the way she had come.

She cursed herself for a fool as she ran. Of course Robert had found their lace shop as easily as Jonathan had. Of course he had stationed his men nearby. Even Robert could think of that, though she had imagined him too dim.

Fumbling in her purse as she ran, she pulled out her shop key. It was her only hope. Just behind, Robert's shouts threatened. Reaching the shop, she thrust her key in the lock and wrenched the door open. Whipping inside faster than she had ever moved before, she withdrew the key, slammed the door, and locked it from inside. Panting, half sobbing, she darted into the small back room away from their view.

"Open or we'll break down the door!"

Robert's shout had Margaret cringing. God's eyelid, she had to get home without their seeing her. Oh, she would do as Bertrande told her. She promised herself, if she made it home safely, she would stay inside!

The single window in the back room looked out on a dirty alley. She remembered the odor from yesterday when she had washed the glass. Holding her bundle of goods close, she pushed open the casement, planning to slip out and away. Climbing on a crate, she stuck out her head and looked around.

"Mistress Willful, god'den."

Margaret leaped a foot into the air, propelled by surprise and terror. Jonathan stood in the alley, wearing pistols along with his sword. "God's eyelid, I detest it when you do that," she panted, "sneaking up without a sound." But the joy had let loose its fireworks inside her. She was so glad to see him she wanted to sing.

"I didn't sneak," he answered nonchalantly, as if passing the time of day. "I was just waiting here, hoping you would stop by your shop. What's the news?"

"I should think that would be obvious," she hedged, casting a glance over her shoulder, trying not to show her fear as the battering at the door continued.

He glanced at the shaking door, as if it were an interesting oddity, then spoke in a courtly manner. "May I help you down?"

"Help me down?" she spluttered, climbing up onto the sill. "God's eyelid, aren't you going to insist on saving me? Get me out of here. Hurry! Now!"

Jonathan made her wait a minute. She looked damned pretty crouching in the window, her hair falling in wisps around her face and her skirts tucked up around her knees. A sly glance gave him a view of her trim, smooth ankles and calves . . . more if he bent over. A wave of sensual heat rolled through him as he reached for her and clasped her around the waist. He had to remind himself he was furious with her for not awaiting his escort this morning. Half the day had been wasted hunting her down. Where else would he find her but with the viscount hot on her heels.

Landing her neatly on her feet, he resisted the urge to draw her into his arms and kiss her—a long, devouring taste of her sweetly bowed lips to release the pent-up rage and frustration, that was what he wanted right now. Instead, he let her go quickly. She seemed glad to see him, but with Margaret, you never knew. "I wouldn't want to be hasty," he assured her in his most gentlemanly manner, "and make a wrong assumption. After all, you didn't want my help this morning, since you went off—"

"Are you going to scold me for that now?" she hissed, darting frightened glances over the windowsill at the quaking door. "I admit my foolishness. I was wrong to go off alone, do you hear me? I admit it. Now please, please . . ."

"Allow me to carry your bundle, mistress." He took it from her and added it to the pack on his back. "Now then, you were saying?"

"Jonathan!" For the first time ever, he thought she looked desperate, her face flushed and frightened. "Robert is out there. He's going to break the door down!" She grabbed his arm and shook it. "We've got to run."

"I wouldn't do anything without your permission. You said I should ask first." He cast a calm smile at the door. As the viscount and his men rained blow after rhythmic blow, the middle panel of the stout oak cracked. When he turned back, she looked fit to kill him. "Milady"—he bowed and took her elbow—"the door will hold for another minute. Are you sure we're agreed?"

"I said I was. Do you want me to beg? God's eyelid, what do you want?"

"I want the truth from you. Will you resent me after if I help you? Will you think of things you have to do to pay me back?"

"I want your help. In all honesty, I do."

"No, you don't. You never will, until you learn to do one thing."

"What? What is it? I'll learn it on the spot. Just tell me and have done."

She was truly distressed, he noted, blocking her fragile beauty from his brain. In fact, she was nigh on hysterical. But this might be his only chance to change her ways. "There are certain things you're good at, and certain things you're not. Will you stop trying to do all of them. Leave some to the rest of us?"

She stared at him, fear in her golden eyes, then nodded vigorously.

"I'm not convinced this makes sense to you now. We'll talk of it again later," he said quietly. "But I'd have your promise. Swear you'll do as I say?"

"I swear!"

"Very well." He nodded, well pleased with his achievement. Sometimes only total terror could make a person see reason. "I'll see you home now. Up you go."

She was a lot of trouble, he told himself as he boosted her up on the windowsill, then levered himself up beside her, and climbed onto the low, slanting roof. With ease he pulled her up behind him, leaving her to dangle only a second, just as he heard Robert break through the door. While the fools rampaged into the shop, tearing it apart looking for Margaret, he led her, clinging hard to his arm, across the roof to the flat warehouse roof next to it, then to the leads on the house beyond.

He hadn't slept last night because of her, hardly a wink. The sleeplessness was upon him as always, along with the ravaging dark. He needed to be back in the Netherlands, where his enemy was. But he was required here. Conflicting needs tore at him, keeping him awake at night. Margaret must be no more than one of his many duties. He reminded himself sternly of that.

Robert's men hadn't thought of the rooftops. Not yet. Jonathan led Margaret with ease from one house to the next, down the row, then over to the street that ran on the opposite side.

Margaret had latched on to his arm with fingers like a vice. Within minutes he had her down to the ground, a mere street away from her dwelling place above the fishmonger's. He slipped them both into a dark, silent alley where they could talk.

"You didn't like our route of escape?" he began cordially. He still had one arm around her shoulders. Now he drew her close. "Are you afraid of heights?"

"I came this close to being caught back there, that's what I'm afraid of." She held up a thumb and first finger to show him a tiny gap. Her hand shook.

His heart went out to her. She had been frightened, and he felt a mad urge to clasp her hand and kiss it, to clasp all of her against him and protect her with his strength. "I wouldn't have let him," he said softly, cradling her fragile form against him. "But listen to me. Did my earlier words make sense? Will you stop trying to do the impossible, stop trying to be all things to yourself and others. Let someone else have a part."

"But I want to stand on my own two feet."

"You are standing on them."

"No, I'm not. You're holding me up," she accused. "If you let go, I would fall down."

It appeared true. He could feel the trembling of her ripe body, so close, so torturously close, asking him to taste.

"This is an extreme moment," he said as evenly as possible. Lord, he appeared to be hardening. "Ordinarily, when you're doing the things you're good at, you stand very well on your own two feet. Go upstairs and stay inside. Robert won't find you. At least not tonight. If you don't come out, he may not find you at all for a few days. Ah, and your grandsire has not only arrived and opened his house in the Strand, but he has a large party of men searching for you."

"I must go in," she moaned. "He must not find me. Pray give me my things."

He had to let her go to take off his pack. He did so with great reluctance. When he produced her bundle, she clasped it to her middle. "I will make the pillow tonight, but your lace piece will take a while. I hope you can wait."

"Of course I can wait. In the meantime, you can do the other thing you agreed to. Tell me the truth."

"I have tried. What do you want to know now?"

He hadn't meant to ask her anything, not just now. But since she asked, a wild desire leaped within him. "I would like to watch while you make lace."

You would have thought he asked for something indecent. Her face, her eyes, turned stricken. To her, lace making must be intensely private. It plunged him into deeper despair. Because he had a mad, desperate need to be close to her. Watching her work her bobbins might appease this tearing hunger inside him. Mayhap. Unless it made her feel something more for him than he was able to return. Right now he was as capable of feeling love as a broken door—half unhinged by his constant thoughts of death—someone else's. Eventually his own.

"What is the matter with you?"

Her question took him by surprise. As did the new anguish in her voice.

"What did they do to you in that place? I would kill them if they—"

Her fierce vow sent cold fear to his heart. "Don't ever talk of killing so easily," he interrupted. God help him, he had to keep her pure.

"But why, if they disrespect the lives around them? They don't deserve to—"

"No!" his fierce whisper silenced her. "That's the danger. Once you think you have the right to make the decisions about who *deserves* to live and die . . . it's bad enough to commit the act itself, but to judge who deserves it." He groaned with torment. "That's what they . . . what *he* did to me. Made me decide I had the right to judge. And I do judge him. He deserves to die."

"Is he here in England?"

The intense, direct nature of her questions surprised him. "He's in the Netherlands."

"Then you'll have to go back, won't you?" Her voice was bleak, her face distressed. But she did something most people didn't—she saw what he needed and told him to go. Her strength, the way she faced the ugly truth, hammered at him like one of his heavy sledges. He couldn't give her feeling when he was full of this all-encompassing hate. But she had feelings in plenty for him—soft, tender feelings. He knew she poised on the verge of giving them to him, like a gift he so miserably failed to deserve.

"On your way," he forced himself to say briskly, guiding her toward the opening of the alley. "Your friends will be worried about you."

Margaret let Jonathan hustle her out of the alley and to the stairs that led to their dwelling above the fishseller's shop. Her body felt numb and her mind hazy. She could hardly move or speak.

She parted from him with great reluctance. With all her heart she longed to help him, as he had just helped her. Several steps up, she turned to regard him. His face was hidden in shadow, his spare, muscular body guarded her entryway, keeping her safe. Might she accept his strength without losing her integrity? The things he said made sense.

She descended two steps so she was exactly his height. The afternoon was waning, and the western sun touched his hair with gold. Despite the burnish to his beauty, that mad, haunted look in his eyes turned his face cold and grim. Quickly she leaned forward and brushed her lips against his cheek. "Thank you, friend," she whispered. "I honestly thank you for what you did."

His face changed. She couldn't help it if this was the first time she really meant it. But he had done what he was good at, rescuing. And she had let him do it.

"Come on the morrow if you like," she told him. "Watch me make lace and welcome. That's what *I* do well."

With that, she turned and hurried up the steps.

Chapter 33

The candles burned down to stumps at Whitehall Palace, and still Elizabeth Tudor paced the floor of her private cabinet, where she conducted her government business. Though ten of the clock had struck, she swished up and down the chamber, hands clasped behind her, waiting. A tap sounded on the door.

"Enter," she barked. "Ah, Sir Spirit." She welcomed William Cecil, chief minister of the royal privy council, using her favorite nickname for him. "I have rich news for you that could not wait for the morrow. I intend to take a new lady-in-waiting. You shall see her by week's end."

"A replacement for Lady St. John?" Baron Burghley entered with the heavy tread of his aging frame. "How did you find someone on such short notice? You have been busy without telling me." He wagged his finger at her in friendly fashion, then seated himself on the chair she indicated while she took the opposite place. He tugged at his gray beard.

Elizabeth bestowed a brief smile on her old advisor. She had made a baron of this commoner for his faithful service throughout her persecution and imprisonment under Queen Mary. It chagrined many of her nobles that he was only the son of a yeoman farmer, but she rewarded loyalty, not birth. "I would not trouble you with such trivialities as household vacancies when I need you for more important matters, but you'll never guess. We have a chance I've wanted for years."

She clasped her hands with pleasure, and it was Burghley's turn to smile on her. "What is that, Your Grace?"

"I'm taking on the Dowager Viscountess of Longleate, who was recently left a widow. And you know her grandsire, the Earl of Clifton? He has no male heir. Burghley, we shall decide her next marriage!" She rose to her feet, all but crowing with triumph. "Think what this means. I'll make her son the next earl, and *I* shall control her husband, along with all those vast Clifford holdings. Here is the key to the northern families handed to us with nary a struggle. Do you know how long I've wanted this?" She pulled a face, remembering the Duke of Norfolk, whom she had had to behead in '72 for leading a northern uprising. "The old earl meant to wed her to Solsover," she muttered angrily. "I would never have approved it, but then Clifton would have done it in secret, telling me after he had a grandson. God's blood, it makes me angry, his sneaking around behind my back when I'm engaged with weightier matters. Clifton served me well in his younger years, but he'd best have a care."

Burghley sat forward. "An excellent opportunity, indeed, Majesty, but where is the dowager? Surely she didn't come to London on her own?"

"She ran away from her grandsire, and he's come after her. He visited yesterday, demanding I turn her over when she arrived. Bah!" The queen snorted in a most unladylike manner. "Why should I do that? So he can wed her to Solsover? That nephew of mine is a rutting goat. Can't keep his hands off my maids-of-honor, particularly Jane Shelton. I've never trusted him. Now let me see." She settled back in her chair and propped her finger against her chin.

"But how is the dowager keeping herself without her grandsire?" Burghley asked practically.

"She's somewhere about London." The queen gestured vaguely. "Come, Burghley, help me decide the proper match for our little widow."

"Somewhere about London?" Burghley's bushy brows shot up in astonishment. "What if the earl finds her before we've made the match? I'd better call the guards." He half rose from his seat.

The queen motioned him down again. "She's safe enough. Clever wench, or so I perceived her. She'll outwit him for a time, but mark my word, she'll be here within a seinn'ght, ready to take the post. Now then, we want someone impeccably loyal to us, naturally. Someone strong enough to serve as guardian of the borders, but not a spendthrift. Let me think, Burghley." She drummed her long fingers on the wooden arm of her carved chair. "Lord, I promised her three choices. I must have been mad."

"Sir Anthony Clives?" Burghley suggested.

"Excellent! I'll put him on the list. Who else? Sir Christian Grieves," Elizabeth said. "What of him?"

"Too old, Your Grace." Burghley searched for a more comfortable position on his chair.

"What difference does his age make?" Elizabeth stated. "He's loyal. He goes on the list. Who else?" Elizabeth frowned. "We need a third choice."

A tap sounded at the door.

"Enter," the queen called. "Who would come at this time of night, I can't imagine . . . why, Captain Cavandish." She looked up in surprise as Jonathan entered, a lady in waiting hovering behind him. "What is it, Captain, is something wrong?"

"Your Grace, just checking on your safety. I've been about the city tonight and feel increasing concern for you. If you agree, I or one of my men will stay near you by night. Somewhere near your chamber. Would your antechamber do?"

Elizabeth examined him and gave a slow nod of acquiescence. Turning to Burghley, she smiled at him sagely. And Burghley seemed to understand.

Chapter 34

Raw scrape of chains crossed stone. Damp and decay invaded the air. Deep in sleep, Jonathan groaned, turned on his hard bed, pleading for the dream to leave him ... to no avail.

Bare stone floor, bare stone walls. Bracken water and moldy bread. Heaven compared to what awaited him. That first time in the inquisitor's chamber, arms and hands shackled, his mighty strength leashed. Hero? What was a hero? He had been helpless, bound to a wall while the master loosed his diabolic mirth.

"You will answer my questions, Captain." The cultured whisper settled over him, its prophesy ugly as a curse. The bite of dread raced through his vitals as his shirt was stripped away to bare his back.

Next to his ear, the whip's hiss stung the air. He gasped as the lash plowed its first agonizing furrow into his flesh.

The inquisitor stepped near to admire his handiwork, tracing a finger across Jonathan's shoulder. "A clean cut of the muscle. Where shall I place the next one, eh?" Devil eyes of onyx blazed behind that black mask. The taunting voice provoked him, full of triumph. "What a pleasure to destroy that proud, masculine back."

"God!" With a shout, Jonathan sat bolt upright, sweating, gripping the bed. He found himself in the queen's antechamber, the silence heavy around him, the eyes of the tapestries watching. Rising from his pallet, he moved to the window, breathing furiously. Never should he have permitted himself to sleep.

The glow of Margaret's golden eyes came back to him, the brush of her kiss against his cheek—both as new and glorious as the touch of her silken lace. Today he had shaved away his beard and mustache so that next time, if there was a next time, he might feel the glide of her precious lips along the full length of his face.

At least Margaret had remained inside for three days running, and Robert had failed to find her. He had had Cornelius check for the easiest entry besides the door, then had sent the women fresh fruit and vegetables. The dark-haired maid, Marie, could nip down to the fishseller's for water without being detected. They might remain hidden for a while more.

How long would that last? He couldn't say, but when his relief man came, he was going to see her, as he had for two nights running. She hadn't seen him though. He had watched her through the window. But tonight she would. He had a compelling, pressing need to sit at her side while she worked her lace.

Three whole days confined to these rooms! Margaret sat near the open window, longing for escape. Patience, Marie, and Bertrande were all abed some time ago. By the light of her candle stool's reflection, she worked her bobbins, approaching the end of the lace for the Spider Queen.

The night hung so heavy and humid, it was a blessing when a breeze sprang up. Margaret put aside her pillow and went to lean against the sill.

She felt alone and lonely tonight, immured in a vast lake of night, with her candle the only isolated point of light. In a city of thousands of souls, she brimmed with sorrow. Her head listed against the window frame, and she watched smoke blow from chimney pots on row after row of roofs.

A distant rumble of thunder startled her. Turning, she stared at the moon, which was hugged by clouds tonight. Wind gusted. Her candle winked out. Alone in the dark, her soul reached, looking for something. Longing filled her, its intensity unbearable. Desperately she yearned for someone to hold her . . . her beloved father. Like the day as a child when she had fallen from the apple tree and knocked herself senseless. She had awakened to his touch, a cool cloth on her forehead, the safety she knew as he gathered her into his strong, loving arms. With a silent sob, she buried her face in her hands.

She had let Jonathan help her yesterday, and it hadn't hurt one bit. Or had it? Tonight she felt the old, dangerous longing for him. Lord, she didn't know. Why shouldn't she feel it?

Because, a voice answered, he would do exactly what Oliver and her grandsire had done—put her under his thumb and make her obey his dictates. And she hated dictates. No, she could accept his strength only if he saw hers first.

But tonight, loneliness gnawed at her. Behind her, the fire had fallen to embers in a bed of gray ash. More fuel would revive it. Turning, she felt her way to the hearthside, fed in scraps of wood, one by one, blowing gently, coaxing the thin flame. The damp log she put on next quelled it. In a hurry, she raked it away and rebuilt the smoldering embers. Trails of smoke curled in the air like ghosts.

When a tiny fire was once more burning, she reached for her lace pillow and worked open a bottom seam to withdraw a letter. Her fingers traced Her Majesty's royal seal, then she reopened the letter she had received that morning and once more studied the list of three names.

The moaning wind called her back to the window. With a moan of her own, she thrust the letter away and went. Away to the south, lightning drew forked flashes in the darkened sky. An excitement gripped her, potent and powerful, brought on the wings of the storm. Though she could see nothing, someone joined her just beyond the window ledge. His gaze teased her in the dark.

Anticipation flashed through her. Margaret's hands fisted at her sides, straining to see in the cavernous dark.

Wind rattled down the chimney, filling the room with smoke. It billowed from the fire, stinging her eyes. She rubbed them as thunder crackled and the storm drew closer. Nothing stirred. Inky night wrapped its arms around her. She clasped her hands together, waiting and hoping. She needed Jonathan so much, tension mounted, tightening all her muscles to the point of pain. His name formed on her lips, fighting for release.

Chapter 35

The Magician emerged from behind a distant chimney, rising like a wraith from the smoke. Margaret swallowed her cry just in time. Black against magical black in his midnight cloak, he blended so well her eyes surely deceived her. She blinked hard and looked again.

As he advanced, she recognized that powerful stance, the proud carriage of his head—unmistakable. Wind ruffled his cloak, making him ethereal. He seemed to float to her across the roof leads, borne on the broad back of the dark.

Wordless, she accepted him, needing his presence.

"I've come," he whispered, "to watch you make lace."

No greeting. A statement like an order. Without removing his cloak, he stripped off his black gloves, pushed back his hood, and sat on a stool. Motioning, he indicated she should take up her pillow once more.

"My candle is out." Margaret's voice sounded small to her in the huge, hungry night.

"Do you need it to work?"

"No. But you need it to see."

He found the flint and steel for her and struck a spark. If only he knew he struck fire in her heart as well. But he wanted to watch her lace making. If ever the torment lay upon him, it was tonight. His face had that taut, steely look to it, his mouth grim, his eyes stark, as if he were only half there. Feeling intensely self-conscious, Margaret took up her bobbins to begin.

Twist, cross, place a pin. Pattern of beauty, pattern of grace. Within minutes, she had caught the rhythm. Mayhap she could work with him watching. The patterns flowed swiftly through her mind, making order of chaos, the twining threads following their given paths.

Midway through a sequence, he spoke over her shoulder, startling her so that she dropped a bobbin.

"You stopped here last night." He pointed to an earlier spot in the finished trim. "You did all that work since?"

Margaret nodded, pleased that he had noticed. "How did you know?"

"I watched you last night. And the night before."

She felt as embarrassed as if he had watched her undress. "Why didn't you come in?"

He abruptly changed the subject. "What is this stuff on your pins?"

"Bits of candle wax," she answered, obedient to his mood. "I use a pin with wax to mark places in the pattern. In this one, it tells me where I used a triple twist."

"Ah." He leaned over her work, studying it minutely, then strode back to his stool. Brushing aside his cloak, he reseated himself. "Continue," he commanded, as if she were a driver of oxen or horses.

She took up her bobbins, trying not to mind his scrutiny, but after a minute, she stole another glance at him. He didn't look any better. How deeply his hate must be lodged.

Leaving her pillow, she hurried to his side and fell to her knees. She gripped his hands, his dear hands that had once been young and smooth. She ran her fingers over the right one, feeling the thickened calluses on his palms. The nail of his third finger had been broken into the quick. "My lace isn't helping, is it?" she asked, her voice shriveled to a whisper. She pressed his poor finger to her lips, unsure what else to do.

His face twisted in a sardonic smile. "Don't be a fool, thinking to help the likes of me. I'll destroy you." He shook off her hands and stood up.

Margaret surged to her feet, darted around, and planted herself before him. So what if he towered over her, looking like an avenging warlord girded for battle, sent to strike down enemies of the light. "I'm not a fool, and you're not worthless, as you imply. So don't you dare storm out of here, thinking to go to the devil or wherever it is you go when the fit's on you." Stridently she demanded his attention. "You're going to find your own healing. I demand you find it and let me help." She had no idea what she was saying. The words flew from her mouth of their own volition.

He returned her gaze, his eyes filled with that dark power. "You're better off without me. Remember that when next we meet." He moved for the window as if to leave.

"Wait!" She seized his arm and pulled him around again to search his face with anxious eyes. "You have to oust these thoughts that plague you. You can't just hope they will go away. Think hard—something must help."

His face was beautiful by the candlelight, perfectly sculpted. Once his eyes had lit from within, showing his humor and love for life. Now what a tragedy to see the change. If he wasn't the devil, he was the devil's nemesis, a warring angel brought to scour evil from the earth.

"One thing does help, but you can't let me have it." His husky voice deepened, beguiling her just as in their youth. His magical hands, stripped of their gloves, reached for her, their touch alive and warm. "Because if you dare, all I will do is this."

His mouth descended. Instinctively Margaret tipped up her face, eager to meet his kiss. Thunder boomed beyond the window, shaking the floor beneath their feet. Lightning crackled, and Jonathan's touch sent sparks racing through her body. Trepidation shook her. "What do you mean, all you will do?" she whispered. "I *want* your kisses."

"But they lead nowhere." His voice thickened with denial. "Not to the bliss of wedded life nor the joy of children to be raised in a loving home. I'll take everything you have to offer, if you let me, and give you nothing in return. Because I have nothing ahead of me but destruction." He snarled the last words. "That is my trade."

"It's not!" She caught his hand and carried it to her cheek. Suddenly she saw everything that had happened to him. The clever, sensitive boy, plunged into war. He had to justify what he did, maiming and killing to help the helpless. He had to judge his enemies, but as he did it, he judged himself. "Your trade is not destruction. You're an armorer. You also create."

"Armor is just another implement of war."

"An implement of life. Your work helps people live." She lowered his hand, an inspiration coming to her. "You have a workshop. I know because I saw it. Do you make armor there? Take me to it now."

He sent her a skeptical glance. "You saw it? When?"

"The guild master told me its location, and I went by yesterday but you weren't there. Never mind." She pulled him toward the door. "Let us go. I'll show you what I mean."

"Not that way." He resisted, looking toward the window. "We must go the way I came."

Margaret's heart thudded in sudden fear. There was at least a four-foot span between their window and the flat warehouse roof lead next door. Probably more. "I can't go that way." She had held him fast by the hand. Now he reversed the hold, closing his fingers around her wrist, though she strained to get away.

"Now who won't be helped, Marguerite." He grinned down at her. "One more kiss for courage, I think." He pulled her to him and enfolded her in his embrace. His mouth came down on hers, rich and sensual, startling awake the surge of blood in her veins. Her heart thudded harder than ever.

He broke off the kiss. "Do you feel braver?"

"I feel frightened to death."

"I can imagine the thought that frightened you. Don't worry." He smoothed her cheek with the curve of his palm and gave her a smoldering gaze. "The thing you were afraid of won't happen tonight. I'm in control now."

"You always think you're in control, but you're wrong." She hauled back hard as he drew her toward the window. "I refuse to go that way."

"I won't let you fall." With a chuckle he picked her up bodily and placed her by the casement. Standing behind her, he leaned over to nuzzle her ear. His lips nibbled their way down her neck. "Sweet little daisy, always resisting me. I meant in control of myself, not of you."

Beyond the window, lightning sizzled, blistering the sky. Thunder rent the night with another mighty crack. A series of storms was brewing, but she had Jonathan to protect her. She sighed and let herself lean against his massive chest.

Lord help her, he was wrong about control, she thought, fingering his doublet ties, smoothing her hand across his cheek. He had shaved away his beard and mustache, and he looked more than ever like the old Jonathan, her first love, her only love. At the slightest word, she would have given herself to him with all her heart, let him take control, but for some reason he didn't even try. He seemed eager to leave for his workshop.

"Come, Margaret." With smooth motions he stepped onto the window ledge, as easily as if it were a stair step. "Let us venture out."

The gap between the neighboring roof leads and her own window loomed wide, growing wider as she stared at it. Below was nothing but a black hole, lost in shadow. Jonathan leaped across without a qualm.

"Don't look down," he cautioned her. "Stand on the sill, gather your skirts, and jump."

Margaret tilted her face skyward and squeezed her eyes shut. "I can't."

He snorted with exasperation and crossed back. "Here, we'll practice." Back inside, he showed her the movement, how to spring forward. "Now, we'll go together."

Back at the dizzying height, he clasped her firmly at his side, linking her arm around his waist. Margaret's heart thumped in her chest, so hard that she, who never fainted, felt her head spin. She clung to him tightly as they leaped.

The abrupt thud of flat lead roof beneath her feet startled her eyes open. She had made it, praise God!

"This time let me teach you," he ordered, keeping his hold on her. "Move slowly and match your steps with mine."

She felt like a dancer engaged in a dangerous, fascinating dance. She moved and paused with her partner, placing her feet with care. He guided her around loose shingles and past chimneys, from a balcony, to a flat roof, to a pitched roof, and on. Silent as mist, merged as if one, they crossed the night-ridden city until he brought her safely back to the ground.

The freshening swell of storm wind streamed through her hair, feeling marvelous. The wide sky stretched above her head. Margaret's entire being celebrated! Three days cooped up in two rooms had her close to raving. When they came to his workshop, she almost didn't want to go in.

But it was her idea, so she descended the stone stairs. Margaret had expected a damp, subterranean cavern. Instead, the room was dry and smelled faintly of sweet woods. A row of windows stretched from the ceiling halfway down the wall on one side—the building must be on a hill. During the day, the windows would bathe the depths with light.

Jonathan kindled the forge fire, crumbling a handful of something on the flame. The room bloomed with exotic scents—cinnamon and sandalwood—while she inspected his domain.

An astonishing array of tools marched in perfect order across the workbench, their pattern speaking quantities about their owner: truth and strength coupled. She applied the words, knowing they were eminently suited. The things spoken to her by the Magician always carried a special ring of truth to them. Truths that changed her view of them together—she was learning to think of him foremost as her friend.

Her gaze lit upon a row of hammers, each one a different size and weight. She touched them as she moved down the workbench, examining each item in line.

When she came to the end of the bench, a strange monster of a machine stood there. Margaret reached for the handle and gave it a turn as she tried to guess what it was for. A mysterious, intricately made thing, it was as puzzling as the man who owned it. She stole a glance at him, where he bent over his anvil. The aura of mystery clung to him, making him as exotic and otherworldly as the rare woods he heaped on the flame. How she longed to penetrate his secret fire, to lay herself like a sacrifice on the burning pyre of his heart. He posed an extreme challenge, yet she wanted to meet it, to unlock his pain and free it to the wind.

He stood over a piece of metal balanced on a helmet stake. Like the magical god of the forge, his fingers and tool changing the curve of the steel. But she saw the eagerness had left him. His eyes lacked the heat of concentration.

"What are you working on?"

He started, as if surprised to remember her presence. "A morion, nothing more."

"It is something more." She strolled over, ran her fingers over the metal helmet. "Amazing, how a seemingly inflexible material as metal can be molded and shaped to our requirements. Yet *we* remain immobile, refusing to be shaped or changed to our good." She shot him a significant glance.

"Speak for yourself."

She wrinkled her nose at him. "You don't care about it,

do you." She indicated the helm, her flat statement confronting him.

He glared at her. "I care more about returning to the Netherlands."

"You expect to be in control of everything around you," she continued. "What happened when you lost control?" She referred to his time in prison, though she ran a risk in reminding him.

Sure enough, his face hardened into a mask of hate. "I was at his mercy."

She writhed at his pain but refused to back down. "So was I in my marriage! But I decided what I thought. I know it's not the same—you were in terrible . . ." She couldn't bring herself to speak of his physical torment. "I'm not saying you could change your thoughts then. No one could. But you're free now! Free of him and what he did."

"I'll never be free, even if I kill him."

"You're mad to think that way."

"That's what I've been trying to tell you." His voice diminished, threatening to flicker out like a dying flame.

"No!" Margaret cried. "I won't let you feel this way." She sounded petulant and childish even to her own ears, but she was beyond caring. She refused to let him give up.

She paced the room, studying his work as she went. "What's this?" She stopped before the odd machine.

"A wire drawer. It draws steel out into thin rods of varying thickness." He indicated several heavy pieces of wire.

Margaret nodded and continued on. Halting before a strange metal construction, she pointed. "This looks like a woman's corset."

"It is." He loomed at her side, his physical presence warm and tempting despite the cold despair inside him. "But it's meant for the queen's protection, not to change her physical shape. I have yet to perfect its construction. At first I tried making it all of plate; it was too hot and heavy. But Her Majesty is forever going among people with only a few guards. Even if she had an entire army, she couldn't avoid a dagger thrust from close proximity. With the state of international affairs, the likelihood of someone trying to take her life is growing. It drives me insane."

Margaret was only half listening. She studied his worktable, then suddenly crossed the room. "Can you make these rings smaller? About this big?" She showed him a size by curling her thumb and first finger.

"For certes, though it takes more time."

"If you make a very fine mesh of this same strength steel, couldn't you line the frame with that?"

He studied the pattern, then the frame. "That's it!" He crossed the room to his worktable. "A fine mesh of this size . . . no, this." He chose one of several dowels and wrapped a piece of thick metal wire around it. "I'll measure and cut the rings. You can flatten the ends for the rivets." He whipped out the hammer from his belt and showed her how to use it, then they both fell to work. Margaret concentrated on keeping pace with his furious tempo, but she smiled to herself as she did it. Her idea had captured his interest. She prayed it might somehow help.

When they had enough rings, Jonathan fit them together in the customary interlocking pattern. He had just fastened the first one when Margaret stopped him.

"Wait, I have an idea. That pattern is pretty but too open. Try this." She showed him another way of interlocking the rings that doubled them.

He tried it out, rejoining the rings in the new pattern. "Brilliant! How did you think of that?"

His smile blinded her with its splendor. "It's something we do in lace to give a different effect, double or even triple the twists," she said, making light of her idea. "It also doubles the strength." To her vast surprise, he leaned across the table and delivered a swift kiss to her cheek. His grin was endearing. She wanted to clasp him to her heart.

"Let's see how it looks made up." He bent over the work, swiftly joining rings.

Margaret touched her cheek, then looked at her hand, awestruck. A kiss from a man meant in friendship, not just passion—Oliver had never given her such a thing. "I'm brilliant?" she asked hesitantly, afraid he might change his mind.

He rolled his eyes to the ceiling. "I'll probably regret having said so. You'll get a puffed head. But yes, you are brilliant. In ways I never understood as a lad."

He thought she was brilliant! Margaret folded her lips tightly to hide her smile of pleasure and the warm glow of satisfaction that filled her being. At his side, she attacked the rings with her hammer, eager to do her share of the work.

Chapter 36

For the next few hours they labored in harmony while rain beat on the windows. Jonathan wrapped and cut rings, Margaret flattened the ends for the rivet, then bored the rivet holes and wove them into their chain. Jonathan drove the rivets and burred them over, sealing them permanently. When they had about a hundred sets of double rings joined, Jonathan threw aside his hammer. He held up the sheet of chain mail. The interlaced rings rippled and draped with fluidity. "Excellent," he exclaimed, "but 'tis enough for to-night. We need fresh air."

He didn't wait for agreement. Closing the forge's damper, he drew her out of the workshop. As they as-cended the steps, cool, wet wind greeted them. Triumph filled Margaret. She had brought some relief to Jonathan's obsessed mind.

But as she followed him along the cobbles, watching signs swinging on their poles above shop and tavern doors, she recognized a change in herself as well. She was no longer the young Margaret, nor was she Oliver's wife. She was marvelously, miraculously, in control of her life, and the thought, coupled with the pressure of Jonathan's hand wrapped around hers, sent thrills up and down her spine and spiraling through her middle, as swift as the scudding clouds fleeing overhead. She had acknowledged his strength, and he, amazingly enough, had acknowledged hers. Life seemed rich and full of wonder tonight.

Thunder rumbled in the distance. "It's going to storm again." Margaret fairly danced behind Jonathan as he guided her through the dark, his walk confident and full of mastery. When he brought her to an open area studded with trees, she stared around in awe at its wind-lashed beauty. "What is this place?"

"A wild place for this wild night."

She gazed into his eyes and felt passion crackle between them. Dropping his hand, she gathered up her kirtle skirt and ran through the thick, wet grass. The park sat some distance from the river, but a stream must have flowed nearby because she could hear rushing water, along with the rushing of her breath. A deep stand of majestic, old trees lay before them, beckoning. Their wisdom spoke to her, and she spread her arms wide and whirled about in the wide space, yearning for their knowledge of the years so she could do even more for Jonathan. Stopping, tipping her face to the storm-tossed sky, she let the wind billow her hair and skirts. Clouds raced above them, dark shapes against the sky. Jonathan came toward her, his hair and cloak likewise whipped by the wind, his face full of desire. Slipping up to him, she wove her arms around him. Never had she felt so free with a man.

As if he were indeed lord of lightning summoning the elements, the storm broke around them. Rain pelted down, thrown from on high. Thunder crashed, its voice immense splinters of sound. A stab of silver fire lit up the heavens, transforming the park into a dazzling dreamscape.

When Jonathan opened his voluminous cloak and engulfed her, entwining her body with his, their sudden closeness needled her with excitement. While wind surged around them, gaining momentum, his fingertips tipped her chin until she met his eyes.

Rain beaded in cold droplets on her cheeks, and he smoothed them away with gentle, roughened fingers. "What does this remind you of?" came his voice, husky with longing. The tip of his finger tugged against the sensitive flesh of her lip.

Memory! Suddenly she was intimate with it. It sprang from him like lightning, from both of their pasts—memory of autumn in West Lulworth, when the last sweltering air settled on the land like a robe. Ever since that night when her father had died, the strength of her wanting had haunted her, tracking her through her days like that diabolic heat. Now he brought the same slow heat with him, and she admitted she needed it in her life, needed him.

Just as he had that night, he bent over her, removed his finger, and replaced it with his lips.

Lightning snaked across the sky, striking the peak of a tree, breaking it into sparkling flecks of wood. The hunger of his lips demanded, filling her with ecstasy so intense that her blood ran sparkling in her veins. The air sizzled with the strong odor of burning. Something equally potent burned in the Magician's eyes. His soul's dark fire. His gaze demanded, full of hunger, drawing her into his dangerous life and his dangerous need.

"Jonathan," she moaned softly. "The things I said I felt for you back in Lulworth . . . I might have deceived you about who I was, but my feelings were real. I didn't deceive you about that."

"No need to tell me," he interrupted, his voice a whisper of anguish. "It was a long time ago and no longer important. Let me take you home now. I should never let you keep company with me." But he made no move to go. The touch of his hands on her face was rough and tender.

She closed her eyes to savor his caresses—his finger tangling in her hair, the imprint of his hands on her cheeks and neck. "Jonathan, take what I offer and be glad of it. My father took what I offered and gave me great wealth in return."

Jonathan looked down on Margaret's lovely, innocent face turned up to him like a flower to drink in the rain. How he craved the rare gleam that burned inside her. Tonight she had sent the dark flood receding. The midnight of his soul grew light. If only he could stay this way. The fragile inroad she made had become a pyre of passion. He blazed with her blessed light. Need raged through him—a painful, starving need. It honed his senses. Heightened sight took in the way delicate drops of moisture beaded on her perfect cheeks and glistened in her hair. Heightened hearing caught her quick intake of air, her gentle exhale as soft as a sphere of down on the breath of the gods. He could smell the sweet scent of her flesh and hair, so like flowers that they became one. Her shining eyes he treasured most of all as he cupped her face with both hands. He saw love glowing there, and it aroused his body, made him harden with wanting. He wanted to hold her naked in his arms and quench his thirst on her beauty. If she were so foolish as to let him, he would take and take and take . . .

He was dangerous to her—he would ruin her slight chance at happiness by tying her to half a man. She had reawakened something within him tonight, but he wasn't whole yet. And he must stop their intimacy before control left him. He knew the surest way how. "You continually speak of your father, but he failed to give you the most important thing he should have offered. Listen to me for once," he chastened as he felt her shoulder and neck muscles tighten. "You bristle when anyone says the slightest thing against him, but I don't mean you should hate him. You must see his weakness and his—"

"Don't you dare speak ill of my father," she cried, seeming shocked at his words. "I won't permit it."

Just as he had predicted, she pulled away from the shelter of his cloak. Rain pelted her, wetting the tight cambric of her smock that stretched across her breasts, which heaved with her rising emotion. Her face had lost its earlier serene calm. The new look of hurt pained him, but he put up his barriers and plowed on.

"You didn't let me finish. His love for you was unflagging, but he had a weakness. Everyone has them. He wasn't a god."

"No!" she cried, clapping hands to her ears, the joy gone out of her. "I won't listen to you. You didn't like him, that's all."

He followed her relentlessly, closing in with the truth. "I don't like what he did, letting you struggle alone for the family's money. That was his weakness. He let you do his work."

Another bolt of lightning shot the sky. Thunder spoke.

"How can you say that about my father," she demanded, on the verge of tears. The rain was soaking her hair so that it hung in wet strands and her smock had turned transparent, clinging to her skin. "After what I did tonight. I helped you."

"You did, but you also hurt me. I accept that as necessary, but you have no idea how it felt." He clenched his teeth, suddenly overcome by a blinding jolt of his own pain. She had opened him up to feeling, and that meant torment. She looked more beautiful than ever, with her clothing clinging to her body. His wanting for her redoubled, but it had to be denied.

Tears ran down her face, mingling with the rain. "I could

never hate my father," she insisted, stubborn to the end. "He did nothing wrong."

Jonathan raised his cloak, wanting to shelter her once more, but she shook her head. "He did his best," he assured her, "as we all do. Don't stop loving him, Margaret. But think what he made you inside."

That ended their intimacy. He had meant that it should. She let him take her home, even let him cover her with his cloak, but it wasn't the same.

"So you intend to return to the Netherlands?" she asked, greatly subdued as he helped her across the roofs.

"Not immediately, but I will confront the inquisitor eventually, and one of us will be destroyed."

He guessed she rebelled against the idea, but she didn't say so. Not this time. He delivered her safely back to her chamber, where she sat down despondently before the cold hearth, clearly hating the confinement.

He knelt, pressed her hand, caressed her beautiful, wet hair. "Stay inside. Stay safe." Then with one massive leap, he left.

After a scant hour of sleep, Margaret roused herself to finish her lace piece. As she reached the end of her pattern, prepared for the finishing stitch, she saw how one part of her life was like this lace piece, drawing to a close. The intense love she had once felt for her father paled ever so slightly. Jonathan had made her realize that she hung on to a dream. Now the queen's letter decreed that a new part of her life must begin. She wasn't sure she was ready, but if the pattern changed, so must she.

Just as the church bells rang out the noon hour, she completed the finishing stitches. She must meet Tim by one of the clock. Quickly she assembled things in a basket—bread, cheese, and some beautiful strawberries Jonathan's man had brought them yesterday. With that she was ready. Having wrapped the lace in a square of linen and added it to the basket, she climbed up on the windowsill.

"You're not going out the window!" Marie came out of the bedchamber, holding Patience by the hand. She regarded Margaret as if she had sprouted horns.

"Marguerite, what are you about?" Bertrande demanded, coming to the door behind Marie and Patience. "Tell me at once."

"I must deliver this lace to the customer or we can't buy food or candles or anything else," she told them firmly, smiling at Patience to reassure her. "And I can't leave by the main door. Robert's men will be watching. Be well, all of you. I won't be gone long."

The alley looked a devilishly long way down as she poised on the windowsill. Far different from the crossing last night. How she longed for Jonathan's arms to keep her safe. But he also made her admit things that hurt her inside. If her father had been weak, what had he made her, as a result? She wasn't sure. It was so confusing, after her success with Jonathan in his workshop, that she rushed the thoughts out of her mind. Strengthening her resolve, she gathered herself like he had taught her and made the leap across the gap.

Chapter 37

It was Friday, market day at Smithfield. When Margaret arrived at the flat plain outside the city, she searched the milling crowd for Tim. Silk-garbed gentlemen examined fine specimens of horses being trotted up and down to show their paces. Pens held cattle, swine, milch cows, and oxen. The dust raised from many hooves and feet assaulted her nostrils, while neighing, lowing, and the babble of voices assaulted her ears. Margaret hung at the edge, wondering how she would find Tim in this mob.

He found her minutes later. Margaret thought the urchin dirtier and even more ragged than last time. His hair stuck out from his head in dirty spikes. His jerkin sported a fresh tear across the front—no doubt from another chase by a fleeced purse owner. She gestured him over by the city wall near the ditch.

"Stop and eat first," she said, handing him bread and cheese from her basket.

Tim's eyes lit up at sight of the food.

"What happened to your linen?" Margaret asked as he crammed his mouth full.

"Sold it," he informed her. "Got two pence."

"But you've none yourself now," Margaret pointed out.

"Needed this more." Tim showed her a cheap dagger tucked in his belt.

Margaret sighed and brought out a handful of ripe strawberries.

Tim's eyes grew round with excitement. The berries disappeared, leaving their red imprint on his hands and lips. "Do you have the lace?" he asked.

"Of course. Have you the crown?"

"Not quite."

"I won't give the lace if I'm not paid," Margaret insisted, unwilling to be cheated. She had been afraid of this all along.

"You can come along, then," he said simply, licking the berry juice from his fingers. Without further explanation, he headed south.

"Come along where?" Margaret hurried after him.

"Buckhurst Court."

"Whatever for?"

"Customer lives there. You show 'er the lace. If she likes it, you get a crown. I take the rest to Mab. Fair 'nough?"

"I suppose so," Margaret conceded, though she wondered who lived at Buckhurst Court.

Buckhurst House was set on a courtyard off Fleet Street, near the river just before Temple Bar. They had passed St. Bride's church and were just setting to cross the courtyard to the great house when the rumble of wheels on cobbles sounded. A coach burst from the narrow lane and bore down on them. They scrambled out of its way, and it flashed past, drawing up in front of the house to discharge its passengers.

Seeing the profile of an occupant, Margaret's heart stopped. She grabbed Tim and pulled him into a lane leading off the court.

"What'r'yedoin'," he spluttered, clawing at her to let go.

"That man," she explained when she found her voice again, "is the one whose purse you cut."

Tim eyed the guests with interest as they entered the house. "Wouldn't mind fleecing 'im again. Must be rich, dining with the Spanish ambassador."

God's eyelid, the Spanish ambassador! What was Robert doing dining with England's enemy? "If that is the home of the Spanish ambassador," she told Tim, "I'm not going."

"Don't be a costard head," Tim scolded. "Old Mendoza won't see us. Nor his highty-tighty guests. We'll not even see 'is mistress, 'less we're lucky. Long as we get paid, 'oo cares?"

His mistress? Margaret groaned inwardly as she followed Tim. Apparently Mab provided pretty goods for Don Bernardino de Mendoza's doxy, and she, Margaret, was making the delivery. Heartily she wished herself someplace else.

They were expected, as evidenced by the fact that a maid showed them into a parlor at the back of the house. Margaret admired the windows, which were just like the ones in her grandsire's cabinet. The house must have been built by the same architect as the additions to Clifton Manor. She was just looking for the characteristic decorative cornices when she heard footsteps in the outer passage and tensed. Could it be Robert? Tim fingered the drapes and silk-covered walls, seeming unconcerned.

It was only the maid. Margaret breathed with relief as the girl took the lace, promising to return with payment if it was accepted. They waited for what seemed like eternity, during which Margaret watched a lone spider work in the window, weaving its web to catch its prey. It reminded her of Mab, spinning lace in the bowels of London. After today, she would work for Mab no more.

She had just smacked Tim's hand, making him put back a silver candlestick he was stuffing up his jerkin, when the door opened and a short, pleasant-faced woman entered. In her hand she held Margaret's lace.

"Madam de Mendoza." Suddenly on his best behavior, Tim bowed over her hand like a courtier, calling her after the ambassador's wife though she was none such. "May we hope you are pleased with our humble lace?"

"Humble?" The lady laughed and help up the lace. "This is no humble work. 'Tis far better than what you brought last time. Are you one of Mistress Mab's silkwomen, my dear?" She turned expectantly to Margaret.

"Madam, I did create that lace." Margaret gave the tiniest of curtsies. She disliked being called Mab's worker.

"You are to be congratulated on your skill," the woman went on, catching up a purse hanging from her girdle. She took out her money.

Tim positioned himself to take it, but as Margaret was the elder, the lady gave it to her.

"Are you having a revel today?" Tim asked cheekily, giving Margaret a look about the money.

"Goodness no, only a dinner." The lady smiled at them. "Today the ambassador entertains the new emissary sent by His Most Revered Majesty King Philip. He is an important person back in Spain, so we are honored. He carries special trade treaties to discuss with Her Majesty and her councilors. I trust all will go well." A shadow of a frown crossed her face, then vanished. "You will bring Mistress Mab to us three days hence at one of the clock, as agreed?

His honor says he has business with her, but I think he knows how well I like her lace. You may receive another commission," she informed Margaret, smiling fondly at the thought of the man who fed and clothed her.

"Mistress Mab will attend him as promised," Tim assured her.

"My thanks. The maid will show you out." With a parting smile, the woman left them alone.

Margaret commenced to count the money. One, two, three coins, four.

Tim nipped three of them from her palm.

"I should get at least half of it." Margaret gave him an accusing look.

"Can't be 'elped," Tim told her, rolling his eyes fatalistically. "Mab exacts her due. You want another order, don't you?"

"No, thank you. This one's my last, and should be for you, too. I think I might have wind of an apprenticeship for you. Or some work."

"Say the word and I'll give up the life of crime. But come 'ere first. I want to show you something. 'Ey, what do I call you?"

"Marguerite," she said, letting Tim drag her out the door into a courtyard.

"Just you wait, Marguerite," he whispered, crossing the yard where a pretty fountain played and opening the door to a chamber. Seeing no one, he pulled her inside. "Look."

It was a sumptuous room full of ponderous furniture and dark embroidered hangings. A small, furry form crouched by the window. Looking closer, Margaret saw it was a monkey. "Oh, the poor thing, it's chained."

"You can 'old it," Tim exclaimed, leading her across the room. "It's that friendly. See." He put out one hand and the monkey vaulted into his arms. "You remember me from the other times, do you?" he asked the animal, who stuck a curious paw in his pocket.

"He seems glad to see you," Margaret remarked. "What is he looking for?"

"Food, most like."

"Let me see if I've anything left." Margaret checked her basket and discovered a scrap of bread. As she held it out, the monkey leaped to her shoulder, chattering eagerly. "Isn't he sweet." She gave him the bread, which he took in his clever paws and devoured. His soft brown fur tickled her neck.

" 'Ere're some nuts, Marguerite. He likes them." Tim found a bowl nearby.

"You feed him." Margaret let the monkey go to Tim and turned to examine the chamber. It seemed remarkably similar to her grandsire's. Did it also have a spy hole? After a brief examination, she decided it didn't. No clever ornaments lined the wood paneling. "Really, Tim, we should leave."

"Whose portrait is that, Marguerite?" Tim pointed as he fed his furry friend.

"Some old lady, I suppose." Margaret hadn't noticed it, but now she inspected it more closely. Why would the ambassador hang an old lady's portrait on his wall? Unless it was a relative of his mistress, though if she were from modest family, portraits were unlikely possessions. It was too high to see clearly, so she lifted it down, searching for a name. Something on the paneled wall behind it caught her eye. The spy hole! The portrait probably belonged to a deceased owner and remained in place to conceal the hole.

The hole stood far too high on the wall for her to look through. She quickly retrieved the steps for the high bed and stood on them.

"What are you doin', Marguerite?" Tim left the nuts to the monkey and came over behind her.

"Shhh," she cautioned, putting her eye to the hole. A small banqueting parlor appeared, its table laden with platters of sweets. Around the table sat a party of men, among them Robert. Hastily she put her ear to the hole.

"You will do no such thing," came a firm male voice. The individual spoke in English with a decided Spanish accent. "That is my affair."

"But I want to do it," came a petulant answer. Robert's voice! Margaret knew it anywhere. "Why can I not?"

"We shall see, friend," the Spaniard answered smoothly. "We shall see. You do have ready access to court, I'll admit. Hmm. In the meantime, you must gather information for us. You can do that, yes?"

"For certes," Robert answered.

"Good. Now then, Don Bernardino, as to—"

"Let me listen," Tim jostled her elbow. "Who do you see?"

"Shhh," she hissed at him. "I'll miss what they're saying."

". . . should be no trouble at all once she obtains the ingredients," the conversation went on.

"You're sure she knows her business?"

"Have no fear on that score."

"My turn." Tim chose that moment to push Margaret off the step and leap up in her place.

"Tim!" she protested, "that was rude in the extreme. I need to hear—"

He waved her to silence, ear to the hole. "Hmm, just as I suspected." He stepped down from the height while she scowled at him. "No lace work for you, but you said you didn't want it. They're leaving, so we'll 'ear no more."

Margaret shuddered, suddenly aware of their terrible danger. She lifted the portrait and hung it back on the wall, then put the step back just as she had found it. "Let us go. We mustn't be caught."

They left by the back door, the way they had come. As they passed the lush garden, Margaret noticed two men from the dining chamber, who had evidently come out for some air. They stood beneath a cherry tree, talking. Both of them followed Margaret and Tim with their eyes.

"Mistress, you have dropped something." The taller of the men bounded after her, catching up the white linen she had used earlier to protect the lace.

He had clean-cut, aristocratic facial bones and a swarthy, foreign complexion. If you liked such looks, Margaret thought, he could be considered handsome, with a strong, muscled figure, a manicured black beard and mustache, and wavy ebony hair. He apparently noticed her inspection, because as he handed her the square, he captured her hand and pressed it between his own.

"I thank you, sir." Margaret pulled back, suddenly afraid of this stranger, but his grip tightened. His sensual aura was undeniable. His lips parted and she saw he breathed quickly, as if aroused.

"Such beauty could thank me in ways other than with words."

"You mistake me, sir." A streak of fear stabbed her. She reclaimed her hand and ran after Tim, wanting away from this villain. His laugh followed her, lingering in her ears along with his heavy Spanish accent. He left a firm impression of intense emotional power and something else—a disquieting intensity in his dark Spanish eyes.

"How do you know there'll be no lace request," she demanded of Tim when they had reached the safety of Fleet Street.

"That's easy," Tim told her nonchalantly. "Mab's going to make them a poison and deliver it exactly two weeks hence. Wonder 'oo they're planning to kill."

Chapter 38

The Spanish were planning to poison someone, and Margaret could just imagine who it was. After Tim agreed to mend the lace shop door for several pence, she set off for Jonathan's workshop as fast as she could go. Halfway there, disaster overtook her—in the form of Giles Hampstead, her grandsire's man.

Woe and betide, she should have known he would turn up. Margaret dodged up one street and down an alley, moving so fast she skidded on some old vegetable peels. It was no use. He trailed her with diligence. Heavens, might the game be up at last?

Searching the street, she got her bearings, then realized she was quite near the street of the goldsmiths. Vulcan's workshop lay just ahead.

As she rounded the corner, which took her out of Giles's sight, she pondered this new name for Jonathan. In truth, he resembled Vulcan, god of the forge, capable of molding hard steel. And what she feared was that he molded her as well.

Ah, but there was the workshop entrance! She bolted forward and in her joy to reach it, nearly fell down the steps. They were steeper than she remembered, and she landed hard at the bottom, half sitting on her basket. It stuck her in a particularly tender spot.

With a gasp Margaret pulled herself up, grabbed her basket, and staggered to the door. The handle yielded to her twist and she pulled it open, then slipped into the subterranean room.

Empty. Echoing. She knew no one was here before she entered, her mind taking it in, along with the sharp odor of coal and lingering exotic woods. She pulled the door to behind her and leaned against it, breathing raggedly.

She rubbed her poor buttock where the basket had poked her, but the pain was nothing compared to what she would feel if caught by Giles. Though he was a kind man, he had his orders. He would prowl up and down the street until he found her. Stealthily she edged herself deeper into the workshop. What a terrible turn of luck that Jonathan was not here.

As her eyes adjusted to the dim light, she could see the anvil rearing its sharply angled head, bald but solid like a cliff. The tools on the workbench marched in well-disciplined order, like Jonathan himself. Spotting the hammer she had used last night, she picked it up, thinking it might be useful. At the far end of the bench lay half-completed pieces of armor scattered like misshapen fish, their scales gone dull out of water. Margaret passed them by, feeling as out of her league as those fish would. Deeper she went into the workshop, swimming through patterns of light and shadow. Feeling her way with careful toes and fingers, she knelt in the shadows on the far side of the forge. Crouched in the ashes, she waited for Giles to be gone.

He was far too persistent. Footfalls sounded on the steps. The door opened.

She could feel him enter the subterranean room. Clenching her hammer, Margaret held down the scream winding up inside her, tightening to unbearable tension. A tremor ripped through her, and she swayed, overcome by nausea. She was hell-bound if he found her. Shutting her eyes, she prayed silently, calling on the god of the forge, the god of anything, if only the poor man would go back to her grandsire with a good excuse for failing to find her.

A head poked around the forge. Margaret screamed.

"What are you doing here?" Jonathan asked, looking perplexed.

"God's eyelid!" Margaret dropped the hammer and clutched her chest. Her heart pounded so hard she could feel it in her throat. "You've done it again."

"Frightened you?" He held out one hand to her. "With regret, lady. Of all the emotions I could inspire in you, that's not the one I would choose. I came to get some work done. I never expected you to be here."

Margaret took his offered hand and started to rise, but

shrank back suddenly. "Giles is out there looking for me." She huddled against the wall. "I'm trapped."

"So that's what all those men are doing in the street, going from door to door asking questions." Jonathan inclined his head. "Hmm, we'll have to quit this place. What are you doing with my hammer, by the by?"

"Oh, that." Margaret felt suddenly guilty. "I was going to hit you with it. I mean I thought you were Giles. I wasn't going to hit him hard." She twisted around searching for the hammer in the ashes but bumped her basket. "Oh dear, I've spilled my pins." With a huff that sent ashes flying, Margaret sifted through the gray matter, searching gingerly.

"Come, Marguerite, I want you in this concealing cloak." Jonathan sounded impatient as he rummaged in a far corner of the workshop.

"Brass pins can't be wasted," she insisted, groping for them in the semidark. "I think I've got the last of them. Ouch!" She hastily found the last pin, then the hammer, which she absentmindedly dropped into the basket. She stumbled out from behind the forge, sucking a pricked finger.

"Fussing over pins at a time like this." Jonathan draped the cloak around her. It had once been black but was now rusty with wear. He arranged the hood over her head, then handed her her basket. "Put this over your arm and pretend to be my granddam."

If it had been a happier moment, she would have burst into peals of laughter. As it was, she couldn't think of any way to imitate his grandmother. "Just how am I to do that?"

"Bend over and . . . lean on this." Jonathan handed her one of the dowels to use for a cane. "Limp when you walk."

Margaret hunched over the cane the way she had seen her grandsire do and hobbled several paces. "Will that suffice?"

"Perfect. Let us go. Remember, you're my aged granddam."

She rapped him across the calf with the cane. "If that's the case, you'd best obey me," she ordered sternly.

"Aye, Granddam," he said meekly, offering his arm.

"What of you," Margaret said anxiously as they mounted the steps. "They'll recognize you straight."

"I hope they won't see us long enough, but if you don't stop arguing and come along, they will."

His concern was a valid one, Margaret realized. They sped up the steps and started down the street. Margaret limped as fast as she could, dreading to hear the anticipated direction to halt.

"Ho, there, we've a question for you," shouted a man after them. "Pray you, master and mistress, hold for a moment 'til I catch up."

"That's it," Jonathan said resignedly to her. "Throw aside your cane. 'Tis time to move fast." Catching her arm, he broke into a run.

The alarm was raised. Shouts sounded after them as they flew down the street and rounded the corner. "Jonathan, I pray you, I cannot keep up," Margaret puffed, her side already hurting. They dodged around a cluster of people, who stared at them in surprise.

"This way." Deftly he turned aside and whipped into an alley. "Over this wall."

He boosted her up. The wall was high and she could scarcely reach the top, but somehow she managed. As she tettered on the stone ledge, Margaret saw a beautiful garden spread out before them.

"Whose garden is this?" she wondered aloud, awed by its beauty.

"How should I know? They're right behind us. Jump!"

He practically pushed her. She tumbled into the plot below and landed in some ripe cucumbers. "We've ruined them. What a terrible shame." To her amazement, a tear trickled down her cheek.

" 'Tis no time to cry over cucumbers," Jonathan scolded, thrusting her dropped basket back in her hand.

But as they ran on, she knew it wasn't the cucumbers she wept for. She had made a decision. One she had to act on now. Hidden in her purse, the queen's letter burned in her memory, along with the list of three men's names.

They left the garden by a gate and walked sedately on the street. At the sound of racing feet behind them, Margaret and Jonathan both whirled. She immediately recognized her grandsire's colors, the men's jerkins a deep blue banded with murrey, their master's shield embroidered on their sleeves. And horrors, something more. They had been joined by Robert's men. Several fellows in the viscount's tawny pounded after them.

They took to their heels. Several streets later, a church door loomed, attracting Margaret's attention. "In here," she cried, darting inside. London had churches on every corner. She didn't even know which one this was. Hustling to the altar, she plunked herself down on her knees and bent her heaving chest over folded hands.

"Pray," she ordered Jonathan. "Try to look devout."

"Have you gone mad?" Jonathan knelt beside her, clearly baffled by this newest strategy. "You can't claim church protection. Not these days."

"Just pray and look like you mean it," Margaret insisted tersely as the cleric in charge of the church emerged from a side door. Composing her face, she searched for her deepest calm and found it. The time had come to fulfill the queen's command and her own desires. Feeling in her purse for the letter she had folded and refolded many times over, she drew it out and clasped it tightly between her folded hands.

From his prayful attitude, Jonathan shot Margaret a glance laced with irritation. Once again she was being impractical, planning to fight physical power with will alone. What was he to do with her? Any minute now their pursuers would crash through the church door and force him to fight them. As the curate approached, he leaped to his feet, unable to stand it. If she would do nothing, he must. "Good sir, your keys, if you will."

The stocky little man reared back in surprise and stared at him. "Pardon, my son?"

"No time to explain. We're in desperate straits. The queen will reward you, if you cooperate." Jonathan nabbed the keys from the surprised man's waist and pelted for the door. Within seconds he had it locked and was checking the other entries to the sanctuary, locking them as well. And none too soon, either. The hue and cry rose outside.

"They came down this street, didn't they?" came a man's shout. Jonathan guessed it was Giles, the leader of the earl's men.

"Aye, I would swear it."

"Spread out and search the area. You in there," the voice continued. "Open the door. The Earl of Clifton's men wish entry."

The heat of the moment was excruciating to Jonathan. Battle lust roared in his veins, shouting at him to draw and fight. But not in a church. And not if Margaret didn't want it. Until now, he had controlled their flight, protecting her. Now he had ceded control to her. Up by the altar, Margaret and the curate had their heads together, whispering. She was showing him a paper. The clerk came hurrying down the nave as the shouts from beyond the door escalated.

"Don't touch that door," Jonathan advised as the sandy-haired fellow reached for the handle and found the door locked.

"Good sir, the house of the Lord is open to all," he said, his ruddy eyebrows raised, giving a frightened expression to his pale face. "What is this about?"

"I don't know, but I intend to find out," Jonathan stated tersely. "I'm as in the dark as you. The one thing I do know is the queen would be mightily displeased if the lady meets with these men." He jerked his head toward the door, which vibrated with their pursuers' kicks and knocks. "Hold them off, will you? Say that a private ceremony is taking place," he improvised. "I'm going to look for another way out."

"You might use the door off the choir room," the young man suggested, joining the intrigue with enthusiasm. " 'Tis seldom used and likely to be overlooked."

"My thanks." Jonathan nodded as he strode back up the aisle. He liked Margaret less docile, but this was going too far. When he next got her alone, he was going to talk some sense into her. If she didn't get caught by the earl and Robert first. But then that was his task, wasn't it—to make sure she didn't. And here she was up to something that might be useless in the face of her foes. In most circumstances, he took charge and made decisions, but he was trying to wait until she asked him, as she had firmly insisted. So what in heaven was he supposed to do now?

Chapter 39

"'Tis entirely legal," Jonathan heard Margaret say to the curate as he approached the pair. "I'm under orders from the queen. You can see the letter bears the royal seal."

"I see it, my lady, I see it. But now?"

"What is this letter?" Jonathan held out his hand and the curate gave it to him.

"Look quickly," Margaret urged. "We need to do something fast."

Jonathan squinted at the letter in the dim light. It was written to Margaret from Her Majesty. In the broad, bold hand of a court clerk, it stated the royal decree that she should wed with a man of the crown's choice.

Stunned, Jonathan stared at the paper, unable to read further. One thought dominated his mind, shooting him through with ugly stabs of jealousy. Margaret would once more belong to another man.

Suddenly her sweet presence was before him, her hand softly on his arm. "What is the meaning of this," he demanded, waving the paper in her face. "Do you intend to wed?"

"The letter lists three choices," came her decided answer. "I am indeed going to wed with one."

"Which one?" He glanced at the paper, hardly able to read it. "This Anthony fellow? Or this other, Sir Christian what's-his-name. I can't think he's fitting for you, a mere knight." His torment escalated, but she seemed impatient with it.

"No, I'm taking the last one on the list." She tapped the paper. "I'm choosing you."

Jonathan stared at her, dumbstruck. He looked back at the letter. Sure enough, when he finally focused his eyes, there was his name, the last of the three. For the first time in his life, he was speechless. He shook his head in disbelief.

"The queen gave me a choice, and I've made it." Margaret gripped his arm, her fingers squeezing hard in her urgency. "The curate will join us if you agree. But you have to decide quickly, Jonathan. We've only a minute or two."

Jonathan's mind reeled. Surprise caught him by the throat, shutting off his wind and leaving him mute. To have her for his own, in every way. Yes! he wanted to shout. Yes!

It wouldn't be right, the rational part of his mind warned. He could never be hers. He was wed to the obsessive dark, first and last.

But he wanted her, wanted her, his body shouted. The temptation to agree drove its burning strength through him, urging him to submit to fortune's rule.

"This is permanent, Margaret," he cautioned, forcing himself to consider her needs first. They were far more important than his. "You don't want to make a wrong choice. You can't change your mind later. We'd be wed for all time."

"I'm sure of my choice, Jonathan."

But he wasn't. He watched while her eyes darted nervously to the far door that jolted with pounding fists, then to the anxious curate and back again. Yet this was no decision to be made in haste.

He caught her chin and forced her to stop, to look deeply into his eyes. "Why should you want to wed with me. I was horrible to you last night. I made you cry."

"For good reason," she said briskly, without emotion. "You were right about my father. He gave me such power, I believed I could control everything. What a shock to learn I was wrong." She grimaced. "I still want to control things . . . and people. I admit that. But I see there are some things I can't." Finally, as if reluctant, she met his gaze.

Jonathan saw her longing then. In her large, glowing eyes, he saw her love burning bright, a golden treasure for the man who deserved to claim it. Such a terrible waste for her to lavish it on him. It would bring her misery and anguish. And set lose a wrenching pain of his own. "The question is," he said slowly, "can I return your feeling, and you know I can't. I have grave matters to attend in the coming months, matters that could easily make you a

widow, should you wed with me now. Ev[illegible]
I can offer no guarantee for your happiness. I w[illegible]on't, [illegible]ish
you all the love and joy you deserve in your next marri[illegible]g.
I no longer have the capacity to give you that. I can't be the boy I once was."

"That boy doesn't exist anymore, nor do you want the girl I was, all sham and deceit," she stated firmly. "If I have to choose, I want a friend, and that is you, as you stand now. If I can make a difference in your life, I will do it gladly. In exchange for what you do for me."

The ring of sincerity in her voice decided him. She was willing to compromise, to accept understanding and companionship from him if she couldn't have love. "Then if you will take me, I will vow to honor you always, as long as I live." Still, he felt the shadow of the inquisitor, looming over him. Soon it would overtake him, would show him the road to his death.

In response, he saw the characteristic tightening of her jaw, the upward tilt of her chin when she encountered resistance. "Your life will be far longer than you think. Especially if I have anything to say about it."

"You must not hinder me in my duty," he warned. He could be equally determined. "Just having a family can make a man vulnerable to attack from new directions."

"I won't hinder you," she scoffed. "If you insist on going off to the Netherlands, I won't say a word. Only do this for me." She curled one hand around his neck, brought his face closer to hers. Her voice softened, lilting and lovely, warming him all over. "Let me be the Magician's bride. Bring me your magic once more."

It burned on the tip of his tongue to ask what magic he could possibly give her, that her own was a potent, dazzling force within her that many longed to steal, himself included. But their time was dwindling. The urgency of the moment was upon them, and her ripe lips begged for his kiss. He gave her one—a sweet, lingering joining of the flesh that made his blood heat in his veins and rush to his head. Better than battle lust—far better—the delicious, agonizing desire for her slender form.

This was wrong, his mind told him, to wed in wild haste with no thought or advance preparation. There must be another way out of Margaret's trouble. But he followed her back to the altar after their kiss, knowing he didn't want

way. He wanted this way. Just looking at Margaret
an him burn inside, wanting her magic fire.
m Your name please," began the curate, clearing his throat.

"They're beating down the door. I can't hold it much longer," called the clerk.

"Hold firm, my son. We are conducting a ceremony." He turned back to Jonathan expectantly.

"Jonathan Edward Cavandish."

"Hmmm, seems in order." He paused to study the letter again.

"Hurry, please!" Margaret urged tersely.

"All in good time. Now let me see. Dearly beloved friends, we are gathered together here in the sight of God, and in the face of this congregation—"

"Good sir," interrupted Margaret gently. "Might we move directly to the vows? There will be a more formal ceremony in the queen's presence later. I'll see you're invited, if you wish."

The curate's eyes lit up at the offer. "I would like that. Very well. Do you, Jonathan Edward Cavandish, take Margaret Mary Longleate, to be thy . . ."

The vows were exchanged quickly, as there were no rings. Jonathan gave the curate several silver coins to bless, but after, he bid the curate put them in his own purse.

"I'll have to open the door," yelled the clerk, easing the key into the lock, "before they do it damage." It flew open, admitting a piercing shaft of light.

Giles strode down the nave and approached them in the echoing depths of the sanctuary. Margaret whirled to face him, and Jonathan braced himself at her back.

"My lady"—Giles bowed—"it is my duty to bring you to your grandsire. Pray come quietly and no one will be hurt."

" 'Twill do him no good," Margaret answered firmly. "To have me in hand. I've wed again, so I can't wed with Robert. I've already married someone else."

"We'll make short work of him," countered one of Robert's men. "Whoever he is."

Jonathan looked to Margaret, expecting her to announce that he was her husband and that they most certainly wouldn't make short work of him, at least not without a fight first. Instead she rummaged in her basket. What was she doing? He was about to answer Giles himself when he felt something thrust in his hand. It was his little pearl-handled hammer.

"Use this," she hissed at him. "Give him a tap in the head. 'Twill delay them while we go out the back."

She should have been a military commander, he thought, wanting to applaud her ingenuity. Balancing the hammer in his hand, he took aim, heaved it with a light touch. It hit Giles squarely in the forehead. Not too hard, he hoped sincerely. The huge man toppled backward like a stone.

Chaos erupted in the sanctuary. The earl's men rushed to aid their fallen leader, but Robert's men charged their quarry. Jonathan clasped Margaret's hand and pulled her through a door beside the altar. "To the choir room," he urged her. "The clerk said it was this way."

Footsteps raced behind them as they blundered down the passage and found the room. Inside, Jonathan shot the bolt and searched the high-ceilinged chamber. The old door mentioned by the clerk stood against the far wall. It was swollen shut from damp and long disuse, but after some prying and a few well-aimed kicks, Jonathan wrenched it open. They escaped into a tiny shed used for grave-digging equipment. From there they crossed the churchyard, dodging gravestones, striving to disappear before their pursuers discovered them.

"This is too close for comfort," he told her as they approached the black iron fence. "Let me stop and fight them."

"You don't have to be a hero," she panted at him. "There's no need. Pray make a graceful exit and not a fuss."

It made him furious, nonetheless. He followed her, frowning, as they approached the fence.

"Temper?" she asked, looking at his face. "Why don't you tell me what's wrong?"

"I don't like being rescued by a woman."

"You're not rescued," she said emphatically, her color high and her face animated. "You're in more trouble than ever. So am I." She lifted one foot and waited for him to boost her. With a toss he landed her on top of the fence, then joined her. "Robert is working with the Spanish," she hurried on. "I should have realized before, but I couldn't see it. Now I do, because I've learned they plan to poison someone. We have to stop them." She gave a decided nod and jumped to the ground.

As he jumped after her, Jonathan let her words sink in. Poison? Lord in heaven, they were in terrible trouble. He had to get to the queen immediately, and Greenwich stood many miles away.

Chapter 40

"First I must fetch Patience." Margaret raced after Jonathan across an open garden, tugging at his hand to slow him down. She could never keep up with his long strides. He refused to halt until they reached the shelter of some clustered trees and shrubbery. He drew her into their protective shade.

"Yes, I suppose you must." He checked their concealment. "Though it makes things more difficult. Come, follow me."

The path they took to the fishmongers' street wound and twisted. They stopped innumerable places, in shops and at stalls where Jonathan knew people who hid them for a moment while he looked to see if they were followed. But at long last they mounted the stairs of her lodgings and were greeted by Marie, who opened the door at Margaret's call.

"Marguerite, we have been terrified for you. Are you well?" Marie's face was pale and she seemed shaken. Behind her, Margaret caught a glimpse of Bertrande, sitting forward anxiously in her chair.

"I am well, though I can't stop to talk. I've come for Patience. What of you, my friends?"

"I—I fear we have ill news for you," Marie stammered. "I am ashamed to say . . ."

Marie twisted her hands and looked so miserable that a frozen lump of fear solidified in Margaret's stomach. She swayed and grasped Jonathan to steady herself. "Tell me. Tell me quick."

"Your grandsire's been here," Marie moaned. "His men followed me from our shop. I am so sorry, Marguerite, but he's taken Patience."

Margaret caught her breath in a sharp, painful gasp of despair. Spinning around, she sped for the door.

"It's happened again, and it's all my fault. Oh, God." They were halfway down the street when Jonathan saw Margaret's back sag, her pace slow. "He'll beat her for the least transgression. What can I do?"

"You must hurry to Greenwich, that's what you can do." Jonathan caught her around the waist and tried to move her forward, but the fire had gone out of her. The determination she had shown in the church and after drained from her like water through a sieve. "What is it you consider your fault?" He would have to get to the bottom of this before they could move on. She acted as if her feet were lead. "Are you blaming yourself for something again?"

"It is my fault," she insisted. "Whenever I go off to tend my own affairs, something terrible happens to Patience."

He felt a shiver run through her body, saw the despairing droop of her head. "Nonsense!" he insisted firmly, determined to keep her moving. "It isn't your fault your grandsire took Patience."

"But if I had been with her—"

"You would have been taken as well," he cut her off sharply, taking a right turn into the next street. "Don't you see it's much better this way. If he had come while you were home, he would have taken both of you. As it is, we go to the queen, show her you have fulfilled her command as set forth in the letter, and Patience is given back into your care."

"It's not that easy," she mourned. "You have no idea . . ."

Jonathan pulled her into a doorway, gripped her by the shoulder and searched her face. Her sudden lethargy worried him. "What don't I understand? Explain."

"It's you," she whispered, refusing to look at him. He caught a glimpse of the conflict thrashing inside her. "I neglect my child for your sake. I've done it in the past, neglected my duties, and look what comes of it. Patience suffers because of me."

He only half understood her, and when he shook her gently, wishing she would say more, she shifted beneath his hands, unsteady as a willow in the wind. "That can't be all there is to it. What else do you blame yourself for?"

She sagged in his arms.

"What else?" he insisted. "Tell me what else."

"My father." Her voice had sunk to a whisper. "When I went upstairs that night, after I was with you, I found him in his chamber. He . . . he died while I was out."

The memory caused her torment and her face showed it. Her suffering over the years was written clearly in the amber of her eyes, as clear as the etching of acid on steel plates. Urgency filled him to erase that pain. He knew exactly how it felt when all the torment of hell afflicted you. And she was pleading for forgiveness for something she hadn't done.

"Margaret, you didn't cause his death." He kept his voice calm and reasonable. "It could have happened at any time of the day or night. There must have been other times when you weren't attending him."

"You know I was at his side night and day except when I went to see you."

"It was still pure coincidence. You must not blame yourself." He was getting nowhere with her.

"I should never have left him. I should have stayed. But I didn't. I wanted . . ."

Jonathan knew how she would have finished that thought. She had wanted to be with him. So many people equated physical desire with weakness. The depth of guilt she must feel wrenched at his heart, causing him equal pain. But for once it was good pain, because it meant he had a heart again. Although that throbbing organ hurt, it was caused by something besides hate for his enemy and himself. "You're mistaken," he said firmly. "You admitted earlier that you can't control every situation you're in. That goes for the people you love as well. We can only control what *we* choose to do."

Still her tears fell, and he clasped her close, comforting her. In broad daylight, too. He knew they were mad to linger here, but her anguish was total. Ridiculous as her thought might be, she seemed to believe it. And he must work to banish it from her mind.

"Come, we must get out of the street." He lifted her in his arms, and she made no protest. "We'll go to where the cavalry is quartered and get horses. We'll go to Greenwich and I'll prove you wrong. You will have Patience again soon."

Chapter 41

"Wake up, curse you. Wake up and answer me!"

Jonathan stepped into the earl's sickroom just in time to hear the angry words resonate in the stifling air. As his eyes adjusted to the gloom, he made out Margaret's rigid figure poised at the foot of the four-poster bed where her grandsire had lain prone since last night.

"You're doing this to spite me," she told the mound beneath the coverlet. Her entire posture radiated impotent fury. "Tell me where Patience is! I want her back!"

"He isn't fully conscious, Margaret." Jonathan moved forward. "The poppy juice relieves his pain, but he can't respond."

"Good heavens!" Margaret started like a coney bolting from its burrow. "I thought you'd gone to town."

"I did. I've returned." Despite the half dark, Jonathan drank in her beauty, especially the way the smooth cloth of her bodice molded her breasts and waist, making his hands itch to do the same. Slowly, he reached out to make his claim on her, but she bristled.

"This is between him and me. I'd rather you leave us be."

"Not yet." He held her firmly while he placed a kiss on her right cheek. Then he released her, sighing inwardly as she hugged herself with both arms, trying to resist their jolt of attraction. He had felt it; without a doubt so had she.

Moving around the bed, he examined the earl. The poor fellow was rolled into a ball, his face the color of dull wax. His breathing scarcely stirred the counterpane. Jonathan touched his forehead and found it cool.

He couldn't blame Margaret for being upset. In a scant few hours they must go through a second wedding ceremony, and she was in a frenzy over her child. Last night had been enough to unsettle anyone. He hadn't cared for it himself, standing by while Margaret did the queen's bidding and met with her grandsire. Their quarrel behind closed doors had been strident. Her Majesty had finally been called to intervene. When she decreed Margaret's marriage valid, with a witnessed ceremony to take place the next day, the earl had collapsed in a fit. Conveniently, the attack came before he revealed where he had sent Patience. And none of his servants seemed to know where she was.

"Your grandsire is very ill," he advised Margaret.

"He's not ill," she vowed, clearly grown irrational in her worry. "He's had a fit as an excuse so he doesn't have to give up Patience. And his servants won't say a word."

He sent her a sympathetic stare, but she didn't see it. She was glowering at her grandsire. "Margaret, I understand how you feel, and I regret not being able to retrieve Patience for you, but I know she's well cared for, wherever she is."

"I can imagine Grandsire's idea of 'well cared for.' Probably a crust of bread, a drink of water, and a hard bed. And I still say someone among the servants knows."

"Margaret, I questioned the servants personally," Jonathan reasoned, "and they honestly know nothing. I can generally tell when people are lying. Your grandsire confides in few people, but especially not them. He's apparently sent her off with Giles Hampstead, but no one knows where to." He put his hands on her shoulders, but she shrugged him off, moving on restless feet around the room.

"If he can't control who I wed, he wants to control my child. He wants to control everyone and everything, the miser, but I won't let him do it. I won't."

"Come away." It was time to interrupt her tirade before she became hysterical. Jonathan took her hand and guided her from the darkened chamber, with its heavy odor of herbs. He wound through Greenwich until he found her rooms, the two tiny chambers they now shared. He had sent her to bed alone last night, but tonight he would not. The thought made his loins heat as he pushed the door open and pulled her after him into the room. "Sit down."

She went to stand stiffly by the window. "I don't want

to sit down. You're always telling me to come here and do this or that."

Jonathan was losing patience with her. No, it wasn't with her, it was him. A raw rush of heated emotion flashed through him, and he wished the ceremony were behind them, that he might have her here and now, might strip away the simple garments she wore and lose himself in the ripe promise of her body. But it wasn't time yet. They still had much to discuss. "I need to know about the poison, Margaret," he said gravely. "I didn't ask you yesterday because there wasn't a reasonable moment, but you must tell me everything you know. Then I hope you will wipe it from your mind."

"And how do you expect me to do that? I'm not feeble-witted. My mind retains the things I've learned."

"What I'm saying is that you must stop being reckless." Jonathan struggled to contain his rising anger. "I give you reasonable instruction and you refuse to obey."

"But, Jonathan," she pleaded with him, "the information fell into my lap. How could I turn away from it? You never would."

"We are not one and the same person."

"Is that so?" she flashed at him. "Then what is the ceremony we're to go through later? I recall that marriage makes one flesh of two."

He sent her a reproachful stare, letting her know that was quite irrelevant. "Just tell me the facts, Margaret. Slowly, from the start."

"I was at the Spanish ambassador's house," she said, biting her lower lip.

"What were you doing there?" Rockets of red fury went off in Jonathan's head. "You deliberately disobeyed me. I gave you express orders not to be involved."

"I was delivering lace to a customer," she declared haughtily. "I didn't know it was the ambassador's house until I got there. I was entirely within my rights."

"What were you doing selling lace without guild approval? The hearing isn't until tomorrow night." She looked guilty at that, and he put on his most intimidating expression, which wasn't difficult to muster. He was furious with her. She had no idea what she had risked. "We'll come to that later," he told her grimly. "Go on."

"We went to see the monkey and I—"

"Who were you with?" he demanded, wanting to shake the details out of her.

"Tim," she answered calmly. "I wish you would apprentice him, by the by. Will you if I bring him around?"

He was getting angrier by the moment. If she continued this way, he might just throttle her. Many times he had wanted to do the same to Rozalinde, his headstrong sister. He had liked Margaret in the start because she seemed the complete opposite. "We'll come back to him later as well," he said, eking out his limited patience. "After the monkey, then what?"

"I listened to the dinner guests, saw one of them was Robert, and heard about the poison."

He waited for her to go on, but she seemed to have finished. "That's all?" he asked suspiciously.

"Yes," she said serenely. "That's all."

"Damn it, that's only half a story. Not even that."

"Are you doubting my word?"

He crossed the room, caught up a brush from the table, and twisted it so hard it almost broke. "I need to know about the poison," he ground out.

"You said I was to forget everything." She flipped a loose curl over her shoulder. "I don't know if my weak woman's brain can—"

"Stop it, Margaret." He smacked the brush on his open palm. "Stop your goading and talk."

"Well," she said conversationally. "In thirteen days, the person who supplies the poison will bring it to the ambassador. I suppose you could find out more then."

"*Now* you may forget everything," he ordered her, exerting ever more pressure on the brush. Of all the reckless, mutton-headed, idiotic things to do, to eavesdrop on the Spanish while they plotted to kill someone. "You could have been caught, Margaret. Did you ever think of what they would have done?"

"Aye, I did. At that point, I left."

"Oh, you left, did you? As if it were a revel and you tired of it," he mocked. "Gathered your gloves and took yourself off to more interesting activities. Not once did you consider the danger of what you were doing!"

"I knew I should tell you what I'd learned," she said defiantly. "I thought you needed to know."

The brush snapped in his hands. Jonathan flung the

pieces to the floor. "Damn it, Margaret, you call your grandsire a miser, but you're just like him. You want to control everything. And you never let me inside."

"I've told you more than anyone else, even Bertrande," she cried, leaping to her feet. She glared at him, then spun away, unconsciously showing him her profile. It was pure and radiant, and a raging desire filled him. He wanted to rob her of that purity, to wrestle her to the bed and make fast, furious love to her, wrenching the secrets from her and claiming them for his own.

"That may be so." He forced the calm to enter his voice, if not his body. "But it isn't enough. Not for the venture we're about to undertake. I need your complete trust. I need you to confide in me. Tonight, for instance, after the marriage ceremony, what are your intentions?" His demand was harsher that he had intended, but to him this was the real issue and far more urgent. "Husband and wife are meant to share a bed."

"You can assume I will do what is required."

Her voice tripped in a nervous catch as she answered. He noticed she avoided giving the act words. " 'Wedding' is one word," he told her, modulating his voice further, turning it tender and tantalizing. " 'Bedding' is another. I never heard you use the second word of the two."

She looked startled to hear him speak so bluntly. "I've agreed to produce an heir. Isn't that enough?"

"I won't bed an unwilling maid."

"I'm no maid, so don't let it trouble you. Oliver never did, even when I was."

So that was it. Jonathan recognized it now, the stiffening of her spine, the tightening of her shoulders, the way she held her neck, pulled back and rigid. Thanks to her first husband, she didn't like bedding. But she would with him. He would soothe away her fear.

Jonathan let his eyes savor the delicious swells and curves of her body, imagining how it would be. Until now, he hadn't given himself the pleasure of deliberately arousing her passion, but tonight he would. Away fell thoughts of poison and Spaniards and how she had disobeyed his orders. What a pleasure it would be to play her sensitive body like a finely wrought instrument until he drew the marvelous music from her, giving her ecstasy in exchange. Because more than anything else, he had to possess her.

At last the time had come when he could. And now he could admit the truth—she was the only female who held the dark at bay. He reached out and caught her fragile hand in his own.

Margaret let her hand be captured, felt Jonathan's claim on her flesh, and slowly raised her gaze to his. The sun rode lower on the horizon. By the light of its slanting beams, she drank in the welcome pleasure of looking upon him, wanting to cup the splendor of his face in both her hands and drink of his essence. The raw magic he exuded captured her utterly, making her lose control. And she did think it a weakness, yet he said it was not. If only she could believe him. With a tiny moan, she gave in to her need, carried his hand to press against her cheek.

"Marguerite, let us dwell in the present and try to forget the past." The warming tones of his voice wove agile patterns around her, making a shiver of delight twist its way to her core. "I want you to give yourself freely to me, not because you must."

"And you?" she asked plaintively, rubbing her cheek against his hand, hiding her face from him. "Can you forget?" She knew he couldn't. The demon tore at him, without a doubt. "You're only doing this to protect me. And because of what I did at Clifton. You can't give yourself freely either. How can you expect that I should." They each had their separate regrets, which isolated them in their suffering. Yet his next words built an astonishing bridge across that gap.

"Because I need you."

The statement floated to her through the rising gloom, shocking her, thrilling her. "Because you . . . what?"

"You heard me, damn it." He pulled her to her feet, clasping her to him. "Come here if you don't believe me. I'll show you what I mean."

His growl made a pleasing prickle dart through Margaret's belly. His face had transformed again, donning the rigid mask meant to hide things from her. But she went into his arms without resistance. Her fingers rose to his shoulders, eager but hesitant, wanting to banish the pain she knew lurked behind the mask. While she fluttered, uncertain, he looked down on her as if debating. Suddenly he claimed her mouth in a hurried, hungry kiss.

When he released her several minutes later, Margaret's

blood pounded, her head spun, and her thoughts ran thick and deliciously cloying like fragrant honey. If this wasn't right, it was too late to escape. Their marriage would be official within the hour.

Chapter 42

"Must I wear this stupid stomacher?" Margaret stood in her chamber amidst a rainbow array of petticoats and sleeves, partlets and ruffs. Her mood didn't match the gaiety of the clothing. In a fit of pique, she flung the beribboned garment on the floor. "I don't want all these hot clothes, and I don't want to wed. I've changed my mind. I won't do it until I have Patience again."

Marie, who had been trying to assist, hurried to pick up the stiff stomacher.

Bertrande moved forward and spoke reassuringly. "Marguerite, you are well enough arrayed. Leave the stomacher. Mayhap Marie should go on to the chapel. You and I will have a word."

Discreet as always, Marie gathered up her fan and went out, closing the door softly behind her. Margaret closed her eyes. She wanted to be alone just now. In fact, she wanted to go somewhere and hide.

"Why did it happen?" came Bertrande's surprising question.

"Why did . . . ?" Margaret opened her eyes reluctantly. "Do you mean why did Jonathan and I part? The reason we never wed?"

"Mais oui."

"It wasn't my fault! That is . . . it was only partially my fault." Margaret groaned, dropped into a chair, heedless of the elaborate gown and farthingale she wore. With one hand she rubbed her aching temple. "It was both our faults and neither. We were young and could not defy our elders unless we dared run away and try to live on nothing."

"Is that the only reason? Your father had just died." Bertrande came straight to the point, as always.

Margaret sought to evade it. "If anyone was to blame, 'twas Grandsire. I had nowhere else to live. And he insisted I wed someone else."

"And did you let your grandsire know you wished to wed with Jonathan?"

"I didn't wish it, I—"

"Yes, you did. But you wouldn't let yourself. Why?"

Bertrande's questions were so sharply focused, for a second Margaret thought they were spoken by her own conscience. "I . . . I didn't dare wed with him," she said finally. "I betrayed my father, and—"

"You did nothing of the kind!" Bertrande had come closer. Now she seated herself on the stool facing Margaret and felt for both her hands. "That is wrong, my child. Without even knowing the details, I am sure."

"But, Bertrande," cried Margaret, stricken. "He *died.* And I wasn't with him. I was out with—"

"It doesn't matter where you were or what you were doing. You go too far, believing everything depends on you. If you were making a piece of lace, and someone ruined it while you were out, would you blame yourself? You should not . . ." Bertrande gestured in frustration. "But you probably would."

Margaret's eyes prickled, but the tears did not come. She was far beyond tears now; her mind stumbled ahead desperately trying to understand, to believe, to accept. "I want to believe you. Jonathan says the same thing." Margaret shook her head. "Mayhap it doesn't make sense, but it was so terrible losing him. Bertrande, there was no one to blame but me."

"Why must someone be blamed? Marguerite, you must take life the way you do your lace, one stitch at a time. You can plan the pattern you wish to produce, you can look back and do your best to correct mistakes, but do not spend your time judging your work and yourself harshly. The lace maker can only create the quality of lace equal to her stage of development, regardless of her gift. You will make yourself miserable by demanding more." She smiled encouragingly and got up to bustle around Margaret, rearranging the drape of her skirt by touch in her gentle, soothing manner. "Come now, 'tis your wedding day, and you will wed with the man you love. Your father would rejoice for you. You must rejoice also. Promise me you will try."

"I will try." Margaret gladly accepted the embrace Bertrande offered, along with the sense of her words, but as she did so, she felt a rush of uncertainty. How could she forgive herself for something that had devastated her world? And how would she possibly get through tonight?

A brief time later, Margaret stood alone at the entry to the royal chapel at Greenwich. She clutched the bouquet of gold and white daisies Jonathan had sent her, paralyzed. Her mind raced through the past with dizzying speed—Oliver had once waited for her in the Clifton chapel, looked on her with ravenous eyes that conveyed his eagerness to bed her. Like the blood of a sacrifice, she had given him her virginity. He had claimed it with vigorous enjoyment, determined to subdue her, to hold her under his control. After his death, she had vowed never to take another master. Was she making a horrible mistake?"

You are about to wed the man you love. Bertrande's words ran through her memory, a thought so startling, Margaret hadn't even responded at the time. She dared not even think the word "love." Not after all that had gone wrong in her life. As she stepped into the chapel, her stomach turned over with a lurch, as if the ground had been whipped from beneath her feet. Steadying herself, she forced herself to move.

The last rays of sun streamed through the stained glass window above their heads. Raising her gaze at last, she found the beam, saw how it touched Jonathan's hair with gold as he waited for her at the altar. His broad-shouldered figure loomed ahead, blocking all others from her notice, imposing in velvet that turned him tawny like a great lion. Her mind sifted through the images and sensations deluging her, then came slowly to focus like the light of that beam as she imagined how it would be this time, tonight when that sensuous, lithesome lion took possession of her body. The sudden, unbidden image of molten metal came to her—his scorching heat would melt her control as easily as the forge fire softened plated steel.

With difficulty her feet did her bidding and moved her toward him. Bertrande and Marie stood to one side, humble in their simple kirtles. Jonathan's sister hung on the arm of her husband, the Earl of Wynford, who held their four-year-old son. The boy wiggled and snagged his stocks on his father's rapier, reminding Margaret of Patience, which made her want to cry. Quickly she moved on to scan the satisfied face of the London curate, Jonathan's friend Cornelius, and beyond to Lord Burghley and the queen's secretary, Master Walsingham.

The queen was resplendent in a costume of glacial blue silk that stood out in semi-transparent embellishments on shoulders and skirt tiers, making her an ice queen, erect and regal, her expression frozen in place. Margaret felt that same way inside, cold as ice and equally unyielding. How would she ever cede control to Jonathan tonight? She curtsied to Her Majesty and offered a wan smile to the four ladies-in-waiting before moving on.

Her grandsire was, of course, absent. He had regained consciousness for a brief time that afternoon but immediately demanded redosing by the physician. "I won't bless your joining," was all he would snarl at Margaret. "Let the cur sire the child and be gone to the Netherlands. 'Twill leave me free rein to raise my heir."

It wouldn't, Margaret vowed. Her widow's jointure raised its golden hand to her, beckoning. She would take a modest, well-built house beyond the city, hire a few servants to buy their food, to cook and clean and do their washing. A place with a garden and stately trees to shelter them. And beyond the heat and dirt of London, she would raise her two children without men to dominate them. But she resented her grandsire's words about Jonathan. *He'll sire the child, then be gone.*

He was undoubtedly right, which made her even angrier. She was about to become a demon's bride. He would leave her forthwith for his business with the devil. And though being alone would give her great freedom—to raise her children, to run the lace business—she had never felt less glad.

As she reached the altar, Margaret looked straight ahead, avoiding Jonathan's penetrating gaze. But when she came to a halt beside him, her stomach lurched again, because she felt him capture her frightened hand.

That simple meeting of his flesh with hers—it sent a torrent of longing through her, causing her world to tilt. If only he could work his magic to make her life once again whole.

"The new gown well becomes you."

His words, his closeness, whispered around her, softly unraveling her defenses the way a bobbin's thread is unwound. " 'Tis the queen's gift," she answered, "one of her own, altered. And 'tis monstrous with the farthingale, as well you know."

"The woman within is not monstrous." Subtly he sent his magic to encircle her. " 'Tis you I admire, not the gown."

The heat of telltale blood crept into her cheeks and neck. She knew her low-cut bodice revealed it. Augmented by the day's great temperatures, the heat within her soared. "*I* am monstrous at times." She tried desperately to contain her response to him. They were in the midst of company, the focus for all eyes.

"You're not. You just think you are." His hand tightened on hers in a compelling squeeze.

His impassioned words wove their web around Margaret. Though it was the queen's chaplain who led them through the ceremony, she heard only Jonathan's voice, saw only his strong face and the depth of his autumn brown eyes.

"With this ring I thee wed, and this gold and silver I thee give, and with my body I thee worship, and with all my worldly chattels I thee endow."

She gripped the daisies and rosemary so tightly the daisy stems bled their sap on her hands. *My miracle, my Marguerite.* She would be that to him, if only she could, but the shadow of another man stood between them, holding Jonathan just beyond her reach.

She wouldn't let that stop her. Because now she bound herself to him for time irrevocable. She would stand up and defy the devil in him, send him back to purgatory where he belonged. Of all the things she wanted to be to Jonathan, this one stood foremost in her mind—to defeat the demon within him so he could heal.

And then would he love her? She wasn't sure. Once he had loved her with an open, honest heart and she had turned him away. What a marvelous fool she had been, impeded by her own torment. Even now that torment gnawed at her, but she wouldn't let it stop her. He still offered her something she needed and wanted: his strength and his friendship, and something more. The chance to rise to a challenge, to redeem him with her own inner strength.

The ceremony ended. As a couple they turned to the sparse congregation and were introduced as the new Captain and Madam Cavandish. She would no longer be called "dowager." For that, at least, she gave thanks.

"May you be blessed by the Lord, who made the Universe out of nothing."

The chaplain spoke the benediction. Margaret gripped Jonathan's hand hard and thought of that universe, trying to draw strength from it. Because her stubborn will to claim what she needed in life was never greater than now.

Chapter 43

Food and drink were served in the queen's antechamber, before the tapestry Margaret learned was called "The Wise and Foolish Virgins." After the blur of the ceremony, she felt like the latter, though she wasn't a virgin. Everything slowed for her, moving with ponderous toil. She felt dazed and disoriented, as if she walked on unstable ground. Why had she gone and tied herself to a man?

Servants had lit branches of candelabra around the chamber. The burning candles starred the room like a dazzle of fireflies. The queen's ladies flitted about serving cakes, wafers, and spiced wine. The London curate fawned on Her Majesty, obviously thrilled by the chance to talk to his queen. "And such a stunning cuff and ruff set," he went on. "I have never seen the like. The ruff sets off your beauty to perfection," he added, focusing on the queen's person rather than the adornment.

The queen seemed well pleased with the compliment. " 'Tis a gift from the Duke of Alençon," she answered with undisguised pride. "But to my way of thinking, his accompanying letter was the more lavish gift of the two."

Beside Margaret, Jonathan turned aside. She was intensely aware of his strong masculine scent enhanced by sweet woodruff, wafting to her like a message of passion. The slight sheen of perspiration on his forehead made her want to lay his head in her lap and wipe away the strain. "What is it?" she asked. "Is something wrong?"

"Nothing's wrong." He played with his dagger hilt, seeming annoyed. "She may wed this knave, but 'tis no affair of mine."

"The French prince? You don't want her to wed with him?"

"I don't favor the match. It's a political error." He seemed cross since they had left the chapel. Or mayhap it was since they had entered the antechamber.

"Let me get you some wine. It was just brought from the cellars." She bestirred herself. "It will cool you." Though she knew that was nonsense. The heat within them both would grow as the night progressed.

The far door opened and one of the queen's maids, Jane Shelton, entered, trailed by Robert. Serpents of tension coiled through the room, thick with warning. What was he doing here? It took Margaret a handful of heartbeats to remember. The queen had commanded his presence. He was to see her wed in all finality to another. His full lips were drawn into a pout as he followed Jane.

The riot of last night played again through Margaret's head. "Your Grace," her grandsire had protested, "I wish to match my granddaughter with your own great nephew, Viscount Solsover—"

"But he is meant for my dear and favored maid of honor, Jane Shelton," Elizabeth had finished.

Robert, upon hearing this, had blanched. Everyone knew Jane was the daughter of a commoner, impeccably loyal to the queen and elevated to knighthood for that express reason. Elizabeth played her cards wisely by controlling the bloodline of her relations. She decreed a marriage that would yield no competition for her throne.

"My lord Clifton," the queen had continued, having let loose her political cannonball, "pray be so good as to return the child to madam, your granddaughter. Tonight, sir. Tomorrow there will be a formal wedding ceremony to join these two individuals. Their charge is to create the next Earl of Clifton." She regarded them all sternly, eyes flashing. "You will all be present to wish them well."

With that, the earl had bent over double, clutched his middle, and passed out.

"You'll pardon me if I leave you a moment, but I need to speak to Kit." Jonathan's voice called Margaret back from her reverie.

"Of course," she answered automatically. But after he had left her, she stood alone by the wine bottles, feeling bereft. She lifted her flagon and took a swallow of water, determined to drink no spirits and muddle her mind. She felt confused enough as it was.

Jonathan meandered his way through the clusters of people, nodding to the queen's chaplain, saluting his sister. Firmly he guided his mind away from the time when he would be alone with Margaret. Having her would by no means solve his problems. In fact, it complicated them. But then that was the way of the world. You might get halfway to paradise but never closer. You could catch a glimpse of it ahead, beckoning, but it was always just beyond reach.

Jonathan flagged down Cornelius as he passed. Making sure they were at the farthest point from his least favorite tapestry scene, the one with all the eyes, he beckoned for the Earl of Wynford to join them. The boy in Christopher's arms shrieked with laughter from his father's tickles.

"Now then, young Kit"—Lord Howard laughed, setting the boy on his feet—"I see your uncle coming. Run along to your mother so the men can talk."

"Don't want Mama," insisted young Christopher in his best wheedling tone. "I want to be one of the men."

Kit chuckled and steered his son toward Rozalinde. "You want to be one of the men because you can eat more cakes on the sly while I'm busy. I know you, young ruffian." He ruffled the boy's hair affectionately. "Run tell your mother you want to talk to the bride. She looks lonely, don't you think?"

"I suppose so," young Kit said reluctantly, his feet dragging. He hunched up his trunk hose which were a matching miniature of his father's.

"Go now," insisted his father. "If you do as told, mayhap Uncle Jonathan will teach you a new rapier cut later."

The dark-haired boy's eyes lit up at that, and he looked to Jonathan, who nodded in agreement. The lad scuttled obediently away.

"What news?" Secretary Walsingham joined them, looking expectant.

"Yes, Jonathan." Christopher brought all attention to bear on his brother-in-law. "What did you learn in the city today?"

"There's a Spanish poison plot afoot," Jonathan answered, inwardly wishing for a different source of his intelligence. "We can't verify the target, but I believe the guard around Her Majesty should be doubled. That's in addition to the man on watch at night in this room. I'll be here personally most nights. Cornelius will relieve me, along with a few trusted others. There will be more information available in a few days about the poison. I'll let you know what I learn."

Master Walsingham folded his hands and digested this information before turning to Christopher. "My lord, what of the ports?"

"No new Spanish ships since the trade delegation arrived. The Spanish fleet has been busy in the Channel, but I see no threatening pattern to its traffic. What did your men learn?"

Walsingham smoothed his beard. "As you know, my men have been keeping watch at the Tower. Last night someone tried to reach the prisoner's window. We had set an ambush for him but . . ." He gestured to indicate the man got away. "Since he was not able to make contact, he will undoubtedly try again. We will wait."

"What is Her Grace's decision about the prince?"

"The date has been set," said Walsingham briskly, looking around the room to be sure everyone was engaged. "The sixteenth of August, he's to be at Calais waiting for you."

"The *Swiftsure II* will be ready to convey him," Christopher stated.

"You have our grateful thanks." Walsingham scanned the room and found Viscount Solsover, who sat on a settle sipping a glass of wine and fondling Jane. "What of him?"

"Suspicions confirmed," Jonathan answered tersely.

Walsingham's eyebrows shot up. "Reliable source?" he asked, clearly doubtful.

"Yes," put in Christopher, "you didn't tell me. How did you learn?"

"All I can say is that I have it on the best authority," Jonathan answered, tight-lipped. "I won't say more."

"Protecting someone? But of course you are." Christopher quickly canceled his question. "I must say he surprises me, after all the queen has done for him. Weak sort of fellow. You'll put an extra watch on him?" he asked Jonathan.

"I already have," Jonathan said. "I intend to make him help reveal the plot."

The talk broke up after that. Rozalinde strolled over to tease Jonathan, saying he was keeping her husband working, and he did his best to act lighthearted and tease her back, saying she worked all the time at the drapery business and was a fine one to accuse him.

After that, though, he retreated to a far corner with Cornelius, where they talked idly about things of little consequence. All the while he watched Margaret flit from one guest to another, her beauty sparkling like the ephemeral fireflies in the candlelit room. He was protecting someone, he thought darkly, just as Christopher had said. And that person didn't even want protection, didn't even grasp the importance of having it.

He would have to remind her, that was all. As her husband, he must look out for her safety. She wouldn't like it; of that he had no doubt.

He stood, ready to make his rounds and bid the wedding guests god'den. He was eager to get on with it. The paradise of her arms awaited him tonight, and he would partake of her warmth with a willingness he couldn't deny. Soon. Very soon.

Chapter 44

Margaret awaited Jonathan in her tiny bedchamber. Earlier a maid had assisted her out of the monstrous gown, and she had donned a soft blue kirtle skirt and bodice. Now she sat fiddling with her bobbin box, sliding its ornamented lid open and shut. Memories of her first wedding night had been lining up in persistent quays in her head, demanding she notice them, one after another: the repelling odor of wine on Oliver's breath as he stripped off her night smock and gloated over her body; her shock when he yanked up his own nightshirt and revealed the inflamed part of his male anatomy meant to make her a wife; the pain of his thrust when he finally took her after pawing and kneading her for seeming hours; the final crush of his weight as he made their marriage real.

Hating the thoughts, Margaret jumped up. She pushed the box back under her chair where she normally stored it, stood, and peered in the looking glass. Her face seemed a stranger's, pale and frightened by candlelight. Yet she had sought this marriage. Better to choose Jonathan, she thought, than a stranger from the queen's list.

Furthermore, her choice had pleased the queen and reaped the promised reward. During the reception in her antechamber, Elizabeth had told Margaret to visit her on the morrow about her jointure. That had cheered Margaret, and shortly after she had pulled Bertrande aside and dumped every last shilling she possessed into her friend's hands to tide them over.

Restless, Margaret prowled the chamber, making plans for that "later." She feared increasingly for Bertrande's health. Her friend had pain of some sort—Margaret could tell by the tightening of her mouth, by the pause in the midst of her work, though she said nothing. Now she could insist that Bertrande see a physician. Lack of funds could no longer serve as an excuse. When she was well again, they would live quietly, running the lace business after Jonathan returned to the Netherlands, as she knew he must.

The door creaked behind her. Margaret straightened, knowing her husband had arrived and she must give him all control. But it was hard for her . . . so hard.

She started at the sight of Jonathan's enigmatic figure looming in the doorway. No reason for nerves, she told herself, trying to calm her racing heartbeat. Except for one thing: she hadn't anticipated his effect on her.

Her breathing sounded frighteningly loud in the silence as she clutched a comb and stared at him. It wasn't just his shadowy, mysterious looks that filled her with rampant anticipation. It was the excess baggage that came with him—their past wants and future desire. He was everything she longed for and feared—a sorcerer with hidden depths so vast she could never plumb them, a fascinating mixture of vitality and pain. One moment he exuded a potent male aura so strong she was suspended in it like a fly in syrup, drowning in too much bliss. The next moment he tamped down that aura to a wholesome, companionable friendliness just like he cut the air to his forge fire to control the flame. And here she was, as rigid as a steel plate, ready to crack at the hammer's slightest false touch.

She reached for another candle, attempting to swallow as she did so, and found her throat had gone dry. Worrying her lip with her teeth, she concentrated on lighting the candle with its neighbor, then placed them both in their holders. Mayhap more light on the subject would stifle her ridiculous qualms.

Without warning, he was at her side.

"What did I tell you about that habit of yours?" His hand closed on her shoulder, his hand tipped up her chin, his finger tracing her poor bitten lip. He was kissing her the next moment, and without meaning to, her body tensed, as rigid as an iron bar. The night would be a disaster if she couldn't relax.

He sensed this immediately. Breaking their contact, he stepped back to study her. "Would you like a cup of wine?"

Mutely she shook her head in the negative. All she wanted was to survive tonight without failing miserably.

"Nor I, but I would like some water. 'Tis hot tonight." He loosened his shirt at the neck while he checked the ewer. He had discarded his velvet court clothes in favor of simple garments. The white shirt molded to his chest and shoulders, its tight fit advertising his muscular strength like a broadside seller. "Is it spring water?" he asked. When she nodded, he poured two flagons full. "Drink. 'Twill cool you."

She knew nothing would cool her at this point, but she seated herself and drank away, obedient for once.

He lounged beside her while they both sipped, running his hand across her back and shoulders in a comforting motion, reminding her of their Lulworth days. In his generous way he was trying to calm her, but she had ill news for him: he could not succeed tonight.

"Penny for your thoughts."

"Did you tell Walsingham about the poison?" She blurted out the first thing on her mind.

He grimaced. "That wasn't the thought I wanted."

She sniffed. "You get what you pay for."

He sent her a stern look.

"Are you intending to go to the ambassador's house when that witch visits him?" Margaret persisted. "Do you need me to draw a floor map?" Their purpose tonight was pressing, but she hid behind her questions. "What of Robert? He can't be permitted to visit court as if he were innocent. Something has to be done."

He didn't answer because he was searching his wallet for something. "Stand up," he ordered, rising and drawing out a roll of tape.

She stared at him. Why didn't he answer her questions? But that was obvious, she thought with resentment. He refused to discuss such matters with the likes of her—for a woman it wasn't safe.

When she didn't rise, he leaned over and caught her beneath the arms. Lifting her from the chair, he set her on her feet.

She should have protested, but her body resisted no more than a rag, while the heat of his touch turned her mind soft and pliant. Suddenly she had the urge to see him as Vulcan. If he planned to melt her into a puddle of passion, she wanted him dressed for the part—or rather undressed. An intense wish gripped her, wonderful because it could now be fulfilled—she wanted to strip away his shirt and experience the smooth ripple of his bare muscles beneath her hands.

But he had control just now, and he turned her around to face him so that the strength of his closeness struck her. Words hovering on her lips guttered into oblivion like a candle wick drowning in a vast pool of molten wax. The sweet scent of woodruff soap accosted her, sending her senses swooning. Without asking permission, he wrapped the tape around her head.

"What are you doing?" Her question came out half squeak, half hiccup. Embarrassed, she clamped her mouth shut, trying to subdue her thrill. He was too close, too breathtaking by far.

"I'm measuring you for armor. Stand still."

Margaret stood stark still, afraid her smallest move would bring them into contact. His supple hands moved with surety, measuring around her temples, across the crown of her head. "Why?" she forced out.

"That's what I ask myself. Why should you be so reckless that you need armor? But you do." His hands drifted to her hair, which she had let down when she discarded her farthingale. Now his fingers tangled in it. Margaret's vision swam and she tipped back her head. A needle of desire shot through her insides. It pierced without warning, sweet and delicious like the anticipated magic each time she sat down to her lace work, except this went further. It swirled through her brain, dizzying her senses, then assaulted her belly with a sharp signal of desire.

"You insist on being forward," he said. "A corselet like the queen's could save your life."

"Then why do you measure my head?"

"So I can be sure it passes with ease down to your shoulders." Those warm hands—they stopped their tangling in her hair and swept it into a cascade so his right hand could trace the shape of her skull, rounding her ear gently, touching her mind. She steeled herself against him, but his fingers made an enchanted band across her forehead, his palms burning at her temples with compelling heat.

"Here is the seat of the intellect." His words fell like shining, shimmering sparks around her in the semidark. "All thoughts and actions emanate from here. Whatever blame and guilt you bring with you tonight, Marguerite, cast them aside."

She squirmed beneath his touch. She didn't want him probing her wounds like a surgeon searching raw flesh for a lost piece of steel. She wanted to forget everything and lose herself in this magnificent moment. His spellbinding fingers had finished with her head and now wrapped the tape around her neck.

Margaret's hands leaped to her throat, afraid . . . of what? That he would strangle her? He wouldn't do that; he didn't have to. She was already choking on the strength of her own desire. "So you think to make me a corselet because I'm like to get in trouble? Very well, but I can't think when I would wear it."

"If I had my way, you would wear it all the time when you're out and about. Here, in our chamber, I would remove it myself." His voice carried the broad innuendo of things to come, and she shivered as he noted the measurement on the tape. His hands then drifted lower.

"Jonathan, you're making me nervous."

"Nervous? Is that how you feel?"

He moved to her left side. Cupping her elbow, he bent and flexed her arm.

No, she admitted silently, she wasn't nervous. Her body was growing marvelously, amazingly pliant beneath his hands; her mind was rejoicing. She was the young Margaret again, at least in her longing. For years she had wanted to wed with Jonathan, to have the right to touch him and be touched. Now the blessed moment had come. Sudden joy drove everything else from her mind, and she reveled in the release, though Jonathan couldn't know it. He manipulated the measuring device in silence, moving around to her back, standing within a hair's breadth so that his body heat loomed behind her like a towering wall of flame. She welcomed it with elation, though he stupefied her so, she couldn't tell him. "What are you doing now?" was all she managed to say.

"I'm checking your breadth of movement so the arm opening fits." Holding her left arm with a light touch, he maneuvered it straight out to her side, then down and back. "You have a long reach for one so small. It would stand you well in a fight."

Margaret couldn't think clearly about such things—not

now. Nor did she feel like a fighter. She felt like a heap of combustible tinder, urged to burst into flame by his lightning touch. As he moved to her right side, his fingertips floated across her shoulders, exerting a subtle claim. A tiny spurt of fear returned, and she shivered. "I didn't know armorers noticed such detail."

"The study of anatomy is essential to an armorer. I've spent many hours examining the human body and its possible range of motion." His words sent delight mixed with astonishment ricocheting through her as he took her right arm and repeated the motions. She could just imagine some of his studies, though that brought a rush of jealousy and she refused to think about other women in his life. He was hers tonight. All hers.

"Otherwise," he continued, "a piece of armor might impede the wearer rather than protect. I take great pains to refine a work so it flexes just where required."

Despite her fear, Margaret gave in totally to her desire. In her imagination, he ruled as Vulcan, master of the forge. She liked to envision him at his anvil, wooing the iron's shape with his hands. Or sitting before the table, lovingly grasping the pincers and coaxing the tiny rings of mail closed. The strong touch in just the right place to mold a work of art. Tonight, she was that work of art. She felt raw and molten, ready to be shaped to his will.

"I would protect you." His voice had turned silky like his insidious hands. Both of them smoothed their way downward, admiring as he measured across the swell of her breasts. Spreading his palm, he covered her speeding heart. "We must proof your armor well so your heart cannot be pierced, for here is the source of your life's blood."

The throb of her heart rose in answer, its cadence beating out of control.

"Mayhap it's too late," she whispered.

"Aye." His voice insinuated a grin she couldn't see. "The life's blood reveals a person's passion. Yours speaks for itself."

Excitement rippled through Margaret, building to fever pitch. He was right, she couldn't hide her answer. Yet fear came as well, its ebb and flow alternating with desire in a most unnerving manner. She fought a desperate urge to step into his arms while his hands left her heart and crept lower still. They encircled her waist with the tape and drew it taut, which made her tighten with excitement. Her heart—that foolish, uncooperative organ—raced in her chest, speeding toward its own destruction. His breath whispered on her neck, so light it reminded her of the leather bellows hanging in his workshop, breathing with the faintest touch.

"I don't think I want armor after all," she choked out. He must stop touching her or she would do something rash. "Pray leave off."

"You wear armor within, anyway. You always have." Finished with measuring, his hands settled on her shoulders, his thumbs and fingers massaging the bare flesh of her neck. "Invisible armor," he muttered, half to himself. "Especially proofed against me. But at times it weakens and leaves you vulnerable, which you fear greatly. Will you submit to me tonight?"

Margaret gulped, realizing she did need a suit of steel, made as strong as could be. Because tonight she faced the ultimate danger, greater than any the Spanish imposed. She was going to do more than submit. She was about to give her heart away—had already given it. She loved Jonathan—and he couldn't love her.

"No need to answer," he whispered, his voice husky rich in the vicinity of her ear. "I am sorry to take advantage of your womanly gentleness." His hand slipped down to apply pressure against her heart again, and she thought he pressed the breath out of her. Her lungs seemed unable to expand far enough; her head swirled. In another minute she would give up and become his for all time. She could think of nothing else.

"But I need you," he was telling her. "And you chose me when I would have refused the honor. You convinced me with your reason, and I agreed. Now we must suffer the consequences."

His hands took a more aggressive motion—one found her left breast, stroking the peak with his palm, making her tighten between the legs and grow moist. The other molded the shape of her hip and buttock with excruciating intimacy. She didn't think she could take much more of this. "It's . . . terribly hot in here."

"Unbearable, yes," he agreed. "This will help."

Before she could utter a word, he had loosened the laces on her bodice and stripped it away. Her soft kirtle skirt followed suit, settling limply at her feet. It looked just the way she felt. Within seconds she stood gaping in nothing but her smock, too dazed to do more than watch while he peeled away his netherstocks, canions, and trunkhose. His exquisite calves and thighs emerged, leaving him in only his long-tailed shirt. His legs and the curve of his buttocks she glimpsed were so flawlessly made that she was consumed by a rushing desire to see all of him. So pliant of limb, so noble of face compared to Oliver—Jonathan's presence overrode every thought or image left from her former marriage. A hungry pang surged within her—for Jonathan to remove his shirt so she could see the rest.

Ah, but she still wore her smock, she realized. Only fair for her to dispose of it first. Crossing her arms, she bent and grasped the fabric, whisked it over her head. His sharp intake of breath as she revealed her body fueled her pleasure. The cloth rippled from her hand. She stretched her arms high in exaltation, sharing her beauty with him openly, smiling up into his sober face.

His eyes mirrored her own need; his gaze flickered over her body. She saw his intense desire and reveled in it. Placing her hands on his shoulders, she enticed him. "Let me help you with your shirt."

"Are you sure you want to?"

The dark note came back into his voice, startling her. "Of course," she insisted. "Why not?"

He awaited her pleasure. "Remove it at your own risk."

Her own risk? Puzzled, Margaret undid the several remaining buttons, then grasped the shirt on both sides. Obligingly Jonathan raised his arms, bent so she could pull it over his head.

"You're as beautiful as I thought you would be." Her eager, reverent hands slid along the bare flesh of his chest, his sides, his hips. She winced shyly as she encountered his rampant arousal, the evidence that he found her equally compelling. Seeing it sent a racing torrent of want through her. Everything about him was so urgently resplendent, and this was the wedding night they had both desired but never had. With a sigh of pleasure, she clasped her arms around his middle and felt . . .

"God's eyelid, what is that?" Without letting him answer, she half turned him, half leaned around him to see. The sight that greeted her made her shrink back with a cry. His back was a mutilated mass of deeply furrowed, criss-crossed scars.

Tears leaped to her eyes. A sob blocked her breathing. "That—that unspeakable, disgusting, filthy . . . I would like to . . . Oh, Jonathan, I had no idea."

"Of course you didn't."

"But what he did to you. It's beyond words, it's . . ."

He nodded.

"Oh, God." A new vision of his agony accosted her. She put her arms around him, holding him tightly.

He returned the gesture, cradling her gently against him, as if she needed comfort. When he was the one . . . Suddenly the need burned within her to offer the bounty of her spirit. "Let me make love to you, my darling. Let me."

"I thought the man was to conduct the lovemaking for the maid."

"I'm not a maid," she reminded him, holding one finger before his face, scolding him lovingly. "And does it matter? Tonight, let the pleasure be mine."

Chapter 45

Jonathan wasn't sure what to expect, but he acquiesced to Margaret's proposal without hesitation, letting her guide him to the bed. What he did know was that he felt like a man abandoned in the heat of the desert, so dry he must plunge himself into her thirst-quenching, shimmering depths very soon or die.

She began by seating herself on his lap, the feel of her silky thighs and buttocks against him driving him mad while she caressed his face, his hair. She smiled and teased, pressing her tantalizing lips to his, sliding down to place provocative nips on his neck. He caught her palm and anointed it with a kiss. Her nimble fingers on his face and shoulders sent shafts of pleasure coursing through him, down through his torso, into his loins to engorge him further. Hadn't she noticed? He wanted to tumble her on her back and ram himself into her blessed female sanctuary, but he forced himself to wait and let her have her way with him.

"By heaven, Margaret," he groaned as she traced the muscles of his shoulders, then his chest in delicate, sweeping motions. "You drive me wild. You have magnificently clever hands."

"I'm a lace maker." She grinned at him between caresses. "I make my living with my hands. They have to be clever." Those agile, pleasure-producing fingers wove a graceful series of patterns over his body, seeming to know the many things a man would like—the most erotic way to smooth his thighs and stomach, the sensual way to cup and caress him. Clearly she had learned things in her first marriage, however unwillingly, that proved to his benefit. Gradually she pushed him back on the bed, stretching out her luscious, nude length beside him. Never had he let a woman do this, take control of his passion and his pleasure. But he trusted Margaret. Trusted her . . .

Her hand encircled him. He groaned and jerked with the ecstasy of her stroke. Her sensitive fingers wove a magic spell of excitement in him, an excitement that escalated into an overpowering hunger. It was true, he didn't mean to use her. But she had chosen him out of love; he knew that well though she had never admitted it. He longed to return the favor, but if he felt any high-flown emotions for her, he couldn't find them in the morass of aroused energy seething in his brain. But he knew one thing—he needed her urgently. She washed his mind clean with her golden serenity. Even now his mind was a haze of blinded ardor focused on her alone. She became his entire world, and he praised that world, wanting to laugh and cavort and . . . God, what he really wanted to do was penetrate her golden depths with all the power of his manhood. If he didn't soon, he would probably explode.

Ah, but she knew that. She seemed to sense his every need. Just when he thought he could bear it no longer, she parted her glorious, creamy thighs and straddled him. Grasping both her hips, he urged her to move lower. Her wonderful hands guided him. One more shift of her pelvis and he found himself plunged abruptly into her tight, silken depths.

He thought he had reached heaven, but there was more to come. All his dreams of the past six months, the agonizing days in prison, had focused on her. Now he admitted it. Now, when it was too late for him. Margaret, with her brightsome spirit, her unflagging strength, had been the embodiment of hope for him. Her soul was fresh and untouched, unaffected by her former marriage. She was one of heaven's pure.

And he was the supplicant. Eagerly he set her in motion, slipping to the brink where he would lose control, giving it all to her. Yes, that was it. They both had a burning need for control, yet he handed that right to her. Because he seethed with raging need for her. "Ah, my Marguerite," he rasped as she undulated her hips, sliding and tightening on him. "I need you. I need this from you. You cannot begin to understand how much."

She had passed the point of pleasing him and now moved to please herself. It drove him wild, the way she squeezed strongly around him, the charging stabs of pleasure coursing through him with her every movement, making his body shudder with joy. For years he had wanted Margaret. She tilted her head and let her golden stream of hair dangle, jutting out her beautiful, full breasts as she rode him, a ride that might mean his salvation, because only she could give him the gift that kept him sane.

Catching her attention, he sought her eyes and locked his gaze with hers. Her tenderness for him lit up her face the same way the bedside candle illuminated her features—in a golden aura of light. Her shimmering hair sparkled with it, her healing warmth blazed from her eyes, moving him toward redemption. If only he could leave the darkness behind forever. If only he could.

"I love you, Jonathan," she whispered, her excitement pushing her harder. She moved swiftly on him, her face a vision of fervent beauty, her rocking hips a gift of grace. "I never meant to fall in love with you, but I couldn't help it. I've always loved you and I can't stop." She sank down on him in one last, deep thrust, her womanly muscles tightening. Throwing back her head, she cried out, soaring into fulfillment, taking him with her.

He blazed inside like a smoldering scrap of tinder that finally found its flame point. Light and heat sprang into being, a glorious explosion of splendor. Of all the things he wanted, he craved her love, and like a miracle, she gave it. With a cry that matched hers, he soared to join her, reveling in the peak of his journey. They convulsed and rocked together, moaning their mutual pleasure, and the rare light she possessed transferred to him. The midnight of his soul turned to shining daylight, with Margaret as the sun, pouring her joy of living from the heavens. The dark flood within him swept away, and he blazed with her inner light. For the first time in months, he experienced ecstasy; he was thoroughly, completely glad to be alive.

In the aftermath of their passion, contentment infused him. He lay beside her, their limbs entwined, and stroked her peach- and ivory-tinted flesh. The chamber was awash with the lingering fragrance of their lovemaking. In his mind, it was spring and he felt young again, a giddy, laughing lad.

"Thank you, Marguerite," he said softly, letting his voice reach out to her.

She turned her face to his, and he could see the longing for love in her eyes. "Did I please you?"

"How can you ask? I've never felt more contented with a woman. You're a miracle, Marguerite. I'm amazed."

Tears sparkled in her eyes at that. An arrow of pain pierced him. He wanted to curse himself for a base churl, unable to return her love the way she deserved, not even able to pretend. "God, I've hurt you. I told you I would." He turned away with a groan.

"No, no." She followed him, her miraculous fingers caressing his ruined back, worried and tender. "It's just that my father called me that first, then you. I never expected to be called that again by someone I loved."

"That's just the point," he ground out, hating himself. "I'm not deserving of your love."

"If you can't say you love me in return, it's my fault."

Her voice was too humble. He felt every bit the knave, taking her golden light for himself and leaving her with nothing. "What are you talking about, it was your fault? I told you to stop blaming yourself. Please stop."

"Very well, I won't use that word. But I did send you away to war."

He twisted around to grasp her by the shoulders. "You did nothing of the kind, Marguerite. Your family would have prevented any attempt on our part to remain together five years ago. You did what you had to by obeying your guardian. I made my own choice when I joined the cavalry." A wonderful memory formed in his mind of a blond woman and her child at Lieden, when he had brought food to the starving city. To him they had been Margaret and her unknown child, and the spirit of their smiles that day stayed with him always, reminding him of why he went to war—to offer his gift to them and others—a second chance at life.

The feeling conjured within him by that glimmering, precious memory was the closest thing to love he could manage at the moment. If only he could tell Margaret he loved her and mean it. But all he felt was an insane, savage relief to feel pleasure again. And a kind of reverence that she wanted to give it to him. " 'Tis I who owe something to you. You're saddled with a man who is half crippled, but I will try to make it up to you. I swear I will."

"For a cripple, you manage some things frightfully well," she told him with a saucy flirt of her lashes. She cast a wry glance at the apex of his thighs.

He answered with a chuckle, but then continued more seriously. "I don't wish you to receive short shrift in this partnership."

"You do bring something precious to me," she assured him. "You give me a gift I've never had."

"What is that, pray?"

"Companionship." Her gaze lowered. "I realize now that my father was somewhere else in his dreams all the time. He loved me, but he wasn't with me, not really. I was a child, after all. How could a grown man find the things he needed most in me?"

"What makes you think this?" he asked, running his fingers along her forearm.

"I realized it when you watched me at my lace making. You asked questions, you made observations, you could point out the exact place where I had stopped the night before. My father"—she gulped and rubbed at her eyes with one fist like a child—"when he watched me making lace, he never said a word. I know he liked sitting with me, but he didn't notice which piece I worked on from one day to the next. It wasn't lack of love," she said hastily. "But his mind was in a fantasy world he had built for himself."

"Marguerite, I didn't mean to make you doubt your father."

"I don't doubt his love," she declared staunchly, her chin quivering. "I know he loved me. But now I see his limits."

"And what of your own? We all have limits. Do you still blame yourself for his death?"

"I am trying not to. But with Patience gone, it is hard."

And with that, she put out her arms, just like she used to, and the poignancy of her simple, unassuming gesture brought him both a wealth of pleasure and a heritage of pain. "Patience is not gone, my Marguerite," he told her tenderly. "She will be back with you soon and none the worse for her experience. I am sure of it." He took her reverently in his arms, cradling her against his chest. The only thing he could do now was pray—that for her sake, he might change.

Chapter 46

They settled down to sleep, and Jonathan sank blissfully into the featherbed, realizing he hadn't felt this contented in months. The bed was soft and Margaret's silky flesh lying full length against him even softer. He was drifting, drifting . . . He jerked awake, remembering something. "When did you say that woman would visit the ambassador with the poison?"

"In thirteen days," Margaret murmured, half asleep.

"Mmmm." He said nothing further, instead letting the drowsy languor brought by her sweetness creep over him. Tonight she had given him the gift of her miraculous serenity, and he thanked the heavens for her. With relief, he looked forward to a restful, dreamless sleep.

That dreamless sleep was denied him. He didn't have the tormented, recurring nightmare about prison, praise heaven. Instead, he wandered through the labyrinth of his past until he passed into it fully, believing it real. There he found Doña Elizabeta lying beside him, her black hair curling like her spirit, dark and lecherous. Wife of the prison garrison commander, Dutch loyalist wed to a Spaniard, she was a practiced minx if ever he had met one. But he was glad she had craved him on first sight.

Not that he had been much to look at then. Back mangled and bloody. Only half conscious and babbling delirious nonsense. The hero stories that preceded him must have been exciting on a grand scale, because despite his broken appearance, she put in gear her devious machinations. An innocent guard took fatal blame for Jonathan's escape, and for once in his life, he found he couldn't care.

Gingerly he rolled to his other side, careful not to touch

his back. The month seemed like forever, hiding while Elizabeta nursed him secretly back to strength.

At first he had thought he would die. Not now. The fact that he lived was brought back all too vividly when Elizabeta performed the daily ritual of removing his bandages and smoothing salve in the jagged valleys of his back. The raw wounds burned like red hot irons. But after the devastating pain that had made them, it was nothing. No, his writhing was mental and came for another reason. He had sunk low to save his scurvy hide.

Elizabeta rewrapped his bandages with sly, devious fingers. Oh, she was cunning, that woman. Wickedly so, and eager for her reward. After the dressing of his back came another daily ritual. Elizabeta threw away the scissors and shrugged out of her gown, exposing her voluptuous body—full breasts, a tiny waist, plump thighs. Again her fingers worked, relieving him of his clothes. Then he closed his eyes.

His miracle, his Marguerite. Memory of her golden gaze returned to him, sweeter than a thousand beddings. Right now he would give his eye teeth for just one of her smiles. If he thought about her very hard . . .

Imagination was a forgiving thing. Eyes closed, he willed himself to believe she came to him. Marguerite, his golden-eyed daisy, the woman he had once loved. The old dream of her returned to haunt him, sweet mixed with bitter. *Cross, twist, half stitch and whole,* the weaving of her bobbins had once captured his heart. Motif of roses, purled and picoted, the pattern of her bounteous spirit, the plenty of her love.

With his body he worshipped her. The tinted gold of her silken flesh, glossy hair, and whispering lips. His fingers explored every inch of her, throat of the lily, breasts tipped with rose. From her flesh came the scent of luscious womanhood mingled with flowers. He traced kisses along the flat plain of her stomach and parted the twining stems of her legs.

Margaret moaned as he urged her toward climax. Almost to ecstasy himself, he surged deep. On and on it went, pure heaven, until she bit his shoulder and cried aloud. Rudely he was jerked back to reality and found she wasn't Margaret . . .

Damn, it made him furious every time. He hated Elizabeta and himself more for a barterer of sex and a lying rogue. It was true he had bedded women by the dozen after he left Lulworth. But in prison, he had recognized what drove him, that he loved Margaret still and could never stop.

After that, the inquisitor had annihilated all emotion, making Jonathan numb to everything but hate. He had lied, killed, and betrayed to escape prison. Without hesitation, he had betrayed her memory with another woman, whispering lies to the impostor that he never meant.

Worse still, he fully intended to capture the inquisitor or die trying. And when he did, he would secure the creature to a stake and give him a taste of his own evil. He would raise the whip, watch its braided, deadly lash curl through the air, and bring it down on the wretched monster's . . .

Jonathan wrenched himself out of the dream and sat upright in bed, panting. Vile, disgusting dream. His eyes sought his bed partner, checking frantically. Margaret lay at his side, wrapped in a veil of slumber, her innocent beauty shining like treasure in the night.

With trembling hands he drew up the linen to cover her loveliness. Then, without disturbing her, he eased himself from the bed. Pulling his garments on one by one, he flung himself toward the door.

His foot collided with something. Craning to see if he had awakened Margaret, he held his breath, waiting. She slumbered on. Bending over, he started to push the thing away, then saw it was a bobbin box. A question formed in his mind. Picking up the box, he slid back its carved cover and discovered the answer. There lay the ivory bobbin he had given Margaret years ago.

My miracle, my Marguerite. His own words haunted him, tearing at his soul. The look of love etched on her face when he had first said the words—he had seen that blessed look again tonight. Smoothing the inscription reverently with his fingers, he placed the bobbin back among the others and put the box away.

Halfway to the queen's antechamber, he paused and leaned against the wall. In that horrible, torturous dream he had thought Margaret was the dream, that he had never returned to England, had never wed with her or held her in his arms. All the bounteous gifts he had received he expected to vanish like water drying in the sun. Gone forever as punishment for his sins.

With a muted curse, he moved on, furious. He was an undisciplined savage, used to controlling everything around him, but he couldn't control his emotions. He needed Margaret to stimulate them. And despite her marvelous success, he couldn't summon the one emotion she needed most. Hating himself, he moved on to the antechamber. He would send the guard away and take his place.

No more sleep for him tonight, that was sure. Jonathan lay on the rude pallet in the antechamber, his loins longing for Margaret. Having her once should have sufficed, but it didn't. The urge to drink of her golden light consumed him like an unholy thirst.

A small click caught his attention, so faint he might have been mistaken. No, there it was again. Lie still, lie silent, here behind the settle. The secret panel across the room slid back.

He couldn't see the panel; it was covered by the tapestry, right at the place where the foolish virgins clustered. The minute it opened, Jonathan caught the draft of air, saw the ripple of the wall hanging. Another of his follies arose to torment him—in prison, he had spilled the secret of this door. Here was his folly, come to fruition. Slowly, a man's form emerged from behind the cloth.

For over a year Jonathan had awaited this moment. Now he exercised rigid discipline, kept his body relaxed in a sleeping posture, even though he longed to leap to his feet and plunge a dagger in the fellow's heart.

He did neither. He had waited this long—he could wait a little longer to catch the assassin in the act of threatening the queen's life. When the black-clad figure moved through the door leading to the inner sanctum of the queen's privy chamber, Jonathan swiftly gained his feet.

"Stop it, Robert. Don't." A giggle sounded in the next room.

Jonathan pressed himself against the wall of the adjoining chamber and listened.

"I don't wish to stop," came a man's answer, presumably Robert. "And neither do you."

"Well"—another giggle—"mayhappen not . . ."

"There you have it. Give me another kiss. And let me take a peek here. What have we? Mmm, very sweet."

More giggles. The sound of muted scuffling, then moans of pleasure. Jonathan wrinkled his forehead, analyzing these pieces. Robert trysting with Jane Shelton, his intended? But why had he entered by the secret passage? It made no sense . . .

Then again, it did. Robert did not have free admittance to court. Of the several hundred people waiting on the queen, not a one did so without express invitation. And people competed viciously for the privilege, despite the cramped quarters allotted them in the respective royal palaces. Without the queen's summons, Robert stayed at his town house in London and came to court only when sent for. Grandnephew or no, the queen held him at arm's length, thoroughly cautious of him. Jonathan recognized that as eminently wise.

"Did you bring me the trinket?" came Robert's voice, coaxing.

"It's right here, as I promised, but why do you want it?"

"A bit of a jest, that's all."

"The queen won't consider it a jest if she finds it missing," warned Jane.

"Shhh," he soothed, probably stopping her mouth with a kiss. Jane's further words were lost to Jonathan. Whispering ensued that Jonathan couldn't make out either. "Sweet, you have my word on it," he heard Robert say. "Now, Jane, I must go."

A second later, Robert skulked into the chamber and, looking neither right nor left, headed for the far door. He passed within several feet of Jonathan without seeing him, too bent on his purpose. Jonathan waited until he heard Robert open the door in the next chamber. Sure that Jane had retreated in the other direction, Jonathan followed his quarry back to the secret passage, back to the source of his folly and his own hate.

When Margaret awoke, it was still dark, and she sensed immediately that she lay alone in the chamber. Patting the empty space beside her confirmed her fears. Where had Jonathan gone? Did he suffer insomnia tonight?

Climbing from the bed, she pulled on a mantle and padded in bare feet to the door. Mayhap he had gone to the queen's antechamber as he often did, to stand guard. She would seek him there.

Margaret entered the antechamber just in time to see Jonathan pull back a corner of the tapestry and disappear. Astonished, she crossed the chamber on tiptoe, her heart racing. Her fingers explored the tapestry edge, then lifted. She peered behind.

A rush of stale air struck her, emerging out of a black, gaping hole. Quickly she flipped the tapestry back in place, alarmed. No wonder she had never liked this room.

But the next moment her mind was asking questions. Had that hole been there all along? Surely not. She would have noticed, as would many others. Cautiously, she pulled back the cloth again and stuck her head inside.

The hole went on forever. Blast, but how did she keep running into dark holes lately? First with Tim, now this. But Jonathan had gone down this secret passage, and she was bound to follow him. Drawing a deep breath, she plunged after him into the dark.

Margaret descended a steep ladder, feeling the temperature grow cooler as she went deep into the earth. After that, she felt her way down a straight passage for a long time, running both hands along the rough walls. Occasionally a branch shunted off right or left, but always the main tunnel continued. Until she came to a spot with multiple branchings. She stopped, baffled.

Which way should she go? How many ways were there? The close, tight air of the tunnel lay dank and unmoving about her, giving no clues. Starting on her right, she tested the dark with her hand.

One opening to her right, two. The third was straight across from the one she stood in. A fourth gaped to the left, and another after that. It had a pattern! A straight tunnel with two openings radiating left and right like the rays of a star.

And judging by her direction and the speed of her walk, she must be somewhere in the vicinity of the closed tennis court, which lay near the river. Determined to catch up with Jonathan, she had just picked up speed when she bumped full face into something warm.

A terrifying tangle of arms closed around her, pinioning her own arms to her sides. Margaret struggled as groping fingers searched her body, passing over her lips, breasts, and waist.

"Good God, Margaret," a voice rasped, followed by the distinctive sound of nostrils drawing in air. "Just what do you think you're doing?" came Jonathan's furious reproach.

"How did you know it was me?" she asked in a small voice.

"You smell like flowers, that's how. And you've been biting your lip again."

Her hands flew to her face, guilty. In her nervous state, she had bitten her lip so hard, it probably bled.

"You've ruined my work tonight," he barked harshly. "Back the way you came. Now."

Though he said not a word during their return journey in the dark, he was clearly incensed with her. Margaret went meekly.

"I suppose I've trespassed in your domain again," she said sulkily when they were back in her bedchamber and he had lit a candle. "I am sorry if I ruined something."

"You should be. If I meddled in your lace making, you'd have my head."

"I don't claim to be a soldier," she said, climbing into the bed, "or an intelligence agent, but occasionally you might find a need for my services. If so, I hope you will admit it. And I hope I could do the same."

"Is that a fact? What of tomorrow night at the guild meeting? Would you like me to—"

"Don't you dare do a thing, Jonathan Cavandish!" she cried, crossing her arms and glaring at him from the bed. "That's entirely different. I want Bertrande in the guild on her own merits. I refuse to play games."

He nodded incisively. "I said it at Clifton and I'll say it again. I don't see a part for you in my business either, so stay out."

With a huff, she pulled up the coverlet to her chin. "I suppose I'm where you want me. Are you satisfied now?"

Jonathan took a long look at his wife, especially at the way her body's inviting swells and curves rose in beguiling shapes beneath the bed linen. She was, indeed, where he wanted her. He wanted her in this particular place all the time. The trouble was, he couldn't join her just now.

He chose not to answer her provoking question. Instead,

he went to a coffer and pretended to search for a blanket, not that he really wanted one. He wanted her aroused and moaning in his arms.

"No wonder I never liked the queen's antechamber," she was murmuring while he searched, half talking to herself, her voice turned plaintive. "With that secret passage there all along. Is that why you guard that room?"

He grunted and rooted deeper in the coffer.

"Does the queen know about that passage?" she persisted. "Does anyone else?"

"Yes," he cried suddenly, swinging around, filled with an alarming rage and the need to spill his secret. "I couldn't keep my mouth shut in that blasted prison. I babbled every important piece of information the inquisitor wanted and begged for the chance to tell him more." He could scarcely bear to look at her, but he had to see her reaction, had to know if he disgusted her as much as he did himself.

"Why, Jonathan." Her face bore that sweet expression he recognized from old, the one that meant she loved him utterly. "You're ashamed of what you told him? But you're human. You feel pain. Of course you had to tell."

"I should have remained silent." His fists tightened around the blanket he had found.

"Nonsense. A dozen people must know about that tunnel, mayhap more. If you hadn't told him, someone else would have. Listen to your own good advice and stop taking the blame."

"Whether I'm to blame or no, I have to guard that entry. Day and night."

With that, he stalked from the room. Could it be he *was* only human, that he didn't have to be the hero; with all his being he prayed she was right.

Back in the antechamber, he resettled himself on his hard pallet and prepared to watch the panel. But he didn't expect any more activity. The performance was played out for tonight.

Margaret tossed and turned after Jonathan left. No position was comfortable. On her right side, the bed seemed lumpy. If she lay on her left side, she was forced to confront the empty space at her side.

"Drat!" She rolled out of bed and fumbled again for her

mantle. She needed someone to talk to, and Bertrande was far away with Marie in the new house she had chosen. Opening the door, Margaret stepped into the passage beyond.

Chapter 47

"I can't sleep." Margaret pushed the door to her grandsire's chamber closed behind her. A single, fat night candle burned at his bedside, and she could see his humped figure in the bed, rolled into his characteristic bent position. "I used to talk to my father when I couldn't sleep," she went on as she crossed the chamber and stood by the bed. "I know, you're not my father, but I need someone and you'll have to do. You won't want to hear what I have to say, but 'tis my great fortune that you have no choice just now."

It gave her great satisfaction that he couldn't protest. "Move over," she ordered sternly, as if instructing an errant child. "I want to sit down." She had never done such a thing before when he was in health, had never even been in his chamber when he was abed. 'Twasn't proper. He would have been outraged.

Now he lay without moving a muscle. Just huddled there, his breathing slow and even. That was a good sign. Before his breathing had been rough and broken. He had thrashed and clutched his middle, moaning in pain. Gallstones, the physician had said, but they must have passed. His color was better. Brazenly she plunked herself on the edge of his bed.

"It's Jonathan, Father. You don't mind if I pretend you're my father. I wanted you to be when I first came to Yorkshire. You seemed in some ways like him. Fair in your reasoning . . . most of the time. Highly intelligent. I had hoped you would love me as he did. You seemed delighted to see me. I misjudged you, I admit, but I wasn't wrong about my first impression. You were glad I'd come, though for all the wrong reasons. I understood that eventually, but I was slow about it. You fooled me well.

"It was when I became with child that I was happiest." She tilted her head to one side and viewed the bed canopy's cunning embroidery. "I thought you loved me, because of the care you lavished on me, the pride in your eyes as my belly grew. No, no"—she held up both hands as if he were protesting—"don't deny it. You were extremely proud of me. And not just because I carried your great-grandson, or so you assumed. You liked it when I stood up to you, when I argued you down and was right. You just wouldn't admit it, but you found my intellect stimulating. No wonder, too, with my aunts and my mother the way they are. Which is partly your fault," she scolded. "You act as if they are mindless chickens, and to prove you right, they behave that way. If you expected more, if you gave them tasks to occupy their minds and stopped lavishing gifts on them, they might change . . . Oh, but why am I bothering to say all this?"

She let her hands drop to her sides, discouraged, then left him to pace the chamber. "This is coming out all wrong, but it doesn't matter. You can't hear a word." She gave a wry laugh, half ashamed of herself. "I came to talk about Jonathan, and instead, I talk about you. But you see, I need someone to love me, now that my father's gone. Bertrande is a precious friend, but I'm separated from her too much. Besides, what I really need . . ." She stopped, letting her head droop.

"I miss my father so," she said finally. "And I was hoping Jonathan . . . Of course I'm foolish to imagine such a thing. I can hear you telling me so. You said you understood him, so you know what I mean.

"As I said, I wanted to love you when I came to Yorkshire," she went on reproachfully, addressing the cold hearth, her back to the bed. She picked up a smooth quartz stone ornamenting the chimney piece and fingered it as she talked. "I realized you were many things I could admire. You had strength of character, you had discipline. It's not that I compared you to my father; I wasn't a traitor to his memory. You weren't better than he was, just different, with strengths in different places. And because of them, I craved your love."

She banged the stone back in place and scowled at it. "How fitting that you rejected my foolish feelings. You with your heart like this stone. Have you ever loved anyone?

No, you like nothing but your rules and being right all the time. Instead of feeling love, you feel satisfaction that you've exercised your power that day and kept your property and your people safe from encroachment by others. But you only care for those people because they're yours. You're obsessed with power and you don't want anything else. Is there nothing that gets through to your hard heart?"

"You do."

Margaret let out a yelp of surprise and spun around at the sound of the gruff, grating voice.

Her grandsire had his eyes open, was staring intently at her. While she watched, he labored to draw himself into a sitting position. "Damn it, granddaughter, come here and help me. Don't just stand there gaping like a beached fish."

Margaret didn't move. "How much of what I said did you hear?"

"Enough." Having found the right position, he sank into his mountain of pillows, panting with the effort. "Come here." She still refused to approach. "Oh, very well, send for pen and paper," he snapped. "I'll send a message to my town house telling my servants where to find Giles. He'll fetch Patience."

" 'Tis the middle of the night."

"I'll write the letter and it can go off first thing," he snarled at her.

"In truth?" Margaret probed, suspecting another trick.

"In truth," he wheezed, clearly disgusted at having to concede the issue. "Will you stop being so blasted stubborn and come here?"

She approached the bed slowly, stopping a foot away.

"Damn it, I want you here." He smacked the edge of the bed. "Sit."

Margaret studied her grandsire warily. He was a crotchety whoreson and she wasn't sure she could trust him, but as long as he had Patience, she had nothing else to lose. "I object to being ordered about like your dogs." She half sat, half leaned against the edge of his bed.

He punched a pillow whose position didn't suit him, then studied her. "Not willing to yield a thing, are you? No, I suppose not. That captain of yours told me you were as stubborn as I am. I'd say twice as stubborn and be right, too." He snorted and reached for his pomander, held it to his nose to breathe in the refreshing scent of pine and cedar. "Did you mean all those things you said about me?" His abrupt question held no hint of tenderness.

"I meant them." It was not a good moment for testing her devotion, Margaret thought derisively. But then he would never understand that. "Especially the part about your obsession with power."

"I have no such thing," he flashed at her, then caught himself. He looked at her glumly. "You remind me of someone I once knew. A woman."

"Your wife, the other Margaret?"

"Lord, no. She was the one with a brain of a peahen, as you so aptly put it."

"Brain of a chicken."

"Be silent and listen. You remind me of my mistress, Elizabeth Grieves."

"I'm charmed to know it. I remind you of your bawd."

"Don't speak that way of Bessie. She was no coarse woman to be slandered. She was the village dairyman's daughter and well liked until I became her protector. Because of me, she was scorned. Damned fools, she was better than any of them, keeping her dignity despite their slights and insults. She was no whore, for she clove only to me."

"Was this before or after you wed with Margaret?"

"Both."

Margaret frowned at him. "You could have wed with Elizabeth and you didn't? You let her be ruined instead." She didn't know if she was pleased or disgusted with him. He had loved, yet he had made nothing of it.

"Of course I didn't wed with her. I had a dynasty to carry on, an estate to manage. I couldn't marry beneath me. My father taught me that."

"And did you never once wish to go against your father's wishes?" she challenged. He hesitated. It was only a second, but Margaret saw it. "Ah, you did. Did you discover too late that you loved her? After you were stuck with Margaret, may she rest in peace, my poor grandmother. I feel sorry for her the most. She had to live under your iron thumb."

He had the grace to look uncomfortable, her hard-hearted, stern-willed grandsire. Mayhap she could get through to him yet.

"What happened to Elizabeth?" she asked more gently.

"Died of some fever."

He had a haunted look in his eyes, and her heart went out to him then, though only for a second. She wouldn't let him bully her. "At any rate, you're better now," she said briskly. "The gallstone must have passed. But I don't want you up right away. I intend to nurse you, feed you strengthening foods, dose you if I see fit."

The look of horror that crossed his face was enough to make her laugh outright. The ruler and the warrior couldn't abide the thought of being entirely at her mercy.

"You'll do nothing of the kind, madam," he roared, tossing back the linen and thrusting out his feet. He stood, but immediately leaned heavily against the side table, perspiration breaking out on his brow.

"You're not ready to get up." She bustled over and pushed him back in bed. "And I won't brook any arguments." She hoisted his heavy feet onto the bed and retucked his linens. "Whew, you need a bed change. I'll see to that in a minute, but first I will send for pen and paper. I would like that letter."

"You would," he growled at her crossly. "I haven't a doubt."

Chapter 48

When Margaret next awoke, the sun reached through the casement to tickle her closed eyes with its rays. A giggle sounded across the room, filling the chamber with sweetness.

Margaret's eyes flew open and she struggled to focus. A huge bubble drifted past her nose, rainbow-hued from the morning sun. It burst, making her jump and blink as it wet her face with its tiny splatter. As she turned, another bevy of bubbles floated her way. Looking farther to the window, she beheld a marvelous sight. Jonathan sat on a stool by the washbasin, blowing soap bubbles through his circled fingers. And on his lap sat . . .

"Patience!" Margaret cried, leaping from the bed. "Patience, you're back!"

Patience sent her a merry smile. "Look, Mama, bubbers," she pointed, her face wreathed in smiles. "Magic make bubbers for Pat."

Margaret didn't stop to correct her daughter, to tell her not to call Jonathan Magic. She swept Patience into her arms and hugged her, laughing like a madwoman. "Patience, my sweet, Mama missed you, missed you, missed you!" she sang out. "I'm so glad you're back."

"Happy to see you, too, Mama." Patience wound both arms around Margaret's neck and gave her a dozen wet kisses.

Margaret nestled on the bed and proceeded to cuddle her baby. They laughed and kissed, patted each other's hair, and babbled nonsense to each other. Jonathan stood by, smiling benevolently, but at one point he went to the door. Paying him scant heed, Margaret gave her child another kiss.

"Giles!" Patience cried, looking over Margaret's shoulder.

Surprised at the interruption, especially since she was still in her night smock, Margaret turned around.

"You see, your little charge is doing well." Jonathan led the broadly smiling serving man into the chamber. "I promised to let him see Patience," he explained to Margaret, "before he set off for Clifton again."

"Clifton?" Patience's happy smile turned into a frown. "Want Giles here." She wiggled out of Margaret's arms and went to Giles. Though she was scarcely as tall as his knee, she crossed her arms and gave him an imperious stare. "Horsy ride now. Morrow, too."

Margaret looked on in amazement as the huge man meekly took her child on his back and gamboled around the room, obeying her every order. Her baby had never behaved like this before.

"Little lass is just like her grandsire." Jonathan seated himself beside Margaret on the mattress, making it dip. "She's learned much from watching him. A quick one, she is. Master Giles, you've spoiled the lass," he said reprovingly to the older man, but he smiled as he said the words.

"Aye, Captain, if you say so." Giles shuffled his feet and looked at the floor. "But 'twas worth it to see her laugh. She cried so at first, even when Mistress Crandle tried to cheer her. 'Twas the lady who cooked for us and did our wash."

Margaret's insides contracted hard at that. She wanted to weep, remembering how she had felt to find Patience gone.

"But 'tis over now," Jonathan pointed out. "What say you, Margaret? Are you assured of your child's well-being."

She managed a tremulous smile. "She won't stop calling you Magic," Margaret apologized. "I hope you don't mind."

"I don't mind anything she does."

"That's a relief. Oliver found her irritating. I had to keep her out of his way."

"You needn't do that for me, but I must take her to see your grandsire later. He won't hurt you," he told Patience, who started to wail. "He may roar and grumble, but that will be all. Come now, what if we find some fresh bread and honey to begin our morning. By the by, did anyone tell you I'm your new papa?"

"You are?" Patience's eyes grew as wide and round as two pennies.

With her child well in hand, Jonathan headed for the door, sending Margaret a significant glance. "I must speak with you in private later today, after we've both seen the queen. Oh, and Giles," he clapped the serving man on the shoulder. "I'm sorry about your head."

Giles touched the fading bruise on his brow and grimaced ruefully. "All for the sake of duty," he said. " 'Tis forgiven, sure. Here is your hammer." He handed the little pearl-handled tool to Jonathan. "I thought you would want it back."

Margaret heard Jonathan thank the older man as they quit the chamber. Trepidation about the coming talk formed within her. Now that they were wed, Jonathan was probably going to dictate her behavior. The thought turned her into a quivering bundle of nerves.

Chapter 49

She was wed to the lover from her youth, she had her child, her beloved father had died but she was learning to accept that it wasn't her fault. All these things considered, life should have been perfect, Margaret thought with despair later that day. But it wasn't. Not in the least.

"I require a service of you, madam," Jonathan said to her. They were back in her bedchamber while Patience napped in the outer chamber, with Giles on watch.

"In truth?" The time of their talk had come, but it wasn't starting the way Margaret had expected. "I thought you didn't want me to—"

"None of your pert comments."

Surprised, Margaret fell silent. His gaze flickered over her, a restless movement, and she realized what a concession it was for him to ask at all. She also sensed a seething volatility in him today. It was more intense than last night when she had followed him in the passage, worse even than on the night at Clifton when he had captured the courier.

"I require the secret of the ambassador's house," he stated, displaying a generous view of his back as he stared out the window. "You mentioned a spy hole. Where?"

He didn't ask nicely. She felt like kicking him but instead calmly fetched paper and ink and sketched out the arrangement of rooms at the ambassador's, including his bedchamber and the location of the spy hole. "First you should check to see if they are in the dining chamber," she advised his back, pausing in her sketch to rub the feather against her chin. "If they aren't, the spy hole won't help you, but I believe that chamber is used for receiving and all manner of things besides dining. After you're sure, you might—"

"That is sufficient." He cut her off as he came over and

took up the paper. "Pray forget we ever discussed the matter. I'm bound for the city and will return in time to escort you to the guild meeting tonight." He took up his dagger and strapped it on.

She tried not to make anything of it; he wore the dagger whenever he left court. But when he took up his pistol, too, she despaired all over again. "I can go alone to the meeting." She whisked the cover cloth from her lace pillow and fingered the bobbins, anything to avoid watching the warrior ready his weapons. "Bertrande and Marie require escort, so you might bring them. Otherwise, you need not be present, you know."

He spun around from loading his pistol. "There you go again—"

"No, there you go!" she flashed at him, leaping to her feet. "I may not want your help, but you're worse. You expect to open my brain, pick out the information you want, close it up, and I'm to forget everything. As if I could! You don't even say thank—"

"Thank you." He stopped her flow of words. "Before you harangue me on my shortcomings, let me say I know a few things about architecture and would have found the secret myself in time, but I need to spend the next twelve days at other things. I do thank you for sharing your knowledge, but it's a dangerous thing. I have no wish to see you—"

"Your wishes! What about mine? You want to wrap me in swaddling bands like a babe and I can't stand it." Even now the close, inhibiting atmosphere of court wore on her. "You remind me so much of my grandsire, I—"

"Who you've been fighting with again." His accusation silenced her, and he went back to loading his pistol. "How do you expect a sick man to recover when you continually stir him up?"

"He enjoys an excuse to shout," she retorted, turning back to the quill and paper. She ran her fingers over the quill, absorbing its smooth texture. She must not lose her temper, not now that they were wed. Not even if he lectured her, not even if he scolded.

"The entire palace heard the pair of you," Jonathan was saying in that stern tone she hated. "I thought you had no complaints now that Patience is back."

"They're not my complaints." She eased herself into the

answer, assessing her control, deciding she had enough to continue rationally. "He fussed the entire time I bathed him, but he must be bathed, don't you agree? And he refused to eat the vegetables the physician ordered, shouted for mutton and wine instead, which are not allowed. And Patience wanted Giles to stay here with her. He isn't what I imagined for a nursemaid, but I told her to ask Great-grandsire. Well, he roared at her, frightened her half to death, though she stood up to him with my help." She warmed to the story, unable to hide a smile at the memory of her daughter, stalwart before her great-grandsire, telling him she wanted Giles. "I believe it does him good to consider other people's needs, and once he was forced to hear her, he gave in, which didn't hurt him in the least."

Jonathan shook his head. "I see nothing amusing about baiting a helpless old man. You should behave with more respect."

"He's not the least helpless," Margaret told him, the smile fading from her face. She rose and stood before him, planting her feet squarely like his. "He's had his own way all his life, commanding others, and he still wields a great deal of power. But he insists on eating the wrong things, the physician says, and he won't stop unless someone makes him. I'm going to take care of him whether he likes it or no."

She stared up at him, ready to defy him on these two points—caring for her grandsire, and refusing to forget the things he deemed dangerous. The tight compression of his mouth, the way he measured her with his dark eyes while he rammed the ball into his pistol, suggested he didn't like it. But then she had her own strength, more than enough to match his. It roiled inside her, along with her love for him, for the beauty of the magic he carried inside. If he had forgotten that magic, she wanted to remind him, to liberate it so he could work his wonderful spells once more. "I'm going to take care of you, too," she said, "whether you like it or no." Letting out a deep sigh, she stepped forward, slid her arms around his neck, and put up her face to be kissed.

He seemed disinclined to respond at first, but that changed rapidly. Especially when she sent her tongue on a brief foray to search for his. At that, he groaned and gathered her to him, kissing her harder. Once they were started,

Margaret's control wobbled dangerously. It crashed into ruins as he took her hand and led her to the bed. She closed her eyes against the dazzle of his lightning and let him work as he would.

"I believe I'll fetch that feather," he whispered in her ear as he removed her bodice.

"That's my writing quill." She sat up, half shocked.

"I'll get you another for writing." He put one finger to her lips, pressed her back on the bed. "Right now I have a task for this one."

He returned bearing the feather, smoothing it between his fingers. Margaret's gaze fastened on those fingers, imagining how it felt to be that feather. If he stroked her that way, she would bend and moan and do anything he wanted, anything at all.

He stretched himself full length beside her and placed the feather, like a painter would his brush, against the slant of her cheek. Propped on one elbow, he swept it across her face and out to her cheekbone, leaving a tingle of gooseflesh in its wake. All the while his eyes worshipped her, speaking his desire. If he couldn't love her, for certes this was second best.

The feather whispered its way to her ear, then down her neck. It came to tickle the hollow of her throat. Margaret smiled, suddenly shy, and turned her head to hide her blush. He teased her with the feather and his bountiful humor—teased and tempted. "Jonathan, no tickling." She put up one hand.

"No tickling. I promise." He sent the soft tufts of the feather to smooth the flesh of her arm, calling attention to where the pale, delicate hairs had risen in tingling response. His suggestive grin sent her blushing again as he tempted her body. Her arousal in answer to him was complete and immediate. He need only exert his will.

Margaret moaned as his lips followed the path of the quill, feathering their way along her neck, tantalizing the dip of her throat. He knew exactly what to do to her and where. Path of the feather, path of his sensual lips, they traced their way downward to where he had freed her breasts from her smock. Ah, bliss, the feather swirled a new teasing pattern on the full tips of her breasts, and she strained for him, for more of his kisses. She arched her back as his mouth followed the feather. She wanted more of him—and more, and more.

The feather wanted to travel lower, but her clothing barred the way. Away with her kirtle skirt! Away with her petticoats! She flung them aside herself, probably like a wanton, but she couldn't wait to see what he would do next with that feather, wielded by his magical, imaginative hands.

"Do you like this?" The feather swirled its way down her belly, trailed by its faithful followers, his lips. The patterns arabesqued and whorled, pleasing her body and her mind. With firm but gentle hands, he parted her thighs, searched between her legs with the feather. "Tell me the truth," he instructed with mock sternness. "How does this feel?"

"Ahhh. Oh!" Margaret moaned and twitched as the feather found the sensitive core of her womanhood, then lost it. "A little to the left, my love. A little more."

Jonathan stopped moving the feather and peered at her. "What did you say?"

She stretched with languorous enjoyment and smiled at him. "You almost had it. Please try again."

Jonathan threw back his head and laughed uproariously. "I asked for that, didn't I? I vow, I've never known a woman like you."

"You imperiously demanded the truth," she said, making a moue at him.

"No one but you would interpret that to mean you should tell me how and where to pleasure you."

"Am I to let you rub away at the wrong spot and pretend it's perfect? I did that with Oliver and I'll do it no more!" She sat up, indignant. "He insisted *he* knew the right way to bed me, and if I didn't enjoy it, there was something wrong with me. I thought you would be different. At least I hoped—"

"I am different." He grasped her shoulders and pinned her to the bed, his face filled with intensity. "Never compare me to Oliver. When you tell me you feel pleasure, I want it to be real, not feigned."

"Then try again." She relaxed and grinned at him as he leaned over her. Stretching up her hands, she pulled him down for a kiss. "I'll tell you the truth when you find the right spot."

"With pleasure, Marguerite. You have no idea how

much." He parted her thighs with eager hands and reapplied the feather, his own arousal apparent now.

Margaret clutched his arm as the feather's delicate tip found its target. "Oh," she cried. "That's the place!" She squirmed in ecstasy as he fueled her excitement, driving her to greater heights of pleasure. Suddenly the storm he brought broke over her. It filled her body, driving her into a frenzy of wanting. Here was what she needed—this man who brought her the tempest, who changed her life and moved it forward with his lightning touch. Her father had loved her, but Jonathan offered something unique, an acute caring for whether she was fulfilled.

Jonathan chuckled in delight as his tender manipulations sent Margaret's beautiful body convulsing into paroxysms of pleasure. Within minutes, he could stand it no longer. Tossing the feather aside, he replaced it with his fingers, letting his body hover above her. When she sat up and grasped her hips, guiding him toward her spread thighs, he was more than ready. With eager hands, she coaxed him into her wet, smooth depths.

His own excitement flared as he drank in the blazing patterns of her glorious light. The rare flame that burned inside her transferred to him. The midnight of his soul grew light. Each of his footsteps in the temple of her beauty burned with light. If only he could stay this way. The fragile inroad she had first made became a massive bonfire. He blazed with her inner, precious fire. With each thrust of his hips, with each of her answering cries of pleasure, they moved closer to heaven. He was so close, so close . . .

Margaret gasped with pleasure as Jonathan's hands wove patterns of excitement through her body, gliding over her breasts, her hips, her thighs. His eyes were closed, his full, sensual lips half parted, his chest heaved with the passion she inspired. Avidly she drank in his arousal like a gift, reveled in the kisses he brushed on her cheeks and hair. "Jonathan, I love you," she whispered, feeling herself approach the summit. "Open your eyes."

He obeyed, and she saw a tender light burning for her in the smoky depths of his eyes. It was the closest he had ever come to escaping his torment, and she cried aloud her triumph, arching her hips upward to take him deeply inside her. With a series of quick, hard thrusts, she found fulfillment. Joy swirled through her body, making her want to sing, to laugh, to spill her exhilaration for them both to share.

In the aura of their spent passion, Margaret lay on her side and unwound her hand from her beloved's neck, let the back of one finger trail along the rasp of his cheek. "I'm glad you shaved off the beard. It makes you just like the old Jonathan."

He chuckled and stretched, a satiated movement of muscled arms and legs. "Not quite. The old Jonathan never had an opportunity like we just shared." His hand admired her, curving along the slope of her ribs, down into the valley of her waist and up the rise of her hip.

At his words, she snuggled against him and buried her face in the shadow of his neck.

"Tonight, Margaret, will you let me help you at the guild meeting if necessary?"

He did ask, she noted, unable to rouse herself to anger now. Not even to anything as vehement as irritation. "Only if absolutely necessary." She toyed with a lock of his hair. "Only if it seems Bertrande will be turned away. But she won't be. I'm sure."

"So if things don't go your way, I have your permission to intervene?" At her nod, he continued. "If that happens, say yes when I wink at you and all will be well."

"I'm sure if they study the samples I've asked her to bring, they will agree—" She stopped as his last directive sank in. "When you do what?"

"When I wink at you, say yes."

"I'll do no such thing. I'll—"

He stopped her mouth with a kiss. "You'll be an obedient wife for once."

She couldn't fight him. Instead, she draped one leg over his and pressed herself against him, wanting the bliss to last.

It couldn't, of course. Within minutes he rose and began dressing. Resentment filled her. Each lovemaking brought her closer to being with child, and therefore brought him closer to leaving. Mayhap she should resist him in future, but she never could. She needed his startling lightning to change her life.

"Jonathan, where are you going?" The impetuous question leaped from her lips before she could stop it.

"Nowhere in particular," came his sober answer. "Around London to see what I can learn."

She knew he was lying. He was going to skulk around the Spanish ambassador's residence, and if he had a chance to use the spy hole, he would. His tension, which had dissipated totally with their lovemaking, returned now, a teaming energy that roiled just beneath the surface, threatening to break out in reckless action, to take him away from her into danger's path.

"Marguerite." His voice caressed, working its way back under her defenses. "You have to accept the fact that I may not survive."

"I don't have to accept anything unless it's a done deed," she stated crossly. "And it isn't. Besides, why should I be the widow? Why not his wife?"

He grinned at her demand. "He doesn't have a wife. The Inquisition is an ecclesiastical court. The men who serve as inquisitors are usually members of a religious order. They never wed."

"Is this beast a religious? Does he have a name?"

"I neither know nor care. All I know is that he had the authority of the Inquisition in the Netherlands, and that he considered me a heretic, doomed to the stake."

"Well, whoever he is, I refuse to let him have you. I intend to fight him, Jonathan. I'll oust him from your life and your mind."

"He's firmly implanted in both, I'm sorry to say." He pulled on his shirt.

"Was he there a minute ago?" She hopped from the bed and moved against him, rubbing her bare thighs against his. "When you and I were, ummm, you know . . . were you thinking about him then?"

He turned around and captured her firmly, pulling her against him, fondling her bare breasts. "No," he groaned, capturing her lips in a probing kiss. She wanted to laugh in triumph as she enjoyed the feel of his fingers on her sensitive skin. "I didn't think of him for a second, and that's why I need you, Marguerite. You make me forget everything else but you, and for that, I thank God!"

With satisfaction, she noted he was hardening again. The inquisitor couldn't do that or anything close to it. When he was with her, in the heat of his passion, she burned away the darkness. But as soon as he got her with child, he had to leave England. And for his sake, she must let him go.

Chapter 50

"God's wounds, 'tis gone!"

At the queen's shout, Margaret dropped the linens she was folding and raced for Her Majesty's bedchamber. Everyone said Elizabeth sounded like her father when she was angry. That seemed possible indeed as Margaret entered before the other ladies and found her sovereign with her face livid, her voice deepened to a ferocious roar. Elizabeth shook a ruff box in Margaret's face.

" 'Tis gone, damn it. I tell you 'tis gone." She shoved the box into Margaret's hands and strode over to jerk the bellpull.

"What's gone, Your Majesty?" Baffled, Margaret opened the satin-covered box and inspected its contents. A beautiful lace ruff reposed on the velvet cushion inside.

"One of the cuffs," roared the queen, angrier than Margaret had ever seen her. "Look below in the drawer. Someone has taken it to make me look the fool. I'll have his head. I swear I will."

"What is it, Your Grace?" Three other ladies in waiting and the mistress of the bedchamber clustered at the entry. "How can we assist, Majesty?" asked Kate Carey, whose calming influence on the queen was well known.

"Someone has taken my lace cuff," Elizabeth shouted. "They're trying to ruin my marriage."

Kate hurried forward to soothe her mistress. "There, there, Your Grace, we will find it." She signaled to the others. "Pray you begin looking while Her Majesty takes her ease in the next room."

Two hours later, the cuff was still missing, despite a thorough search and questioning of all the staff.

"Those cuffs and ruff were Alençon's gift," exploded the

queen when her ladies had reassembled to tell her the bad news. "When he arrives, he will ask me to wear them as a compliment to him."

"Then you explain that your foolish women have mislaid one of the cuffs," Kate answered. "You may place the blame on me."

Elizabeth stopped her pacing and shot Kate a furious stare. "You're either more naive about such matters than I thought or incredibly stupid, Kate. He will take my excuses as insults. You know how the French are. And so does whoever took the cuff."

The queen was right, Margaret realized with foreboding. This seemingly trivial incident could wreak havoc in English-French relations, and that must not happen. France was England's strongest, nay, England's *only* strong ally against Spain. She would have to do something. She stepped forward decisively.

"Your Majesty."

"What?" thundered the queen, whirling around, clearly at her wit's end. Her dark eyes flashed as she brought them to bear on Margaret.

"I believe I can help, Majesty, with your permission."

"What can you do, Mistress Cavandish?" Elizabeth demanded, looking down her nose at Margaret, "that all those other good ladies have not."

"I can make a cuff just like the lost one," Margaret said calmly. "If you will permit."

The queen examined her. " 'Tis a complex piece of work. Not for a novice. Unfortunately, the French are far ahead of us in this skill, though I like it not."

"I assure you I can do it." Margaret kept her voice strong and confident. "I have been well taught by a skilled French lace maker. If you will but lend me the matching cuff, I can reproduce the pattern. 'Twill take some time, though."

"How long?" The queen tapped her foot impatiently.

"All the time between now and the duke's arrival," Margaret stated. "And I will need help. May I send for my teacher and lodge her here at court?"

"Send for any help you require," ordered the queen. "Begin at once."

"First, Your Grace, I must go to the Drapers Guild, whose monthly meeting you kindly gave me permission to attend. In fact, I will barely make it if I leave now."

The queen scowled. "I want you back here immediately after. You will start work then."

Armed guards rode on either side of the coach as Margaret was borne toward London and the guild meeting. She didn't much like it; they made her conspicuous, but it couldn't be helped. The queen and Jonathan had insisted on it, in case Robert tried to stop her. Margaret rearranged her simple kirtle skirt and bodice and stared out the window anxiously. Bertrande must be admitted to the guild tonight.

Just as she had predicted, the search for the missing cuff made her late to the meeting. Bidding the guards wait outside with the coach, Margaret slipped into the passage off the main hall, unobserved.

Nigh on a hundred people crowded the assembly room. She spied Jonathan seated with the officers on the raised platform at one end. Various speeches were going on, but Margaret couldn't concentrate on them. She had to find Bertrande. There she was with Marie, sitting toward the front with Master VanderVorn. She hoped the applications for membership would come soon and be approved speedily, because she must get back to Greenwich to begin the cuff. The very thought of the task before her made her feel nervous. She had never attempted quite so complex a work.

At long last, they came to the new-member portion of the meeting. She had been warned, Margaret admitted. Still, her temper slipped the first notch as she listened and realized the requests were all for relatives of influential members who had clearly arranged for their fellows' positive vote before the meeting ever took place. She scowled at the speakers from her hiding place in the darkened passage and bit her lip.

When the Capell request for consideration was announced, Margaret drew closer to the door.

"Mistress Capell," said one of the officers, "with due respect for your experience, we would welcome you as a sister in our fraternity, to worship and feast with us in friendship, but we only take new working members if they can better our standing in commerce. Do you have anything to say?"

In the passage, Margaret gasped. Bertrande couldn't speak before an assembly like this. She wasn't used to it, and if flustered, she was likely to relapse into French. They weren't even going to discuss the merits of having Bertrande as a member. Naturally, she thought angrily, because there was no one to smooth her way.

Master Thirstan and the other officers were shaking their heads in the negative. Everyone looked solemn. "Well, my friends, shall we put it to a vote?" Thirstan asked.

Margaret wanted to shriek, to leap on the platform where the guild officers sat and confront them. Outrage lent wings to her heels. It moved her forward through the door. "Wait," she cried, "you must not take the vote yet."

Everything stopped. Thirstan swung around, his face suggesting the interruption was most unwelcome. The other officers examined her, their mouths closing in stern, strict lines. The women stopped chatting and gossiping and hushed their children. All eyes in the guild hall turned her way.

From her place on the wide, low platform, Margaret noted the women who craned to get a better look at her and was glad she had removed her court gown and dressed simply in a style befitting the tone of the meeting. But most of all, she felt Jonathan's gaze on her, and she was glad her hair was done up neatly in a knot, not hanging down like a wanton's. Bad enough that it shone gold around her head by candlelight. It was an embarrassment to her in moments like this. Jonathan and these other men would not see anything past her hair color and her sex and deem her useless. Yet she was not useless.

"What if Mistress Capell offers something substantial to your guild?" she demanded loudly. "What if she offers something beyond price?"

A hubbub arose in the room. People bent to their neighbors, whispering. What did she mean by priceless? Was she talking about silver or gold?

Margaret dared not look in Jonathan's direction. She straightened proudly and addressed the audience. "Consider that there are only two qualified lace makers in the city of London who belong to your guild. I know"—she paused significantly—"I met and spoke to them and assessed their skill. Two is hardly enough to supply a city with lace products. The guild has not done its job."

Angry mutterings broke loose in the hall at that. People leaned to one another, expressions indignant. The guild master's voice rang out. "Madam, pray state your qualifications to say such a thing."

"I am a skilled lace maker. I have made bobbin lace in the English style since I was a child, and in the last five years, I have mastered the traditional French patterns, having learned them from Mademoiselle Capell."

Master Thirstan turned to where Bertrande sat in the front row. "Is this true?"

"Mais oui." The answer came strong and clear. "She is the most miraculous student I have ever had the privilege of teaching. She learns and retains like magic. Her fingers work of their own volition. She even knows patterns by heart."

The master turned back to Margaret. Renewed respect could be heard in his voice. "What is it you propose that would benefit our guild?"

"A school for lace makers," Margaret answered crisply. "With Mademoiselle Capell as its mistress. It will strengthen the lace industry in London, and in England. You say yourselves that England relies too much on imports from the Continent. But how can you prevent that if you cannot make lace yourselves? Mademoiselle will teach your wives and daughters and sisters to be lace makers, which will add to their families' livelihood. You will hold the London lace market, nay, the lace market of all England, in the palm of your hand."

She paused, and once again pandemonium broke out, rising and falling in waves throughout the room. But this time the women broke into smiles at the prospect of increased income and a personal skill of their own. At their urging, their menfolk agreed, nodding their approval.

"And what is your role, madam? Pray state your name and part in this venture."

Margaret drew a deep breath and cast an apologetic glance at Jonathan, hoping he would forgive her for what she was about to say. "I am the Dowager Viscountess Longleate, nee Smytheson," she added for the benefit of Master Thirstan, who wore a surprised look. "I would be happy to serve as patron of the school." She had plenty of money now and could outfit them all, and her noble title lent credence to her offer.

The officers of the guild had put their heads together and were whispering earnestly. One of them eyed Bertrande, then returned to the discussion. A tiny doubt pierced Margaret. Was something going wrong?

Jonathan stood up. She had not dared look him in the eye before this. Now she met his gaze and saw approval. A splendid feeling of victory rushed through her. There was something else in his gaze, too, but she couldn't quite make it out. While she looked at him, he gave her a decided wink.

"Captain Cavandish?" Master Thirstan acknowledged him. "You wish to add something to the discussion before the membership votes?"

"Aye, master." He grinned roguishly. "I wish you to consider. Mistress Capell is no longer young in years. She does not have the strength to teach all day."

Margaret's gaze locked on him in astonishment. What was he saying? What was he doing?

"And her niece, though a steady lass, is too young. She has neither the experience nor the skill to serve."

Fury shot through Margaret. He was ruining everything! Her temper flared, bypassing every notch likely to hold it back. She wanted to yank the jeweled dagger from his belt and plunge it in his black heart.

Jon turned toward her, his mouth lilting teasingly at the corners. "For this reason, the dowager has something more to offer." He winked again, then turned back to harangue the crowd.

Margaret followed him with her gaze, wishing she could be alone with him and a rope. A nice long one, not too thick but plenty strong, so she could throttle him. She would draw it slowly around his throat and tighten it gradually, so that he would understand the depth of her fury. Her temper caused a roaring in her ears.

"The dowager says she is a skilled lace maker," he continued, speaking to the crowd like the pompous knave he was. "She has testified to that fact, and her claims are confirmed by Mademoiselle Capell, who is her tutor."

Margaret gritted her teeth, hating it when he called her *the dowager,* as if she were sixty and decrepit.

"I will add my testimony to theirs," he continued. "I have known the dowager since her youth and will verify that she is even more skilled than she claims."

God's eyelid, Margaret thought furiously. Why didn't he finish and be done with it. They would lose the vote now.

Why didn't he go ahead instead of keeping her standing here.

"For this reason," Jonathan said solemnly. He had the attention of every living soul in the hall now. They all were enraptured by him, the men wishing they could be like him, snared by his charisma, the women enchanted by his beauty. He was beautiful. His glorious facial structure, his muscular form ensured that. All of them sat on the edge of their stools awaiting his mandate. "For this reason, I wish to advise you that the dowager will take the position of head mistress herself. She will run the school and teach the most eligible women, who will in turn become teachers to the others. Ah, and do not fear that this is too much to ask, since the dowager has recently become Madame Jonathan Cavandish. She forgot to mention that. What say you, gentlemen? To have both the patronage and the skill of so charitable a lady. Need we even vote to record your unanimous consent?"

A roar of approval broke out. Margaret's jaw dropped in astonishment. Was the man mad?

He turned toward her and winked again, his wicked eyes sparkling. And she was furious with him. Rage claimed her. "For certes I shall—"

"She accepts!" he cried, moving to take her hand and press it between his two. "What a noble sacrifice she makes."

She glared at him. Sacrifice? She would make a sacrifice of him given half a chance, on a block with a cleaver. God's eyelid. No, God's holy foot and arm and every part of Him, including his eyelid. She swore she would show them all, including Jonathan Cavandish, how to teach the making of lace.

Chapter 51

"What did you do that for?" Back in their chambers, Margaret looked up from the parchment she bent over as Jonathan came in. She had so much work to do, it was late, she was tired, and he had to go and do that. After the guild meeting, she had hastily settled Bertrande and Marie in the tiny chamber allotted them at Greenwich. Now, despite her exhaustion, she must begin the lace cuff. But she intended to give Jonathan a piece of her mind. She would *make* time for that.

"Why did I do what?" Jonathan asked calmly, looking fresh and collected, as if nothing had happened tonight.

"As if you didn't know!" Margaret wanted to shriek with frustration, but she held on to her temper. "Why did you volunteer me to teach the lace school?"

Jonathan sent her a penetrating stare. "I should think that would be obvious. Complete control of what will be taught of lace making in London belongs to you now. In fact, the city's entire lace making future rests with you. You got everything you wanted. Or didn't you know you wanted that control?"

"I hadn't thought of it that way." Margaret leaned back in her chair, trying to take all this in. He had handed her a tremendous chance to exercise her skill.

"You will do well," he said as he stripped off his buff doublet. "You only resisted because *I* was the one insisting on it. Now it's my turn," he continued, pulling on his dark magician clothing. "Why did you do what you did?"

"What do you mean?"

"You brought that young ruffian back with you from the guild hall," he said, slanting his eyebrows together in a frown. "I understand bringing Bertrande and Marie, but that fellow is a thief fresh from the stews."

"Oh, Tim." She gave a little laugh, half pleased to thwart him in something—he had so thwarted her. "Remember I told you about him? He knew I would be at the guild meeting so he met me there. I thought he ought to come to Greenwich. He needs a home and care."

"He needs a good hiding, that's what he needs."

She gazed up at him with innocent eyes, holding her thick needle suspended in midair. "But Jonathan, I thought to set him to work as your apprentice."

"No!" Jonathan exploded. "I'll have no scurvy stripling to apprentice until he can show manners and restraint."

Margaret winced. She hadn't expected quite this reaction. "He's a bit uncouth, but I can't see any other reason for complaint. I'm sure he would work hard."

"He cut the guard's purse," Jonathan barked at her. "Call that reason for complaint?"

"He did?" A slow burn of anger went through Margaret. "He'll have to stop that. I'll speak to him." She bit her lip and reapplied herself to the parchment.

"Better yet, I'll take a birch to him." Jonathan exchanged his boots for shoes with soft, silent soles.

"You'll not," Margaret contradicted, glad of the chance to tell him a thing or two. "After he's been bathed and clothed properly, I'll . . ." What would she do with him? "I'll set him to work serving my grandsire. He'll teach him restraint," she declared. A satisfied smile tugged at her lips. "Are you coming to bed?"

"I fear not. I have work to do. The duke is due in August." He came to look over her shoulder as he fastened his dark trunk hose. "What are you doing?"

"I'm copying this cuff because the mate was either lost, misplaced, or stolen. It's part of the set Alençon gave the queen, and she *has* to wear it when he arrives. So that is what I must be doing every waking hour, not teaching at the lace school."

Jonathan drew back, astounded by the revelation. The cuff was gone and Margaret would replace it? He looked at her with admiration. And now he knew what Jane had given Robert in the queen's chambers. He let out a long, low whistle. "Serious business, this."

Margaret methodically punched holes in the parchment. "It is, Jonathan. I don't think the cuff was lost or misplaced. Someone took it, but why? If I wanted to hurt relations between France and England, I could think of worse things to do."

Jonathan shook his head, unwilling to share his suspicions. If he were so reckless as to do that, Margaret would undoubtedly do something even more reckless with the information. He was better off pretending he had no idea. Besides, he had more immediate things on his mind. Throughout their conversation, he had found it difficult to take his eyes off Margaret. She was arrayed in a pale amber night smock that could hardly be called a smock, it was so delicate. In fact, it was semitransparent, offering him a superb view of her breasts, their lush tips jutting against the fabric as she leaned against the table.

"Put that needle down," he instructed, taking it from her hand and dropping it on the parchment. Bending over, he swept aside the silken trail of her hair.

"I told you, I have work to do, I . . ."

Her words faded as he kissed the nape of her neck, let his lips travel across the fragrant texture of her skin, nuzzling until he found her ear. Taking the lobe in his teeth, he worried it gently, awaited her answering tremor. Ah, there it was.

"You can take some time for this," he wheedled, reaching for her lips, which were still slightly swollen from his earlier kisses. "But tell me one thing, first. What is that called?" He waved vaguely at the parchment.

"It's called a pricking," she answered, giving the corner of his mouth a tiny nip. Her hands abandoned their work, reached for his body instead, targeting a particularly sensitive spot. "I thought you had to hurry off?" She sent him a sly grin.

"This won't take long," he chuckled, tugging her to her feet. "Not with the way I feel about you tonight."

She didn't seem convinced, though. Jonathan noticed immediately. As he watched, she became engrossed in a crack of the floor, rubbing her bare toes along it in a fragile, frightened movement. This was one of those times he had feared—when he wanted to destroy all thought of the inquisitor in his mind, to burn it away with the piercing gold of her purifying light. But instead, she needed something. "You're hesitating," he stated bluntly. "Why?"

"Jonathan, there are things I said on our wedding night . . ."

"You can take them back any time," he assured her, unable to suppress the sarcasm that leaped into his answer. "They weren't required."

"That's just the trouble." She turned up her sweet face to him, her clear brow drawn into a pained frown, and he felt a stab of guilt at his harsh answer. "I can't take back what I said," she went on in plaintive tones. "I can't unfeel what I feel. I tried to over and over for years and it was no use. It makes me afraid."

"You still think love is a weakness?" he asked baldly.

"Not the way I once did. But it does make me . . . you called me reckless, and I am. Mayhap it's not weakness but stupidity. For your sake I do things I would never otherwise dare to do."

Like killing a man. Like spying on the Spanish. She didn't have to say the words. They both knew what she meant.

"Margaret, has it ever occurred to you that your love is a strength? It gives you the power to achieve."

"It gives me madness."

He couldn't argue that. He had felt that very madness himself after he first lost her. "The question is, can the power override all else—the madness, the weakness, the stupidity, whatever you call it. I believe it can. You have a strength in you far greater than you ever dreamed."

"I do?" Margaret found this to be the most astonishing conversation she had ever had before a bedding, not the least like the ones with Oliver. She searched Jonathan's face, the face she had learned to love so well. Not a trace of mockery did she find. Only a depth of sincerity that stripped away her defenses. His forceful essence took possession of her, filling the moment with his magic, like seeing light through a crystal, a dazzling rainbow of many-faceted new beginnings.

He held out one work-roughened hand. She knew he had been working on the mail corselet for the queen, and she took his hand and caressed the callouses tenderly.

"Come to bed, Marguerite." He summoned her with a voice that swirled around her with the spark of his wizardry. "I need that strength of yours. I need your healing touch."

And because of her weakness or her stupidity, or her strength, she wasn't sure what to call it, she went to him gladly. With a new hope in her heart.

Chapter 52

The days before the French duke's visit flew by rapidly. Twenty days remained, then nineteen, then only eighteen more days.

On the fifteenth day before the visit, Margaret sat in her chamber, working the cuff. She had known her court appointment would be demanding, but she hadn't counted on hysteria. Though the visit was officially "secret," everyone at Greenwich knew. Tempers had built to the breaking point in the last week. Fights broke out between those who favored the match and those who did not. The queen's mind changed daily about marriage, swinging from pro to con and back again at the slightest provocation.

In the midst of the frenzy, Margaret tried to keep her equilibrium. She had started teaching at the lace school, and her pupils were attentive, but she *must* finish the cuff. Day and night she labored, having finished the pricking and begun construction. Bertrande came daily, to sit with her and advise, but it didn't always go well.

"This part is impossible." Margaret threw down the pair of bobbins she held, frustrated and tired. "I'm not sure I interpreted the stitches right."

"Your interpretation is flawless. 'Tis merely your temper, chaffing." Bertrande's gentling, magical voice instilled its calm. "This is the first time you have attempted to copy such a complicated work, but you progress beautifully. You were meant to reach for ever greater achievements. You are growing, *ma chère*."

Margaret put down her bobbins and caught up one of Bertrande's hands. The fragile wisp of flesh felt leaf-fine against her cheek. "Bertrande, you are too good to me. You offer so much and I give little in return."

"You give more than you know," Bertrande answered tranquilly. "Now that I can no longer work, you are my worldly tie to the thing I love best."

Her back suddenly sagged and Margaret caught her around the waist, alarmed by this confession. "*Ma tante,* you are ill," she cried fervently. "And have been for some time. Pray let me send for a physician, as I have so often urged."

Bertrande let her breath escape in a prolonged sigh as she leaned against Margaret. "No physician can cure me. I have such pain here." She placed a hand across one breast, for the first time admitting to a specific malady. "Do you see now why the captain was right to insist you teach the lace school? I have not the strength."

Tears stung Margaret's eyes at this proof of her friend's increasing weakness.

"But we can help each other," came Bertrande's wise council, even in the midst of her pain. "You make a miracle for me each time you work your lace, and I hope I strengthen your resolve. You *can* finish that cuff." She placed her left hand on Margaret's right. Margaret took up her bobbins again.

"Ah, that is most comforting." A smile played around Bertrande's pale lips and she closed her eyes. "You are working the motif now. I can feel it."

"Yes. And now I place a pin." Margaret hurried on. Bertrande was right. She had to finish the cuff.

They worked for an hour thus, letting the serenity of the lace wrap itself around them like a cloak of calming grace. But all the time the echo of her father's words pierced Margaret's heart. *You have a gift, daughter.* But that gift had been her father, and then Bertrande, and she was going to lose both. She lifted her face to the heavens and pleaded, "I don't know if I can bear it. It's too much."

"If something costs too much, I'll steal it for you," interjected a sympathetic voice.

Startled, Margaret whirled about to behold Tim. "Oh, Timothy. It's you." She raised one hand and gestured him back. "Don't come in unless you've been deloused again," she instructed. "We can't have fleas near Bertrande."

He immediately turned sulky. "Me 'air's been near plucked from me head and me skin scrubbed off. Does that suit, Marguerite?"

Margaret rose from the bed and inspected him. "You look greatly improved, Tim. Doesn't it feel better to have a full set of clothes, new shoes, and clean hair. But don't you dare steal anything," she warned solemnly, remembering her promise to Jonathan. "You're to ask if you need something, and if it's reasonable, you'll have it. If I decide you're not to have it, I won't be disobeyed. Furthermore, no purse cutting."

"Aw, Marguerite." Tim pulled a long face and looked dejected.

"And you may not call me Marguerite here at court. You must call me madam. I'm entirely serious about the purse cutting," she admonished. "There's to be none of that if you want to stay."

"Aww." Tim scuffed his feet in the new shoes. He was doubly put out, Margaret knew, because she had forbidden his cursing. "Do I 'ave to wait on that old man? He's a regular coney catcher. Wouldn't put it past 'im to slit me throat."

"You do have to wait on the earl." Margaret put on her most authoritative expression, but she almost chuckled, imagining these two together. Yet how could she laugh when she was frightened for Bertrande. "If you do your tasks well, you'll be considered for an apprenticeship, but you must impress the captain first."

"Let us go to the earl now," Bertrande proposed. Margaret whirled around to behold her friend sitting up straighter, looking much improved. "And take Patience with us, if she is awake from her nap."

Tim had left the door to the outer chamber open. Beyond, Patience sat on the hobbyhorse that Jonathan had bought her, listening to Tim's reprimand with big eyes.

Margaret bustled out to scoop up Patience and balance her on her hip. "Yes, let us go watch Grandsire make faces over his remedy." Nothing cheered her like that ritual, she had to admit. It was naughty, but now that her grandsire couldn't hurt her, could barely clothe himself let alone enforce his will, it gave her a mischievous pleasure. "I believe 'tis time he met Tim."

"Stories?" Patience asked, tugging on Margaret's sleeve. "Gran'sire tell?"

"We'll see if he's in the mood to tell stories," Margaret agreed. "Mayhap, if you ask sweetly, he will." Astonishingly enough, her grandsire knew a wealth of stories and could keep the child spellbound if he chose. With a nod, Margaret led them off to the earl's chamber.

The earl didn't like his new servant. He scowled as he drank the ugly herbal brew Margaret brought and refused to look at Tim.

"What am I supposed to do with him?"

"He's to do your bidding. Whatever you need or wish."

The earl banged the empty mug on the table and snapped his fingers at Tim. "Make yourself useful, gutterscum. Take this away. Then fetch my mantle."

"Aww, do I have to let him call me that, Marguerite," whined Tim, pulling another of his ugly faces as he removed the mug and brought the mantle.

"That's what you are and that's what I'll call you until you can prove to me otherwise!" the earl roared. "And don't you dare to address my granddaughter in that insolent, slovenly manner. She is 'Madam Cavandish' whenever you are in company. You will learn to address everyone properly here at court, especially when you are serving. If you can't do it correctly, you'll be locked up with naught but bread and water for a se'nnight. Stand up straight. Look me in the eye and say 'Yes, my lord.' "

Apparently the threat of lost freedom frightened Tim more than any other punishment could, for he jumped to attention, visibly shaken. He who was so used to going his own merry way feared loss of liberty more than a beating.

"That's the way to handle him," the earl said decidedly to Margaret. "I know his type. And you, madam, can get back to work."

Margaret looked down and remembered her lace pillow before her.

"You have a great deal of lace to make," her grandsire said with a knowing nod. "I have ears and I hear things. Not everyone at court knows about the missing cuff, but I do, so you'd best keep the secret better. Go on, what are you waiting for? You, too, mademoiselle," he ordered Bertrande, clearly enjoying himself, though there wasn't a trace of a smile on his face. "No one can stay here without helping. You can thread up the spools or whatever the blasted things are called. Tim, mull some wine. No"—he put up a hand before Margaret could contradict him—"Don't you dare remind me what to drink and what not. Go to the kitchens and get me some unfermented cider. I assume that meets with your approval, Madam Meddlesome." He glared at Margaret.

"Me, too?" piped up Patience, apparently thinking she should be doing something since all the others were.

Her grandsire cast a glance at his great-granddaughter, and Margaret could have sworn she saw a fleeting hint of pride in his eyes. "You, young mistress, can practice being quiet, since it is clearly a difficult lesson for you. And I," he added, "when Master Gutterscum returns, will tell a story. Tim, before you go . . ."

Tim stopped in his path to the door and bowed stiffly, obviously uncomfortable with the gesture. "My lord?"

"Don't you dare mention a word about this lace madam is making or I'll personally kill you." He whipped out a dagger from beneath a bolster.

Margaret gasped. "Grandsire, put that away. You must not—"

But Bertrande was chuckling. The low sound filled the room, growing into a gay laugh. "Marguerite, I do believe his lordship is improving. I am so glad!"

The earl leaned back against his cushions, apparently spent from his efforts, though he wouldn't admit it. "There are ill plots about and we're going to unearth them. Send me that husband of yours when he returns," he ordered Margaret. "I'll tell him how it has to be done."

Fourteen days before the duke's visit. Thirteen. Margaret worked the cuff furiously, hardly resting, scarcely eating. Early on the morning of the twelfth day, when she entered her grandsire's chamber with her lace pillow, a dagger whizzed past her nose.

"God's eyelid, what—"

"Don't you knock?" snapped her grandsire from the bed. "Foolish woman, I might have pinned you to the wall. Now that's the way 'tis done," he told Tim, who stood beside the bed at attention. "Poxy boy, thinks he can throw," he muttered at Margaret, "but he goes about it wrong. Here"—he handed Tim the second dagger of a matched pair he owned—"let's see you have a try. Get out of the way, Madam Meddlesome," he growled at Margaret. "Lest you want some blood let."

Margaret scuttled over by the hearth. She didn't approve of dagger practice inside, even if they used an archery target. She watched as Tim made a remarkably good throw, just missing the circle in the center.

"Too low," corrected her grandsire, motioning Tim over. "When you aim, pull your arm back like this." He grasped the boy's arm and demonstrated the swing. "Now fetch the pair."

As the lad retrieved the weapons, Margaret spotted Jonathan sitting on the far side of the earl's bed in the shadow of the bed hangings. She studied him, suspicious. Since when had he been friendly with her grandsire? Yet the earl had sworn to advise him, and it made sense.

"Come here," her grandsire grunted, as if sensing her curiosity. "We have news of the lace cuff."

They were going to confide in her? Margaret approached the bed, eager for the information and willing to ignore his commanding manner for its sake. "Where is it?"

Her grandsire glanced at Jonathan. "Robert has it," Jonathan stated tersely. "We questioned Jane Shelton and it appears he asked for it, swearing it would be returned."

Margaret regarded the men with astonishment. "Then why did she not say so when it was discovered missing?"

"How would she dare, with the queen in such a temper?" Jonathan answered. "But during our discourse with her last night, Walsingham, Burghley, and I, she confessed it. And though taking a cuff is hardly treason, it seems highly suspicious. Particularly because Solsover has dined often with the Spanish ambassador of late. We are also sure Solsover was the man the Spaniard tried to contact at Clifton. I searched his town house while he was out last night and discovered a pair of rough shoes in his chamber, exactly like the weeder folk wore."

Margaret's eyes widened. They had all suspected this, but her information proved it.

"That knave," snarled her grandsire, "trying to drag me into his illicit business. I should have never trusted him, but all I saw were his lands and his relationship to the queen. To make my heir a relative to royalty, that was my hope. Hopes have a way of being dashed."

"And what of Jane?" Margaret asked, not wanting to discuss her grandsire's dynastic dreams. It was miracle enough that he sat with her merchant-soldier husband, discussing state secrets. "Shouldn't she demand that Robert return the cuff? My work on a duplicate would not be required." She indicated her lace pillow.

"Ah, but that is where the Spanish come in," Jonathan advised her. "Robert didn't take that cuff for his own purposes. Jane is continuing in her duties as a maid of honor, but she is to watch Robert carefully. You and Lady Nottingham are to watch her when you are on duty. Do you understand?"

Margaret nodded slowly. "What do you hope to learn from her?"

"The details of the plot from Robert. She is to report anything suspicious to me."

"Jane has ever been a loyal subject to the queen."

"We believe so." Jonathan glanced at the earl, who indicated he should continue. "This task will test her loyalty. She was chosen to wed with Solsover because he requires guidance, and oddly enough, she seems to love him. We believe she can guide him away from this treasonous plot. You, on the other hand, misjudged him."

Margaret couldn't deny that fact. It still seemed impossible that Robert, the dim-witted, was involved in a serious intrigue. "I think," she said, "he is easily swayed. They must have promised him something—"

"They promised him *you* when I was dead, among other things." The ugly look crept back into Jonathan's eyes.

Margaret cast him a glance of concern before turning to her grandsire. "What is the next step?"

"We capture the poisoner," said the earl.

"After I observe her delivering her poison to the Spanish tomorrow," Jonathan said, "Master Tim will show me where she hides."

Margaret thought her eyes would pop out of her head, she stared so hard at Tim. In mere days he became privy to their trust and their secrets. She began to smile. She had judged someone a-right.

"I'm not safe in London as long as she's 'ere," Tim told Margaret by way of explanation. "She don't take kindly to them as leaves her service."

"But why don't you just arrest the Spanish now?" Margaret wondered aloud.

"We have nothing worth accusing them of," her grandsire interjected. "How would it look, arresting the Spanish ambassador because of a missing lace cuff? We would appear mad. Keep your kirtle on, Madam Impatience. We'll have our evidence in good time."

She was getting impatient, Margaret thought to herself as she settled down to work on the cuff. The Spanish could poison the queen at any moment without warning. But at least her grandsire and Jonathan were finally including her in the plot, which was something, though she felt danger all around.

Chapter 53

A single pair of lascivious Spanish eyes increased Margaret's sense of danger. For two entire hours the next day, those eyes bored into her while she danced attendance on Her Majesty during the first visit of the Spanish trade delegation. They belonged to the same man she had seen at the Spanish embassy, the one who had stopped her in the garden. He recognized her, too, no question in her mind. And his question? His probing gaze spoke it clearly: what had she, one of the queen's ladies, been doing unattended that day at the ambassador's house?

Summoning a maid who had just entered the queen's antechamber, Margaret relieved the girl of her tray and rose, needing to hide her disquiet. First she poured more ale for the queen. Then she moved along the paper-strewn table, offering wafers and fruit to the visitors and English representatives.

The men talked and talked, both sides demanding many things, neither side agreeing. Not today. Not for many days while their discussions went on and on. The queen presided over them, gracious and interested. Every fan in the chamber, including Her Majesty's, churned the air in the vain attempt to dispel August's sultry heat. And all the while that pair of onyx eyes followed Margaret's every move, making the hair prickle along the back of her neck.

Odd in the extreme that he caused such a reaction. There was nothing unusual about him. His name was indistinguishable from dozens of other Spanish names: Don Luis de Alvarez, a wealthy gentleman who represented his country's interests. She took in the white hairs punctuating his temples, the lines traveling his face, as well as the austerity of his dress. Yet beneath those black garments, behind that broad, aristocratic forehead, lingered something sinister and sexual about him.

Fantastical nonsense! Margaret scolded herself, returning with her empty tray to her stool behind the queen. Because of the secret panel, she waxed macabre every time she entered this chamber. Busying her hands with her fan, she thought of the cuff instead. She had made a good start on the task, but it was only half finished. So much more remained to be done, she wished she might be at it even now.

"Mistress Cavandish, you are not attending."

Margaret jerked to attention at the queen's words. "A thousand pardons, Your Grace. What did you say?"

"I said, pray escort Don Luis. He wishes to see the tennis courts and gardens."

Conflict erupted inside Margaret as she moved to obey. A second ago she had longed for escape from this interminable meeting. But not this escape. She didn't want to be alone with this man.

She had no choice. While she daydreamed about her lace, it seemed he had requested her services. As Margaret moved through the doors, de Alvarez's palm contacted the small of her back, making a possessive imprint. Despite the day's heat, a wave of cold foreboding swept up her spine.

"You are enjoying your visit to England?" Margaret kept her eyes fastened on the pebble-strewn path of the Greenwich gardens, anxious to avoid any meaningful discussion with this man.

"Indeed. I enjoy the views." His insolent gaze suggested the front of her bodice was particularly to his taste.

"Will you be staying much longer?" She hoped he would say no.

"I will stay until our business is complete." His voice lingered in her ears, oppressive like the heat. He shrugged, a swift, animal-like movement. "Who can say how long that will take."

They lapsed into silence. Margaret fanned herself as they walked, training her gaze stringently away from his. She indicated the trimmed shrubbery that took fantastical and intriguing forms, of animals both real and mythical. But she knew he was looking at her, waiting for the right moment to ask her the question she didn't wish to hear.

"The closed tennis court is here, Don Luis," she exclaimed, hurrying ahead to open the door and enter. The great building was empty at this time of day when the heat was most intense. "You see, there is a gallery for spectators."

So one of the exits from the secret passage came out here, Margaret thought as she examined the structure herself. De Alvarez strolled the vast, echoing chamber in a leisurely manner, seemingly untroubled by the heat. While he studied the design of the building, Margaret speculated on where the exit might be.

"I find the customs of the English curious."

Was it her imagination, or did his voice carry a hint of innuendo? "In truth?" she responded nervously. "How so?"

"The women folk go about freely." His eyes suggested he liked that freedom. They were decidedly alone in the tennis court. "Much more so than is the custom in Spain. In my country no woman of status would dream of venturing beyond her household without several male retainers to guard her person and her ladies to see to her belongings and ensure propriety."

Margaret tossed her head, determined to ignore his veiled suggestion. "Such is the custom here as well, but I am no great lady. I go about as I please."

"The granddaughter to an earl is not a great lady? I find that hard to believe, especially when the lady waits upon the queen. Mayhap the woman fails to recognize her own importance. Such a one might be accustomed to going about without escort, or to doing all manner of things. Mayhap making goods for delivery to others, eh?"

Margaret narrowed her gaze at him. Here, at last, was the question she dreaded. Adroitly, she skirted it. "In our country, the queen chooses her servants by what they offer her, not their birth. A person of any class can earn her favor."

"Ah, I have offended the English flower. Permit me, madam, to make amends. The daisy is your namesake, is it not?"

He had taken her hand, was rubbing it in the most insolent, intimate manner that sent spirals of revulsion up her arm.

She pulled away and hurried back toward the entry door. 'Let us proceed to the tiltyard. You will find it even more interesting than the tennis court, which is not the finest specimen of its kind," she said.

She jerked open the door and went out, away from his questing gaze. As he followed, she knew he was speculating. She hadn't answered his question, but he was drawing his own conclusions, and they weren't comfortable ones for her.

As patiently as possible, she showed de Alvarez the tiltyard and the gardens. When they met with Marie, who was walking with Patience, he welcomed her daughter and insisted on sending Marie inside. He made her vastly uncomfortable, and her anxiety was augmented by another thought. Today, the Spider Queen had visited the ambassador. What had Jonathan learned?

Nothing! Half the day spent skulking around the ambassador's, and he had learned nothing! Nor had his man sent to the trade talks learned anything. Jonathan paced the Greenwich gardens, frustrated and furious. He had made no progress in exposing this plot so he could get back to the Netherlands. And right now he was making no progress in finding Margaret. She was somewhere in the gardens, escorting a visitor, he was told.

Lengthening his strides, Jonathan sought to outwalk his tension. His work protecting the queen wore on him. He had finished the corselet and Her Majesty wore it in public, though she complained heartily about its weight and heat. Now her tasters would have to redouble their efforts, since the Spanish had the poison. It was hopeless . . . hopeless. No, he must not think that way. He must move forward in his efforts. It was time to confront Robert, and to do that, he needed . . .

Madness, he needed Margaret. She came naturally to mind now whenever he planned his next move. He might as well admit he included her in his every thought. Whether he wanted to or not, he couldn't exclude her—from his work or his pleasure. She was in with him too deep.

Speaking of deep . . . His mouth curved up at the corners as he thought about Margaret's beautiful, silken depths, how he liked to twine his body with hers and submerge himself, forgetting all else. At times of late, the hate, the desperation, and wildness in him evaporated, and for one blessed moment he was the young Jonathan again, holding his beloved, full of tenderness worshiping at the sweetness of her shrine. Those moments faded too soon. Yet the fact that he had them at all left him lusting for the next one, and the next.

With still no sign of her, he paused in a quiet part of the garden. A marble bench beneath a shade tree invited, and he gave himself a minute to sit down. She was here somewhere in this garden, and he would find her. He needed her like a drug to numb his mind.

The sound of a voice drifted to him from beyond the thick hedge behind him. A woman's voice, sweetly modulated. Margaret's voice—talking about a fountain, its Greek god statue. Jonathan rose to go to her, craving her blindly, needing her welcoming smile to soothe his soul. Until a man's voice answered, asking a question.

Jonathan froze on the other side of the thick yew. He couldn't see the man with Margaret, but he heard his voice.

The musty damp of the stone cell deluged his memory, the resonance of pain and torment mingled with death. They hit him hard, sent him reeling emotionally. Physically, nausea welled up from his stomach, filling his mouth with bile, the horrifying taste of hell.

With a snarl, he pounded to the end of the hedge, rounded the corner, and beheld them together. His worst nightmare, Marguerite and the devil . . .

"You!" Jonathan let the single word drop into the well of silence, a long, low sound of derision. It sent out ripples like a stone, stirring the pool of antagonism that had sprung up between him and this man upon sight. Deliberately he wrapped his right hand around his rapier hilt.

"Patience, come here." Margaret put out her arms for her daughter, shaken by Jonathan's furious face and the deadly challenge in his voice. She had been making the best of de Alvarez's unwanted company by playing with Patience, merrily tossing pebbles in the fountain. Jonathan appeared out of nowhere, astonishing as a lightning bolt. The look on his face must have frightened Patience also, for her child obeyed her instantly. Margaret clasped her arms around her protectively. Something terrible was wrong.

One swift assessment of the two men as they faced each other filled Margaret with dread. It was worse than something wrong; something terrible was about to happen. The look of rage on Jonathan's face horrified her. In contrast, the Spaniard's face had split into a grin, as if he had just received a coveted prize.

Understanding came to Margaret so suddenly she swayed and had to lean against the fountain's basin to catch her balance. This man was no merchant bartering for favorable trade relations. This was the Spanish inquisitor general of the Netherlands, the man who haunted Jonathan's past.

Part Three

Chapter 54

The Inquisitor General of the Netherlands

"Margaret," Jonathan's order slashed into her thoughts like sharp steel. "Take Patience and go inside. I don't want you near this filth."

"Good sir"—de Alvarez spread his hands palm upward in a friendly gesture—"what can be your trouble? You seem eaten up with . . . could it be hate?"

Despite his innocent tone, Margaret detected the hint of delight in him, as if he liked the idea of someone filled with so much loathing it hurt. The heinous smile still adorned his mouth.

"You know damn well how I feel. Don't play games with me." Jonathan seemed to gain stature as he took an insidious, gliding step toward the Spaniard, one hand on his rapier. As if he had used his magician's powers to transform himself, he assumed the grace and lissome strength of an enraged predator cat. "I know who you are."

His voice curled through the calm of the garden in a sinuous snarl. Suddenly Margaret saw more than the magician. The demon leaped forth, bitterly superb. She stood riveted to the spot, as if her feet had put down tap roots. Whatever Jonathan did next, it must not be violent. If he killed the Spanish emissary in cold blood, without obvious reason, there would be trouble of the worst kind.

"Your wife and child?" inquired de Alvarez pleasantly.

"I should have guessed you were behind this." Jonathan held his stance, ready to fight, hand never moving from his rapier.

"Lovely lady. Charming child."

"I know exactly what you're up to. You'll not succeed."

"Is this fellow sane?" De Alvarez turned to Margaret, raising his thick, black brows. "I compliment his family and he babbles nonsense."

"Touch them and I'll kill you."

"I admire loyalty in a man, but this one seems to go too far," de Alvarez continued to Margaret. "He seems to worship his family. False ideals. Or should we say false idols."

"Take your stinking sermons and go home. Before it's too late."

"I'm here on invitation from the woman you call 'Her Majesty.' " His tone carried the slightest hint of insult. "I intend to call England my home for a time."

"Those who are too sure of themselves can be given a rude awakening."

"Is that some sort of an English proverb? I do believe I'll stroll back to the palace and take my leave of Mistress Tudor for the day. Would you care to accompany me, Madam Cavandish?" He inclined his head, held out his arm, his enjoyment evident.

Jonathan half drew his rapier from its scabbard.

"My dear!" Margaret hurled herself forward between the two men. "I—I suddenly feel weary. I prithee, escort me to our chamber." She sidled up against him and caught his gaze with hers. Fumbling under the cover of Patience's garments, she pressed his rapier back in its place.

Mentally, she had to reach a long way to find him. But she managed, dragging him back the long, painful road from hell to everyday life. When he saw her, really saw her, she pressed Patience into his arms. Turning her back on the inquisitor, she led her beloved away. Jonathan must not be guilty of provoking a battle. The Spanish must be the ones to attack first.

The noose was tightening, Margaret saw that now. All the way back to their chamber, she realized it, while Patience's tiny hands gripped her gown, radiating fear like heat of the day. Slowly, insidiously, Spain put its evil machines in place and set them in motion. Now they were grinding toward their final destination, and she was powerless to stop them, could only be carried along on the relentless tide as it moved forward, going God knew where. To death and destruction . . .

No! It must not be! She wouldn't let this happen. She flung back a strand of trailing hair and stared at the heavens, the dull gray clouds in a pale, watery sky. She must find a way out of this deadly coil. Because if she didn't, she would be back to nothing, alone and desolate once more.

"You're to stay away from him. Do you hear?" Back in their chamber, Jonathan's rage burst forth. "He would like nothing better than to kill you, or Patience, or both, in order to torment me. If you so much as speak to him again . . ."

His face had become a death mask riddled with savagery.

"I'll not speak to him," she vowed earnestly. "I'll mind my own business and make my lace. I swear." At the moment she said it, she really meant it. She wanted to stay as far away from de Alvarez as she could.

"You think *you* have a weakness." Jonathan whirled and clasped her about the waist. "*You* are mine. Think about that before you place yourself in his way again. He can get at me through you, and now that he knows it, he will."

"It's not a weakness in yourself." Margaret stared at the bed curtains, understanding fully for the first time—love made a person vulnerable, not weak. Because the more love in your life you had, the more you stood to lose. "No one can be everywhere at once, to guard those they love."

"But I intend to guard you." Jonathan's voice wove a fierce pattern of magic around her mind, just as his hands encircled her waist. "I have no intention of losing you again." The warmth of his lips found her cheek, slid back to her neck, his intimate whisper at her ear. "I couldn't bear it a second time."

It was as close to a vow of love as she was likely to get. Margaret turned to him blindly, wanting more, having to settle for less, but only for now. He would heal further, she told herself. And just now the immediacy of the moment filled her, making her need his physical presence. Tears blurred her vision, changing him before her eyes—half magician, half devil, filling her life with magic one moment, casting her into hell the next. Just now she felt more frightened than ever. The inquisitor was here, waiting to steal him away.

"We must defeat him," she said aloud, letting her

thoughts take form, "using our strengths *and* our weaknesses. I refuse to let him have his way."

"No more 'we,' " he ordered, turning her about in his arms. "I will do it."

"Then you must unveil him," Margaret urged. "All you need is sufficient evidence."

"I don't have that yet. Even Jane's information about the cuff is worthless until it's clear what they plan to do. What I need right now is for Robert to change sides."

"Oh, excellent idea! That could be managed." Buoyed by the prospect, Margaret ran her fingers up and down his arm, soothing herself with the texture of his skin. "I always said he had a will of jelly. He'll be at the practice for the revel today. I'll speak to him and—"

Jonathan grasped both her wrists and pushed her back on the bed, pinning her. Surprised, she tried to wiggle away. "You promised to work your lace and mind your own business." His eyes were pits of darkness, drawing her in.

"Just this once and I'll step aside," she vowed fervently. "I swear."

He continued to study her, but she knew he wasn't with her. He was back in that Spanish prison, in that desolate wasteland of the soul, with the man she had just met . . .

Raising herself, she rubbed her cheek against his. Somehow she must bring him back to her, because he belonged to her, not that monster. He belonged with the world of the living, the world of light. "What do you think he will do with the poison?" she demanded. They had to expose this plot.

"I don't know," he muttered, releasing her and leaning against the bedpost. "I learned nothing today. The maids were cleaning the ambassador's bedchamber, and though I got in on the pretext of flirting with one of them, I didn't have a chance to use the spy hole until the meeting was almost done. And only while the girl emptied the chamberpot."

His face had that volatile look to it again, the look that told her he was degrading himself because he hadn't heard more, hadn't done enough.

"But you did see Mab and the ambassador together, correct?" she inquired, determined to remind him of how much he *had* accomplished. "And you did hear them discuss a poison. That alone is incriminating evidence. After all, one doesn't acquire a deadly poison for fun."

"Margaret—"

"Nor would one leave it on a shelf after acquiring it. Mark my word—"

"Margaret, would you—"

" . . . that poison will turn up any day now." She was sure he interrupted only to degrade the importance of his efforts. "I will warn the queen's tasters to be especially cautious, just in ca—"

"Margaret, would you stop!"

She halted and looked at him inquiringly. His expression had become so troubled and stormy that when he moved toward her, she met him halfway.

"I just told you I was in a bedchamber with another woman, flirting by my own admission, and you say nothing in return?"

His strong fingers tightened on her arms, betraying his tension, and she knew she must answer this question with care. "I know you did it for good reason as part of your work, so it doesn't matter. Wouldn't you say the same of me, if I were in your place?"

"You're not in my place. You'd better not be." Jonathan flung himself away from Margaret, astounded at her answer. Here he was, an unfaithful, heartless monster, and she had complete faith in him even when he told her he had been with another woman.

He took a deep breath, sucking in air and expanding his lungs to steady himself. He had sought out Margaret, hoping to solace himself for failing to gather the desired information. Reconnaissance was like that at times, full of disappointments and missed opportunities you learned of only too late. Instead he got the inquisitor, come to England to pursue him, reminding him he was also a monster in disguise.

"Jonathan, I trust you."

The understanding in her voice shattered him, the softness of her touch as she came up behind him.

"What do you trust me to do? Anything necessary to get what I want? What would you say if I hadn't just flirted with the woman. What if I had done more."

She moved closer and into his arms, her hands moving over his scarred back in a sensitive motion. "I assume you did do more. After all, you had to play the part, which must have included a few kisses at the least."

Jonathan burned with chagrin. The maid's eager hands came back to him, roving with skilled practice over his sides, his hips. He hadn't wanted her any more than he had wanted Elizabeta, but he couldn't forget the taste of her mouth when she had kissed him, so cloying it made him ill. "What if I had bedded her?" He flung the ugly words at her like a challenge.

Her hands stopped their comforting motion, withdrew. Good, he thought. She needed to know he had been unfaithful—not today with the maid, but with Elizabeta back in the Netherlands, after he had sworn to take no more women even if he never had Margaret. A vow he hadn't kept.

But Margaret shocked him with her surety. "I know you didn't bed her. The situation didn't warrant it. Few would."

"What if the situation *did* warrant it?" he pressed her harder.

"Name me such a situation."

"What if my life depended on it."

The silence that followed settled around him with frightening intensity. Their entire marriage hung in the balance. If she couldn't accept what he had done, when he himself didn't accept it, they had nothing together. And he was mad to test her this way. Why hadn't he left the question alone?

As soon as he asked himself, he knew the answer. He had to know if the love she professed for him was real, or if it was just a game to her, like many women played. Even if he couldn't love her back, he had to know . . .

Her laugh broke the silence, a sound full of hope that fell in glistening waves around him. "So that's what happened in the Netherlands. Jonathan, you had to get away from *him,* and that woman saved you." She was smiling that serene, confident smile, and he could scarcely bear the brilliance of her lovely face as she caught his hands in hers. "I would thank her for doing it if I could. Your life means more to me than some nonsensical ideal."

"But they're not nonsensical, and I failed to uphold them."

"You say I judge myself too harshly. What of you? You're right about the ideals, but there are limits to how far we should go with them." The grip of her hands tightened on his. "You are a hero because of the things you did in the war. You were the one who pierced the dikes at Lieden, flooded out the Spanish, and raised their siege of the city. You were the one who saved families from the Spanish Fury. That doesn't change."

"But it was my reputation with women that made her want to save me."

She smiled gently, wrapping her fingers around the pearl-handled hammer tucked in his belt and caressing its brass head. "You're wrong about that. It was your brave deeds that made her want you. It was your reputation with women that made her believe she might have you. Without that, she would have passed by your cell, knowing her wish was hopeless. Where would you be now?"

"Marguerite, you have the most astonishing way of looking at things. I tell you I bedded dozens of women, and you practically thank me for it."

"That's because I made you do it," she stated with that maddening conviction of hers. "It was my fault."

He was incredulous. "You weren't even there. I've told you before, you blame yourself—"

"Yes, yes, you're right. I'm trying to get over that," she conceded hastily. "Let us say instead that I sent you away. I *let* you do it. You had every right to those women, Jonathan. If you wanted them and they wanted you, it's hardly my place to disapprove."

"Marguerite, I don't think—"

"You don't complain about Oliver, nor do you complain about Patience being his child, though you are more a father to her than he ever was. And I have had little trouble forgetting I was wed to him. I forgot it while I still was. Clifton is a big place with many people, and it was easy to go off somewhere and pretend he didn't exist, except when he turned up in my—"

"Marguerite, listen to me!" He captured her chin with his fingertips and lifted her sweet face to his. "I know you didn't love Oliver, so I don't resent him. But you need to know I never wanted all those women. I haven't had any at all since I realized it, except for the one who saved my life. Because all the time I really wanted you." He fell silent then and let his eyes do the speaking. Hers were deep pools of gleaming, shifting light, now golden brown, then amber, always clear like calming waters flowing in secret places, sheltered by depths of shade. And he had a driving thirst for her that required slaking. Reaching out, he pulled her into his arms. He wanted to consume her like a tall draft of startling gold liquid, until he felt her buoyant peace.

He buried his face in her golden shock of hair, which hung in a sparkling trail, bound by a blue ribbon. But after a minute, he faced her and spoke in utmost seriousness. "Marguerite, when we wed, I made vows I intend to honor. I promised to worship only you with my body, and I do. I promised to honor you always, and I shall. Ask no more than those vows of me and you can trust I will fulfill them. In return I ask you to share your strength with me. I know I should offer you more, but *he* stands between us. I . . ."

His words trailed off as Margaret caught his face between her hands. "I need you as well," she whispered. "Don't think about what you don't offer. Think of what you do. You believe in my strength. You're honest and forthright in caring for me, and I need those things more than anything else right now. And I want you to forget that monster. Put him out of your mind."

Margaret's fingers rasped against his hint of beard. She let them float up to push back his hair before standing on tiptoe and kissing his lips.

She heard his deep groan and felt his shoulder and arm muscles tighten as he bent over her, his torso rigid as steel. At the same time, she sensed he was rigid elsewhere. With her teeth, she caught his earlobe and worried it, sending him a sharp, sensual message.

"Marguerite, I mean what I say. I don't want you involved with him."

"I won't be involved," she insisted, rubbing her body against him, claiming his senses and his full attention. "But neither should you be. Forget *him.* Think only of you and me."

He stifled another groan and let his fingers trace her throat, drawing a slow line to her breasts. Her smock slid from her shoulders, propelled by his clever hands.

"You saw how glad he was in the garden at your torment," she went on, not done with the subject. "How delighted he was that you hadn't forgotten. Imagine how it would be if you didn't even recognize him, or didn't care when you did. He would be devastated!" With a groan of her own, she gave in to the racing of her blood, to the rush of lightning he sent streaking through her. She sent her own hands exploring and found his finely modeled hips and waist as she waxed eloquent. "He would be utterly devastated to know his evil had no long-lasting effect. If he knew you had moved on with your life and found happiness despite him, that he was nothing but a task to accomplish, he would despair!"

"I would like that." He laid her down on the bed beside him and slid his hand up her skirts, parting her thighs with singleminded concentration. It left her unsure which Jonathan would like, to pleasure her body or for the inquisitor to despair. It didn't matter. She would settle for either one, but just now, she realized with a tingle of anticipation, she wanted the former quite intensely herself.

Their lovemaking progressed rapidly after that. He was rampant with desire for her, and within minutes she had helped him discard his clothes, then tossed away her own. God's eyelid, she never understood how her body accommodated him, he was utterly massive. Between her legs she felt slick and ready for him, driven by her own want. Of her own volition, she spread her legs and brought him down on her. For a split second he hovered above her, kissing her neck and breasts, touching her flesh, sending the beloved thrill through her like silver lightning.

Then he made the plunge and she forgot everything else, her work, her fears, and the man who had come to steal her lover like a shadow of death. She thought of nothing except Jonathan's immense length filling her, and she gave herself up to him, let him surge inside her over and over with complete abandon, lifting her hips to meet the stunning beauty of his body. On and on they went, shocks of excitement coursing through her body, each thrust drawing the two of them away to another realm, a place of beauty and justice that chaos could not touch.

His groans of enjoyment raced through her mind, uplifting her. He was the lightning, lighting up the landscape of her life, bringing her change. His face was a vision of wonder as she approached the pinnacle and thrust from its ledge, so that she was riding in glory, Jonathan's glory. Stars flashed before her eyes, dazzling her body, making her shake with the spasms of release. And still he showed no signs of relenting, no hint of satiation. Just the driving of his body into her center, relentless, unending. But to her it meant everything.

She could hold him; she had power the inquisitor lacked. She had not thought to confront the devil incarnate, but now that he was here, she would show him the strength of love. And tenuous though her hold on Jonathan was, she vowed to keep it. She had her freedom and her lace school, and she would have Jonathan. She would not surrender him to the dark lord.

Chapter 55

"Good sir, would you partner me?" On the sixth day before the duke's visit, Margaret stopped before Robert in the great hall where the queen's ladies and gentlemen were rehearsing. The master of the revels ran to and fro, giving orders. Everything had to be perfect for this entertainment of the French duke, even if the guest of honor dared not show himself on the night of the revel.

Robert looked at Margaret in surprise. "I thought you wouldn't have me for your partner."

She gave a wry smile. "I'm a staid old married woman now, and you're soon a bridegroom. What's a dance between old acquaintances?" She caught his hand, and though it was still clammy, that troubled her less now. She coaxed him out for the pavane.

"I notice you say acquaintances, not friends." Robert twirled her through an intricate sequence. He had always been an impeccable dancer. Pity he was not impeccable of mind.

"Are we friends?" Margaret countered. "You keep such terrible secrets." She sent him a meaningful stare, and he had the grace to redden. She shot a glance at Francis Walsingham, who had come to watch the practice, then at Jonathan, who sat with the musicians discussing the selections. "Robert, I know what you're doing with the Spanish," she continued, knowing her reinforcements were at hand. Robert looked ready to bolt, so she held to him firmly throughout the next figure, though it didn't call for it. "Jonathan knows. As do Walsingham and Burghley, and Hatton and Sussex and more than half the queen's privy council. We told them all."

He looked horrified. If it had been an amusing topic, she

would have laughed at him. As it was, she set her lips firmly and continued to dance. "You're meddling in treason. You're asking for the Tower and the block."

"If someone is accusing me, there is no proof," he blustered.

"I saw you meeting with the Spanish ambassador and his other men. I heard you discussing the poison."

"You spiteful little bitch." He dropped her hand in mid-figure. "You hate me because I'm to wed with Jane instead of you. You want to—"

"Give it up, Solsover." Jonathan clapped one hand on Robert's shoulder from behind. Jane stood nearby.

Robert's eyes darted in furtive rushes from one to the other, searching for escape, seeing none.

"You'd best come back to our side, Robert," Jane said. She held up her hands, pleading. "I told them everything I know. Put together with what the others know, well . . ." She let her hands fall to her sides. "I love you, Robert. Please don't make me a widow as soon as I'm wed."

Jonathan led them away from the dance floor to a quiet nook. Though everyone had been eyeing them curiously, Walsingham collared the master of the revels and set them back to work. The music sprang up again, gay and lively. Though furtive glances shot their way from time to time, the couples resumed the dance.

"Look here, Solsover, you'd best get that cuff back to Her Majesty," ordered Jonathan. "Straight."

"I can't." Robert put on a petulant expression. "I don't have it anymore. I gave it to them, and if I'm not to see them anymore, I can't—"

Jonathan rolled his eyes. "You're impossible even when you're cooperating. Take him away, Jane, and talk to him. Explain to him what a double agent is. Tell him what he's to do."

"Double agent?" Robert brightened, captured by the concept. "I would be working for both sides, wouldn't I?"

"Horribly romantic," Jane assured him, leading him away, leaving Margaret and Jonathan alone.

"Not that we'll tell him any of our plans." Jonathan heaved a sigh and sat on the window seat. "I wouldn't trust him with the hour of the clock."

"At least that part's done. I told you 'twould be easy."

"Jane did well. I briefed her beforehand and she caught

on quickly. It still astonishes me that she sees some good in him, but it serves our purposes. Burghley and Walsingham will take him to the Tower for the night, just as a safeguard. He'll come back tomorrow convinced the Spanish haven't a chance in hell of succeeding with their plan. At least not in supplanting our sovereign."

Margaret quickly twined her fingers in his, demanding his attention. The look hovered in his eyes again, as if he had met the devil and been summoned to his side. And she knew he had been. De Alvarez was calling, exerting his lure for revenge.

On the fifth day before the duke's visit, the *Swiftsure II* sailed for France. For Margaret, the remaining days passed in a whirl of anxiety. In the early hours of the sixteenth of August, Marie ducked into Margaret's chamber, flushed and smiling. "The duke has arrived. Just imagine! He's here at Greenwich, and he is even more *charmant* than they say."

Margaret started up from her work at the cuff. "He's here? Kit's back?"

"Both of them are here, Kit and the duke, and the court's agog, at least those who are up. I chanced on him as they arrived at the water gate. I was terribly bold, but I wanted to meet him, since we are fellow countrymen. Lord Christopher obliged and made introductions. He . . ." She blushed so red Margaret would have thought she wore paint if she didn't know better. "His Grace kissed my hand and said the most amusing things. Oh, 'tis wondrous exciting. A great prince come to woo Her Majesty in secret, and only we know."

"Everyone at court knows, Marie. We're just not allowed to tell." Margaret felt unaffected by the excitement, probably because she had too much work to do. "So he is not ugly like they say?"

"Not the least. He is not tall of stature, but he has the most . . ." Marie stumbled over her words. "I heard one of the ladies say he has a 'well-turned leg.' And his manner, oh, so imperial, yet I confess, I believe he could woo the feathers from a duck."

"He's to do that with the queen and no other," Margaret cautioned, working her bobbins steadily. "Best stay away."

"And you'd best stay out of the queen's way," Marie

cautioned in return, becoming sober. "At least until she's met with him. Her maids say she's nigh hysterical with excitement that he's arrived. She wanted to meet with him immediately, and he with her, but Simier managed to get him to bed instead, for some rest so he might look his best when he presents himself."

"A sensible suggestion," Margaret agreed. "You can be sure I'll not go near Her Majesty until after the dinner hour. I'm almost done with the cuff, but not quite. Believe me, I'm staying right here."

Jonathan had no such intentions of avoiding the queen. In fact, since he knew she had been with the duke for several hours, he lay in wait for her, leaning against the wainscotting of her antechamber. The room was situated so as to receive little morning light, and he endured the dimness, staring at the foolish virgins. Fitting that the wise ones stood in the other corner, avoiding the Spanish and the hidden panel. The time drew near when those menacing Spanish would attack. He could feel their encroaching power in his bones. Every fiber of him tuned to the inquisitor's next move, his body poised to deal the death blow or receive it himself.

The door to the queen's inner chambers clicked open. He came to the center chamber and sank on one knee.

"Cavandish, what are you doing here? Oh, guard duty, I suppose." She held up her candle, hunting for a book along a shelf, tapping her long, slim fingers on the leather book bindings. "Now that the prince is here, no harm will come to me. Why don't you do something else today? Go to your wife for a change."

She was in rare good humor, Jonathan saw. Word had spread that the duke's deft wit and apparently honest appreciation of Her Grace's feminine charms had put Elizabeth in his thrall. Making this the perfect moment for Jonathan's request. "Your Grace, on the morrow, at the revel you planned, will you wear the corselet I made? You have left it off of late."

" 'Tis infernally hot, Cavandish." She hummed a galliard to herself while she searched for some specific book, a volume of poems to share with her lover, mayhap. "I would prefer not."

"And King Philip would prefer you dead."

Elizabeth stopped, her hand outstretched toward a book. She turned around. "What do you mean by that?"

Jonathan had not moved from his kneeling position. "I suspect that Spanish trade delegation," he said, repeating with care the words he and Walsingham had chosen. "At least one of the emissaries is not what he seems, a simple merchant. I wish you to take special precautions. They may be necessary to preserve your life."

"The emissaries?" Elizabeth shrugged them away. "They haven't been back to Greenwich since the last meeting."

The devil, you say, Jonathan thought silently, stealing a glance at the tapestry. He had sprinkled a fine veil of wheat flour on the floor last night just in front of the hidden panel. No one had entered the room all night, yet the flour had been disturbed. The panel had been opened so someone could watch. "I beg you to wear it on the morrow, Your Highness. Pray oblige me. Remember the attempt to shoot you only weeks ago?"

Elizabeth whipped back to the shelf and took down the book she wanted. She thumbed through it, as if searching for a passage, but he could tell she was thinking. She hadn't been shaken by the shot at the time. It had happened too quickly and missed her entirely. Yet he had to impress her with the danger. "Having missed you the first time, they will be even more determined the second, Majesty," he insisted. "And I believe that second try will come soon."

"Oh, very well." Elizabeth snapped the book shut and prepared to return to her suitor. "If for no more reason than to be rid of you. If you think 'tis so powerfully important, I'll wear the cursed thing."

"Your *life* is important, Your Grace," Jonathan assured her, getting up and moving ahead to open the door for her. "Your good health is paramount to the survival of our country." He swung open the panel with a bow and his best smile. "May I add that you are looking especially charming today?"

Elizabeth touched her beautifully coifed auburn hair, then snatched up her fan to hide a sudden smile. "Let us hope Alençon agrees with you." But she was looking well, and by all accounts, Alençon thought so, too. "And tell your wife I must wear that cuff on the morrow."

"She knows, Your Majesty," Jonathan answered, praying

Margaret would have it ready. "She is working on it as fast as she can."

"You can't go, Grandsire," Margaret said definitively as she bent over her lace pillow. "The physician says a revel will be too taxing for you. You must stay in bed."

"Damn it, you get a great deal of satisfaction giving me these orders!" Her grandsire rounded on her from his place by the window. "I won't stand for it. I intend to meet this French duke on the morrow whether you like it or no."

"You'll have another attack," Margaret warned, her fingers moving so fast they seemed a blur, even to her. Lord, would she ever finish this cuff? It was midafternoon now, and she must have it by the revel that next night. "You'd best stay quiet with Patience here."

She didn't mention there might be trouble tomorrow night, or that she wanted them both somewhere safe.

"Gran'sire have?" Patience sat across from Margaret, devouring a huge slice of bread ladened with dripping honeycomb. She offered him a bite and a sticky smile to match.

"Lord, no! Don't come near me." The earl dropped heavily into a nearby chair and mopped his perspiring face with his huge kerchief. "You're a fright."

Patience's smile disappeared. She screwed up her face to cry.

"Oh, Patience, don't listen to him." Margaret put down her bobbins and caught up a wet cloth. She mopped Patience's sticky hands. "He says the most foolish things at times. Come now, don't cry." Patience hung on her mother, struggling to straighten out her face. "There now, that's better." Margaret smoothed back Patience's dark hair and made a face at her grandsire. "Let's pretend he's a horrid, cross old bear, trying to frighten you. But you know he can't hurt you because I'm here. I want you to walk right over and give him a big kiss. He'll pretend to hate it, but secretly he likes it. Go ahead."

Emboldened by her mother's encouragements, Patience approached her great-grandsire. She was still slightly sticky, Margaret knew, but she had gotten the worst off. As Patience pulled a stool next to her great-grandsire's chair and climbed on it, Margaret hid her smile. The earl would be mortified—kissed by a female, but she made him endure this ritual on a regular basis. Part of her training for him, she reminded herself, to make him human again. But then she grew sober.

"I expect you to stay in your chamber tomorrow night." Margaret bent back over her lace making, unable to waste a second. "Or mine if you please, with Patience. I'm going to tell Tim to keep an eye on the pair of you. And no dagger throwing with Patience around."

She gave him her sternest look, but he had his eyes closed. He leaned back in her best chair, his face a picture of pained tolerance, while Patience latched on to his arm and put her sticky lips to his wrinkled cheek.

Chapter 56

The queen adored her French suitor. By the next day she had nicknamed him her Frog, and he called himself her devoted slave. He was said to be enamored of her and certainly acted it, by all accounts.

Margaret imagined how they must look, with the queen so tall and stately and the duke so short. Yet they would not spend much time standing side by side. Marie had run in and out all afternoon, carrying the latest gossip to Margaret. It was said they could not get enough of one another's company. They talked and dined, walked in the garden, stole kisses behind the shrubbery, and talked some more. Her Majesty, Queen Elizabeth I, was in love.

The courtiers and all of London were hysterical with contention. If this meeting went well, Alençon might leave England in forty-eight hours as good as wed. Unless Margaret failed to finish the cuff. Even if the queen did not want to marry Alençon, the Spaniards' way of ruining her chances would destroy French/English relations. No one wanted that.

It was the hour of supper, and Margaret's tiny chamber was packed with such a crowd, she could scarcely draw breath. Six people! This must be what it felt like in Bedlam. Or prison.

Speaking of prison . . . Jonathan had returned from the city, bathed and dressed for the revel. Just looking at him made her tense and nervous, the way he held his body taut and seething, the tempestuous storm in his eyes. It frightened Margaret so, she couldn't think clearly

For comfort, she let her gaze slip to her grandsire. Imagine that, her grandsire a source of comfort. He had stayed all afternoon, even to sup with them, and had actually spun Patience's top for her. Tim lurked in a corner, fiddling with a new dagger the earl had given him. Patience snuggled on the great bedstead, playing pat-a-cake with Marie, while Bertrande sat at Margaret's side.

"Can't you all run away and leave me alone?" Margaret's hands seemed weighted with lead as she moved the bobbins, she was so tired. "Except for Bertrande, of course." No one moved. They all wanted to hear her announce she was finished. But they helped nothing by staring down her shoulder. She had been working this piece steadily for twenty-four hours, barely sleeping, never stopping. She was almost finished, but almost was not close enough.

"You can do it, Marguerite," Bertrande encouraged her. "This is a great triumph for you. Not only do you have your own shop now, through which Marie has been selling her lace, but you teach and have achieved a masterpiece of copying. Not even the maker of those cuffs would know her work from yours."

Margaret leaned and kissed her friend's cheek. "Thank you, Bertrande."

She was interrupted by a tap at the door. Giles opened it to admit a flustered, frightened-looking Jane.

"Madam. Captain. My lord." Jane dropped quick curtsies to each of them. "I came as quickly as I could. Her Majesty would like to see you, Captain. You won't believe it, but when I went to fetch the queen's ruff and the one cuff, to get them ready for tonight, the missing one was back."

Dead silence greeted her announcement. Margaret stared at Jane, then the cuff before her, stupefied. She had done all this work for nothing? Suddenly everyone talked at once, babbling, speculating. Everyone had an opinion about why the cuff had reappeared.

"Silence!" Jonathan gained his feet, and mouths closed at the sight of his grim countenance. "Jane, fetch the box with the returned cuff here and do not touch it until I can examine it. I will go advise Her Majesty, then return. The rest of you, clear the room. I need quiet for this work."

He didn't need quiet, he needed solace, Margaret thought, examining the tight bind of his lips, the cold fury in his eyes. Oh God, that wasn't what he thought he needed. He still believed he had a need to kill.

"But why has it been returned?" A short time later, Margaret bent over the two cuffs that lay side by side. Jonathan was still with the queen. "I can't understand it. Nothing is different about the stolen one." She puckered her brow in puzzlement. "Except that someone has been careless and spilled something on it. Feel here." She passed the cuff to Bertrande. " 'Tis oily."

"I don't understand it either," murmured Bertrande, who sat with Marie. She took the cuff and studied it, moving her fingers over the pattern with minute care.

"Are you sure you wouldn't rather lie down?" Margaret asked solicitously, touching Bertrande's arm. Her friend had that tight, pinched look around her mouth today, suggesting she was in pain again.

"Mais non," Bertrande answered briskly. "I feel no better lying down than I do up and about. I would rather make myself useful while I can."

As Margaret searched her friend's face with sorrow, wishing she could banish her illness, Jonathan returned.

"Let me see the cuff," he ordered, coming straight to the table. "None of you were to touch it."

"Here it is," said Bertrande, holding it up. "We did it no harm, I'm sure. I was just saying—ouch!"

"What is it?" Margaret leaned over, concerned. "Oh, 'tis only a pin." She plucked it away as Jonathan took the cuff from Bertrande. He dropped it on his handkerchief, as if afraid of soiling it. "Let me see your finger," she said to Bertrande while Jonathan studied the lace. Margaret took up the pin from the table. "Your finger has a tiny prick," she explained to her friend. "I will wash off the blood." She looked up and saw that Jonathan had frozen like a marble statue, enraged and tormented both at once. Her heart stood still as she stared back at him in shock.

"Mademoiselle Bertrande should lie down." Jonathan suddenly came to life again, focusing his solicitude on Bertrande. "You have been hiding your pain from us, my friend," he chided as he helped her to rise and led her to the bed.

To Margaret's amazement, Bertrande obeyed him without protest.

"Don't touch that!" Jonathan's roar made Marie jump in fright.

She had reached for the pin where he had placed it on the table. "I only wanted to—"

"No one's to touch that pin or the cuff. Margaret, wash

your hands thoroughly. Now! Marie, did you touch either one?"

"*Mais non,*" Marie quavered.

"Good." All the rage of hell seemed to possess Jonathan as he strode across the room, caught up the cuff by the handkerchief, dropped the pin on top and popped them in the box. Turning the key, he pocketed it and returned to Bertrande.

"Now, then, mademoiselle." He knelt by the bed and took her hand gently. "I must perform a slight surgery on your finger. Margaret, light a candle. Quickly, please."

"Jonathan, is this necessary?" Margaret protested. " 'Tis only a prick. I can wash it with soap if you wish."

"Do as I say," he ordered tersely.

She hurried to obey, baffled and frightened.

Jonathan heated his dagger blade in the flame, then let it cool until he could touch it. "I am losing precious minutes, but it can't be helped. Now then, are you ready?"

In answer, Bertrande gave him her hand.

Margaret gagged as Jonathan neatly sliced the flesh of Bertrande's finger twice in a crisscross pattern and pressed blood from it into a cloth. As she watched, he glanced up and met her gaze. His eyes were so hard and full of fury that a lance of fear smote her heart.

"What is wrong with Bertrande's finger?" she demanded. "Tell me, please."

"Get me a clean piece of linen," was all he would say.

Margaret wanted to weep as she hurried to obey. When he had bound the finger, he continued to hold Bertrande's hand. Grimness had turned Jonathan's features to granite, but now they gentled as he spoke to the French woman. "I have ill news for you, mademoiselle, but I know you would prefer to hear it than not. The tip of that pin was coated with curare, a poison made from the night blooming cereus plant. The Spanish meant to kill the queen with it. Either that, or more slowly with the poison oil that saturates the cuff where it would touch the queen's skin."

"No! Jonathan, no!" Margaret shrieked, unable to believe what she was hearing. Her fear was a rabid, breeding thing.

"I pray you be still, Marguerite," Bertrande ordered. "Could the procedure you just performed help me, Captain?" she asked rationally.

"Curare is a strong poison, so I have grave doubts. We can but wait and see."

"How long do I have?"

"At full strength, curare can kill in thirty minutes."

"Bertrande." Margaret edged herself in near Jonathan. Marie hovered at her shoulder. "My dearest friend, I cannot believe this. I will see that vile man put to death my—"

"*Non, non.* 'Tis a blessing come to relieve me of my pain. Don't you see?" Bertrande smiled and embraced her fate with a sigh.

"Is it so bad as that?" cried Margaret. "You never complained."

Bertrande clasped Margaret's hands with her own, shaking them gently for emphasis. "It is bad, my friend. Even without help, my end draws near. How will the poison act?" she asked of Jonathan.

"The poison will freeze your breathing. You will be aware of things around you until the heart stops shortly after, but you will be unable to speak. I do not think it causes pain."

"Fetch your pillow, Marguerite, and sit at my side." Bertrande issued orders, letting them fall from her lips as crisp and precise as the finished lacework she had made over the years. "Marie, fetch Patience and sit with her here, on my other side. Captain, I would be honored if you would fetch the earl and the two of you would be present. *Mon amie,* you must finish that cuff so the queen can wear it," she instructed Margaret, who returned with her pillow, tears streaming down her face. "Marie, are you there?"

Patience had been half asleep in the outer chamber with Giles. Marie brought her, and she gave Bertrande a kiss on the cheek, then snuggled up against the old lady on the bed and fell asleep.

"Now then, Marguerite, I wish to enjoy the splendor of the lace one last time. Weave your enchanted web with your magic hands, to save queen and country. And I will see the pattern with you in my mind. Tell me where you are."

The lump blocking Margaret's throat prevented her immediate answer. Putting Bertrande's hand on her left, she took up her bobbins and began. "I've come to the end of a motif," she choked, almost breaking down. "I'm putting in the pin for the first linking bride before I finish the last motif, then return for the closing stitches."

"Ah, I can see it. Your bobbins are all to the right?"

"Yes. That's it."

"Go ahead, Marguerite." Bertrande squeezed Margaret's hand, and Margaret subsumed herself in the movement of her bobbins, entering the enchantment with Bertrande. *Cross, twist, place a pin. Pattern of beauty. Pattern of grace. Eyes in the heavens, feet on earth, the pattern moved in her mind like a blessing.* The responsibility that rested on Bertrande's shoulders lifted, freeing her tired friend, and settled on her young, strong shoulders. For the first time she understood Bertrande's words, that the poison came as a blessing. The daily pain that had tightened Bertrande's face lifted. She looked younger and at peace.

"How much more to go, Marguerite?"

Bertrande's voice came to Margaret, her gentle touch a wisp of fading leaves on Margaret's hand. "I will begin the finishing stitch soon, *ma tante.* I love you, my friend. I will miss you unbearably," she whispered as she worked. Tears slipped down her face, and she pulled back to avoid dripping on the lace, never stopping the movement of the bobbins while Bertrande's hand followed. *Not Bertrande,* her heart cried in agony. *Not her dear, precious Bertrande.*

"I didn't say you wouldn't miss me." Bertrande's face had a serene, other worldly look to it already. "I would not wish to be forgotten. I hope each time you pick up your bobbins, I will be with you, the same way your father is with you."

"Do not say that." The tears sprang thick and fast, blurring Margaret's sight. "I cannot live without you. God would not—"

"God knows best, Marguerite. He brought the two of us together. And you have been a blessed gift to me."

"Not as much as you have been to me."

"We have been a help and comfort to each other, and for that, we must both give thanks," Bertrande admonished, as always her voice gentle. "And I want the work that lies before you to be our supreme triumph."

"She is right." Jonathan's hand was a poignant pressure on Margaret's shoulder. "You must be brave, Marguerite, and finish the cuff."

She worked in silence. How much time passed, she did

not know, but she kept her eyes on the beloved face of her friend, felt the strength of her magical hand on her own. Mother and mentor, offering the key to her memories. Those memories had enriched Margaret's life, allowing her to bring the beauty and order of the lace into the world. The cherished gift lived on in her, to be passed to her daughter and the children of her daughter—works of art that chaos could not touch.

At long last Margaret felt Bertrande's grip relax, and she let the bobbins fall from her own hands, their thread flaccid.

"She can still hear us," Jonathan whispered to them. "Each of you say a final word to her. Your lordship, I pray you go first."

The moment of death was considered sacred. For this reason Margaret mourned being absent at her father's death, at the moment when the door to the next world opened and those who were earthbound might catch a glimpse of the path beyond. If you were very fortunate, the departing dear one might hold the door for an extra moment, filling your soul with light. Now Margaret watched a miracle wrought by death as her crotchy, cold grandsire, incapable of such an act mere weeks ago, knelt beside Bertrande, a woman of humble peasant origins, and gave her his grave respect. He was followed by Jonathan, then Marie, who kissed the woman who had been mother to her, then lifted Bertrande's limp hand and ran it over the sleeping Patience's dark hair.

When it was Margaret's turn, she wanted to rebel, to cry out her hate of the inquisitor. Instead she forced herself to lean over Bertrande, to gather the living hands in her own for the last time. The skill of those beautiful hands would be lost to the world. She pressed them tightly between her own, whispering her love.

Evil has made a gift of compassion. Remember that and have hope.

Margaret's eyes jumped to Bertrande's face. The words seemed to have come from her lips, yet that was impossible. Jonathan had said she could not speak. Her sightless eyes were closed, though her chest still rose and fell in rhythm. Gripping her friend's right hand, she gestured to Marie, who came to the other side to take Bertrande's left. Together they kept the vigil until Bertrande breathed her last. Her body went completely still.

Margaret released Bertrande's hand and bent over her lace pillow, weeping painful, stormy tears. She caught up her bobbins again, worked them hard and fast. "No! It can't be. She can't be gone."

Jonathan was at her side, kneeling. She knew her face was a twisted mass of misery. Suddenly she threw the bobbins aside and flung herself on his chest, weeping wildly. "Oh, God, I can't go on."

"You can," he soothed, folding her in his arms, rubbing her back and gentling her. "You must for Bertrande's sake. This is the test your friend has spent years preparing you for. You are so close to succeeding. Don't let her down."

Margaret took a tight hold of her sorrow. Pushing away from him, she forced the sobs down inside. Bertrande's wealth of experience must let her accomplish the impossible. She must get on with it. "I will continue working," she said when she could trust her voice again, "but I wish to sit beside Bertrande while I do it. May I?"

Jonathan nodded. "We will all sit with you. Come."

When Margaret had completed the last stitch, had unraveled her bobbins to give herself long threads for finishing, and had sewn the edge firmly in place, she leaned forward. " 'Tis finished, Bertrande," she whispered. "I will send it on to Her Grace."

Jonathan's hand claimed her. She rose and went into his arms.

"Put on your most beautiful gown and shine like the Marguerite," he whispered into her hair. "Give me strength."

And Margaret went to dress, knowing exactly what Jonathan meant. There was still a battle to fight. But she would be the victor. She swore she would.

Chapter 57

Elizabeth was in her glory that night. For that reason alone Margaret was glad they hadn't told her about the cuff. How could a person enjoy herself, thinking any minute she might be murdered?

Murder. Margaret avoided the dancing because she couldn't face it. How could she be gay at a time like this? She arrayed herself in a corner, and watched for Inquisitor de Alvarez. He had not yet made his appearance, but he would not resist the temptation to be there. He would wish to watch the effect of the poisoned cuff.

The new cuff, the substitute she had made, gleamed on the queen's arm, snug to the skin of her wrist. *Fickle fortune,* Margaret cried inside, *to save the queen yet strike her friend.* The country would not suffer, but she would. She wanted to bow her head and weep.

Bright music poured forth from viol and recorder. Great branches of candles glowed. A walnut sideboard set along one wall held a lavish offering of dainties. Margaret had no stomach for any of it. *Bertrande,* her heart cried. *Oh, Bertrande.*

Jonathan was proud of her. She knew without looking at him where he stood behind Her Majesty, a stark figure in gilding and brown velvet, punctuated by the gleam of his weapons. His gaze caressed her, praising her skill. She had completed the cuff and no one knew the difference. Not even the duke who had originally chosen the gift.

"Mama?"

Margaret jerked around, seeing no one.

A giggle drifted to her ears. "Mama, here."

"Patience?" Margaret noted the arras behind her rippled slightly. "Child, what are you doing back there? Grandsire!" Margaret frowned mightily. "I said you were to stay in your room."

"We're conversing with His Grace, the duke," her grandsire said matter-of-factly. "I told you I would."

"My good woman." A smooth, masculine voice startled Margaret. "Would you be so kind as to bring a poor gentleman a taste of wine? I thirst so, watching my ravishing mistress. She makes my mouth run dry with want."

"My lord, of course!" Beside her grandsire stood François de Valois. Margaret was so astonished she fetched the wine without further ado. Now she understood what Elizabeth had known all along—that Alençon hid behind the tapestry in a sheltered alcove, enjoying the revel presented for his pleasure. Many others shared the secret. They sent pointed stares in that direction, yet went about their amusements, feigning ignorance.

"What's astir?" came the duke's voice as she returned and handed him the wine.

She turned to study the room and answer his question. Her lungs felt suddenly so small and tight she could hardly expand them to take in air. "Some new guests are arriving," she choked out.

The duke peered around the edge of the tapestry. "Spaniards?"

"Yes." Margaret labored for breath as the inquisitor entered the chamber. She wanted to pour out the danger to Alençon, the threat to the queen's life. France disliked and feared Spain every bit as much as England. But Margaret must not upset the diplomatic balance. The Spanish must be the ones to do it first.

That was the trouble, Margaret thought as the night lengthened. Nothing was happening. The tolling of the tower clock announced it was eleven of the clock, then midnight.

By then, Elizabeth had reached the peak of her enjoyment. She danced with Sir Christopher Hatton, leaping high, showing her trim ankles the way she loved to do, seducing her subjects and her hidden paramour with her vigor. Her charisma, too, was in abundance. She jested as she danced, teasing her partners, tossing her kerchief on the floor beside the arras. It disappeared, swept up by a stealthy hand, no doubt to be clasped to a beating, yearning heart.

De Alvarez and his companions watched, ate the dainties

supplied, and chatted among themselves, but they did nothing more.

A slow trickle of perspiration ran down Margaret's back, right where she couldn't reach it. She shouldn't touch it anyway. If it soaked through her smock, it would stain her gown, and it was the only monster of a court costume she owned, not that she minded. She didn't want another. What she wanted was a confrontation with de Alvarez. Here on their own ground, with armed palace guards nearby.

De Alvarez sat on his satisfied backside and smirked at her, tilting his lofty eyebrows in superior disdain. Determination propelled Margaret to her feet.

She marched herself over to where the Spaniards lounged on their stools and gave him a charming smile. "Don Luis, would you be so kind as to walk with me?"

"The lady of my dreams, and she comes to me." De Alvarez elbowed his associate. "But of course I will walk with you, gracious madam." He unfolded his sinuous body from the chair and offered his arm. When she let the tips of her fingers rest on it, he clamped his other hand on hers, capturing her with an iron claw.

She gritted her teeth and guided him toward the queen. The galliard had ended, and Elizabeth was taking her ease, her color high, her talk animated, while Sir Hatton fanned her and the Earl of Sussex brought her refreshment.

"Her Majesty will be interested in the progress of your trade talks," Margaret said, unable to think of another reason to bring them together. She caught a glimpse of Jonathan's warning gaze from across the chamber. Tossing her head, she ignored him. They were going to have this out once and for all, and not in some obscure corner in the dark of night where no one could remark on who died as a result. Now! In public! Where everyone would know, including the queen.

"I can't think she would wish to discuss such things tonight," de Alvarez replied smoothly. "I would rather go somewhere quiet and hear your opinion of them. Besides, no doubt the queen will soon be weary." He inspected Elizabeth minutely from where they had paused at the sideboard, a half-dozen paces away. "She will have to retire for the sake of her health."

"Don Luis, I see you admire the queen's costume," Margaret said boldly, furious at his veiled reference to how the poisoned cuff would affect the queen's person. "Do I perceive you study her lace cuffs and ruff? The set is French, a gift from His Highness, the Duke of Alençon. Do you know much about lace?"

"I know a few things about its making," he answered. "But not as much as you. I hear you are a skilled lace maker." He fastened his malevolent gaze on the lace trim adorning her smock.

Margaret wanted to clap both hands to her breast, to hide herself from his virulent stare. He was making fatal inroads on her temper. In another minute she would say something terrible, and she had been doing so well, leashing her anger of late. But not tonight. "So modest," she said loudly, pitching her voice to carry to the queen, who was exchanging a private word with Burghley. "You do yourself an injustice. I think you know a good deal more about lace than you confess, particularly this set of cuffs. I think you know about one cuff in particular. Come, admit you do."

Her words were bantering in manner, but her tone was deadly serious. As she had planned, the queen fell silent, listening, watching them with suspicious eyes.

"Really, madam?" De Alvarez had narrowed his gaze as he studied Margaret. "Would you care to be more specific?" He would bluff his way out of this trouble if he could. Margaret searched for her next words.

Jonathan materialized magically at her side. "Keep out of this," he hissed at her, his voice low. Then more loudly, "I would care to be more specific. We know you took the queen's lace cuff. We know you put poison on it with the intent of killing Her Grace."

The queen let out a gasp. Her unconscious signal stopped the musicians, who paused in midmeasure, plunging the entire great chamber into silence. Every courtier present twisted around to see what had happened. Alençon, who had been careful not to show himself all evening, put his head around the tapestry, but no one noticed. At Walsingham's signal, guards grouped around Her Majesty, halberds raised.

Margaret had never seen a smoother performer under pressure. The inquisitor cast his disarming, puzzled smile around the room.

"Good sir. Madam. What can you mean? I took no lace cuff." He looked pointedly at Robert, who had come to stand on the queen's left with Jane.

"No," said Robert, recognizing his cue after Jane gave him a swift kick in the shin. "You had someone else take it for you. I know who it was and I'm prepared to say. So does Mistress Jane here, for she saw the man."

"This is silly discourse." De Alvarez laughed. "The cuff is right there, as we all can see. In truth, you English are strange folk. Your idea of a jest is odd."

"That's not the cuff originally given to Her Majesty," Margaret spoke up. "The other one has been impregnated with poison, which is quite evident upon close examination. I know, because I made the one she now wears."

"You made that cuff?" De Alvarez's face wore a look of disdain. "Impossible. No one could do that in twenty-four days."

Margaret felt a slow smile spread over her face. "Don Luis, how does it happen you know the exact number of days the queen's cuff has been missing? You are remarkably well informed." She paused and gave him a meaningful look. "Isn't it about time you admitted your real identity, Don Luis de Alvarez? You're no humble merchant. You're really the member of the Spanish Inquisition in charge of the Netherlands."

The intake of breath by every person present constituted a vast, simultaneous hiss. In one corner, a woman withered into her partner's arms in a faint. The inquisitor fell back a step from Margaret, his eyes blazing with rage.

But the fury emanating from Elizabeth was equal in intensity. She drew herself up to her full height, which was considerable for a woman, and assumed her most imperial demeanor, her gown of gold and gems sparkling, her anger crackling. "Don Luis, do we understand correctly that you come here as a trade emissary from King Philip, that you let us lavish our hospitality on you, and you repay us by attempting to take our life?"

"Your Grace, these are false accusations," began de Alvarez, donning a facade of outraged dignity. "I cannot think—"

"Silence!" shouted Elizabeth. "Don Bernardino, is this true? Have you placed this adder in our bosom?"

Alarm suffused Ambassador Mendoza's face. "Majesty, I assure you, Spain would never—"

"Don't you deny it!" Margaret cried, her temper spinning out of control. "I saw and heard you discuss the poison with Don Luis, and so did our English spy." She flashed Robert a significant glance that said he had better agree if called on. "I saw you with my own eyes. You plotted the queen's downfall, and so did he." She pointed at de Alvarez.

"God's blood, I hate plots brewing under my very nose," Elizabeth shouted. "Do you think me weak-witted? Guards!" The burly leader of her yeoman of the guard stepped forward. "You had best take these gentlemen to the Tower for questioning. I've had to expel ambassadors from my country for conspiracy before. For certes I can do it again."

Burghley stepped forward. "I fear, Don Luis, that we must ask you to come this way and answer some questions."

But de Alvarez moved toward the queen instead. His face had changed from that of a puzzled innocent to a snarling monster. With unexpected velocity, he whipped out his dagger and thrust the shining blade straight for the queen's ribs.

Startling as lightning, Jonathan's blade met his, the two colliding in midair, knocking de Alvarez's aside so he dealt the queen a glancing blow instead of a thrust. She collapsed into the arms of her ministers, a heap of farthingale and feathers. While Jonathan bent over the queen, de Alvarez whirled and ran.

He crossed the chamber, heading for the gilded double doors, and without thinking, Margaret followed. Suddenly she froze. Patience stood at the sideboard, clutching a piece of pilfered gingerbread, right in the path of the inquisitor's escape.

"Patience!" Margaret's scream reverberated in her head. Too late, she saw the inquisitor's hands, those thieving, evil hands that had robbed her of Bertrande, close around her child. Lifting her baby, he charged from the room.

Chapter 58

This was evil. This, true wickedness. Now Margaret understood everything Jonathan had said back at Clifton. She streaked after de Alvarez, with the others just behind her, probably Jonathan and heaven knew who else. The queen might have been murdered, but Margaret had no time to find out.

"Patience, I'm coming!" she cried as de Alvarez dodged from room to room, but she knew where he was heading. For the queen's antechamber. Using the secret passage, he would make his escape, taking her child with him. Her innocent child, always the pawn of adults.

Margaret's breath came in jagged gasps as she dodged around a corner and made for a door. De Alvarez slammed that door just as she reached it, catching Margaret's hand. Oblivious to the pain, she dealt the panel a violent blow with her shoulder and raced after him. She must save her child.

The antechamber lay just ahead. Margaret skidded through the double doors just in time to see the tapestry ripple and resettle. Flinging herself across the room, Margaret tore back the cloth to find solid wall, intact, uncommunicative, without a trace of secret panel to be seen.

"Where is it!" Margaret beat on the wall as if demented, cursing herself for failing to learn the panel's opening charm.

"Let me open it."

Jonathan materialized at her side, startling as usual, but his magic had never been more welcome. She let him elbow her aside.

He fumbled for a second before the hidden panel responded. It slid back to reveal the dark maw of the tunnel, and in the wink of an eye her husband disappeared into the gaping dark.

Margaret hesitated a second. Of the many branchings in the tunnel, which would de Alvarez take? She couldn't stop to consider. She hurtled herself into the tunnel, following Jonathan, trusting that if anyone could guess de Alvarez's choice of turns, he would.

Just as she made her decision and let the tapestry settle behind her, she glimpsed her grandsire and Tim racing into the chamber. How nice, she thought with sarcasm as her many skirts impeded her climb down the ladder. They had brought Patience to the revel and were now concerned for her. The devil! She kicked at the skirts and the clumsy farthingale. Why had she worn it? Bad enough to be fumbling in pitch darkness, cursing her grandsire's stubborn will, without a clue herself as to which turn de Alvarez would take.

He must have gone straight ahead, Margaret decided when she reached a first branching to the left. At least that's what her ears told her as the scrambling of feet drifted back along the tunnel. Echoes could deceive in these musty depths, but tonight she must trust them. Feeling the hated kiss of spiderwebs on her face, she dived into darkness, plunging ahead.

Heat generated by her body bred irritating trickles of moisture that ran down her chest and back. The dark of the tunnel clung tightly, stinking like her own fear. Sense of touch and hearing increased in the black pit. Sense of terror ran at fever pitch. Her child, her beloved, everything she valued hung at the edge of a precipice, about to plummet off and cast her into the depths of despair.

Living death. All at once she felt the things Jonathan had felt, knew the same crazed wish to close her hands around another person's throat and squeeze and squeeze and squeeze . . . This is how it had been for him, dwelling in Hades day after day after day.

And she had done this to herself. She had forced the inquisitor's hand. Why hadn't she stayed safe in the palace and let Jonathan handle things. But that meant letting them fight out her future somewhere far from her sight. No! Her mind rebelled. She had to take action, to exert control. While she groped and hurried, she weighed their chances of winning. With Jonathan's fighting skill and the palace guards . . .

But there was only one of Jonathan, and de Alvarez had Patience to act as his shield. A man accustomed to torture and death would think nothing of sacrificing a child for his own life. And if he escaped with Patience . . .

Blackness of the tunnel, black despair. Yet a mad, unflagging determination drove Margaret forward. At the juncture where the tunnel diverged in six directions, she stood herself squarely in the passage hole and felt for the opening directly across from it. She must not take the wrong turning. She must stay to the main tunnel. She must catch up.

It didn't take long. Just as she despaired, Margaret's hand found a ladder on her left. Halting, she listened. Had they gone up here?

"Margaret?"

The voice, the touch of a hand shocked her body into a violent jerk backward.

" 'Tis your grandsire," came the voice again.

"How did you get here?" Her blood was racing, racing. . . .

"No time for chatter. Go up this ladder to the tennis court. The hidden door comes out in the tiring room. When you see de Alvarez, talk to him, stall for time. The captain will understand and help you. Whatever you do, don't make him angry, and don't let on that he's cornered. He might kill Patience if he thinks that."

"Where are you going?" She groped for him but he pushed her away.

"Do as I say! Now! Up the ladder." His bark filled the tunnel with thunder.

Margaret whirled, instinctively filled with the old fear of his punishments. As she climbed the ladder, she heard his grumble recede down the tunnel. "Stubborn wench . . . for once in her life . . . never obeys . . ."

She forgot him as she topped the ladder and saw the dim outline of a door ahead, low and squat. Bending almost double, she pressed herself and her voluminous skirts through it and came out into the tiny room where supplies were stored and people changed clothes. On the floor lay a clutter of tennis rackets that had evidently stood before the secret panel and been pushed aside when it opened. The next door ahead was her destination. Moving forward, she peered into the covered arena of the tennis court.

The rays of a curved moon streamed through the windows, illuminating the court. In the center she could make out the dim figure of the inquisitor holding her daughter. Halfway between her and the beast stood Jonathan, dagger in hand, crouched at the ready.

"Ah, Madam Cavandish," the inquisitor's voice rang out in the court, sending the ghosts flying and the chamber echoing. "Here at last. I assume you have come to talk some sense into your husband. I have an urgent appointment elsewhere, and you'd best let me keep it. Or mayhap you prefer to see your daughter die?"

Chapter 59

"Patience, it's all right." Margaret stepped into the court and moved toward Jonathan, holding out her arms so Patience could see her. "Don't be frightened, darling. The man won't hurt you. He's just playing a game."

Though Jonathan's body tensed, he never looked around. His full attention was trained on the inquisitor. "Margaret, go back," he ordered coldly. "Get out of here at once."

"She can't, friend," de Alvarez answered for her, pitching his voice low, yet strong enough to reach them both. "You see, I have her child." He hefted Patience and turned her about to face Margaret. Patience hung from his hands, drawn tightly into herself, eyes closed. He let his naked dagger lift one of her locks, uttered a satisfied laugh, and tucked her back under his arm as if she were a bundle.

Margaret took an outraged step toward him. Jonathan had been right—he knew exactly how to get at her, and therefore at Jonathan. She wanted to fling herself on him, to tear him to pieces. "You . . . you . . ." She ground to a halt, remembering she must not make him angry. "There is no reason to frighten a defenseless child," she stated, gathering her strength, forcing her voice into rational argument. "She is not the object of concern here. Your quarrel is with us."

"Ah, but there is reason," he retorted, apparently willing to engage in dialogue with her, which was just what she wanted. "A pity we had not the time to become better acquainted. I have a profound appreciation for your lively imagination, but it tells you nonsense. You forget one important thing. You are all heretics who must be punished, and half the punishment is fear. Along with the letting of blood, which we will have soon. The captain could tell you about that." His voice flowed with icy cold.

Margaret's gaze leaped to Jonathan, and she saw him wince involuntarily. "Don't look at him," she whispered. "Look at me."

"I must be ready for him," Jonathan whispered back, his speech rigid with tension like the dagger in his hand.

"Then feel my touch if you can't look." She planted herself beside him and encircled his upper arm with both hands. "Think of me, not him. Remember what I told you. You hurt him by forgetting," she slid the answering whisper back at him. "I'll let go the instant I feel you move."

"Do that," he replied. "All I need is an opening so I can attack."

But how were they to get that? Margaret scanned the night-dappled court, wanting that opening with all her heart, despairing of finding one. Had no one managed to follow them? Where had her grandsire gone?

"Yes, Captain." De Alvarez released his voice into the empty court, a subtle, unearthly sound. "You, too, have a vivid memory and a keen imagination, just like the lady. Remember our hours together? You were reluctant to confide in me at first. Quite stubborn, in fact. I had to coax the words out of you, but I can be convincing, as you know. Eventually you told me everything. Everything you knew, including the details about that passage, which has served me well."

"Stop it!" Margaret commanded. Vibrations of disgust shook her. "Enough. You're in England now, not Spain, nor are you in the Spanish-occupied Netherlands. You have no claim here, no right. And he doesn't remember, not the way you wish him to. He only wants justice for you now, as you deserve. But you don't fulfill the work of an inquisitor because you believe in justice. You do it because you like other people's pain."

"I uphold the righteous teachings of the church." Clearly offended by her lack of respect, de Alvarez drew himself up and thundered at her, assuming the guise of judge meting out a sentence. "My masters approve my work and I fulfill my duties with a thoroughness that earns me praise."

"Yes, you did especially well tonight," Margaret countered, thinking this was the moment to share Bertrande's words with him. "Your little pin made a gift of compassion to a woman in great pain. She rests peacefully now. Did you have any idea you could do something so kind?"

"That pin was prepared to destroy."

"It gave a gift of love," she told him defiantly, keeping her eyes fastened on Patience. Far to her right, she caught a glimpse of a movement.

"I have killed your queen," de Alvarez countered. "Within days, the Duke of Parma will be here from the Netherlands with ten thousand men to secure the throne for Mary Stuart. In the meantime, I must take my leave of you. But we shall meet again. I have plans for you, lady, when this country is firmly under the control of my king." He began edging toward the door, near where Margaret had spied the movement.

"Can he escape?" she whispered in fear to Jonathan.

"The boat he came in is most likely waiting at the water gate," answered Jonathan. "Release my arm."

Helpless, Margaret watched while the inquisitor moved steadily away, taking her child. The agony of the knowledge burned in her mind, infusing her with a whirlwind of desire to lay hands on her child. Determined to do just that, she inched forward with Jonathan as he took cautious steps, moving with the inquisitor toward the door.

A bright flash of steel spun through the air from the door. It struck the inquisitor in his left arm, sending him heavily to one knee, clutching his arm. He released Patience, dropping her to the ground like a limp sack.

"Patience! Come here!" Margaret's cry rose, matched by an identical masculine shout. As she sprang forward, someone else much closer leaped from behind the entry doors. He scooped up her daughter and retreated with her to a safe distance.

"Grandsire!" Margaret fell back a pace, clasping one hand to her chest. Air rushed back into her lungs, and she gulped several greedy breaths. Miracle, he had saved Patience! From the shadows by the door, she saw Tim step forward and salute her jauntily. He hefted her grandsire's dagger adeptly, the mate to the one he had just flung.

"Stay back!" Despite the pain, the inquisitor pulled the dagger from his bleeding arm and readied it in his right hand, aiming for Tim. Then he bent forward and grasped the weapon he had dropped, aiming for Jonathan. He couldn't kill both, but he could try.

"One of you dies tonight." The inquisitor's threat curled itself around them, thickening the complexity of their decisions. "Which shall it be? Madam Margaret?" He trained his dagger on her. "Or the captain?" He adjusted his aim. "Can the great captain's magic save you both? I think not. One or the other must go."

He was too close to miss, Margaret realized. They might kill or capture him, but he would wreak destruction, too. For the first time since the start of the encounter, Margaret looked at Jonathan. She expected to see the darkness burning in his gaze, expected to see all the signs showing he was gone from her, visiting that rocky, barren country of his hate. To her astonishment, his expression was clear. He seemed alert and poised to act when required. No torment riddled his face! No black despair radiated from his eyes!

"Give it up, de Alvarez," Jonathan ordered calmly. "You don't stand a chance."

"Ah, the trait that earned the famous captain his name shows itself at last. Nonchalance always was your way until I broke you of it. I would have destroyed you, Cavandish, given a little longer. And I will destroy your soul eventually, because it belongs to me. Even if I die, you're ruined inside."

"You're wrong about that," Jonathan retorted. "I'm free to turn my back on you this minute and walk away. Admit you've failed in your mission and come quietly. Or would you prefer I call the guards?"

"The palace guards have no idea where we are."

"They do, though," Tim volunteered cheerfully. "The Earl of Clifton tol' 'em you'd be 'ere. They're just outside the door."

"Your queen is dead, Cavandish," roared de Alvarez. "Or mortally wounded. If you kill me, 'twill go the harder with you later. The Spanish now rule this land."

Jonathan's laugh rose in the court, astonishing Margaret with its clarity. "You haven't killed the queen. She was wearing a corselet of chain mail beneath her gown. You might have bruised her, but dead? Not in the least. And you have no hold on me anymore. I'm free of you, do you understand? Tim, bring in the guards." He snapped his fingers, then turned to Margaret. Linking his left arm around her, he pulled her toward the door as a score of guards poured in through the double doors.

Margaret saw the inquisitor's mouth turn to a slash of fury against the blackness of his beard. He let fly one of his daggers, which struck a guard in the thigh. She couldn't bear to see more. It was over and done with, and she was free to turn to Jonathan, to verify the miracle. But as she let Jonathan draw her away from the inquisitor, she caught a glimpse of something from the edge of her vision—de Alvarez pulling back his arm in a swift move.

Jonathan didn't see anything but Margaret. Having called the guards, having pronounced those liberating syllables and turned his enemy over to others, he felt a sudden lightness of spirit he hadn't known for years. De Alvarez no longer ruled him. Because in that moment he had found all he had lost, found he did have a heart, and it beat that very minute, with relentless force, with love for Margaret.

The startling advent of the change astounded him. When had he thrown off the shackles? The miracle caught his attention fully. In a move totally uncharacteristic of his military training, he retreated, drawing her toward the door, wanting nothing but to have her, his golden beloved, standing at his side.

He forgot everyone and everything, wanting her. His only love, his life . . . he looked down on her, a smile lifting the corners of his mouth. And she answered him with a sigh, torn from those lovely lips of hers, her gaze locking with his because she saw instantly, she understood . . .

Pain pierced his shoulder. His brain didn't register its source. He had one thing on his mind—moving the woman he loved out of harm's way. But this time his soldier's instinct ruled. It brought him into a whirl. As he moved, he let fly his own dagger, propelling it from his fingers with ruthless force.

For a second everything moved too slowly to be real. The blade of his weapon pierced his attacker squarely in the chest, causing his legs to buckle. The man thudded heavily to the ground.

Jonathan stared at the fallen form, caught in a stupor until he felt Margaret's hand on his.

"Jonathan, come away, love. You are wounded."

He turned and saw her with new eyes once more. She was strong and regal and he loved her. He swept her to his heart and kissed her hair, her face, unable to get enough of her. Blessed beauty. Serene grace. He felt the wondrous pulsing of his heart in his chest. He could love the way she loved, the way she deserved to be loved. He could feel his life's blood spurting . . . A wetness spread at the back of his shoulder, and he was struck by a sudden wave of weakness. With a smile on his lips, he slumped forward into his beloved's arms.

Epilogue

When Jonathan came to, he was lying in their chamber, the silk curtains drawn to keep out the early-morning sun. His first impulse was to sit up, but the flexing of his muscles sent hot blades of sensation knifing through his shoulder. Then he remembered.

"Margaret—"

"Here." She leaned forward from beyond his head. "I'm right here, and so is Patience." Patience toddled forward and climbed up the bed steps to put a soggy kiss on his cheek.

"But the queen," he asked. "Did she—"

"I am here also, Cavandish." Her Grace unfolded herself from somewhere in the chamber and came into his line of vision. "Thanks to you and your insistence that I wear that blasted corset, I am well."

"So it—"

"Worked? Aye." Elizabeth chuckled wryly and rubbed her ribs. "I'm sore, I confess, but far from dead."

"Will anyone let me complete a sentence," Jonathan grumbled, propping himself up on his good side. "I knew the corselet would work if you would wear it, Your Majesty. But I wasn't entirely certain you would."

"Of course I wore it. And will again, if I think 'tis necessary. Quite an ingenious device."

"William. Where is he?" Jonathan said suddenly, looking about the room.

"Who?" Margaret's face held a blank, puzzled expression.

Jonathan chuckled. "Your grandsire. That's his name, remember. Where is he?"

"In the outer chamber." Margaret rose and opened the door, and in sauntered the earl, trailed by Tim.

"Thought you'd grace us with your company another day, Cavandish?" William thumped him on the shoulder.

On his good shoulder, thank God. "I am, thanks to you and Tim."

"Tim did the throwing."

"But you did the strategizing," the queen interrupted from where she sat enthroned on Margaret's best chair. "I recognize your tactics from old."

Jonathan noted that the earl's gruff countenance retained its stern expression, but a gleam of pleasure twinkled in his eye. He stretched out his right hand to the earl. "My thanks. But how did you know about the tunnel and which exit de Alvarez would take?"

The old earl let out a bark of laughter. "I've known about that passage for ages, ever since Her Majesty showed it to me once when she had to make a swift departure in secret." He sent the queen a conspiratorial grin. "The tennis court was only logical, being near the river. He wasn't going to escape by land."

"And what of de Alvarez?" Jonathan found himself able to ask easily, impersonally.

"A tragic story," said the earl, sending the queen a sly wink. "It appears that he was set upon by ruffians last night and murdered while prowling the bawdy district of London. A horrible thing to happen, but what was he doing there? Everyone knows 'tis dangerous in the extreme to go about there at night. His body will be shipped back to Spain in state. The ambassador will accompany him and not return for a while."

Jonathan felt his tired mouth stretching into a grin. What a clever solution to the diplomatic difficulty. England couldn't afford open war with Spain.

"Enough talk. Time for kisses for our heroes," Margaret interrupted, signaling to Patience. "We gave him some before but we'll give them again." She picked up Patience and flung herself on her grandsire, the two of them covering his wrinkled cheeks with kisses.

"Good God, you'll smother me."

"And you don't like it." Margaret laughed. But suddenly she grew sober.

Jonathan noticed immediately. "Where is Bertrande?"

Jonathan saw tears rise in his beloved's eyes. He still couldn't believe it—his beloved. He loved her. "I would like to see her," he stated quietly.

"She has been laid out in the queen's chapel," Margaret hastened to say.

"Then we must go to her. Together, you and I." He levered himself with difficulty from the bed and found his feet. To his surprise, the earl was there in an instant, offering his support. Their hands met, and the look in the earl's eyes told Jonathan that bloodlines no longer mattered.

It was an idea that overwhelmed him, and he followed Margaret in a daze after that. Or mayhap it was the loss of blood from his wound. Whatever it was, as he knelt before the empty shell Bertrande had left behind, and whispered prayers for the dead, he couldn't keep his eyes from Margaret. The sight of her pure, golden profile, the liquid crystals of her tears beading in her amber eyes. He had fought the enemy by not fighting him, and had regained his love. She was totally, thoroughly, his sweet Marguerite.

Candles flared in the great hall of Hampton Palace a week later. Gay music laced the air, and the queen and her ladies danced and celebrated. The Duke of Alençon had returned to France, but not without many tender words of love to the queen and many passionate kisses. French-English relations had never been so strong.

Margaret was just going to join the others in the great chamber when her grandsire sent for her. She entered his room, pleased to hear Patience's merry laugh. The two of them were bent over a chess board, moving the chess pieces about in a playful game.

"Don't you ever knock?" he said when he caught sight of her. "Never mind, I have something for you, madam." Pointing to a wooden box on the bed, he turned back to his game. "Mistress Patience," he corrected teasingly, "this is the proper way to move your knight, and when you do, heaven's you've captured my bishop."

Patience laughed with pleasure, and Margaret sat on the bed to open the box. To her surprise, inside lay her lace pillow, the one her father had given her. She took it from the box to cradle it lovingly. A letter lay beneath it. Picking it up, she stared at the writing. It was to her grandsire at Clifton, and she would have sworn it was in Jonathan's bold hand. She opened the letter and scanned its words. Tears gathered in her eyes and fell in profusion. Five years ago, Jonathan had written to ask her grandsire for her hand.

"They're both yours. Thought you ought to have them," he said gruffly from the chess board. "Little lass, I believe you've checkmated me," he told Patience.

It was as close as Margaret was likely to get to an apology. She took it at face value. Getting up, she headed for the door, but she dropped a kiss on his head as she passed. He caught her hand and gave it a squeeze, then turned back to smile at Patience, who was trouncing her black king all around the board in a victory celebration.

Jonathan lounged in the great chamber, on a comfortable settle with his friend Cornelius, enjoying the music and nursing his wounded arm. He had never been so happy. And yet . . .

"Are you in the dumps, my dear?" Margaret danced up to him, in a sweeping golden gown that matched her golden hair.

"I'm not sure," he answered, not wanting to spoil her fun.

"I think you are. Out with it straight."

"You never made me a piece of lace like you promised."

"I didn't. I'm sorry." She came closer to study him. "But that's not what's troubling you, is it? Come now, confess."

"The queen wants to knight me, but I don't want a title. I hate the things."

"Be of good cheer." She made a delightful little moue at him. "It might be worse. My grandsire might expire before our son is born and you would have to be earl. Come dance."

"An earl?" he complained, struggling to his feet, protecting his shoulder. "Never. We'd better get to work on that son."

"Just come along."

The musicians began the galliard "Sweet Marguerite." And the strains of it cast him back to the days of their youth, when he had first declared his love for her, first found himself drawn to her golden light. Now it blazed forth in glory as she sang before the company, brandishing the cushion, laughing with joy. When it came time for her to choose a partner, she came to him and threw the cushion at his feet like a gauntlet. Laughing, she stepped back.

"You expect me to kneel on that thing?" he demanded teasingly.

She pointed at the cushion, her face mock-stern. "I do, indeed."

" 'Tis undignified."

"I've chosen you for the dance."

"Oh, very well." He knelt with a show of reluctance, but he chuckled the entire time.

To his surprise, she went down on her knees before him, so close that their thighs touched, and pressed her lips to his. All the golden treasure she bore inside opened up to him, and he took it with gladness, knowing they were both worthy.

She leaped up, laughing merrily. "Come dance with me and our son."

"I don't have a son."

"You will soon. He'll save you from being earl." She looked down at her belly, gave it a caressing, tender look.

"Great heaven, if you're with child, I'll be anything you need me to be." He held out his hands, astounded. He was going to be a father?

"Is that an avowal of love?" she asked saucily, dancing ahead of him onto the floor.

"Yes, it is. I love you. Come here."

"I don't want to. You come to me."

"Are you being pert again?" he bantered.

"I'm telling the truth. You said I don't do it near often enough. I want you to come to me."

He gave a snort of mock disgust, but he went to her gladly, clasped her by the waist, and whirled her around.

She screamed, pretending to be frightened, but it was really an excuse to cling to him. "How is it you always do that, sweep me off my feet?" she chided when he finally put her down. She wobbled dizzily and clung to him more.

"It's part of the pattern," he told her firmly. "And you, my love, are the maker of that pattern. The weaver of the enchanted web that snared my heart."

"You, snared?" She laughed with lilting delight. "What of me, El Mágico? I gave in to your magic long before you even earned the name. I knew you from the first to be the lord of lightning who made me burn inside. And"—she pulled him away from the dance floor and showed him the letter—"I never knew about this."

Jonathan recognized it immediately, his letter to the earl, asking that Margaret be his bride. "He gave it to you?"

She nodded. "Aye, Jonathan. I believe he's sorry, which is a miracle, wouldn't you say?"

"The miracle," he answered, looking deeply into her eyes, "is your incredible persistence, Marguerite. How could he resist you? I know I can't." And he clasped her to his heart, his golden beloved, knowing she had her lace, her independence, and his love. The pattern was complete that brought them together for all time.

Author's Note

Elizabeth Tudor did not marry her French suitor, the Duke of Alençon, nor did she marry at all during her lifetime. She remained until the end, the Virgin Queen. But of all the foreign nobles offered as matches for her over the years, she certainly came closest to taking François de Valois for her husband. Royalty did not typically meet their spouses until the marriage agreements were all signed. Therefore, the three secret, idyllic days Elizabeth and Alençon spent together in 1579 represent the only time the queen was wooed in person by one of her foreign suitors (he visited her again publicly later that year), and historical records suggest that she was every bit as swept off her feet by the duke, at least initially, as I have represented in this story.

As for the founding of the English bobbin lace industry, according to the many history and research books I consulted, the exact details of its origins during the sixteenth century are lost to us today, obscured by the passage of time. Continental history is a bit more detailed, but by and large, individuals and institutions that supported its establishment around the same time remain unknown to us save for an exceptional few.

The records that remain available to us today about bobbin lace in the sixteenth century are paintings from the period in which such lace is depicted, lace pattern books that show the designs favored, plays of the period in which types of lace are mentioned, and such documents from the period as wills and household inventories that mention bobbin lace. Because the stitches that made up various patterns were trade secrets guarded by the craft, even the pattern books did not explain how to execute the patterns displayed. For the same reason, there were no "how to" instruction books on the craft until later. As a result, the precise terminology used to discuss construction was undocumented. I have therefore taken certain liberties in this area, drawing on later or modern-day terminology in part, other times making assumptions based on discussions of lace found in old documents or dramatic works of the period.

Without a doubt, the Elizabethan age was a fascinating time, even more exciting to me than the seventeenth century when more precise documentation came into being about lace making and lace-making schools. In keeping with the plan of my first historical romance, *Pirate's Rose,* I again put a woman behind the events of history, as progenitor, in *Lord of Lightning.* My fictitious Margaret Cavandish naturally went on to run a flourishing bobbin lace school in London, which served to establish the craft as a formal industry in England.

If you wish to write to me about *Lord of Lightning,* or if you wish to receive my periodic newsletter, "The Lynnford Letter," contact me at P.O. Box 21904, Columbus, Ohio 43221. Please be sure to include a business-sized, self-addressed, stamped envelope for reply. I read all your letters, and though I'm sometimes slow in responding due to deadlines, I always answer you personally.

May my stories fill all your dreams with the beauty of romance!

- What type of story do you prefer?

  a: Very sexy b: Sweet, less explicit
  c: Light and humorous d: More emotionally intense
  e: Dealing with darker issues f: Other

- What kind of covers do you prefer?

  a: Illustrating both hero and heroine b: Hero alone
  c: No people (art only) d: Other___________

- What other genres do you like to read (circle all that apply)

  Mystery Medical Thrillers Science Fiction
  Suspense Fantasy Self-help
  Classics General Fiction Legal Thrillers
  Historical Fiction

- Who is your favorite author, and why?___________________________

  ____

- What magazines do you like to read? (circle all that apply)

  a: *People* b: *Time/Newsweek*
  c: *Entertainment Weekly* d: *Romantic Times*
  e: *Star* f: *National Enquirer*
  g: *Cosmopolitan* h: *Woman's Day*
  i: *Ladies' Home Journal* j: *Redbook*
  k: Other:____

- In which region of the United States do you reside?

  a: Northeast b: Midatlantic c: South
  d: Midwest e: Mountain f: Southwest
  g: Pacific Coast

- What is your age group/sex? a: Female b: Male

  a: under 18 b: 19-25 c: 26-30 d: 31-35 e: 36-40
  f: 41-45 g: 46-50 h: 51-55 i: 56-60 j: Over 60

- What is your marital status?

  a: Married b: Single c: No longer married

- What is your current level of education?

  a: High school b: College Degree
  c: Graduate Degree d: Other: ___________________

- Do you receive the TOPAZ *Romantic Liaisons* newsletter, a quarterly newsletter with the latest information on Topaz books and authors?

  YES NO

  If not, would you like to? YES NO

  Fill in the address where you would like your free gift to be sent:

  Name:____

  Address:____

  City:_________________________________Zip Code:__________

  You should receive your free gift in 6 to 8 weeks.
  Please send the completed survey to:

  Penguin USA•Mass Market
  Dept. TS
  375 Hudson St.
  New York, NY 10014